CW00621974

DOUGIE McHALE

The
Girl
in the
Portrait

VINCI
BOOKS

Vinci Books

vinci-books.com

Published by Vinci Books Ltd in 2025

I

Copyright © Douglas McHale 2018

The author has asserted their moral right to be identified as the author of
this work in accordance with the Copyright, Designs and Patents Act 1988
This work is a work of fiction. Names, characters, places and incidents are
the product of the author's imagination or are used fictitiously. Any
resemblance to actual persons, living or dead, places and incidents is
entirely coincidental.
All rights reserved. No part of this publication may be copied, reproduced,
distributed, stored in any retrieval system, or transmitted in any form or by
any means, including photocopying, recording, or other electronic or
mechanical methods, nor used as a source for any form of machine learning
including AI datasets, without the prior written permission of the publisher.
The publisher and the author have made every effort to obtain permissions
for any third party material used in this book and to comply with copyright
law. Any queries in this respect should be brought to the attention of the
publisher and any omissions will be corrected in future editions.
A CIP catalogue record for this book is available from the British Library.
Paperback ISBN: 9781036700744

Printed and bound in Great Britain by Clays Ltd, Elcograf S.p.A.

BY DOUGIE MCHALE

The Hellenic Collection

The Girl in the Portrait

The Flight of the Dragonfly

The Boy Who Hugs Trees

The Homecoming

A Moth to the Flame

Where the Sky Falls

Beneath a Burning Sky

Under a Broken Sky

PROLOGUE
1905

Corfu, Greece

S he has a vivid image in her mind.

The smoke silvered olive trees glisten in the sun. Lemon and orange orchards sprinkle the country-side, like abundant tiny forests. As she looks upwards, the sky is blue without a wisp of a cloud. Flowers of every variety dust the ground in splendid colour, their globes like showy fireworks. Around her, the air is still, salient, to the accompanying rhythm of cicadas.

She sets a good pace along the track, and in front of her, rising like giants, are pine trees, undulating against the crystal blue sky. She keeps her pace even, as the track climbs steeply and unfolding valleys open themselves to her eye with every step.

A bend in the track brings her to a stream. She trails her fingers on the surface. The water so clear, she cups her palm and drinks thirstily. Butterflies flit from flower to branch, black, orange, red... she can count at least ten. Behind her, the Ionian spreads towards the horizon, and in her mind, she can hear the constant murmur of waves caress white sands on a beach she once visited. Her mind drifts, as the memory is soothing.

At that moment, she decides there is an unequivocal link between what is around her and the surge of wellbeing that drains her mind of worry and pain, of loss and vulnerability. This is extraordinary. This has never happened to her. It is absolute. It feels as if the embers of a fire have begun to smoulder in her chest and radiate a heat that is becoming so intense; it takes her breath away.

She carries on, not knowing where she is going. She can feel beads of perspiration on her forehead, down her back and along her arms. She frees her hair off its pins and it falls around her shoulders, unrestrained. She unfastens her buttons and rolls her sleeves. Her sense of time lost. There are only the olive trees, the sky and the sun. She is reinvented in a great sense of weightlessness. Her perception of this new sensation is profound. It seeps into her bones. She is lost in the excessive pleasures that surrounds her and she is smiling.

On a hill, stand three distinct trees, each separate from the other. There is an undisputed elegance surrounding each one, their green foliage striking against the incandescent sky. She views the trees as a diary of time, of the men who have touched her life. Alfred, John and Reuben. Each has left their mark, forever. And for different reasons, she is grateful for each one. At times, extraordinary and wonderfully happy, intimate and saddened. A life lived.

CHAPTER ONE

ELIE

The beach is long and sandy, curving like a crescent moon. Stone steps descend from wooden doors that sit in a protective wall hiding the gardens of large houses and cottages along the length of the beach. When the tide is out, as it is today, it stretches at least a hundred yards from the shore.

He is not alone, he never is. People come to walk their dogs, and couples stroll in long padded coats shielding themselves, hunched against the biting wind that whips over the wet, ridged sand. The potent smell of seaweed hovers around black rocks, as little pools of seawater wait for the incoming tide where children explore under the watchful eye of statuesque parents.

The sand is wet and sticks to his shoes. He almost stands on a dead crab and watches as a dog catches its scent, puffing nostrils combing the sand in frantic anticipation. He walks alongside footprints, and paw prints, and wonders about the lives of those that left these marks.

Wisps of clouds float across the crystal blue sky, and on

the horizon, a dark bank of menacing grey seems to wait patiently, and he watches as a sweep of rain falls. It fascinates him how quickly the sky can change its mood.

Mark wonders if it is raining in Edinburgh. He is missing the streets, the buildings, the rush of civilisation, its presence around him. Some days, he feels he is in exile.

For the past few weeks, Mark has been renting a friend's holiday cottage in Elie, Fife. His friend and business partner, Joann, an art dealer from Edinburgh, had bought a holiday cottage a few years earlier. Amongst a certain business type, buying a holiday cottage in a coastal village in North East Fife is the latest hip purchase. Such ventures are not always appreciated by the locals, as the owners often only visit during the summer months, at weekends, and seldom contribute to the local economy.

On the outside, the cottage has all the hallmarks of a nineteenth-century building, but inside, it reflects Joann's modern taste. She has spent a small fortune installing a German designed kitchen, an ensuite and further bathroom with their imported Italian tiles. The bathrooms themselves are the cost of a good-sized family car. These days, Joann rarely uses the cottage and has put it up for sale. Mark's self-isolation is ending, viewers will arrive next week, and he has already taken advantage of Joann's goodwill towards him.

It has become his habit to go for a walk twice a day. Early in the morning, he wanders along a grassy headland towards a white lighthouse where he watches as the River Forth meets the North Sea. To his left is a stone tower. It has probably been there for hundreds of years and he wonders, each time he looks upon it, what it might have been, what function did it serve? He keeps forgetting to Google it.

This is his favourite time of day. As the electric orange

light of Elie shimmers like a heatwave, he watches crimson light streak an ice blue sky, diffusing cloud in salmon and fiery peach, a spectacular light show that dilutes the River Forth in a violet sheen.

Each day, after his second walk, he has lunch at The Ship Inn where the young waitress smiles warmly. Now he is almost a regular. He has become a familiar face, and pleasantries are often exchanged when he is out and about in the village, buying milk or bread.

Mark visits St. Andrews once a week for his household shopping. He loves the drive. The road is like a ribbon, threading along and hugging the contours of the coast. He takes the coastal route in his 4 series BMW and is so enamoured with the views that he has, at times, just avoided leaving the road and ending up in a field. The land is flat, fertile and green. He passes through villages: St Monans, Pittenweem, Anstruther and Crail. He will turn left, pulling away from the coast for a while until the skeletal ruin of the old cathedral comes into view and the contours of the town's skyline emerge.

At this point, he can take in the sea again and the large seagulls that glide above the foam waves. It is the time of year when the sun hangs low, blinding the unprotected eye; he often must shade his own with his hand as the sunlight pushes at the windscreen.

He often parks the car, unfolds his limbs from the seat and walks a stretch of beach lying just beyond the road.

One time, he stopped to let three long black cars of a funeral cortege pass. The occupants staring into space, solemn expressions hinged on their grief. The car with the coffin was adorned with flowers and a bouquet that said, '*Mum.*' It reminded him of his own mother's funeral. Even now, her loss can catch his breath, something in his day can trigger the reaction and it folds over him like a blanket.

He often wonders about the heart attack that killed her, the disease that took his mother from the family. Is it now spreading inside him, and if not, is it just a matter of time?

Her eyes are green, mesmerising green. She smiles a greeting now. It was not always like this. She averts her gaze most mornings as they pass each other, going in opposite directions. Mark is always heading for the beach; she disappears into a lane amongst the cottages. He often contemplates following her, but always thinks better of it; it wouldn't do to draw attention to himself after all.

One afternoon, whilst sitting outside at the Ship Inn having a drink, she walks towards him. Should he say hello or just nod a greeting? She makes the choice for him.

'Hello again. We need to stop meeting like this. People will start to spread rumours.' She smiles at him with white teeth.

Mark returns the smile. 'Maybe they already have.'

'I wouldn't be surprised.'

'I'm Mark, by the way.' He extends his hand.

'Gill.'

'We keep meeting each other.'

She smiles. 'I know. I'm not following you, honest.'

'Would you like a drink?'

'No. I'm fine. Have you moved into the village?'

'I'm just staying for a few weeks.'

'On holiday?'

'Not exactly.'

'Sounds mysterious.'

'Not really. I'm staying at a friend's cottage.'

'Where are you from?'

'Edinburgh.'

'Nice. Not far from home then.'

'If I get bored, I can be home in an hour or two.'

She smiles. 'You're still here, so you're not bored.'

'I like it so far.'

'It's a big change from Edinburgh.'

'A nice one, although I'm starting to miss it now.'

'Will you be going back soon?'

'I will, I need to see to a few things,' Mark says reflectively.

'I might see you around then.'

'I was just leaving. I missed my usual walk today. I usually go to the beach. You're welcome to join me.'

'All right.'

Mark drinks the remainder of his coffee. They walk along The Terrace and South Street before reaching the beach. Mark can feel his shoes sink into the sand. Gill pulls off her sandals and rests her hand on Mark's arm to steady herself.

'I used to play here when I was a girl.'

'Have you always lived in Elie?'

Gill looks out towards the waves that are rolling towards them and secures a stray hair behind her ear.

'No. I went to Manchester University and studied English Literature and History with all my East Neuk innocence and returned fifteen years later. My innocence long vanished.'

'What did you do after university?'

'I was a journalist in London, The Times, The Telegraph, all the highbrow broadsheets. I travelled a lot. I was a foreign correspondent. That's how I met Robert; he worked in Paris at the time.'

'Oh.'

'It's ok. We're not together; we're having an amicable separation, a mutual break. He's in New York working for the New York Times.'

Mark nods.

She pulls a cigarette from a packet. 'Do you mind?'

'No. Of course not.'

'Do you want one?' She gestures with the packet.

'I stopped years ago.'

'I wish I could.' Gill turns her back to the wind and lights the cigarette, inhaling with relief.

'What brought you back here?'

'London was like a goldfish bowl. When I did escape, I was always working, and I began to hate the constant travelling. Robert got the opportunity to work in New York. It put a strain on us. That's part of the reason why I came back.'

She looks at him. 'I shouldn't be telling you this, dumping all my woes on you.'

'It's fine. Honest.'

He feels her gaze on him.

'What?'

'What do you do... when you are not here, aren't you working?'

The wind is tear-inducing, and it catches her hair again, which she flicks from her face. Gill inhales her cigarette avidly. Her skin is pale, but her cheeks have a slightly rose tinge to them. Her hair is dark and wavy, her eyes snare him, and Mark feels he can stare at her face forever.

'I'm an art dealer.'

Gill looks at him curiously. 'I'd never have guessed.'

'Why not?'

'You don't look like one.'

'We have a look?'

'Well, you know what I mean; people have a certain impression of what people look like according to their professions.'

'They do?'

'Well, yes. I think most people do. You buy paintings for a living. You're the first art dealer I've met.'

'There's more to it than that,' Mark says, starting to feel hurt. 'I work with collectors, sometimes museums and represent various artists. I specialise in Italian art.'

'It sounds fascinating.'

'I have a gallery in Edinburgh and one in London. We're not big players, but we do all right.'

'We?'

'Yes. Joann, she's my partner in the galleries. It's her cottage I'm staying in.'

'How do you become an art dealer?'

'I read History of Art at the Courtauld Institute of Art in London. That's where I met Joann. We were both from Edinburgh.' Mark smiles. 'There's nothing more gratifying than to sit in a room surrounded by visual beauty that inspires the soul.'

'Very poetic. When you put it like that, it sounds the perfect job.'

'It is.' Mark says, visibly pleased.

'Are you any good? I mean, not everyone can be an art dealer. I suppose it's quite an exclusive profession.'

'I have confidence in my eye. I follow my curiosity. I also have an open mind. I trust my instincts, but mostly I must be true to myself. I constantly visit studios, galleries and museums, exhibitions, read the headlines, listened to word of mouth. That's how the gallery grew.'

'Are you a big player?'

'We do all right. It keeps a roof over my head. It's funny that we keep bumping into each other. I suppose it's inevitable, really, with Elie being a small place.'

'It gets busier in the summer. I'm not sure if I'll still be here to see it.'

'Why is that?' Mark asks.

'I need to work. There's not much call for a foreign correspondent for the East Fife Mail.'

'No. I suppose not.'

'I've got an interview with The Scotsman next week.'

'I hope it goes well.'

'Thanks.'

A small piece of glass catches Gill's eye. She picks it up and turns it in her hands. The cobalt surface is cloudy and smooth to the touch.

'What's that?' Mark asks.

'It's called sea glass.'

He leans forward to get a closer look. 'I've never heard of it.'

'It's just bottles and glass that have been broken, and then smoothed by waves and currents. Some people collect it. You can make necklaces out of it.'

'I love the colour.'

'You can get all different types of colour. Green and blue are my favourite. I collected it when I was younger.' This memory of her past invites her to once more turn the sea glass in her hand before she places the shard in her pocket.

Mark feels a damp breeze on his face and looks at the sky. 'I think it's going to rain; we should start to head back.'

Gill gestures to a gap between the houses. 'There's a path just up there. It'll be easier to walk back.'

'I've been staying in Elie for nearly three weeks and you're the first person I've had a real conversation with. I didn't realise how lonely I was.' Mark thinks for a moment. 'What are you doing later tonight? Have you any plans?'

'I was having a quiet night in... again.'

'Why don't I make us something to eat? Come around, say about seven. Don't worry, it's not a proposition, just an invitation.'

'What's your cooking like?' Gill asks, toying with him.

'I've never had any complaints.'

'Ok, seven it is.'

'I'm staying in Fountain Street, number nine.'

'I know.'

He raises his eyebrows. 'You do.'

'You're already the topic of conversation amongst... let's see... certain available females.'

'Ah, I see.' Mark feels his face flush.

There is a pause. 'But I wasn't one of them.' Gill announces.

CHAPTER TWO

DISCLOSURE

Joann says lightly, 'What happened?'

'It's what didn't happen. I could have stopped it,' Mark says.

'I blame you?' Her voice rises.

'I blame myself. It was my first reaction.'

'And there obviously wasn't a second reaction?'

'No.'

'Is red, ok?' Mark enquires.

'Red or white, I don't mind as long as it has alcohol in it. Something smells nice and spicy.'

'It's just chilli and rice. I made it mild, just in case. Here, let me take your coat.'

Gill slides from her jacket and hands it to Mark, along with the bottle of wine she has brought. Her hair falls onto her shoulders in dark waves. She wears little makeup, just a touch of eyeliner and lipstick. Instinctively, Mark's eyes sweep over her blouse and skirt, and he hopes she hasn't noticed, but her smile tells him otherwise.

'Your friend Joann has done wonders with the place.'

'It's up for sale, just this week, actually. As far as I know, there's been some interest already.'

'I'm not surprised. She must have spent a small fortune. Does that mean you won't be around for much longer?'

'I'm afraid so. It was never going to be long term. Your drink.' He sets a glass of wine on the table.

Mark feels relaxed with Gill and although he hardly knows her, he is already at ease in her company, and he finds her attractive. It is the first time Mark has felt genuine sexual excitement for some time. He hands her a glass of wine and they sit at the table.

'Mm, this is nice.'

'It's a Merlot. I got it in St Andrews.'

'I love St Andrews. I've often thought of moving there, but the price of the property is through the roof, bloody London prices in Fife.'

'It's getting just as bad in Edinburgh.'

'Where in Edinburgh do you stay?'

'The West End. It's not far from Haymarket Station.'

'I know the area. A journalist friend of mine moved from London and bought quite a large flat there. Palmerston Place. Nice area.'

'That's close to where I stay, Eglinton Crescent, just around the corner, really.'

'Small world.'

'It is. I'd better check the chilli.'

Mark spoons out a little portion and tastes it. 'I hope you're hungry. I always make too much.'

'I'm starving. I've been saving myself all day.'

'No pressure then.'

They eat in almost silence. Mark refills their glasses and after the chilli, he serves a cheesecake.

'I'm stuffed. That was delicious, Mark.' Gill wipes the edges of her mouth with a napkin.

Mark smiles gratifyingly. 'Would you like a coffee? A real one, I'm sure I've still got some pods in the cupboard somewhere.'

Gill lifts her empty glass. 'No, I'm fine, but you can fill this again.'

Mark retrieves a bottle from the wine rack. 'A Rioja this time.'

'Perfect.'

'I'll help with the dishes. I need to do something to help quench my guilt.'

'No, you're fine, relax. There's a dishwasher.'

'Are you sure?'

'Yes. I'll load it up later.'

'In that case, then, I need a cigarette. I'll go outside.'

'I'll come with you; we can go into the garden.'

They sit on a wooden bench; Mark has brought their drinks.

'Is the garden nice? I like a well-kept garden. It's hard to tell, it's too dark.'

'It's a bit overgrown to be fair. Joann's hardly here, which is a shame. Even if she was, she's not a gardener, anyway.'

'Are you seeing her?'

'Joann?'

'Yes. Are you together, a couple?' Gill prompts.

'What?'

'Do you fuck each other? God, this is hard work.'

'No... No. We're just friends, good friends. She's my business partner.'

'Ah, I see.' Gill nods. 'So, tell me, Mark, what brings you to Elie? I'm curious, that's all. You're not on holiday, you're not working here, but you're staying at a friend's cottage.'

'There's nothing to tell.'

She looks at him. 'Really. My job has afforded me the opportunity to travel to many countries and interview diplomats, presidents, businessmen and woman, and your ordinary Joe Bloggs. They all have one thing in common when they lie their body language gives them away.'

'So, you think you know my weakness?' Mark grins.

'All I'm saying is your reasons for being here seem to be different from most people.'

'Does that matter?'

'Not really, but since we are getting to know one another, I'm curious.'

He turns it around in his mind, the complications of his past.

She seems full of confidence. Normally, this would alert him to be cautious, but he has an overwhelming urge to tell her. He ignores the contradiction. He is aware his throat is a little dry. She looks at him expectantly and, at that moment, all he wants to do is lean forward and kiss her.

'Ok, you win.'

She smiles then, a warm glow of self-satisfaction.

'It was months ago. We agreed that it should end. When I say we, I mean Abriana and myself. We met at a gallery in Italy, Rome, the Ermanno Del Bramante, it's a culture and arts centre. Abriana was one of its directors. Influential people run it, from the arts and Italian politics. Anyway, we were attracted to one another and before long we were meeting up at other venues and sometimes travelling together when we were both attending the same meeting at a gallery or museum. We tried to keep it low-key, but it was impossible,' Mark sighs. 'It's quite a close community, the art world. She stayed a few times in Edinburgh, I went to Rome. Anyway, it went on for some time until one day she phoned me saying that she'd resigned. Our relationship posed potential damage to her employer's reputation; she was going to "explore a new challenge," that's how she phrased it. Seemingly, we were photographed together several times by the Italian press when we were at galleries and conferences. She was married, you see.' Mark runs the tip of his finger around the rim of his glass. 'The press ran several stories. The adverse publicity that followed her resignation was scandalous. A reporter and photographer from the Italian press came to Edinburgh, harassed our staff for a story, followed me, found out where I lived, and hounded me for days. That's when Joann suggested Elie. Once I'd gone, the Italians lost interest. Abriana did an interview for one of the Sunday papers in Rome, saying she deeply regretted her behaviour, but her personal life was a private matter. I was told she was given a lot of money for her story.' Mark inhales deeply and thinks briefly. 'I suppose she deserved the money.'

'Well, I wasn't expecting that. So, you stopped seeing each other?'

Mark smiles sadly. 'We did. The thing is, she loved me, but because of me, her world fell apart. I hate myself for that. I've struggled with it a lot, you know, what happened. I don't even know if she's still with her husband.'

Gill touches his arm. 'If it makes you feel better, I'm not looking for love.' She leans forward and kisses him.

. . .

Most mornings, he wakes to the laughing wail of gulls. It is another dismal day, the third in a row, as rain continues to peck at the window. The cottage feels like incarceration and an intellectual numbness spread within him.

At first glance out of the window, there is blurriness to everything around the edges. The light reminds him of water-coloured paintings he once saw in his gallery, strangely he can't remember the artist. That morning, there is a milky film over the sea and sky, but by midday, sunlight floods the cottage and Mark ventures outdoors.

Outside, it is strangely quiet. Leaves fall onto the pavement like fluttering snowflakes. There is a chill in the air. He buttons up his jacket.

It is the discreet nature of their meetings that, as he walks, prompts a swathe of exhilaration, excitement, but also guilt, as he draws closer to the house. He rings the bell and the realisation of that guilt grips him, disturbs him, quenching his enthusiasm, but then memories of their love-making add a different dimension to his thoughts, stopping him from turning and leaving. The door opens and at once Gill's smile snags him. He apologises and says he should not have come. She invites him in and instead of leaving, he makes it worse and accepts her offer.

'You were meant to be keeping a low profile, not having an affair,' Joann says, shocked and astonished.

'It wasn't an affair.' Mark is adamant.

'It doesn't matter what it was, the facts are you told her

why you were in Elie. What were you thinking? You weren't thinking that's the point.'

'No, I suppose you're right.' He had no convincing answer.

'I know I'm right. God Mark, you've made a right meal of this.' Joann draws heavily on her cigarette and turns her head to the side as she exhales the smoke.

'I hadn't planned on it. It wasn't an affair exactly.'

'She was married Mark, another one, or has that little detail slipped your mind?'

'He never knew.'

'Lucky you.'

'If it makes you feel better, I feel guilty about that. She didn't tell me she was married. She just said they were having a break from each other.'

'She had a ring on her finger, no?'

'Most women have rings. It was an oversight. Anyway, we only saw each other a few times. She was unhappy.'

'God, you're really making a habit of this. I thought getting your fingers burnt once was enough. And you made her happy?'

'For a bit, I suppose. It was a distraction for both of us.'

'You were both running away then.'

'Well, it wasn't a marathon, more like the hundred metres.'

'She's a journalist. Has that slipped your mind? You told her why you were in Elie. The last thing we need is bloody journalists sneaking around again.'

'That won't happen. She's not like that.'

'How do you know what she's like? You hardly know her. All you know is what her bedroom looks like. I can see the headline she will write, 'The Italian Mistress, the Scottish Art Dealer and the Missing Masterpiece.'

'That's a bit of an overreaction. She's not working now, anyway.'

'What did you tell her?'

'I never mentioned the painting. Don't worry, she doesn't know.'

'All she'd have to do is Google your name and up it would come.'

'Why would she?'

'Why would any of us? Out of curiosity, that's all it would take. She's a journalist, for Christ's sake. It's in her DNA.'

'Look. I didn't go into any detail. It's fine, honest.'

'I hope you're right. Going to Elie was meant to make this mess disappear; you might have just made the whole thing worse.'

CHAPTER THREE

THREE MONTHS LATER

'Hello Mark, it's Abriana.'

It is the last voice he expects to hear. Something levitates inside him. 'Abriana, how are you?'

'I'm well.'

'I never thought I'd hear your voice again.'

'It's me, really. I need to speak to you.'

'Are you sure that's a good idea?' His heart races.

'It's what I want. Look, I'm in Edinburgh. I'm staying at The Sheraton. Could we meet for a drink?'

'A drink. When?'

'Tonight.'

'Sure. I'd like that. Why are you here, Abriana?'

'Not for pleasure. Work brings me to Edinburgh.'

'So, it is a pleasure.'

'I suppose you know me too well.'

'I enjoyed the experience.' He swallows. 'This is so unexpected.'

'I know. But I'm here now. Life seems to be in the habit of drawing us together.'

'Look Abriana, about what happened...'

'Mark, we'll speak later tonight. Are you sure you want to?'

'Of course, yes, it's just that you're the last person I thought would want to see me.'

'I have a proposition for you.'

They meet in a small restaurant on Lothian Road. When Mark arrives, Abriana is already sitting at a table. She glances up and sees Mark. Abriana stands to greet him. Mark, on his part, is unsure how to greet her. Is it acceptable to embrace her like a good friend, after all they have been through? He can see that she is smiling, and it seems to melt his awkward indecision. His relief is immense. He bends his head, lays his hand on her forearm, and kisses her lightly on both cheeks. Her perfume catches his nose; the scent is still familiar to him.

'Abriana.' His voice wavers. It is a name he has said in his thoughts, but not on his lips for a long time.

'Mark. Thank you for coming.'

As soon as they take their seats, a waiter approaches, and they order drinks. They decide on a bottle of Merlot. He remembers her almond eyes, dark and piercing, and when she smiles, it draws him to her arresting lips. She is wearing a white blouse that curves at her clavicle, where a small gold cross rests. He remembers it well. He has already noticed her skirt when she stood to meet him, tight-fitting, but business-like.

Mark nods towards the cross. 'You're still wearing it.'

Abriana touches the cross between her fingers. 'It feels part of me now. It would feel strange not to wear it.'

'For sentimental reasons?'

'Something like that.'

Mark remembers the day in Rome when he bought it. It took him a while to choose the right one, in the end, its simplicity won him over.

He wonders briefly if she still feels anything for him. She has been cordial. He is not certain, however, if her visit is only business. Abriana turns her head to look at a couple who are taking their seats and when she looks at him again, there is something in her smile that he has always marvelled at.

Their wine arrives, and once they order their meal, Abriana smiles. 'I never thought I'd see you again.'

'Did you want to?'

'Not at first. No.'

'What changed?'

'I did. Life did. I was given a fresh start, a new job, a different place to live that didn't remind me, with each turn, of the memories I was trying to forget. I realised I didn't ruin my marriage. It was over before I met you, but it needed what happened between us for it to become obvious.'

'And your husband?' He shifts uncomfortably in his seat.

She shakes her head. 'No. We're not together anymore.'

'I'm sorry, Abriana.'

'Don't be. I found out that even before I met you, he had been seeing someone for over a year. No one is innocent in all of this.'

'I know it doesn't sound right, but I feel a sense of relief in a strange way.'

'What do you mean?'

'I've always thought I was the cause of your marriage break up. This feels strange. You're sitting opposite me. I never thought that would be possible. If I was told yesterday this would be happening, I would have thought it inexplicable, impossible even.'

Her smile is radiant. 'It's me, honest. Touch me if you need convincing.'

Abriana's invitation produces a rush of adrenaline in Mark and around him it feels like the world is holding its breath. She extends her hand. It is a simple gesture that transfers him to another time. He searches for words; none is forthcoming, only memories that are sensual and physical leave an impression on him, quickening his breath. Her fingers are long and slender, her oval nails manicured. He recalls their touch upon his skin. He holds her hand in his, pressing it gently, and her presence in that touch is so familiar that the months of separation melt from him.

She leaves her hand in his for a moment and then removes it. His eyes skim her face, the features still familiar to him.

Mark smiles. 'I can't believe you're here in Edinburgh, with me.'

'I've always wished things could have been different between us. Were we foolish, wanting what we could not have?'

'It didn't feel like that. No. I can't think of it like that.'

'Do you have any regrets?'

'Only that it ended. I wanted to be there for you.'

'But you couldn't be. That was the whole point. It must have been hard for you, too. I'm sorry.' Abriana spreads her hands, suddenly apologetic.

Mark gazes at her. 'Don't be. I think it's good that we can

talk like this. It must have been awful for you. The press are animals.'

Abriana shrugs. 'At the time. Yes. I wasn't prepared for it. How could I be? I wasn't expecting that kind of interest. The gallery's strategy was that once our affair was out in the open, it would all just blow over quietly and quickly, with limited damage to their reputation and brand. Even they weren't prepared for the media interest that followed. It even made the news in Japan; can you believe that?'

'I think I got off lightly,' Mark says, sheepishly. He bows his head.

'Did the repercussions affect the gallery? I hope not.'

'No. I went away for a while,' Mark says tentatively. He thinks of Gill. Now, sitting opposite Abriana, he feels a crushing sense of regret. He tries to push it to the back of his mind. 'So why are you here, Abriana?'

'Are you familiar with the artist, John Sutton?'

'Yes. He was a portrait artist, wasn't he? He also dabbled in Italian landscapes.'

'He did, mostly around the Florence region. But that's not why I'm interested in him.'

'So, why are you?'

'One of his paintings has emerged. Very few people knew about it. A portrait he did of a group of musicians back in the early 1900s. We don't think the painting was cata-logued or ever sold, for that matter. Some rumours have spread that it was lost or destroyed; even its existence was in doubt, until now.

'It had actually been in the ownership of a Scotsman, William Buchanan, a distinguished correspondent of the BBC's Italian Service. In the 1950s, Buchanan received the painting as a wedding gift, from a friend, an Italian wine-maker. I like this part of the story. The winemaker was given the painting by a German officer during the Second World War in exchange for bottles of wine.' She laughs.

'So, how are you involved?'

'By chance, last year, Buchanan's son, Geoffrey, a BBC producer, showed the painting to Anna Webster and the Team of The Commission for Looted Art in Europe, who was researching for a BBC program about the loss of art during the Second World War.'

'How did the painting end up in Italy?' Mark asks.

'Sutton had moved from England to Italy, sometime in the early 1900s. He obviously took the painting with him. We believe he painted it in London. He was living in a villa in Montagnana near Florence. By 1935, he had donated most of his landscapes to the Uffizi Gallery in Florence. I was asked to help with the research and look at the archives and try to establish the provenance of the painting.'

'You're working for the Uffizi Gallery?'

'Yes. I am.'

'Are you still living in Rome?'

'No. Florence. Well, a little village about fifteen kilometres from Florence.'

'Why are you here in Edinburgh?'

'Alan Sutton is a history teacher in Edinburgh. He came across the story on the internet and learned we were investigating the provenance of the painting. He claims that John Sutton is his great-grandfather.'

'And he is laying claim to it?'

She nods. 'Yes. We think the painting was originally taken from Sutton's villa by soldiers of 362 German Infantry

Division. Sutton died two weeks after that. Some German officer gave it to the winemaker, obviously oblivious to its value. It was then given to Buchanan as a wedding gift by the winemaker, who passed it on to his son and then we became involved. It seems that very few people knew of the painting's existence. The Uffizi Gallery is disputing Sutton's grandson's claim. They believe that since Sutton donated his paintings to the gallery whilst he was living in Florence, any other painting, especially one that was in Italy, should hang on their walls.'

'That could get messy.'

'We're hoping it doesn't come to that. We have a contingency plan.'

'What do you mean?'

'It's quite possible that if Alan Sutton wins his claim to the painting, he could threaten to put it up for auction.'

'Oh, that would hurt. A private auction?'

'Probably. Sutton was one of the most sought-after artist of his day. You would have to be seriously jealous of his talent not to admit it. His paintings of Italy are exquisite. People often think of his portraits as iconic, but he is now being recognised for his landscapes. He could express light and detail to the extent it could almost be a photograph.'

'I've seen a few of his paintings. You're a fan then?'

'Not only me. An auction would command international interest.'

'What's the gallery's position?' Mark asks.

'It seems likely that if Alan Sutton's claims are substantiated the Uffizi Gallery will either try to broker a deal with him that allows them to display the painting for a year, for an agreeable sum of money and then Sutton will be free to do what he pleases.'

'I'm sure the gallery would want to buy it if it does go to auction.'

'They're hoping it doesn't come to that. I think they'll offer him a lot of money to buy the painting before any auction takes place.'

'Either way, Alan Sutton becomes a rich man.'

'He does. I was hoping you would be interested enough to help me.'

'In what way?'

A waiter approaches their table and asks if their meal has been to their satisfaction.

'It was lovely, thank you,' Mark replies.

Abriana hesitates. There is a moment of silence between them. 'I want to meet Sutton in a neutral place, not a hotel, certainly not his house, so I was wondering if I could use your gallery.'

'I'd need to ask Joann. She's not going to like it.'

'Do you think she'll ever like me?'

'I'm sure she will.' He pauses. He could never have imagined seeing Abriana again and here she was, sitting opposite him. The guilt he feels at this moment is overwhelming. He has nourished his feelings for her with the prospect that maybe, one day, they could still be together. He often dismisses this assumption for its absurd lack of reality. Yet, she is sitting opposite him drinking a glass of Merlot. How surreal life can be, he thinks, but also full of possibilities.

'Why not?' He thinks out loud. 'Of course you can use the gallery. Would you like me to be there with you when you meet this, Alan?'

She smiles, more in relief. 'I'd hoped you'd ask. Yes, I'd like that.' Abriana sips from her glass with a satisfied glint in her eye. She looks around the room, and as she does so, her hair moves along her shoulder. It awakens a memory in Mark. A glance into the past. A cascade of falling hair, released from a knot resting on the nape of her neck and hiding a dark mole. He remembers brushing the tip of his finger over the curves of her spine...

'You won't have seen the painting, here, I'll show it to you,' Abriana says, lifting her smartphone from the table. 'Instagram is the world's newest art dealer. It's a virtual art gallery. It's the new way to access art. All you need is an iPad and an Instagram account.'

'I feel threatened,' Mark laughs.

'Here it is. You won't be able to really appreciate it, but what do you think?'

She hands the smartphone to him.

Mark looks at the painting for some time, studying the composition, colours, light, and the figures. He can appreciate the effect the artist was trying to convey. In the background, three young musicians are playing instruments, two males and a female. Mark can see the grace in their movements. The music is not absent. The sweeping gestures of their arms and bows transmit the quality and tone of the instruments. The painting has a melody. He can sense the music, the timbre, and flowing notes. The woman and one of the men are smiling, but their eyes are closed. The other man's eyes are open, his face is stern, in concentration, or irritated, discontented perhaps. Mark is unsure? But it is the figure in the foreground that dominates the scene and attracts Mark. Although she has a violin, she is not playing the instrument; instead, it hangs loosely from her fingers.

Mark enlarges the screen and focuses on her face; her head turned from the others, looking out towards him. The look in her eyes catches him. The connection between her and the person or persons she is looking at snares him. Is she gazing at the artist, John Sutton, or are those eyes suggesting she has something to tell the onlooker? A secret perhaps? Her expression is warm. She is a painting within a painting, almost the only subject of importance. Her stare pulls him in and if he looks closely enough, her eyes resonate with a warmth that is as soothing as an evening sky.

But there is something else. A connection is achieved as she looks out from the canvass, it is so tangible that Mark feels it is almost personal. A transmission of sorts. He knows that look; the expression is so vivid, and he feels he knows her intimately. She is beautiful.

'Who is the young woman?'

'Ah, I thought she would interest you. Some art historians believe she was Sutton's lover.'

'So, that could make her the great-grandmother of this guy, Alan, who is contesting the ownership of the painting.'

She shrugs. 'It's possible.'

'I wonder what her story is.' Reluctantly, he hands back the smartphone. 'This painting is really good. It's influenced by several styles. There's a combination of a Florentine school of Renaissance, academic art and romanticism in the early 1800s. Are all his portraits like this one?'

'The portraits, yes. He developed a unique style with his landscapes. They are a hallucinatory play of light.'

'I'll need to look them up. I've not really seen a lot of his Italian work.'

'Yes do. Sutton's proficiency in landscapes was met with great praise and accolades. He continued to get commissions from wealthy Italian families right up to his death. He was a prodigiously talented artist. That's why I like this job so much. I get to discover artist's work and deepen my under-standing of them.

'Yet, we're not sure of this painting's title; he might not have even given it one, considering its history. For instance, why did he take the painting to Italy with him when he relo-cated there? We know it was painted in London in the early 1900s. It obviously had some personal connection. Maybe the young woman you are attracted to knows the answers.'

'If she does, she's not able to tell, is she? Mystery and intrigue are exciting, don't you think?'

'The mystery will add value to the painting, that's for sure. In my research for this assignment, I've studied most of Sutton's portraitures and landscapes, especially the ones in the Uffizi Gallery. I noticed things new in them each time; I'd see things I didn't see before. There are layers which reveal them-selves, gradually. In this one...' She taps the dark screen of her smartphone and it reveals the painting. 'He transmits melan-choly, compassion and tenderness all infused with rich colour. It's a complex and moving portrait, fascinatingly detailed and inventive. I feel Sutton took enormous risks with it, but it's the subtlety and mystery of Sutton's style, his depiction of strong emotion that sets it apart from its contemporaries.

'I read he was fascinated with the characters of those he painted. He tried to capture the character in the model's face. I read a quote he once said, "*I am communicating human experience.*" When I first saw the young woman, I felt as if she was holding a secret in that expression. Some-thing the onlooker would not necessarily know because there's nothing in the painting that would suggest it,' Abriana explains.

'Secrets have an implicit power, but once told, they're devalued, dissolving their enormity and worth. I hope she can keep hers.'

'Did you notice the pearl necklace?'

'I did, but it was her face I was attracted to initially.'

'It's thought the necklace was added a few years later. Whether there's any truth to that remains uncertain. The painting hasn't gone through any testing.'

'Would you like another bottle? We seem to have emptied this one.'

'Maybe just a glass. I need to keep a clear head for tomorrow,' Abriana says, flicking her hair from her face.

'Sure, a glass it is then.' Mark calls over a waiter and orders two Merlots.

'So, Mark, how's business? I hear the gallery is doing well.'

'It is. Which is great, but I don't care too much for the attention that generates. I leave that side of things to Joann. You know me, I love art, galleries, discovering new talent, but everything else that comes with it is so ephemeral and superficial. That's not me, as you know. I want to be involved in projects that inspire and touch people on a personal level. Art is a powerful medium; it can change people's lives. I truly believe that. I love what I do and that can be very satisfying.'

'That's what I love about you, Mark. You can be so passionate and philosophical about things.'

The waiter brings their drinks. Mark smiles at Abriana and raises his glass. He pauses, collects his thoughts. 'To the making of precious memories in this fine city of mine.'

They clink their glasses. 'And to the sweetness of finding

one another, again. Cin Cin.' Abriana smiles through a row of perfect white teeth.

That night, Mark stands at his window, staring into the street below; the wash of streetlamps illuminates the wide pavement, parked cars, the iron, wrought fence and communal garden. The glass of whisky has warmed his throat as he realises now he has found Abriana. He can never feel lost. He can never be lonely again.

He breathes in deeply and squeezes his eyes closed, but the images remain. It has always been like this. The past, their past, has been his relentless companion.

The intervening months of separation have been a barren existence, but outwardly he has portrayed a lie. It stole his judgement, and he has no enthusiasm for it now.

When he thinks of his time in Elie, he struggles to connect with the person he had become. He was in no doubt enthusiastic for the physical pleasures his clandestine meetings with Gill elicited. She was a distraction from his pain. Even then, in the mire of his guilt, he unconsciously detached himself from his feelings. Despite his outward persona, he was empty inside, emotionally disorientated. He looks upon that time as a state of grief. Now, with the measure of distance, he can rationalise it, clarity of thought has descended upon him.

He moves away from the window and sinks into the sofa, tipping the remains of the glass over his throat. There are five stages of grief; he remembers reading about it in one of the weekend supplements. These stages don't announce themselves in a pre-set order. It doesn't work that way, he now recalls. How someone grieves is dependent on that person's personality and temperament before their loss. Mark wonders about this, and a flash of recognition crosses his face. He remembers his deep sense of disbelief that this could have happened to Abriana and himself, forced into their self-imposed exile from each other by events out of their control.

In the early weeks, a deep sense of disbelief and then denial suffocated him. Why did it have to happen? Mostly, he remembers the anger, and it is only now he realises he connected to this anger because it was an outlet. He needed someone, something to blame. And he blamed everyone and everything. It was those who were close to him, the easy targets he offloaded onto most. It strikes him now that it is easy to hurt those we care for and love the most. He must have made Joann's life hell, but she suffered him like a saint. It brings a smile that acknowledges the unconditional bonds of their friendship. She even made him laugh, and when he thinks of her attempts to console him, he can now smile about it.

He looks at the empty glass in his hand; he has been drinking more. His meeting with Abriana had a dreamlike quality to it. He wonders why that is? Was it because it was unexpected? The last thing on his mind was the opening of an opportunity to see Abriana again.

In his mind, he has imagined her a thousand times. The images and memories bring sensations that only they know. The pleasures they have shared are intimate recollections that stir his mind and feed his craving for being in her company again.

He has tried to make judgements on their time together, but the seduction of his senses smothered such judgements of the mind. He tries to confront this change that has come over him with rationality and reason. There has been a shift.

It has brought a sense of weightlessness in him. He still loves her. He never stopped. Now, he feels no guilt. Guilt invites hysteria. There is a possibility, amongst all the complexities, she still feels something for him. His mind races with questions, each one clamours to be answered.

CHAPTER FOUR

A THORNY REQUEST

'I definitely looked at my e-mails.' Mark laughs. 'I did, honest. You don't believe me.'

'I do. If you said you did, then I believe you.'

'Good. I must have missed it.'

'I've told you a hundred times to delete your e-mails as you go along. Keep the ones you want, put them in a file and delete the crap.'

'I know. There must have been about 500 of them.'

'Jesus Mark 500! That's insane.'

'Maybe a bit more actually, now that I think about it. Maybe 500 was the number I got to before I deleted the last lot.'

'Honestly. I don't know how you manage to run the gallery. All I can say is the next time I'll be going to Joann.'

'Probably best. She'll be back soon. Out for lunch.' Mark smiles.

'I'm going to be naughty. I've already had an orange, so that makes it ok. Would you like a chocolate?'

'I really shouldn't.'

'None of us should.'

'Oh, go on then.'

Jane hands Mark a chocolate.

'Mm. These are delicious. Where did you get them?'

'Tesco. They were on offer. They're usually five pounds. Got them for two.'

'Bargain. Especially tasting like this. I've never tried these.'

'They're new, apparently. Would be nice with a coffee, Mark.'

'Of course. What is it again? Milk and two sugars?'

Jane regards Mark with an exasperated look. 'Just Black.'

'Huh. Got you. Hook, line and sinker.'

'Honestly, Mark, it's a good job. I know what you're like. I hope you don't treat your other clients like this?'

'Only the ones I like,' Mark says, heading off to the small kitchen area to the rear of the office.

'Do you remember Alice Calverton?'

Mark returns with two coffees. 'No. I don't think so.'

'You do. Remember. She was at the opening of the last exhibition you did. She was the one who got incredibly drunk at the start of the night and she and her husband had the most fire-spitting row. The best I've heard in ages. It was intense and gratifyingly embarrassing. She threw her wine all over his Armani shirt. Do you remember? He was furious.'

'Oh yes. I remember that now. What about her?'

'They're getting divorced. She has a problem with the drink. A functioning alcoholic, so I've heard. Anyway, her husband, soon to be ex, is applying to get custody of the children. He says she's an unfit mother.'

'How do you know all of this, Jane?' Mark asks, intrigued.

'I know her well. Her daughter went to the same nursery as Philippa.'

'The posh one.'

'Who? My daughter or the nursery?'

'The nursery.' Mark smiles.

'It was a good nursery. It came highly recommended.'

'I don't doubt it.'

'Anyway, you're transgressing. I bumped into her the other morning. She was sucking on a mint, but it didn't disguise the smell on her breath. It wasn't even eleven o'clock. She stank like a brewery.'

'That's a shame.'

Jane looks at Mark sceptically. She wasn't expecting sympathy. She was just about to crucify the woman. It took the flow from her. 'I know,' she says reluctantly.

'She must be in a bad way, knowing her children could be taken from her, yet she's still drinking. It's an illness, Jane. She needs help, not punishment.'

'Yes. I know. I've spoken to her about it, but I don't think she grasps it, really,' Jane says, now changing her tone.

'I've always felt there's a fine line regarding drink. It's easy to get into the habit of having a few every night just to unwind. The trouble is when you start to crave that drink every night.'

'Is this a confession?'

'All I'm saying is it's easy to do.'

She looks at him suspiciously. 'The trouble with you, Mark, is I never know when you're being serious. You sound as if you've had personal experience of this. Are you telling me you have a problem with drink?'

The conversation was heading in a direction he wasn't comfortable with.

'I don't think of it as a problem.'

'Are you sure?'

He had no convincing answer. 'Oh, that sounds like Joann is back.'

'Jane. I wasn't expecting you,' Joann says with a smile, as she slips from her jacket.

'I know. I emailed Mark to tell him I'd pop by to go over the catalogue for the exhibition. I should have cc'd you into it.'

'Better still, you should have sent it to Joann. I deleted it by mistake, I think.'

Joann looks at him earnestly. 'Now why doesn't that surprise me, Mark?'

Mark grins amiably. 'Sorry.'

Joann has a proof of the catalogue from the printers and whilst she discusses the contents with Jane, Mark's smartphone buzzes. It is a text from Abriana. She would like to meet with Alan Sutton the next day and ask if she can still use the gallery as a meeting place.

Mark hadn't been able to tell Joann about his meeting with Abriana. He's sure it won't go down well. In fact, he knows it won't. Her attitude towards Abriana has caused Mark to struggle with divided loyalties. They were the two most important women in his life, each for their differing reasons. Mark knows all too well that Joann is still angry with Abriana. Joann feels that Abriana's influence over Mark had clouded his judgement when he was in Italy. Joann was furious with Mark. She struggled to believe how he could have put his career on the line for an affair that could never have a future; it was damaged. Not only had Mark jeopardised his career, but he had also inadvertently risked the gallery's reputation and that of Joann's.

This pained her sensibilities. Mark realised that to Joann it was what it was. The elation he felt last night with Abriana in the restaurant and later, when he was alone in his house and her voice swam in his mind, was quickly evaporating. Mark waits for the right moment if ever there is one.

Once Jane has left the gallery, Mark finally approaches the thorny subject of his meeting with Abriana. Joann listens carefully.

'She is here in Edinburgh.'

Mark feels a knot in his stomach. 'That's what I said.'

'And you have met her?' It was not a question, simply Joann thinking aloud.

He looks at her uncertainly. 'As I said, she is here on business.'

'Yes, you said. And she wants to come here, to the gallery. God, has the woman no morals? No. I'm having none of it. I'm not having that woman set one foot in here.'

'She wants to meet Alan Sutton in a neutral venue. I can understand that.'

'Edinburgh is a big city. There are lots of hotels, café bars, you name it and it has it. Why here?'

'Because it's safe and I'll be here.'

'You still love her, don't you? After everything that woman has put you through.'

'I still have feelings for her. She's interesting, intelligent and... still attractive.'

'I'd like to think I am too, but what she did, Mark, takes a certain cunningness. It was calculated and at your expense. It's me who picked up the pieces. I'm not doing that again.'

'That won't happen again.'

'How do you know what will happen?'

'She didn't have a choice.'

'There is always a choice. She left you high and dry. She abandoned you.'

'It was difficult for her too, Joann. I was a willing participant in it all. No one is to blame. It's the way it was, that's all.'

'God, I thought you had got over her, Mark?' She sounds disbelieving. 'You almost committed a crime for her; you could have gone to jail. Have you forgotten that, or has it just slipped your mind?'

'She was being blackmailed. She didn't have that kind of money. I just offered to help. I thought it was the right thing to do.'

'That brings us back to choices. She could have refused your offer. She must have known you were taking a massive risk for her.'

'It was my choice to sell the painting.'

'Yes, but unfortunately it wasn't yours to sell.'

'At the time, it seemed like the only option. Abriana needed the money. Selling the painting seemed the only way to get that money. Anyway, as we know, she didn't take it.'

'No, but it cost you. No, I'll rephrase that. It cost us ten grand above the hundred thousand you got for it, to buy the bloody thing back.'

In Italy, an anonymous blackmailer demanded one hundred thousand euros from Abriana to keep them from going to the press about her affair with Mark. Alerting the police was not an option and both Mark and Abriana knew that if the press got hold of their story, the aftermath of the publicity would end Abriana's career. Being in such a senior position within The Roma Art Gallery and having an affair with one of their rivals, she would be asked to resign quietly, or worse still, they would terminate her contract and view her loss to the gallery as collateral damage. Abriana was adamant that the blackmailer was someone or persons who worked for the Roma Art Gallery, or had a close connection to her. They had both been meticulous in their efforts to keep their affair discrete, never allowing any public showing of being intimate. Abriana was sure it was someone she knew. She became easily flustered, which was uncharacteristic of her. Everyone she knew, in her head, became a suspect. Knowing that they had become objects of someone's curiosity and eventually, the recipients of someone's financial gain troubled her, to the point she became more stressed and anxious. It was a defining moment.

Mark persuaded Abriana to agree to his plan, a plan hatched out of desperation and not without risk. Using various contacts, Mark could sell one of his gallery's paintings on the black market to raise the money the blackmailers demanded, making it look like the painting was stolen from his gallery. He convinced Abriana there was no other option and reluctantly she agreed.

On the night, they were to hand over the money; they both stood over the small suitcase and stared at the notes, packed neatly into bundles. She could never forgive herself if Mark was arrested and convicted. How could she live with herself? They were dealing with someone who knew her; someone who probably knew her for a long time. They were expecting to get the money. She tried to put herself in the blackmailer's mind, assess his motives. What did he know about her? What was his knowledge of her? She had two obvious choices: give him the money or give him nothing, and end the affair, go public and resign from her post.

Abriana decided she would not be held hostage. Where would it end? Once the blackmailer received the money, he could ask for more.

Mark remembers it like it was yesterday.

'It's finished, Mark. It has come to this. Is this what we are worth? This will not define what we are to each other. I will not let us be violated by this.'

Shit, Mark thinks. *'But what do we do? It's almost done. I've sold a painting that was not mine to sell. It was the gallery's.'*

'It's the end, Mark, can't you see?' She shut the lid of the suitcase.

The story of the blackmail surfaced not long after the Italian media reported the affair. It was never proven, as two autonomous individuals gave conflicting stories regarding the details of the blackmail attempt.

Mark was left with the dilemma of either try to buy the painting back or keep the money. When he explained to Joann what he had done, she flew into a rage, her eyes blazing, her anger hit him like a storm. She threatened to go to the police and to dissolve their partnership in the gallery. Mark desperately tried to explain the impossibility and complexity of the situation.

It took her a few hours finally to calm down. Deep down she was not suspicious of his motives, there had been no deficiencies in his attempts to explain them and she had heard the emotion in his voice. Mark had sold a painting that belonged to the gallery and although that was bad enough, what really cut her to the core was Mark felt he could not tell her about the blackmail threat and what he intended to do.

Mark had betrayed her trust, their friendship... but then, when he bent his head and sobbed, and broke down in front of her, and his shoulders shook, she knew it had broken him.

Later, after she had wiped the tears from his eyes, he said he regretted keeping it from her; it had haunted him,

continuously.

'I've told you a hundred times, Joann. If I could, I'd do anything to have that time back again and put right what I did to you...' He pauses.

Joann looks at him. 'Sometimes, Mark, I feel like your mother.'

'I'd prefer if you'd said, sister?'

'No. Believe me, I feel like your mother. Why has she got such a hold on you?'

'Truthfully, it's like I have a spiritual orgasm when I look into her eyes. It's a connection of the body, the soul, and my entire being. She makes everything sound exciting and sometimes mysterious. She's very compelling.'

Joann tidies her desk, a distraction she hopes to find in the arrangement. Mark can hear the crackle of paper and then Joann shakes her head. 'You're fucked, Mark.'

'So that's a yes, then.'

CHAPTER FIVE

___

AN UNEXPECTED ENCOUNTER

The next day, Mark is waiting for a tram outside Haymarket Station

'Mark, I thought it was you.'

The voice is unexpected and familiar. He turns.

'Gill. What are you doing in Edinburgh?'

'I got the job.'

What job? And then it comes to him. 'Ah, The Scotsman. Congratulations. That's brilliant.'

'I'm staying in Edinburgh with a friend until I find a place of my own. I'm virtually just around the corner from you.'

He feels a burst of panic. 'Oh, when did you move?'

'About two months ago. I was never going to commute from Elie. That would have killed me. I'm not sure whether to rent or go the full hog and buy a place, anyway.'

'Are you enjoying your job?'

'I am. I'm off to New York tomorrow, covering the final stages of the election. Isn't it crazy? Trump looks like he's going to win it. Who would have thought? If you had said a year ago Trump was the President of the United States, no one would have believed it. A fairy tale. It looks like it's not one anymore.'

'No. It's a nightmare. New York sounds like it will be fun.'

'It will be, I suppose, even if it's work. I never tire of New York. We should get together when I get back. Go out for a drink. Catch up.'

'Yeah. We should. I'd like that.' Mark is thinking, but I'd prefer not to. 'How long are you away for?'

'It depends. I'm covering for the paper's American correspondent. He's ill or something. I'll only be gone a few days. I've still got your number. I'll give you a phone.' And then she smiles. 'Or, how about a coffee? Have you got the time?'

Mark glances at his watch. 'I could spare half an hour.' He regrets the words the second he answers her. 'We could go to *Nomad*. It's just across the road.'

Gill smiles. 'Perfect.'

Nomad sits on the corner of Roseberry Crescent. It is a small coffee shop that sells patisseries, sandwiches and baguettes. Once inside, they sit at the window.

'My treat,' Gill says as she heads for the counter.

Gill is wearing a suit jacket and a tight-fitting skirt. Her hair is long since he saw her in Elie. She looks quite tall in her heels. Was she a mistake? It didn't feel like that in Elie, although there was always something in the back of his mind prodding him. Maybe now, this was what that referred to.

He didn't think he would ever see her again, and now that has changed. He felt safe telling Gill about Abriana. It doesn't feel like that now.

He looks out onto the street. He could leave, make his excuses?

Gill approaches him with a tray of two coffees.

'Did you want a cake? I forgot to ask.'

'No. I'm fine.'

She sits opposite him.

'Good. I'm on a diet.'

'Whatever for? You look great.'

Gill blushes. 'Another of many. I need to lose a few pounds here and there. I must have tried every diet there is, I tell you, it's ridiculous. The Paleo diet, New Atkins diet, Cambridge diet and Slim-Fast, more like, slim bloody never. They all work, for a brief time, but it's impossible to live like that every day.'

'I always say everything in moderation. Watch your portions and get some exercise. Those are my three rules. I don't always stick to them, though.' Mark grins.

'But it works. I've tasted the results, remember?' Gill's eyes sparkle mischievously.

It is Mark's turn to blush. How can he forget?

'This is a nice little place,' Gill says.

'I like it. It only opened a few months ago. I think it used to be a butcher's shop at one time. They've still got the white tiles on the wall behind the counter. I often nip in at breakfast time. Have a coffee before getting the tram into town to go to the gallery.'

'Yes, the trams. They're new. It makes the city feel very European.'

'I suppose it does. Came at a price, though.'

'I know. We even heard about it in London. It's always the same with these kinds of projects, over budget and never completed within the agreed time. I like the music they play in here.'

'Me too. African Caribbean I'd call it.'

'So, Mark, what have you been up to?'

'I'm busy with work. Thankfully. It means the gallery's doing well.'

'Where is your gallery?'

'On the corner of Abercromby Place. Do you know it?'

'I do. I'd like to visit. Maybe buy a painting for my new house.'

'We're putting on a new exhibition, a local artist. He's making a few waves in the art world right now. We were lucky to get him. There were quite a few London galleries in the chase, but since we also have a gallery in London, he chose to go local.'

'I might come along. Maybe buy one of his paintings. You could help me chose. Would that be a wise

investment?' She gives him a flirtatious look.

'I would think so. But only buy if you like the work. After all, it has to hang on your wall.'

There is a moment of silence between them.

'Have you been back to Elie?' Gill asks.

'No. Someday maybe. I love that part of the country. I'd like to see it on a warm summer's day.'

'I noticed your friend sold the cottage.'

'She did. It didn't take long. Some businessman from Glasgow bought it. He probably won't be there much.'

'I've got a viewing today in half an hour. The timing couldn't be worse.'

'Oh. Where about?'

'It's a mews in Gloucester Lane. Number 9. It was by chance I saw it. I loved the front door. It was blue, my favourite colour and I decided there and then to put an offer in.'

'I love that part of Edinburgh.'

'It's perfect, actually. If I get it, I'll have a housewarming. I'd like it if you'd come?'

'That sounds like an invitation. It would be rude to not to.' Although he thinks, he'd rather be rude and not go.

'I need to buy the place first, but I've offered over the asking price, so hopefully, I'm in with a shout.'

'I hope so too.' He is dropping his guard. 'Are you still seeing... what's his name? God, my memory is terrible.'

'Robert.'

'Yes. Robert, sorry.'

'No. We didn't get back together again. There's no love lost there.'

'So, how's the job? Working for The Scotsman must be exciting, especially going to New York.'

'To tell you the truth, I'd rather I wasn't going.'

'Oh, why's that?'

'Well, it's only for a day or two. Six hours on a plane, then I'll be constantly working and six hours back again, possibly all in under forty-eight hours.'

'I see what you mean, not that glamorous.'

'Exactly. They pulled me off another job, much more interesting than Trump, I can tell you. So, when I get back, I'm straight back onto that one again.'

'When do you sleep?' Mark smiles.

'On the plane. I like being busy. It keeps me out of mischief.'

Mark glances at his watch.

'I'm sorry. I'm keeping you here.' Gill apologises.

'No, honestly, I'm not late. It's fine. It's just a habit.'

'I need to go, too. Don't let me keep you, Mark. Look, it was nice seeing you.' She rummages through her bag and pulls out a packet of cigarettes.

'It was nice seeing you too,' Mark says, standing. 'Let me know how the house hunting goes.'

'I will.'

'Enjoy New York.' He feels awkward. If he gave her a kiss on the cheek, it could be construed as something more than just a friendly goodbye. In the end, the matter is taken out of his hand, as Gill smiles at him and offers him hers. Maybe she sensed his indecision.

Once out on to the street, Mark takes a deep breath. He is glad Gill didn't ask about Abriana, for he is sure if she had, he wouldn't have been able to lie about her.

CHAPTER SIX

THE MEETING

Joann was still fuming the next day. Mark can tell as she has been making as much noise as she can all morning.

'The internet is so bloody slow. It's getting worse. Bloody B.T. Sky is always doing deals. I bet they're cheaper than what we're paying now. I'm going to check them out.' Her mug of coffee thumps her desk and Mark can hear the rapid clicking of her computer keys.

Mark is sitting opposite her; their desks face each other.

'How long are you going to keep this up for, Joann? Abriana will be here in ten minutes. Being in a foul mood is not going to change that.'

'No. But it makes me feel better. Ah, here we are, Sky broadband. They can even do deals for phones. Oh, and by the way, I've booked the flight to London.'

'Good.' The timing couldn't have been better, Mark thought. A client wants to exhibit in their London gallery and Joann will be there for a week organising the event.

There is a fluttering sensation in Mark's stomach. He hates conflict.

'Please be civil to her.'

'I'll try. But I'm not promising I'll be able to keep it up.' Joann, incredulous, turns towards her screen. 'I knew it. We've been getting ripped off for years. Look how much less we'd pay if we switched to Sky.'

'I'll go out front and meet her.'

'You mean to keep her away from me?'

'Something like that.'

'Oh Mark, it's alright. I'm sure I can pretend to like her for an hour or two.'

Mark gets up from his desk and taps Joann on the shoulder. 'I'm not asking you to be her best friend.'

'Thank God. I'm not that a good actor.'

He climbs a short flight of stairs that brings him into the front of the gallery. There is a small reception area with two leather sofas and a glass table with art magazines placed neatly in a fan shape. A knot of anxiety squeezes his chest. Mark searches the street outside for a glimpse of Abriana. It's almost lunchtime, so it is busier than normal. A black cab pulls up outside and he can see a female reach over to the driver from the back seat, paying the fare. The door swings open and Abriana steps onto the pavement. She sees Mark in the window and waves. Mark opens the door to the gallery for her.

'I'm a little early. I hope that's alright?'

'It's fine. Not a problem, we can use the meeting room. I'll show you to it and get us some coffee.'

She smiles. 'I'll just set up my laptop. I need to send a few emails.'

'We're just in here.' Mark shows her to the room and goes to make the coffee.

Joann calls out. 'She's here then. I suppose I'd better say hello.'

Mark's anxiety gives way to a stabbing of panic. 'She's in the meeting room. I'll come with you.'

Joann raises an eyebrow. 'You don't trust me being alone with her.'

'It would be rude of me not to introduce you.'

'For God's sake. It's not that I haven't met the woman before. I'm not going to bite her. I will be a model of propriety. Trust me.'

'If I didn't know you any better, I'd say you are enjoying this.'

She gives a quick smile. 'Maybe.'

Mark follows Joann to the meeting room. Abriana is sitting at a large table with her laptop open.

'Abriana. How delightful it is to see you. Mark has told me all about this painting of yours.' Joann extends her hand. Abriana stands and shakes Joann's hand.

'Joann. How lovely to see you again! How are you?'

'I'm well, thanks. And you? Mark tells me you're now living in Florence. It must be beautiful.'

'Just a little outside, Florence, actually.'

'Oh, that's nice.'

'I hope you don't mind me using the gallery like this. Mark did say it would be alright.'

'Of course it is. Well, I won't keep you. Your man will be here soon, I suppose.'

'Well, I'll get those coffees,' Mark says, relieved, but not at ease. 'Would you like one, Joann?'

'I'm fine Mark. I'll leave both of you to it, then.'

Joann turns to leave and touches Mark on the forearm and raises her eyebrow as if to say, 'Told you so.'

When Mark returns, he asks Abriana, 'Is your coffee alright?'

'It's fine, thank you.'

Abriana has taken some sheets of paper from her briefcase and placed a pen on top of them. She checks her watch. 'He should be here by now.'

'It's lunchtime. It'll be busy out there. He'll arrive soon, I'm sure. Are you ok?'

'I'm fine. Just a little tired.'

Abriana sits back and crosses her legs. She is sitting side on to Mark and her skirt rises above her knee. Mark tries not to, but he looks there. The room is intimate. Mark wonders if Abriana feels it, too. She picks up the pen and taps it on the desk. 'Maybe we should go out and meet him when he arrives?'

'Probably best.'

Alan Sutton is a short man, slightly overweight with thick jowls. The crown of his head is bald and shines like a polished surface. There is a shadow of stubble hair that curves around the back of his head, from ear to ear. He is wearing a dark suit that seems to hang on him and Mark notices, as he leads Alan into the meeting room, several lines crease the tail of Alan's jacket.

He looks like a teacher, Mark thinks. How odd that people's appearance can become to resemble the profession they practise. Mark wonders if he looks like an art dealer to others, and then he remembers a conversation he had with

Gill in Elie on that very subject. The thought of Gill makes him uneasy.

Once the pleasantries of introduction are over, Abriana informs Alan that Mark will be present and then proceeds to outline the Uffizi Gallery's reluctance to see the painting leave Italy. If Alan Sutton proves his right to the painting through his family connection, it is the gallery's desire they can still come to an amicable agreement, whereby the painting can be displayed in the Uffizi Gallery alongside John Sutton's other paintings. Rather than contest who is the rightful owner in the courts, which would be an expensive endeavour for both parties concerned, although, Abriana stresses, the gallery has often pursued that course of action in the past; they hope their offer is a more palatable option.

'The gallery will obviously come to a financial agreement that will be suitable for both parties. You will be handsomely compensated for your generosity.' Abriana smiles.

The soft pitch. She is keeping her bullets in her metaphorical gun, in case it turns nasty, Mark thinks. He smiles to himself and wonders if Alan Sutton will find the proposal amicable.

'I hadn't considered that course of action as an option.'

'I've been instructed to inform you that on the open market, the painting could fetch upwards of five hundred thousand pounds. A considerable sum.'

Alan Sutton fidgets in his seat. He massages his temple. There is a considerable sheen of sweat on his forehead and he wipes it with a discoloured handkerchief.

'Christ, that's a lot of money. I'd no idea we'd be talking about that much.'

Abriana is choosing her words carefully, Mark observes.

'It gets better Mr Sutton.'

'Please call me Alan.'

'As I was saying... Alan. If in the event you can prove your claim to the painting, the gallery is prepared to pay you in monthly instalments the equivalent of two hundred thousand pounds over a period of a year. This money would be given in compensation to yourself for allowing the painting to be displayed in Florence at The Uffizi Gallery for an agreed period. After that, you're free to sell the painting. We would hope that as a goodwill gesture you would sell to us for an agreed sum written in your contract.'

Beautiful. Mark grins to himself. He knows the painting could fetch up to a million on the open market. Easily. He has done his homework, unlike, it would seem, Alan Sutton. It was a tactic that could have easily backfired. But, Mark assumes, in such an event, Abriana would have had room to increase the offer. At this rate, they could get the painting for a bargain. Even if, afterwards, Alan Sutton discovered its true value, he would have already signed the contract.

'My, that seems a generous offer, I must admit. I had no idea. So, I know how things stand.'

Abriana sits back and crosses her legs.

'Of course, Alan, such a course of action and contractual agreement can only be undertaken if you prove that you are who you say you are and that you have John Sutton's logs.'

Alan flinches and suddenly looks pale.

Ah, she's loading the gun.

'Yes. Yes. Of course. But your tone is slightly threatening.'

'It's just business. Just business Mr Sutton. We are reputable in all our dealings.'

'Well, then.' He reaches into his duffle bag and brings out

a large brown envelope. He pulls out a sheet of creased and stained paper. 'My birth certificate.' He hands it to Abriana.

She studies it carefully. 'I will also be visiting the registrar's office and making my own enquires.'

'As you see fit, but as you can see on my certificate, it clearly states who I am and who my father is, which by all accounts makes John Sutton my great-grandfather.'

'On first impressions, it certainly looks that way. Do you mind if I photocopy this?'

'No. Not at all, go ahead.' Alan Sutton is smiling now, the look of a man who is perceiving as if in anticipation his life is about to take an astonishing turn of events.

Abriana hands the birth certificate to Mark. 'Would you Mark?'

'The photocopier is in the office.' As Mark gets up and leaves the room, he can hear Abriana say, 'Do you have your father's birth certificate, Alan? '

'Eh, somewhere, I think.'

'It's not a problem. I'll be able to locate it at the registrar's office if I need to. We've already drawn up a contract. Once we finalise your claim, we can go over it for your consideration.'

Mark smiles. She's good.

CHAPTER SEVEN

A PROPOSITION

'Is that how you imagined him to be?' Mark asks.

They are sitting in Amarone, an Italian restaurant on the corner of St Andrew Square and George Street. It is the day after the meeting.

'I was expecting a bit more,' Abriana says, sipping a glass of red wine.'

Mark smiles. 'He was timid.'

'Looks can deceive. Although I thought he would have done some research on the value of Sutton's work.'

'He might be doing that right now.'

She shrugs. 'It's of no concern to me. The Gallery can afford to offer more if need be, but I don't believe they will.'

'How can you say that?'

'They'll probably not even have to part with a pound, as far as Alan Sutton is concerned.'

'I don't understand.'

'I've been doing my own research.'

'Ah. His father's birth certificate.'

'Yes. The General Registry Office is quite efficient online. As is the DX service.'

'What's that?'

'The document exchange Courier Service. I had already applied online to set up an account with the registry office in London. Well, the gallery did all that before I came, just in case Alan Sutton didn't have his father's birth certificate. Which, as it turns out, he doesn't. He thinks it might be in the loft, but he's stalling.'

'And did you find the birth certificate?'

Abriana pulls from her briefcase a sheet of paper.

'Courtesy of the DX service.' Abriana smiles.

Mark studies the paper's contents.

Mark traces the columns of the certificate. 'So, here's Alan Sutton's father, who is called George Sutton, born in 1945 in Lambeth, London.'

'He is. But what interests me is who George Sutton's father is? He is registered as Fredrick, there is no surname. Now, you would expect Fredrick's father to be John Sutton.'

'You would. Have you found that out?'

'Of course.' Abriana gives a satisfactory smile. She hands Mark another sheet of paper.

'Fredrick Sutton's birth certificate, I presume. It says he was born in nineteen hundred and six.'

It takes a little time for the information to sink in and when it does, Mark sits back in his chair, his open mouth almost resting on his chest. 'There's no mention of a father or mother. It's blank. How can that be?'

'So, it is.'

'There's no mother or father,' Mark repeats.

'No.' Abriana takes another sip of wine.

'There's no mention of John Sutton either. That's for

sure. Well, Alan Sutton's going to be pretty pissed off with that.'

'Unless he already knew, but I don't think so. He never knew John Sutton. He died long before Alan was born. We know that. Maybe Alan's dad, this George, he knew the family history, we'll never know if he did. Look at column seven on the birth certificate.'

'What about it?'

'Once the entry has been checked by the informant, he or she signs their name in Column 7. The informant could be the mother or father, a person present at the birth, the owner, or occupier of an institution, or the person in charge of the child. In this case, it's someone from an orphanage.'

'Jesus. So, there's nothing to connect this Fredrick to John Sutton.'

'No, but that doesn't explain why the surname Sutton was used thereafter. That's the mystery.'

'What about Sutton's logbook?'

'It seems genuine. That's the only connection to John Sutton. That alone will be worth something, although I don't think that'll be compensation for poor Alan. There is an entry of a painting named *The Quartet*. It's numbered, and we know Sutton numbered all his paintings. The numbers match. Unlike the birth certificate. Sutton could be the father, we don't know. One explanation could be that if the child was born out of wedlock, Sutton wouldn't have wanted his reputation tarnished and disgraced by fathering an illegitimate child, so he was not named as the father and it was sent to an orphanage. It's possible, but just a theory. I'm sure there'll be others.'

'I guess we'll never know.'

'I know of someone who might.'

'You do?'

'I got a call this morning from one of the researchers at the Uffizi Gallery. She has located an old friend of John Sutton. He's an old man now, but was sixteen at the time. He was the gardener at Sutton's villa in Italy.'

'That's incredible.'

'It is, and it's well-timed. We're hoping he'll be able to shed some light on our little mystery of the missing names. He's living in Greece. Have you ever been to Zakynthos?'

'No.'

'I'm going there next. How would you like to see what Zakynthos looks like?'

'That sounds like an invitation.'

'I just thought you might want to follow this up and see it to its conclusion.'

'I'm intrigued for sure.'

She smiles and takes a sip of her drink. 'They've rented me a villa, big enough for two, apparently.'

He meets her eyes. 'Are you sure this is what you want?'

'Yes,' she says, simply. 'Would you be able to leave the gallery at such short notice?'

He shrugs. 'I'm due some holiday time. I'd need to get a flight.'

'I used my initiative. I figured you'd want to come. I know, like me, you'd want to unravel this mystery. I asked the gallery to book two flights. I said you were integral to the process of reaching a conclusion, given your authority on the subject and your background.'

'That's not exactly true.'

'I know. It worked though.'

'Are you sure?'

'I'm not about to jump into bed with you.'

'I wasn't implying you were.'

'I'd still like you to come, it can give us a chance to get to know each other, again.'

It's a beginning, he thinks. He has thought about being in this position a hundred times, but never has he been so close to the possibility. It is a fragile thing, delicate in nature and can slip from him just as quickly as it presented itself.

'It's funny, for some reason, I must have read it somewhere, but I remember what the actor Hugh Laurie once said: *"It's a terrible thing in life to wait until you are ready. No one is ever ready to do anything. There is no such thing as being ready. There is only now."*

'That's a yes, then.'

He smiles. 'I believe so.'

CHAPTER EIGHT

THE VILLA

Cielo Villa is located 1.5 kilometres outside Zakynthos Town, a short distance from the Venetian Castle that overlooks the capital. Mark's first impression, apart from its modern furnishings and size, is no matter where he stands, he can see the sea.

It is air-conditioned with marble floors, a large open planned living area and all mod cons kitchen. It has four bedrooms and two modern bathrooms. Large sliding doors and the glass frontage on the ground floor offer magnificent views of the countryside and sea.

'It's big. Couldn't they get anything smaller?' Mark looks around the ground floor.

'It was only available for this week. A cancellation, I believe. All the good hotels in the capital are full. What do you expect, it's summer? We're lucky to have got it.'

Mark smiles. 'I'm not complaining. It must have cost a fortune.'

'Over three thousand for the week.'

'Euros?'

'No, pounds.'

'Wow!'

Abriana slides open the glass frontage and steps outside onto a covered veranda. There is a small pool with several loungers around it. Abriana hears voices. She thinks she can hear someone greeting them.

'Ah, you've arrived already. You are early, or I am late.'

She turns to see a man and a woman walking up the driveway. Mark joins her. 'Who are they?'

'I've no idea.'

'My name is Stephanos, and this is Stella. If you need anything, just let me know. It's my job to make sure you have everything you need.' Stephanos is a small man, but next to Stella, anyone would look small as her prodigious frame waddles alongside him.

Mark notices they are both carrying plastic bags that bulge with shopping. 'This lot should have been in your fridge by now.' Stephanos nods towards the bags. 'Stella will soon have lunch ready. If you prefer to make your own food, just phone the office and we won't trouble you again. Some people prefer it that way. The number is in the welcome pack.'

Mark bends towards Abriana. 'Did you know about this?'

'No.'

'I like the sound of it.'

Stephanos explains Stella will cook a meal once a day if required. Normally, these arrangements are pre-booked, but as the villa was booked a few days ago, the procedure would be overlooked.

'It's fine. We'll make our own, thanks anyway,' Abriana says.

'Since we are here, Stella will make your lunch while I put this away,' Stephanos says, disappearing into the villa.

Before too long, there is a spread of Greek salad, salmon fishcakes and stuffed roasted vegetables, wine and water laid out on the table on the veranda.

'Are you sure you won't change your mind?' Mark says.

Her face is noncommittal. She has already decided. 'It's not a holiday, Mark.'

'I was only kidding.'

'Although, when you look at this place, it could be a holiday. We'll only be here for a few days. It's booked for the week; it seems a shame.'

'I might just stay for the week.' Mark smiles.

'That would be nice. It's a working holiday then.'

'Yeah, I like the sound of that.'

'Me too.'

'I've never really thanked you for what you did, Mark. If it wasn't for you, I don't know what I would have done. You saved me.' With these last words, she gulps some air. They resurrect the complications of that time, the unforgivable choices she made.

Mark smiles and says, 'I would do it again.'

Abriana looks surprised. 'I wouldn't ask you again, even if I were in the worst situation, which I will never be. I always worried that you would hate me. I regret leaving like I did and not calling you.'

'It was hard for both of us. Anyway, it was my idea to sell the painting, not yours.'

'Yes, but I didn't stop you. I could have, but I didn't.'

'It wouldn't have changed anything, really.'

'I suppose not.'

'It's different now,' Mark says, searching her face.

At first, Abriana doesn't speak. She stares at the food on the table. 'It has changed me. I'm different.'

'Different? In what way?'

'It was a time that taught me many things about myself. I was driven, ambitious and I could be ruthless, at times if I needed to be. I would strive to be the best at what I did, at any cost, to myself, to others. Some might say I was not a very nice person when it came to business, but that wasn't the entire person I was. There was another side to me. I'd like to think you experienced that. It's who I am now. I've mellowed. I do this because it's important, the work, it has value. It's about people, not just money, galleries and paintings. It's about people's stories, their lives; it's about righting the wrongs, life's injustices. That's what drives me now, not personal gain and building a reputation. I just want you to know that.' She lets her breath out; it is a relief.

'There was no need, Abriana,' he says reassuringly.

'We haven't seen each other for a long time, Mark. I wasn't expecting to see you again until I got involved with this. In fact, I was surprised. When I phoned, I wouldn't have blamed you if you said you wanted nothing to do with me. I'm glad we've met again. Really.'

He tries to imagine touching her hair and letting it fall from his fingers and tracing her skin with his lips. He remembers how she tastes; it is a memory that has not faded from him with time. Mark searches for words, but any word would sound feeble compared to the want inside him. He realises that now is not the moment. He hopes it will come soon.

The sun glints off the pool. Mark has a sudden desire to slide into it and encase himself in the water. Instead, he takes a drink of wine and sets the glass on the table; there is a slight tremor in his hand that has gone unnoticed by Abriana.

'Joann will know about this now, I suspect,' Abriana says.

'By now, she will. She'll have phoned the office. I told Susan to tell her where I was and why. Susan is one of our assistants.'

'I can imagine her response.'

'It doesn't matter.' He means the words. She can hear it in his voice.

'Are you sure you have done the right thing? I mean, I've ruined your life once; I don't want to do it again.'

'That sounds ominous. But really, it's a bit late for turning back. I'm here now. I wouldn't be here if I didn't want to be.'

'Joann will hate me even more.'

'I'm a grown man. Joann needs to know I can make my own decisions. Anyway, it will come as no surprise to her; she would probably expect it of me. I disappoint her all the time; she's used to it by now.'

'I'm sure she doesn't think of you like that. She is fond of you.'

'Oh, I've no doubt,' he says, trying not to smile. 'But I think I've probably stretched that fondness.' The thought of Joann stewing back home, and a slight edge of guilt, made Mark think of phoning her, texting her at least.

'Will she phone?'

'Once she realises, I haven't just dumped everything to come here, and that I've made the appropriate arrangements to ensure the gallery's day to day running.

She'll gradually calm down. Once I get back, though, that'll be a different story.'

Abriana smooth's her dress along her thighs and a longing inside him replaces any thoughts of Joann's reaction. He gives out a small laugh.

'Are you alright, Mark?'

'I'm fine. A little hot, that's all.'

'Have you ever been to Greece before?'

'No. This is my first time.'

'First impressions?'

'I can see how people are attracted to it. There's something special here. I don't know if it's the sea, the colours or the air. They all seem to have a quality of their own. The climate helps, of course.'

'Believe it or not, it gets cooler in the spring and it can be cold in the winter. It rains too. You wouldn't think that on a day like this.'

'So, you've been to Greece before?'

'Several times, but this is my first visit to Zakynthos. The first island I went to was Cephalonia. It's not far, actually. I'm sure you can see it. It's part of the same group of islands, the Ionian Islands.'

'When did you go?'

'Oh, it was years ago. I was just married, in fact.'

'You were on your honeymoon?'

'I was. Cephalonia left me with better memories than my marriage did.'

The villa sits in its grounds and around them the pulse of the cicadas' is magnified in the still air.

'I love that sound,' Mark says. 'It reminds me of when I once went to Westminster Abbey. It was my first time there and there was a service about to begin. I was quite surprised they let tourists in because when you see Westminster on the TV it's usually a state occasion or something like that. So, when I went in, it was filled with the public, sitting in seats. Anyway, once the choir started to sing, my God, it was beautiful. You know that expression, the voice is like an instrument. Well, this sounded like an orchestra of voices. It was truly spiritual. I was mesmerised. I haven't heard anything like it or felt like that since, but now, this comes a close second. There's something about that sound.'

'The cicadas?'

'Yeah, maybe it's just me, but it's almost spiritual.'

He can feel the sun on his face and momentarily shuts his eyes, basking in its heat upon his skin. When he opens them, Abriana is looking at him, studying his face. He stands up and walks towards the edge of the veranda, then down the steps and around the pool to the hedged verge. He looks out over the top of pine trees that descend into orange and lemon groves and then further; they give way to the sea.

Adriana turns and watches him. 'What is it?' She asks, puzzled by his sudden interest in the view.

He doesn't answer at first and then he turns to face her.

'It's been a long time.'

'What has?'

'This sensation. I haven't felt like this for a long time.'

'Like what?'

'Gratified I suppose. I feel like I've just drunk a warm drink that's spreading through my stomach.'

'Has the sun gone to your head?' She smiles.

'If it has, I hope it never stops. I'd love to see the island, Abriana. It wouldn't take that long, would it?'

The suggestion surprises her.

'I don't know. We're meeting Sutton's gardener, Pavlos, tomorrow morning. He stays just over there, on that hill, somewhere.' Abriana points to a hill that is visible on the other side of the harbour in Zakynthos Town. 'The hired car comes with a Sat nav so Pavlos shouldn't be too difficult to find.'

'I'm not meaning now, once this is over,' he says enthusi-astically.

'I'd like that as well.' She smiles at him.

'It's a date then?'

'You'll have to wait and see.'

CHAPTER NINE

A FLAT TYRE AND INDECISIONS

The next morning, after breakfast, they set off along the single tarmac track that winds its way past several high walled, gated villas and houses. The number of olive trees they pass surprises Mark. There are groves on each side of the track and Abriana tells him that there are many ancient olive trees to be seen throughout the island. Mark nods and notes that amongst others he can see a few cypress trees jutting above them, like steeples. They move along at a steady pace, stopping on the verge, several times, to let an oncoming vehicle pass.

Soon the road opens into two lanes and white and mustard houses become more prominent. Before long, Mark can see the sea and then the harbour. A church steeple, like the cypress tree, he thinks, is visible above the terracotta roofs. Soon the town opens up to them. They are in a warren of small streets, confined on each side by shops and homes. Mark gets the definite impression they are now in the capital.

'The Sat nav is going to take me along there.' Abriana points towards a line of cars parked almost the entire length of the street. 'If a car comes the other way, one of us would have to reverse all the way back.'

Mark peers at the screen. 'Turn left, here.' He points. 'It looks like it will take us along the harbour. It looks easier that way, see it will take us right along the coast.'

To Abriana's relief, Mark is right. They are soon out of the claustrophobic streets and into the open space of the road that runs parallel to the harbour.

'That's better. There seem to be a few nice restaurants here,' Mark observes. 'We should maybe come one night.'

'Without the car, I'm not driving through that again.'

'A taxi then, or we could add my name to the hired car. We should have done that at the airport when we picked it up. It would save you having to do all the driving. I've got my licence with me. It's still not too late to do it.'

Abriana shrugs. 'It's ok. We're only here for a few days.'

Mark looks at the Sat nav again. 'I'm sure we could have come along this road in the first place. Yeah, we could have. I can see it now. It's a long road, but probably quicker than the way we came.'

'I'll definitely go back that way then.' Abriana laughs.

'That's a nice church. Greece is famous for its churches, isn't it?' They pass Zakynthos' Cathedral, The Church of St Dionysius.

Abriana smiles. 'It is. Orthodoxy and Catholicism are both theatrical, what with the crucifixion, the candles, the icons, the incense, the Virgin Mary, but their churches are not as nice as our Italian ones.'

'I wonder who has the most churches, Greece or Italy?'

'Italia, of course. We definitely have the most masterpieces.'

'A biased opinion, I'm sure. Oh, wait a minute, I forgot about this.'

Mark reaches into the glove compartment and pulls out a guidebook on Zakynthos. 'I bought this at the airport, remember? I wonder if it can answer my question?'

He looks at the table of contents. 'Here we are.' Mark flicks through the pages.

'Well?' Abriana turns to look at him.

'Oh, that's a shame. It's just a biography of St Dionysius. It says here that his body is in the cathedral, and it remains intact and smells of flowers and frankincense. He was remarkable for his forgiveness. Seemingly, he forgave the man who killed his brother.'

They make their way along the coastal road, the sea to their left, and Zakynthos Town behind them.

'I should have filled the car up at the airport. There wasn't even a quarter of a tank. I'll stop at the next petrol station.'

Five minutes later, Abriana is filling the tank and Mark stretches his legs. He walks to the side of the road they have just come down. He can still see the capital, and like most Greek towns, its white complexion radiates in the sun's light. There is something ancient about it. Around him, he listens. He is aware of birdsong, insects buzzing, the rhythmic chant of cicadas and a white butterfly fluttering nearby some flowers. A sweet scent perfuses the air that is familiar to him, yet he cannot name it.

Something is invigorating about it. He realises this is the first time he has really listened. He turns to look at Abriana. It feels like the past few days have been like a dream, yet here he is, the sensual all too real. An excitement jolts through him.

Once Abriana returns to the car, she hands him a bottle of water. 'You don't want to dehydrate; you need to drink plenty of water.'

'Thanks. Oh, it's cold.'

Abriana combs her fingers through her hair. She has on sunglasses, so he can't see her eyes, but he knows how they look. Mark looks at her, scarcely believing he is with her, that this is happening. He can see her lips, and they are full. He has always found them to be her attraction. She meets his eyes and he can see his smile in the reflection in her sunglasses. He can't resurrect their history, but he can influence the present. He can silently acknowledge his feelings. It is enough for now.

Soon, they are entering Argassi and it doesn't take Mark long to realise it looks like a purpose-built resort.

'It has a Blackpool in the sun feel to it. Not what I'd imagined,' Mark says. He consults his guidebook and frowns. 'Originally, it was a small fishing village. There's not much evidence of that now. It's not what I'd expected.'

They turned right, off the main road, and travelled along a street that took them past restaurants and hotels. They came to a fork in the road and stopped outside 'The Phoenix Grill House.'

'Left, or right?' Abriana asks.

'The Sat nav says right.'

'Then right it is.'

They find themselves on a dusty road, winding above Argassi. They pass several villas, hidden behind large stone walls. Olive groves sprinkle the landscape, where tracks skirt their ancient trunks. The single-lane road continues to coil around blind bends where terraced hills undulate in giant waves against the cobalt sky.

'Look, over there. There's Zakynthos Town,' Mark says, looking to his left. 'The buildings look like marble against the green of the hillside. They're so white in the sun.' He feels an immediate elation.

Ahead of them, they can see a man with what looks like a hammer and chisel. Mark can see he is pointing a stone wall. The top of which is draped in the most striking bougainvillaea, its brilliant hue and complex patterned branches arch along and cascade down the wall in luscious and graceful burgundy and purple flowers. A Golden Retriever lies a few feet from the man, its eyes never moving from him.

Suddenly, Abriana feels the steering wheel shudder. It vibrates through her hands, and she has to apply force to keep the car from veering to the side.

'There's something wrong.' There is a trace of panic in her voice.

'Stop the car,' Mark urges.

Abriana brings the car to a halt. 'What do you think it is?'

'Probably a puncture.' Mark answers already halfway out of the car.

The tyre looks like it has melted into the road. He bends to inspect it, rubbing his fingers along the tread.

'It's a screw. I can just see its head. That's how far it's gone in. I hope we've got a spare.'

Mark opens the boot, and to his relief, finds the spare tyre. He checks the tread and locates the wheel wrench and locking wheel nut adapter. Besides the spare wheel is the moulded imprint of a vehicle jack, but it is empty.

Mark sighs. 'I can't believe this.'

'What is it?'

'The jack's not here.'

'It that bad?'

'Put it this way, the spare tyre is useless without it.'

By now, Abriana has got out of the car and is looking inside the boot. She bends her head as if she knows what she is looking for. 'That's bad then. I'll phone the hire company, the numbers in my bag.'

Mark closes the boot with a frown. Up ahead, he can see the man walking towards them, the dog ambling by his side.

'Is everything ok?' the man enquires.

'We've got a puncture, but no jack, would you believe?'

Abriana throws her smartphone into her bag. 'An answering machine. What way is that to run a business? It's only lunchtime.'

'They'll be in Greek time.' The man smiles. He has short black hair and is wearing a blue t-shirt, long shorts that stop just above his knees and flip-flops.

'Your Scottish,' Mark says, surprised.

'And so are you. Where are you from?' He offers his hand and Mark shakes it.

'Edinburgh.'

'Really, me too. What's the chance of that? This is Abriana and I'm Mark.'

'Hello. Your wall is nice,' she says, feeling she has to make some comment.

'Thanks, it's coming along now, eventually. And you're not Scottish.'

'No, Italian.'

'So was my dad. I'm Louis, by the way.'

'Your dog's gorgeous. What's its name?' Abriana bends to clap the dog.

'This is Floyd.' The dog hears its name and turns towards Louis.

'He's so well behaved.'

'Ah, first impressions can be deceptive. If he catches the scent of a rabbit, he's his own man.'

'I can't believe there's no jack,' Mark muses.

'I've got one back at the house. I'll just be a minute.' Louis walks back along the track, followed by Floyd.

'That was lucky,' Mark says, crouching down and fitting the wheel nut.

'Have you changed a tyre before?'

'One or two. You look sceptical. I've got my hands dirty before, you know.' He grins.

Soon Louis returns with a jack. 'Do you need a hand?'

'I should be fine, thanks.'

'Once you're finished, just come up to the house. You can get cleaned up if you want.'

'That's kind of you,' Abriana says.

Mark looks at his hands, already they are dirty. 'I think I'll take you up on the offer.'

'Are you sure you don't want a hand?'

'No, I'm fine.'

'My wife, Maria, has insisted you have a drink. She'll be pouring the lemonade as we speak.'

'That would be nice, but we shouldn't impose any further. We're just grateful to get the tyre fixed,' Abriana says.

'It's not a problem. Anyway, in this heat, Mark will need that drink. When you've finished, just come up to the house. Maria's expecting you,' Louis assures her.

Once Louis leaves, Abriana smiles. 'He's nice and not too bad looking,' she teases Mark.

'A drink would be nice,' Mark says, wiping his brow 'I'm leaking sweat here. Have we still got time?'

Abriana looks at her watch. 'We're still early.' She looks

at him and pouts her lips sympathetically. 'I think you deserve it.'

'Good,' he says, then thinks, 'I'm filthy already. I can't visit someone looking like this. I'll need to wash my hands.'

Abriana parks the car alongside a Mitsubishi 4x4. The house is large with a modern extension. It has a wrap-around veranda. Across from the house, with its own land-scaped garden, there is a two-storey building with balconies and blue wooden shutters. On a wall, a blue placard with white lettering reads, *'The room with a view'*, where marble steps lead up to a second floor. Mark glimpses the blue sheen of a pool, obscured by a small stone wall, and hears children's excited voices. Behind them, there is a garden and a stone path that leads to a circle of olive trees where an old wooden bench sits, waiting for someone to sit. And what a beautiful place to sit, Abriana thinks, for she can also see oranges and lemons, hanging from branches, like coloured light bulbs above a carpet of wildflowers.

'Over here.' Louis waves, standing on the veranda, as the Mark and Abriana get out of the car. 'Come and have that drink.'

'I wasn't expecting this,' Mark says.

'It's beautiful.' Abriana continues to look around, her eyes taking it in.

They walk over to the veranda and climb the steps.

Abriana ruffles Floyd's fur, as he comes to greet them with a toy animal in his mouth.

'Hello, I'm Maria. I hope you like lemonade?' Marie pours lemonade into four glasses.

After the introductions, Louis shows Mark to the kitchen, where he can wash his hands.

Maria invites Abriana to sit and hands her a glass of lemonade. Abriana concludes they are the same age. Maria's hair is full and falls around her shoulders in curls. It is lighter than most Greek women, but her eyes are unmistakably Mediterranean, dark and oval. Abriana can detect a faint scar above Maria's lip, which doesn't detract from her attractive face, she thinks to herself.

'The lemonades lovely. It's so fresh. Did you make it?' Abriana asks.

'Freshly squeezed this morning.'

'I can tell. My mother did the same.'

'There's no better way to quench a thirst.' Maria smiles.

'I love your home.'

'Thank you. We've added to it over the years.'

Abriana looks towards the apartments. 'Are those yours too?'

'They are,' Louis says, as both he and Mark sit down. He hands Mark a lemonade. 'We've been renting them out now for coming on, let me think, thirteen years now.'

'The house is older than that?' Abriana asks.

'Yes. It originally belonged to my aunt. She stayed with us until she passed away last year.' Maria smiles, sadly.

Louis reaches over and squeezes her hand. 'Anna was a big presence around here. The kids miss her.'

'You have children?'

Maria's eyes widen. 'Yes. Three. Twins, a boy and girl, Manolis and Despina, who are twelve and little Anna, who is eight. They're at school just now.'

'Of course.'

'You'll never believe it, but Mark lives in Edinburgh,' Louis tells Maria.

'Really. What a coincidence. Which part?'

'The West End,' Mark answers.

'This is creepy. What street?' Louis looks at him expectantly.

'Eglington Crescent.'

Louis claps his hands and laughs. 'I was just around the corner, Lansdowne Crescent.'

'God. That's weird. I wonder what the chances of that are?'

'Are you staying in Argassi?' Louis asks.

'No, we're in a villa just outside Zakynthos Town.' Abriana smiles.

'Nice. Have you been to Zakynthos before?'

'First time.' Mark says, taking a drink. 'Mm... this is nice.'

'We just arrived yesterday. Unfortunately, it's just a flying visit,' Abriana says.

'Short holiday, then.'

'Business actually. We're on our way to meet someone. I'm hoping they don't stay too far from here.'

Louis looks intrigued. 'Oh. Who's that?'

'Pavlos Torosidis.'

Louis raises his eyebrows. 'Oh. Old Pavlos. We're virtually neighbours. He keeps me right with the garden. It wouldn't look as half as good without Pavlos' help. He just lives two minutes away.'

'Oh good. That's a relief. The Sat nav struggled up here.' Mark laughs.

'How long have you known Pavlos?' Maria asks.

'We've not met. I need to ask him about something.'

'Does he know you're coming?'

'Oh, don't worry,' Abriana says, sensing Maria's concern. She explains about their interest in Pavlos, without going into too much detail, and that Pavlos has agreed to meet with them.

'That's right,' Louis says. 'Pavlos told me he worked in Italy when he was a young man.'

'We're hoping he can clear up a few loose ends. It's important really, there's a lot of money at stake.'

'His memory is excellent, so you won't have any problems there.'

Abriana smiles. 'I suppose we'd better get going. Thanks for the drink, Maria.'

'And the jack,' Mark adds.

'Yes, I'm so relieved about that,' Abriana says.

Maria smiles. 'I hope Pavlos can answer your questions, it's a long way to come for nothing.'

'It's worth it just to see Zakynthos,' Mark says as he stands. 'I'd love to stay longer and really explore the island. That's a good enough reason to come back. There's something special about this place.'

'I know what you mean. I felt exactly the same when I first came here.' Louis smiles.

'When was that?'

'Almost fifteen years ago. It's incredible when I think about that. It feels like yesterday.'

'That must have been a big decision to make. Coming to a different country and making a go of it.'

'Not really. It was the easiest one I've ever made. I never grow tired of looking at the sea. It has a new composition for me to admire each morning I wake. It's been the same ever since I first set eyes on it. The smells of the herbs, the trees and flowers that rise from the garden and forest and sweeten the air are all the oxygen I need to nourish this body of mine. I'm spellbound by the vast blue sky, the rich colours of the towns and villages and then there are the people, their selfless hospitality and genuine affection, their love of tradition and orthodoxy. This is where I call home. I belong here. I'm living the dream, especially because it involves this beautiful lady.'

'Louis!' Maria smiles fondly at him. 'You'll embarrass me.'

Abriana can see another look on Maria's face. There is an expression that she knows, for she too has known such satisfaction. Also, she realises how relaxed she has become in their company. She wishes she could stay longer in this beautiful place and hear Louis and Maria's story of how they met and raised their family. There is a definite aura of being at home around them. This is how it should be. She believes one cannot model such an existence; it is inherent in the individuals who influence its creation. A love that is pure, a love that is given, enhances it and it needs to be worked at. Abriana knows without having known the pain of suffering, and setbacks, and trials and tribulations, it is impossible to reach such an attainment. It is reassuring to her. This is not a passive relationship; it is real. Abriana finds herself intrigued by them. She has been aware of their body language towards each other. She marvels at their togetherness. Abriana wants to indulge in what has brought them together. She wonders about herself. Is it the revelation that this is what she has always wanted? She is astonished at how this makes her feel. She is profoundly conscious of her own feelings towards Mark. What is she afraid of? Herself? Her own indecision takes her aback.

In the air is the smell of jasmine and lavender. There is

birdsong around them. She can hear the faint cries of children playing in the pool and Floyd's muffled barks as he lies at her feet, dreaming.

'Thank you so much, Maria, Mark.' Abriana smiles.

Maria waves her hand. 'You're welcome and when you visit Pavlos again, I'd love to see you. There's always enough lemonade.'

'I'd like that very much. Thank you.'

CHAPTER TEN

PAVLOS

The tyres crush on the dry earth as they turn onto a narrow track that curves around a thicket of burnt vegetation. The house they face is a small, one storey, pink salmon building.

There is a crouched figure in the immaculate garden as Abriana and Mark exit the car. Pavlos stands stiffly, holding a trowel in his hand. As a young man, his frame was sturdy. He is now a shrunken version of his former self.

'How old is he?' Mark asks.

'Eighty-eight or eighty-nine... something like that, I think.'

Mark makes a mental calculation. 'So, he was either sixteen or seventeen when the painting was stolen? When you think of it like that, it's a long time ago.'

'Yes, it is.'

'I hope he has a good memory.'

'We wouldn't be here otherwise. He obviously convinced the gallery's researchers he has the information they need. I just need to capture it.'

Pavlos wipes his hands together. Slightly stooped with a pronounced limp, he walks towards them.

'Kalispera, I believe you are expecting us,' Abriana says.

Pavlos' hooded eyes strain to focus on them. From his breast pocket, he takes out gold spectacles and, once placed on the bridge of his nose, he says, 'That's better. I can see you now. You must be Abriana?' He has a gentle air about him.

'I am, and this is Mark.'

Mark raises his hand in greeting. 'Hi.'

Pavlos nods towards his hands, that are caked with mud.

'I'd welcome you with a handshake, but I don't think it would be very polite of me. Come, let's go up to the house. We can sit under the tree. It should be cooler in the shade.'

'Your garden's beautiful,' Abriana says as they walk towards the house, adjusting their pace to Pavlos' slower progress.

'Thank you. It's what I've always done. Not only was it my living, but it has also always been my passion. These days I spend more of my time speaking to flowers and herbs than I do with people. I've been looking forward to your visit ever since the nice young woman phoned.'

Abriana smiles. 'That's good.'

'I must admit, I was taken aback when I spoke with the young woman. I thought, after all these years, the painting was lost. Since the phone call, I've thought of nothing else.'

'I'm so glad you agreed to meet with us. You do know the importance of the matter? Ultimately, you may hold the information that decides the future of the painting.'

'Yes, I'm aware of that. The young woman made it quite clear. I have nothing to gain from this and even if I did, it would not change what is the truth.'

'It seems you're the only person who may know the truth.'

'You mean everyone else is dead? Then we'd better get started. I'm odds on to be next.' Pavlos chuckles to himself. 'Just let me wash my hands first.' With that, he disappears into the darkness of the house.

Above them, the tree provides a canopy of shade from the fierce sun.

'He seems friendly enough, and he has a sense of humour,' Mark says in a lowered voice.

When he returns, Pavlos sinks into a wicker chair opposite Abriana. He holds a small pipe between his teeth and spends about thirty seconds puffing vigorously, trying to ignite the tobacco with a lighter. A plume of smoke announces his success and his face washes in a satisfied glow.

'Do you mind if I record you? It's easier that way.' Abriana shows Pavlos a Dictaphone.

'I thought you might. It's not a problem.' He puffs on his pipe. 'I hope the smoke isn't troubling you. I can put it out if you want.'

'No. Not at all,' Abriana insists.

'I don't mind either. I've always liked the smell of a pipe. My grandad smoked one. It reminds me of him.' Mark smiles.

'Where are you staying?'

'We've rented a villa just outside the capital,' she says. 'It has lovely views, just like here, really.'

'You can switch that thing on now.' Pavlos nods towards the Dictaphone.

Abriana places it on the table. 'You can start whenever you like.'

The wicker creaks as Pavlos settles back into the chair. 'I

first saw Villa Casamora when I was fifteen. I was just a boy, really. I didn't know much about tending a garden, planting flowers and pruning trees. That didn't matter to John, he just said, '*I learned how to paint, so you'll learn to be a gardener.*'

'I went to Italy from Greece with my father. He was a carpenter and had come to Florence to work on the many projects to restore the city's historical buildings. I was labouring. One day, my father fell from scaffolding, and he died a few days later. I was a boy in a strange country. I couldn't speak the language, but I knew some English and by chance, I heard some Englishman who lived in a villa in the countryside just outside Florence needed a gardener. I didn't know how big this garden was. If I had known, I wouldn't have gone, that's for sure. Luckily, for both of us, I did go. John taught me English, and I taught myself to be a gardener.

'I often accompanied him when he travelled through the countryside to paint. I remember him wielding a fistful of brushes and washing the canvass in colour. He was the painter of elegant aristocrats and socialites, but he abandoned all of that at the pinnacle of his career. He was part of the British establishment. His reputation as a painter of portraits was insurmountable. He had critical respect, yet he turned his back on it all. I did not know that John Sutton. I never saw him paint a portrait; he had found the freedom to paint what made him happy. The John Sutton I knew painted the landscapes of Tuscany.'

Pavlos speaks warmly of John Sutton. His voice is deep and sonorous. 'I think about it a lot. I'll never forget that day when the German soldiers came and took the painting. How could I forget?'

Pavlos pauses and collects his thoughts. He puffs on the pipe. 'It killed John; you know. The soldiers had to rip the painting from him. It was more than just canvass and paint; it was his connection to Alisha. He found it incredibly painful. As long as the painting was with him, she was as well.'

This piece of information tightens and sears Abriana's chest. It is a reaction she is not prepared for.

'Her name was Alisha?' Abriana asks.

'Yes. Alisha.'

'Were they a couple when he painted her?'

'They were.'

'Where did he keep the portrait? Was it hung on a wall?'

'No. He kept it in his studio. The portrait was only ever seen by a few people in John's lifetime. It was never displayed publicly.'

'But why?' Adriana asks.

'The painting was so much more than just a representation of Alisha. It proclaimed their love for each other. Artistically, it was his crescendo of portraiture and his last. It was a visual manifestation of the woman he loved that made life worth living. If you look into her eyes, you can see that love. Such dynamics shine from the painting. I'd never seen anything as powerful in the way it is communicated. You can see she is in love. John never loved another woman. Very few people at that time even knew of the painting's existence and even fewer ever saw it.'

There is a silence between them, respectful of the revelation of such love.

'Why have you agreed to talk about this now and never before?' Abriana asks.

'I didn't know what the fate of the painting was. As time passed, I thought it must have been lost or destroyed. But then I received the phone call telling me about the current situation. If the portrait belongs anywhere, it should be with John's other paintings. It belongs to the Uffizi Gallery which is fitting because it is near to the villa, the place John loved. When John started to paint his landscapes, he was very keen that they were seen by as many people as possible. So, when the Uffizi Gallery approached him, he was delighted. They also paid him well. Not that he needed the money.'

'What was he like, really? There have been books written about him, mostly documenting his life in London. Very little is known about his time in Italy, other than what has been written in the Uffizi Galleries accounts. They're just guessing. The difficulty the biographers had was Sutton's silence.'

'He was my friend, my best friend, but that doesn't mean I won't speak honestly about him. He could be very sensitive, sometimes stubborn, but mostly, he was charming to be around, first as an employer and then later, as a friend.

'He was a man who believed in the value of principle. He lived his life by them. He rarely compromised. If he felt strongly about something, he never budged, well, not often.' Pavlos smiles to himself, as if remembering a time from the past.

'He was intensely passionate about his landscapes. He came to love the Italian countryside. He once told me he had fallen in love again and I said, *"With whom, who is she?"* John laughed and replied, *"Her name is Italy."'*

Abriana smiles, immediately warming to this image of John Sutton.

'John was always compassionate and generous. Although I was his gardener, and he had a maid and a cook, we were all regarded as his family. We were as loyal to him as he was to us.'

'We are here because we hope you'll have the answers to our questions. In your correspondence with the gallery, you said you know the truth about John Sutton. You know who the heir to the painting is,' Abriana enquires.

'I do. John spoke of it many times.'

The Story of Alisha Hadley

London 1905

They sit in silence for a while.

'Play for me,' he suggests.

'What would you like me to play?'

He observes her, feeling a spontaneous surge of love for her that spreads through his chest, engulfing him in its warm glow.

John Sutton smiles. 'Anything. You decide.'

The violin sits in her lap. Made of spruce and maple, it is over a hundred years old.

'Let me see.' She lifts the violin and holds the lower bout of the instrument between her left shoulder and her chin. 'Mozart or Bach perhaps?' Her face takes on a seriously concentrated look as she presses her fingers to the strings and glides the bow over the end of the fingerboard, making an ethereal sound. Her fingers are delicate, yet she plays with certain precision and agility. There is a grace and an elegance to their movement. He listens intently whilst she plays beautifully phrased runs that are fluid and at times flamboyant. It takes the breath from him.

A pool of warm yellow light seeps into the room, high-lighting the milk-white skin of her face. John catches her eyes under her wavy hair. He is looking straight at her, watchful and thoughtful, his gaze caught in the animated angles and structure of her eyes, her mouth and cheeks. When the last notes of the piece fade, she lays the violin on her lap. He recovers himself.

She is smiling at him now. 'Did you enjoy it?'

'It was wonderful. Just exquisite.' When she smiles at him, he forgets himself. 'I could watch you play all day.'

She is aware he says, *watch*, rather than *listen*.

'Alisha, it's been praying on my mind for some time and if I don't ask now... well, you'll be leaving soon. Would you indulge me and consider a request?'

'Of course. What is it?'

'I'd like to paint your portrait. It would be my gift to you. You give me so much joy and pleasure when I listen to your music that I want to return the favour if I may.' He smiles. 'The only way I know how is to paint you. Would you sit for me, Alisha? I'd love to capture you playing the violin.'

Alisha bows her head.

'I've embarrassed you. Forgive me. It was certainly not my intention,' John says with a tension audible in his voice.

'No. You haven't embarrassed me, John. You could never do that. I'm honoured, being asked to have one's portrait done by one of the greatest artists of his day is beyond flattery, but I'd prefer you didn't paint me.'

'Oh, I see,' he says, quietly.

'You misunderstand me.' Alisha acknowledges John's awkwardness with a smile. 'If you really want to paint me, I'd prefer it was in a group portrait.'

'You mean the Quartet.'

'Yes. Would you object to that? After all, I don't perform in public on my own. We are a group. It wouldn't feel right.

It would be self-indulgent of me to sit for you on my own without them. And there are only four of us. What do you say?'

He senses he is losing the argument. 'It would be my pleasure.' He leans back in his chair. 'We don't have long together. The thought of you leaving so soon presses on my mind?'

'We still have two weeks.'

'Are you still looking forward to it, this Grand Tour?'

'I am,' Alisha says with a mixture of anguish and anticipation.

'And have the travel arrangements been finalised?' John crosses his legs.

'Yes, at last.' Alisha gives an account of the travel arrangements. 'We'll initially be taking a train, then a ship. We'll be travelling to Brindisi in Italy, then a ship to Corfu. It's exciting, but I'm apprehensive about going.'

'Why? It will feel like a holiday, a great adventure.'

'I suppose it will. I've never been that far from you. It feels as if it's another world away.'

'You'll be fine. You're performing most nights and I have my painting; it always keeps me busy. They'll be lots to see. It won't be all work.' His words conceal his heavy heart.

'I know. I do hope I can fit in some sightseeing, especially in Rome and Athens.'

'I never told you I've been to Italy... Florence, Naples and Rome, of course. Some years ago, I had a commission. Some incredible wealthy Italian paid me quite handsomely to paint him in his villa, in Italy. He was ecstatic with the results, I recall. I loved the countryside, that's what I really wanted to paint. I ended up staying for three months just travelling.' He shakes his head. 'Remember Alisha, Greece is not Italy. There are parts that have not reached the level of refinement that one would expect. Athens is different, I believe.'

'We're performing in the main towns and staying in hotels. Alfred has always looked after us in that respect. I'm sure we won't suffer any indignation.'

'I just worry, that's all.'

'I know you do.'

'Well, since we've agreed that I can paint you...'

'The Quartet.'

'Sorry, yes, the Quartet. We'll need to arrange the sittings; time is not on our side. Two or three sittings will be enough, I suspect.'

'I will speak with the others and then we can finalise the arrangements.'

John stands and adjusts his tie. 'Well, that's settled. Would you like some tea?'

They drink their tea in a large room. The walls are wood-panelled but offset by two large bay windows that flood the room with light.

John Sutton first met Alisha when introduced to the Quartet by Alfred Beecham, after a performance at The Wigmore Hall, Marylebone, London where they played Haydn's String Quartet in C No 2, and Beethoven's String Quartet in C No 3, 'Razumovsky.' After that first performance, their music, but mostly Alisha enthralled John. He attended several more performances before finally asking Alisha out for dinner. She had no idea who he was; just a friend of Alfred's, she thought. Yet John was one of the most sought-after portraiture artists of his day, which not only brought him fame, but quite considerable wealth.

Alfred Beecham was the Quartet's wealthy benefactor.

He had made his money in the linen mills of the north of England. His passion for classical music was the driving force behind his sponsorship of the Quartet's tours around the cities of England. His energies now focused on a new venture, setting up archaeological and historical tours of the Mediterranean to Europe's elite and wealthy.

'It's quite a novel concept Alfred has; pretty ingenious, I would say.'

'He's very enthusiastic about it. He said there is a thirst amongst those that can afford such trips, visiting the ancient sites. The first-class travel arrangements, fine hotels and experienced guides who they speak English will guarantee its success. I've never seen Alfred so animated and enthusiastic.'

'He's putting a lot of his own money into it. He wants investors. That's what this trip is all about, as well as promoting the excursions. It's a fledgeling industry, but there's a market. Those who can afford to do so will want to visit the spa and seaside towns of Europe.

'It's becoming popular amongst the middle classes and Alfred can see the potential in that. He was always one for spotting a business opportunity. The manufacturing and trading families, educated professionals - writers, journalists, lawyers, even artists, they'll all want to go, it will solidify their social status.

'He's already looking at developing and publishing guidebooks and travelogues. Such literature has acquired Bible like status recently amongst travellers to Europe.

'I suspect the English will be attracted to Italy and Greece with their paintings, sculptures and architecture, not to mention visiting the historical sites. He needs quality hotels, to a standard his customers will expect. He needs the business community to invest and a big part of that is setting the right ambience and that involves you and your music. You are part of the selling pitch. That's a big responsibility. You'll have to persuade these potential investors to dig deep into their pockets.'

'I don't think that's the reason we're playing. We're there to entertain those that Alfred has invited to hear his business plans.'

He lifts her hand and kisses it. 'I'm teasing you. On a more serious note, I am worried.'

She senses his sadness and can see it on his face.

'There's no need to be. Let's turn our minds to more palatable thoughts.'

John twirls the ring on his middle finger.

He looks at her, contemplating whether to air his thoughts. He crosses his legs, clasping his hands on his thigh. The thought of celebrating Alisha's impending departure is almost too much to bear. She would be gone from him for three months. For a moment, his mind tumbles over such a reality. Alisha is fixing the pins in her hair, securing a stray hair. Something moves inside him. He recalls an image of sliding the waves of hair from her shoulder and kissing her neck. The awareness of desire is brief, but all the same, it pricks at him like a needle. For that moment, he cannot trust himself.

'I thought I might take you out for dinner tonight.'

'That would be nice. Where do you have in mind?'

'I've booked a table at the Dorchester.'

'John, that's a bit extravagant.'

'I know, but you're worth it. I love spoiling you. I'm not going to get that chance for the next two months, so I'm making the most of it.'

. . .

Everyone is in high spirits when they arrive. Reuben, Alex, Sara and, of course, Alisha. John's studio is on the upper floor of his house, where three prodigious windows flood the room with light.

Scattered around the room there are many colours in labelled jars: Cadmium orange, Brown ochre, Cobalt blue, Ultramarine light, Cinnabar green, Cold grey, Titanium white and much more. There are brushes everywhere, all varying in size and state of use. Several paintings sit around the studio on trestles, half-finished compositions of the great and good of the English establishment. It is John's habit to work on several commissioned paintings at a time; it keeps the creative process fresh and challenging, he often tells his subjects. These paintings are shrouded in white sheets, their contents hidden from the eye until John feels he has accomplished a likeness and mood.

The floorboards are splattered in colour as if a child has been given license to cast paint wherever it desires. All in all, the impression the studio gives is that of disarray, which is in striking contrast to John's orderly and functional outlook on life.

There is an exciting tension amongst the quartet. They are all aware of John's standing in the art world and although he has become a familiar acquaintance, there exists a respected admiration towards him.

John instructs them on where to stand, demonstrating their individual poses.

'I want it to look like you're playing a particular piece of music as one, not four individuals, but in unison, you have become the melody. There is no distinction between your instrument and your human form.'

'I've been pondering over what will be best for this particular portrait. I hope you will not be averse to a somewhat deviation from your usual set up.'

'What do you mean?' Reuben asks.

'I would like to suggest that Alisha stands to the fore of the group, side on and looking straight at me. This will give the effect that she is looking outwardly towards those who are viewing the painting.'

Sara seems momentarily flustered. 'But then Alisha will not be portrayed as part of the group.'

'I'm not sure, John,' Alisha says.

'I have done some preliminary sketches to give you an idea of what I mean. Here, pass these around.'

They contemplate the images, drawn in pencil.

Alex clears his throat. 'It's different, not conventional. I think it does make us look interesting beyond just another portrait. It will be different; I'll give you that. I like the idea. It will stand out, that's for sure.'

'You never really wanted to paint us, did you, John?' Rueben says, looking up from the drawings. There is a disturbing manner about him, a provocative veneer. 'You really just wanted to paint Alisha, not us. We're just props in all this.' He thrusts the drawings towards John. 'This is a charade.'

'Rueben!' Alisha protests.

'You're quite right, Rueben. It hadn't occurred to me to paint the Quartet. And why should it have? I wanted to paint Alisha for my own gratification. Alisha persuaded me otherwise, and she was right, of course, but I am right when it comes to matters of composition.'

'This is a charade. So, we must accept your professional judgement, even if I disagree with you. It's intolerable. I'm not sure I want to be part of this.'

'It really wouldn't represent the quartet if you were missing from the portrait, would it, Rueben?' John shrugs. 'It's your choice.'

'Look, let's not fall out over this, please. John, I will stand with the others and let that be an end to the matter.' Alisha is insistent.

John wants to press the matter further; he feels his artistic integrity threatened and because of this, he will not back down. Rueben's interference has bruised him, yet he tries to be tolerant.

'This has the potential to be much more than just another portrait. It can touch people; we can give them so much more. I can add layers of mystery and possibility; it can have an aura about it that will draw people into the scene, stimulating them emotionally. This is my hope.' John is unable to keep the desperation from his voice.

'You're being horrid, Rueben. You're questioning John's integrity as an artist. How would you feel if the shoe was on the other foot?' Alex asks.

Rueben ponders this question. 'Alright, maybe I'm over-reacting... I apologise John.'

'Accepted. Thank you, Rueben,' John says, with some relief. 'You see, great portraits are made in the detail. That's what I try to achieve. When I paint a face, I want that face to tell a story. It has to project that narrative, or I've failed. The painting is then worthless. It may stand up technically and in style, but as its creator, its purpose is lost and so too is the opportunity to communicate emotion and connection.'

Rueben smiles apologetically. 'You've convinced me, John.'

'I think we're all convinced,' Sara says.

'Let's get started then.' John smiles towards Alisha and lays the sketches across a small table. 'The women can get dressed behind the screens.'

Alisha and Sara change into lavender-blue off the shoulder, sleeveless evening gowns with low necklines that allow for an overt display of cleavage. Alisha's hair falls in waves around her shoulders. Rueben and Alex dress in dark suits and white shirts opened at the neck.

John instructs Reuben and Alex on the poses he requires. 'I need to depict grace within the movement of the composition.'

Likewise, he shows Sara how to hold her violin, the placement of an arm and the tilt of her head. 'We need to see sweeping gestures. It is a performance. It is not static.'

He asks Alisha to stand side-on, hold her violin by its neck and let it hang loosely by her side as if it is about to slip through her fingers. Tilting her head, she looks ahead towards the space between herself and John. It is a gaze that gives the distinct impression there is an intimacy between the painter and his subject. Her eyes define it. There is a hypnotic quality to that look, and it is John's desire that it radiates from the canvass.

'The light is perfect today. Alisha, tilt your head. Yes, that's it.'

Alisha slips out of bed and opens the velvet drapery to a mist that seems to have stolen everything that is familiar to her. She opens the large wardrobe and picks out a flecked wool walking suit and lays it on the bed. After some deliberation, she chooses a wide-brimmed hat and gloves. Her eye catches the bulky trunk that sits on top of the wardrobe and it reminds her she has still to pack. It is a task that she has been postponing, as it is a constant reminder of her imminent departure.

There are times she thinks of the prospect of travelling and performing so far away, her mind can't comprehend the distance. She feels like an apprehensive child. She can flit from this state to then feeling emboldened with excitement at the prospect of possibilities and adventures enjoyed to the full.

Alisha sits in front of the dressing table and pins her hair. It is a feature, with its natural waves and curls, which often beguiled men and women alike. She has been told by several of the women who have attended Alfred's gatherings and travelled abroad that the humidity of the Mediterranean leaves the hair damp and limp. Their advice is to always cover the head with a large hat whenever she ventures outdoors.

Alisha wonders if she will get the chance to swim in the sea. The thought of swimming in warm water is a novelty she has not experienced. She has been told it is like floating in a giant bathtub, for in the summer, the water is soothingly tepid, clear like a mountain spring and suffused in shades of striking blue she will think the horizon has melted and the sea and sky have become one. Her imagination feels frozen, for she cannot contemplate such a scene. The recognition that her eyes will fall upon such wonders in the absence of John punctures her bubble of excitement.

Alisha sighs and not for the first-time struggles with the decision she has made. She has often contemplated that John has been hiding his true thoughts and suppressed them in her presence. She knows this, for he will often quash his instinct to reveal his frame of mind on a subject or issue in his desire to please her. It worries her he feels such a need. Such propriety is an effort most men would not tolerate, for it is not in their nature to deny the expression of their inner senses and beliefs.

Alisha fills the bathtub with hot water and tentatively she steps into it, lowering herself with ease, and as her skin turns red, she welcomes the soothing heat. She lays her head against the cold porcelain, her mind full with a new piece the quartet is rehearsing. She can hear a hushed cello pattern, then a rising and falling and a constant, but slightly varied melody, a crescendo of flourishing strings. It is a striking atmospheric and intense piece. Alisha loves its dramatic flair. She inhales deeply. Alisha has a sense of floating, like a feather on the wind. She can feel her muscles relax, the whispery touch of the water on her skin tickles her neck. She is weightless. Still, there is an ache in her.

Alisha's hand jerks and the splash of water wakes her with a startle. She panics. How long has she slept? How could she have fallen asleep? The bathwater is not yet cold, so she assumes not too long. Alisha quickly washes. She dries herself and gets dressed in the bedroom. Breakfast is a hurried affair. She forgoes her usual cup of tea, checks her hat in the hallway mirror and, with her violin case clasped firmly in her hand, she opens the front door and purposefully strides off down the street.

As she walks, Alisha is conscious of the sun, still smudged by the grey sky, is gradually dissolving the mist that recedes with each passing minute. Misty amber light reveals the expanse of the streets, the terraced houses with their glow of electric light and the horse-drawn carriages restoring the senses with familiar sounds and smells.

She walks along Frith Street, thoughtfully, going over the new piece in her head they have been rehearsing for several days. Heading towards the little room that serves as the quartet's rehearsal space above a butcher's shop, Alisha notices a sliver of blue amongst the shroud of cloud in the sky and she is confident it will be another fine day.

To gain access to the room, Alisha must walk through the shop, where Mr Brown, the proprietor, stands behind the counter and greets her each day framed by white tiles and carcases hanging from hooks.

'What will it be today, Alisha, sausages or a lovely piece of beef?'

'Beef will do just fine, Mr Brown.'

Since the day they first rehearsed above the shop, Mr Brown has given each member of the quartet a parcel of meat in gratitude for entertaining himself and his customers, their music heard by everyone who visits his shop.

'It will be a long two months, Alisha. The mornings won't be the same without the wonderful sound of your music. We'll all be poorer for it. I truly feel that.'

'You're too kind, Mr Brown.' Alisha smiles, as she mounts the stairs at the rear of the shop. 'I'll surely miss your delicious treats.'

When she arrives, everyone is already there. Rueben turns his handsome face towards her, and Alisha conceals her disappointment and irritation by smiling a good morning. Since the last sitting for the portrait, which none of them have seen yet, Rueben can't hide his spreading itch of anger towards John. There is a pang of worry in Alisha, and Sara has caught that look in Alisha's eyes.

Alex looks his usual puzzled self as Sara enquires about Alisha's state of mind. 'Are you feeling yourself this morning, Alisha?'

Reuben looks sharply at the two women and then smiles. 'Why shouldn't I be?'

'Oh, I've noticed you've been quiet at times. You're not ill, I hope, not now that we're almost on our way.'

'I'm fine, Sara, honest.'

'It's John, isn't it?'

'What do you mean?'

'That he won't be joining us when we get to Greece. He works too hard.'

'He's already signed the contracts for his next commissions. It can't be helped. The timing of it wasn't kind to us.' Alisha checks her disappointment and irritation with herself.

'That's a matter of opinion.'

'Rueben, that's quite enough of that,' Sara scolds him.

'Well, who does he think he is? We haven't seen the painting yet, and it's almost finished. I don't think we'll ever see it. It's probably his way of getting back at me. I'm sorry Alisha, but that's just the way I feel. I can't change that.'

'What is it with men? They think the world revolves around them,' Sara says, waving her hand dismissively.

'Look, let's just get started, shall we? I thought today we should run through our whole repertoire before we begin practising Bach's, The Art of Fugue. I fell asleep in the bath this morning going over it. I played every note in my head.'

'I hope it doesn't have the same effect on the audience.' Alex smiles.

The thought that John cannot join them strikes her. She remembers when Alfred asked the quartet to go to Europe with him, all expenses paid, first-class travel and a considerable small fortune in payment. The others were ecstatic at the prospect of travel and playing to a foreign audience. When she told John, her words tumbled from her as to why she would stay and not go. John was insistent that she should not let the opportunity slip by. John just looked at her and smiled. It was a once in a lifetime chance. Music was what she did. He has his painting and Alisha has her music.

After they rehearse, the mood has changed, helped by an oblique sun that lightens the room in a golden hue.

'I hope we can play like that on the tour. I didn't hear a single mistake,' Alex says.

Sara places her hand on his shoulder. 'You mean you didn't make a mistake for a change? The rest of us are always professional.'

'You're right, Alex. We've become a tighter unit and we're more relaxed when we play. That's an expression of our confidence. It comes over in the performance,' Rueben says, visibly impressed by their efforts.

'I'm so excited,' Sara beams. 'It sounds so exotic, Italy and Greece. I've never been out of England. Do you think the air will feel different, Alisha? I've been told it has a certain smell; it's supposed to be sweeter, more fragrant.'

'I've never thought about it. It'll definitely feel warmer. The light is very bright I'm told. Don't forget to pack some hats, Sara.' Alisha smiles as she bends to place her violin into its case.

'That sounds like a good excuse to buy some new ones. Do you want to go shopping Alisha? You can help me choose. I wouldn't want us having identical hats. That would never do. We wouldn't be able to swap.'

'It's almost lunchtime. Anyone fancy a drink?' Rueben asks, raising an eyebrow at Alex and flashing a white smile.

'Now that you mention it, I could murder one.' Alex grins.

'Sorry Sara, I'm meeting John for lunch,' Alisha says, with a little too much enthusiasm.

'That's a pity. We'll have to do it soon then; we don't have much time left. The days are going past so quickly.'

'I promise.'

Alisha's mother died in childbirth, leaving her young grieving father to raise his two daughters on his own. Alisha's sister, Julia, was two years old. Her father, William Hadley, worked as a labourer in a local factory. It was a job that fed them, clothed them and just paid the rent with a little left-over. William relied on the charity and benevolence of his neighbours, who looked after Alisha and Julia during the day, when he worked twelve-hour shifts, six days a week.

William's ability to sustain this existence lowered with each passing month. It became increasingly apparent he drank heavily, visiting pubs on his way home from the factory most days. When left in his care, the neighbour's concern for the children's safety grew and often William failed to collect them, too drunk to walk.

A sister who lived in Camden offered to take the children. Two weeks later, their father walked in front of a horse and carriage. The suggestion it was not an unfortunate accident spread like a fire. When the drink numbed him, William often proclaimed his life over.

Alisha's upbringing was unremarkable; it echoed the life of working families who struggled from week to week. She grew into a striking young woman with an enquiring and independent mind. Education was not a priority; children were a means of income for the family, so they often worked in factories. However, Alisha spent part of her days in school, learning to read, to write and do basic arithmetic. When she was thirteen, her academic abilities continued to excel, and she assisted Mr Barker, the class teacher, as was the practice. This allowed her to further her education and often, these young ladies became teachers themselves.

Mr Barker was an avid lover of music; he played the violin and often performed for his class, introducing them to Mozart, Beethoven and Vivaldi. Alisha became absorbed in these limited introductions to an unattainable world. Mr Barker gave violin lessons to the few who expressed an interest. It didn't take long for him to discover Alisha displayed a promising ability. She got better week by week. She improved at a ferocious rate. Her playing of the violin seemed an instinctive obsession. She needed no encouragement; her motivation and enthusiasm were infectious. With each new piece practised and learnt, it astonished Barker how Alisha articulated mood and emotion through her playing for someone so young. In recognition of this, Baker introduced Alisha to Gloria Beecham, the wife of Alfred Beecham. Gloria ran a private boarding school for young, talented musicians.

Unable to have children of her own, Gloria felt it her duty to educate the most promising academically gifted girls, and those who displayed a musical gift. She employed the best teachers, who also instructed the girls to prepare them for a specifically female role in adult society; teaching them how to be committed to female social rituals or duties. Her school was a boarding school with a difference. There were no fees asked for. Alfred financed his wife's ambitions; it was his way of dealing with the reality that theirs was always going to be a childless marriage. It smothered their grief and filled a vast void. It gave his wife meaning to her life; it gave her a distraction.

Gloria was a visible presence in the schools' day-to-day affairs. She visited every day, chaired meetings, observed lessons. She met with the girls individually, took an interest in them and invested time in getting to know them. This was not an arduous task, as there were only twenty girls in

Gloria visited Alisha's home and reassured Alisha's aunt Alisha would undergo the finest education equivalent to any private school in London. And so, it was agreed Alisha would attend the school and board there along with the other young girls.

It did not take long for Alisha's musical talent to be recognised amongst the teaching staff. As well as nurturing their child prodigy, Alisha was often used to give private performances to enhance the qualities of the school to the parents of prospective pupils.

Gloria took Alisha seriously. She admired Alisha's technical skill and found her playing graceful and sensual.

After several years, Alisha outgrew the school, and Gloria, only wanting what was best for Alisha, agreed she should pursue an exclusive education in music. Just after her eighteenth birthday, the Royal College of Music in London accepted Alisha. As the years progressed, Alisha became a contained and elegant woman, immersing herself in the world of music and study. She continued to receive the patronage of Gloria and her husband, Alfred, who had also become fond of her. After a brief illness, Gloria died unexpectant, and it fell to Alfred to continue to support and invest in Alisha's education.

. . .

They meet in a tearoom in *'The Savoy'. It* is their customary afternoon tea and as John is at the peak of his fame, the management always welcomes him with great enthusiasm.

John sits legs crossed, his hands clasped, resting on his thigh. He looks at Alisha carefully. She sips her tea and catches his eye over the rim of her cup.

'Are you alright, John?' She asks, placing the cup on the saucer with a clink.

'Of course, dear. I was just thinking about the painting. It's your eyes, you see, I must capture the light within them.'

'You do say the strangest things when you talk about your work.'

He reaches over and touches her hand. 'I'm sorry, my dear. I promise, from now on, you have my utmost attention. I'm all yours.'

She smiles. 'Good.' She pats her thick and pinned hair, checking it is still in place. 'Actually, I'm going to take back what I've just said.' She frowns.

'Why is that?'

'Rueben has been like a child recently. I don't know what has got into him.'

'What seems to be the problem?' John asks, leaning forward.

'Tell me the paintings are going to be finished and we can see it before we leave for Europe, otherwise Rueben is going to drive us all mad.'

This revelation is pleasing to John. He finds it gratifying that he holds such influence over Rueben's emotional welfare.

'The man sounds tortured.'

'He thinks it's a personal vendetta against him, I'm sure of it.'

'Whatever for?' John is enjoying the moment.

'I don't know, because you argued, I suppose. He feels you only agreed to the painting because I told you to. Which is true, but I tried to assure him you wouldn't delay the completion of the painting just to make a point. Would you, John?' Alisha looks at him sternly.

'Why, of course not. I take every painting seriously. God, I wouldn't use it to air my frustrations publicly. I invest too much of myself in each piece of work. This isn't some sort of vanity project. The man flatters himself.'

'Good. Then you can tell him personally to his face and that will be the end of the matter.'

John moves uncomfortably in his seat. He nods his head. 'As you wish, my dear.'

'Thank goodness that's settled, then. Tell me it's nearly completed, John.' She smiles for a moment, then straightens her face.

'Just about. I'm almost there. When painting a face, the triangle between the two eyes and the mouth must be right. I've achieved that with the others, but I've spent more of my energy on you and now I'm almost there. I have had to see you with a fresh eye. There needs to be that emotional exchange between the artist and the sitter.'

'I think you achieved that with Rueben. I'm afraid the emotion was an unpleasant one.' She smiles.

John clears his throat. 'For the painting to connect with others, it needs to fire their imagination. This means a lot to me, Alisha. I want to get it right.'

'I can see that, darling.'

'It will be ready, I promise.'

'Then let's turn our minds to more pleasant conversation.'

'Gladly,' he murmurs. He reaches into his breast pocket and pulls out a black velvet box.

'I have something I want to give you. I saw it yesterday and felt compelled to buy it for you.' He can see her anticipation turn to apprehension. 'Don't worry, it's not a ring.'

Alisha laughs nervously. John hands her the box. She opens it and her jaw drops. 'John, they're gorgeous.'

'I knew you'd like them.' He stands. 'Let me.'

He takes the pearl necklace from its box and gently fastens it around her neck. Alisha touches the pearls with a finger. She sighs. 'Two months is such a long time.'

'It's not a lifetime. You'll come back, and we'll have the rest of our lives together. I can wait two months for that.'

'I've never been happier. I love you, John Sutton.' Alisha takes his hand and lightly kisses it. 'Are you still coming tomorrow night? It will be our last performance before we leave.'

'I wouldn't miss it for the world.' John smiles.

CHAPTER ELEVEN

THE BEGINNING OF SOMETHING

It has been a few hours since their visit to Pavlos' house. The white glare of the afternoon heat is a by-product of the climate that continues to blur his eyes. They meander down a well-worn track, crushing pine needles underfoot. Around them pinecones scatter the dry earth; their comb shells remind Mark of fish scales. Once in the shade of a pine tree, their eyes sharp, they look out to the sea. It is constantly in motion, a living entity that creates a striking, intricate and detailed aura of almost ethereal translucency. A hush seems to fall around them; the only audible sound is the rhythmic whisper of the sea meeting the sand further down the track.

'Do you think Pavlos has any family?' Mark asks.

'I don't know. You would think so, wouldn't you? But the way he spoke, he sounded lonely. Maybe he doesn't.'

'Or they may live on the mainland.'

'Possibly.'

'Imagine getting to his age and not having your family

around.' Shit, he thinks, but it is too late. 'I'm sorry, Abriana. I wasn't thinking.'

She waves his concern away. 'The thought of having a family is no longer on my '*must-do list.*''

'But you always wanted children.'

'Yes, of course I did. My body was just never going to make them and give me a family. There was a time I couldn't talk about it. It's the worst phrase I've ever heard. *"You'll never be able to have children"*. It felt like my heart had been ripped from me. For a while, my life ended. It had no meaning. I coped by putting every living minute into my job. It's a cliché, I know, but I really did live and breathe my job. I put every ounce of energy I had into the gallery, into art; it became my motivation to live again. I was the dealmaker, the bitch that got things done. No matter what, that was my identity. Surely you saw that.'

'You had a certain reputation. I saw a woman who knew her mind, who knew what she wanted and how to get it.'

'But as we know, it came at a price. My job, my marriage, if you could call it that. We were both unfaithful. Knowing about his affairs justified how I felt, I suppose. It gave me a reason to hate him for a while. I wasn't innocent either, as you know.'

'I don't regret what we had, what we did, Abriana. Do you?

'I think differently about it now.'

'In what way?'

'You brought out the good in me, Mark,' she says with enthusiasm. 'When I was with you, I didn't need to be so obsessed with being in control. You made me see the human side. You were warm and kind, you made me laugh again and I realised how desolate my life had become, but you changed all that. You gave me back my vision. I could see what I wanted from life with a clarity that wasn't influenced by pain and regret. I've still got my disappointments, my shortcomings, but that's alright, it makes me who I am now. I'm finally comfortable in my own skin.' Her throaty laugh punctuates their conversation.

They walk a little further, the sound of waves getting nearer.

Abriana smiles. 'I see more of my brother now.'

'You've made up with him. That's great.'

'There's no point in living with regret. One of us had to make the first move. He has a family. They were strangers to me.'

'He has children?'

'Yes, two girls.'

'So, you're an auntie. Auntie Abriana, it has a certain ring to it. It suits you. I can imagine you spoil them?' Mark smiles.

'Now that I see them more often, I do. I've had them over at weekends. I love having them around. We go shopping, visit the cinema, eat out, they're lovely girls.'

'How old are they?'

'Fourteen and sixteen.'

'Young ladies, then.'

'They've grown up so quickly. Time just seems to be passing so fast. It's scary, it just emphasises how old I'm getting.'

'You're not old,' Mark says.

'I feel it, sometimes.'

'Nonsense, nowadays fifty is the new forty and you're only thirty-five. God, look at you, you are wrinkle-free.'

'How hard have you been looking, Mark? I count them

every morning just to make sure another one hasn't appeared.'

'I don't understand women. Why do you always see yourself looking fatter or being older than you are? It's beyond me. There must be a problem with your eyesight or there's something seriously wrong with your mirror.'

As they talk, they have been walking along a track that has taken them to the shore. Several cafes and bars skirt the beach.

'I could murder a drink. Fancy one?' Mark asks.

'It would be good to get in the shade. I think I've burnt my shoulder. It's tingling.'

'They are a little red. You can never be too careful, even if you're Italian.'

'The sun doesn't discriminate between white or brown skin, that's for sure.'

They sit in the shade looking out to a liquid blue sea.

'You seem interested in John Sutton, not just his paintings, but the man himself, his life.'

'I'm curious,' she says, breaking into a smile.

He loves her wide smile.

She raises an eyebrow. 'Aren't you? My passion for art is not just about its history. It's about the artist's story.'

'I'm intrigued by the girl, Alisha. I want to know about her. There's something about her in that painting. I felt it the minute I saw her face, that expression. Her gesture and posture, she's telling us her story, it's in her eyes.'

Abriana sips her beer. 'They both intrigue me.'

'Do you trust the old man? So far, his story lives up to the hype.'

She tilts her head. 'He's genuine enough. And it was kind of him to invite us for lunch tomorrow.'

'Well, if he's half a cook, as he is a gardener, we could be in for a treat.'

'I wasn't expecting his story, his narrative, actually to be so detailed. It's like watching a movie, scene by scene.'

'He's brought her alive, back to life in a way. She's no longer just an image in a painting.'

'I know what you mean. I was slightly disappointed when he said he was tired, although I was concerned too. It gives us something to look forward to.'

Mark would have preferred if Pavlos could have told them the entire story and unravelled the mystery. 'It's strange how the past can influence the future. They didn't know it at the time, but the choices they made changed and affected other people's lives more than a hundred years later. It makes you think about your own life, don't you think? We need to take responsibility for our own actions and consider how that might affect others. We're all guilty of being complacent in the moment, don't you think?'

Abriana contemplates their past together. I wonder if this is what he thinks of me, she ponders, uncomfortably. She senses a slight tension in her chest. 'You're probably right.' Is all she can think of in reply.

CHAPTER TWELVE

UNCOVERING DRAMA

Mark wakes early. For an instant, he thinks he is back in Edinburgh before the sound of birds coming from the garden reminds him of where he is. He recalls leaving the sliding glass door slightly ajar to combat the heat of the night. He slips from the sheets and pads to the shower.

Once dressed, he checks his smartphone. There is a text from Joann. He opens it. *You're an arsehole, Mark. Enjoy the sun.*

Mark grins to himself. It could have been a lot worse, and she's being quite restrained. She's angry with me, but she doesn't hate me, not yet, he thinks to himself.

Downstairs, he makes himself a coffee. The coffee machine rumbles and vibrates on the worktop. Mark worries the noise might wake Abriana. Although the house is spacious, the tiled floors are not designed to dampen sound. He regrets not having an instant coffee.

He glances at the clock on the wall: 6.45 a.m. For years now, his body clock has wakened him early. He sits on the terrace that overlooks the garden. A small bird takes him by surprise and lands on the table; it ignores him and pecks at some scattered crumbs before flying off.

'And a good morning to you.'

The veranda overlooks the garden and in the pale light he can make out the shape of a hill that looms across the bay from Zakynthos Town. Jasmine floats in the air. It is a violet, grey dawn. The sea is flat with a velvet-like sheen. Green slopes rise gently, and he finds it immensely satisfying to witness the new day begin around him. He thinks about the momentary decision to follow Abriana and leave the gallery behind. It is in such decisions that life's turning points are constructed. Yet, something is nagging him. It sits in the pit of his stomach; it is indefinable, but genuine all the same.

'Good morning.' Her voice is unexpected, she is holding a coffee. That feeling passes through him again, an involuntary impulse where he thinks of making love to her.

'I hope I didn't wake you?' Mark asks.

'No. I didn't even know you were up.'

'Did you sleep well?'

'I did, in fact. You can never trust the beds when you go away from home. They're never the same as your own, but it was very comfy. And you?'

'Not really. I woke with a sore back. I'm not used to a soft mattress.'

Abriana sits at the table and takes a sip of coffee. She is wearing a dressing gown, her hair tied in a bun.

Mark looks at her breasts. He slips his eyes away. To his relief, a glance tells him she hasn't noticed his inquisitive urge.

Abriana looks at him and smiles. 'I could make you a Scottish breakfast if you want?'

'There's no black pudding or haggis.'

'If that's the definition of a Scottish breakfast, then it'll have to be an English one.'

'Second best will do,' Mark smirks. 'Tell you what. You enjoy your coffee and I'll make breakfast.'

Before she can answer him, Mark is in the kitchen, opening drawers and cupboards. 'I've found the tin opener,' he calls to her as if he has just decoded a great mystery.

Abriana smiles to herself, surprised how easy it feels to be in his company again. She surprised even herself when she asked Mark to accompany her to Zakynthos, but with each second she spends in his company that invitation is justified.

Abriana straightens herself in the seat. She had caught him looking at her and she spared his embarrassment by averting her eyes. She inhales deeply. Abriana hadn't expected to be flattered by his attention.

How can she describe these intimate and physical sensations? She feels strangely exhilarated. It feels as if her senses and perspective are being readjusted. What will be the consequence of our reunion? She asks herself. We are playing out our parts discreetly, with a solicitous curiosity, wondering what the other is thinking?

Abriana can often sense the intensity of his look, accompanied by a rise of excitement in her abdomen.

This morning, she is content, and it is a sensation that hasn't always accompanied her days lately. Does she attribute this to Mark or her current environment? She can feel the morning sun grow stronger as it casts its light further along the veranda, melting the shade as each minute passes. The sea shimmers in the light and shaded patches of blue and she knows that before long the sun will melt the cotton wool clouds that dot the horizon.

Abriana thinks of her day ahead, and their meeting with Pavlos, and his promise of lunch. She smiles to herself. Already, she can feel a fondness grow inside her for the old man. Also, she has become engrossed in his story. She compares this to the pull that one gets when reading a novel that can't be put down.

Abriana has found herself gripped by Alisha's world, but mostly attracted to the woman and her story. Alisha is no longer just a figure in a painting. Pavlos' story has brought her alive. She has become real and not just an image in Abriana's imagination.

Abriana wonders about Alisha's circumstances; the choices Alisha has made and how they have determined the events of her life. As Abriana considers this, she thinks of her own life and where it is leading. She knows she will discover how Alisha's story ends. Pavlos has promised to disclose all he knows. If only she had the same benefit of hindsight, a looking glass into her future. Would she still make the same choices that have brought her to this island with a man she has, until a few weeks ago, confined to her past?

'Here we are, two poached eggs, bacon and toast,' Mark says triumphantly. He lays two plates and cutlery on the table.

Abriana smiles. 'It looks lovely, Mark. You have a hidden talent.'

Mark sits down. 'I've been told my poached eggs are a delicacy to die for. Mind you, it was my sister who said that, so obviously it was a biased opinion.'

Abriana slices one with her knife, and the yoke spills

onto the bacon and toast. 'Maybe it's not as biased as you think. These look wonderful.'

'One tries one's best,' he says with a broad smile.

'I'm looking forward to meeting Pavlos again.'

'I think he's enjoying it; don't you think?'

'I suppose so. I'm just worried that we're maybe asking too much of him.'

'I wouldn't worry, Abriana. I'm sure he would say. Actually, I think he could be dragging it out because he likes the company.'

'What do you make of Alisha's story so far?'

'She's not who I imagined her to be.'

'Really.'

'Well, yes. You know, when you construct an image of someone you've never met, and you make up preconceived notions about them. Well, when I looked at the painting, she was always the focus of my attention. All the other figures just seemed to fade into the background. I was drawn to her face, especially her eyes. That look, it was as if she was looking straight at me and she was saying, '*I have a story to tell*' and it fascinated me. She was the painting. It's not a portrait that has four people in it, there is only one subject. She is a mystery, but now, that mystery is gradually being peeled away, layer by layer.'

'She really has a hold on you.'

'She does. This woman, whose name I now know, is revealing herself to me through Pavlos. She's becoming real, but she's not who I thought she was.'

'In what way?' Abriana looks at him, intrigued. 'You've kept this quiet. You've spoken about the painting, obviously, but never like this.'

'I suppose, as I hear more of her story, I'm just beginning

to admit to myself that she has affected me like no other figure in a painting. It's bizarre, I know. I sell and buy art for a living. It's who I am. It defines me, but she has made me question everything I know about what I do because it feels like she is addressing me personally. I need to know about her life, what happened to her. I want to understand finally what is behind that look that has stuck in my mind the very second I saw it.'

'But she's not looking at you. It was painted over a hundred years ago. She's looking at John Sutton as he paints her. So, that look is for his benefit. He was the man she loved.'

'Yes. I've thought about that. And I've tried to tell myself exactly that. Believe me, I've reasoned with that logic, but the fact remains, the impression she leaves upon me doesn't just disappear with that logic, it's remained.'

Abriana smiles. 'We came here to find out about the history of the painting, who the rightful owner is. All we've spoken about is Alisha. She has got me interested in her. She's good at that, it would seem,' Abriana says happily.

'She's irritating,' Mark says with a smile.

'Once this is over, she'll just be another woman in a painting.'

'I don't know, I'm not so sure,' he says doubtfully. 'In all my years in art, I've never come across a painting that makes me feel like this one does. It's not because we're getting a first-hand account of the story behind its origins, it's not that. This is different. With most portraits, you know the look, the expression that the artist is trying to convey. It tells its own story. With this one, I've even neglected Sutton's ability as an artist, in a way. His style is immaculate, luminously detailed and beautiful, but with my preoccupation with Alisha, I've not given him the recognition he deserves. It's Sutton, the artist, who has created the mystery on Alisha's face. He has transferred that onto the canvas. I've been so preoccupied with this woman, to the detriment of Sutton's creative influence. I haven't valued him enough in that process.'

'I think we've both been guilty of that at some point.'

He scratches his head and thinks. 'The word I'm looking for is *drama*. By telling a story, there is inevitably drama in his painting.'

Abriana smiles. 'There's drama in all of us, don't you think?'

'There are different types of drama. We've got a history together that would fit that billing, that's for sure,' Mark says, and he can't help grinning.

Just then, a dove lands on the back of a chair, opposite Abriana.

'Wow, it must be tame. It's probably after our breakfast.' Abriana breaks off a piece of toast and throws it onto the ground. The dove flies off the chair and starts to peck at the toast.

'And it'll keep coming back if you feed it.'

'Oh, it's lovely. We could adopt it as our pet while we're here.'

'You mean him and the rest of his friends,' says Mark, nodding towards the bird that has been joined by another two.

'Oops, the words getting out.' Abriana laughs.

After breakfast and once the dishes have been washed, Abriana showers and gets dressed. She can feel the physical connection return to her. It is tangible. It has settled upon her like a warm coat. It leaves her feeling confused, but all the same, it is there. She admits to herself of fearing it. If she submits to its pull, she knows she will be moving towards a place she has been before. In the past, regret has burnt her. Does she want to travel that journey again? Does there have to be regret? *Live for the moment. See where it takes me.* She tells herself. *Be impulsive. It's not going to kill me, just this once, to let go of the instinct that always forces me to want to be in control and to be calculated in my decisions.*

She senses Mark is waiting for her to make a gesture that will clarify a mutual attraction. Does it make it easier that they have known each other intimately in the past? Or is that what she is afraid of? Is this what feeds her caution? Will it cloud her judgement? Why did she invite Mark to Zakynthos? At the time, it seemed the right thing to do. He was becoming involved, his interest in the painting stoked like a fire. Did she assume he would say no, and she was just being polite by asking if he'd like to accompany her? When he agreed to come, something inside her jumped. She can't deny it. It was a sense of relief, she now thinks.

Being in Edinburgh and meeting Mark again, going out for dinner and talking about their shared past, has left her with feelings that are bubbling to the surface.

Mark has never been good at hiding his intentions. She can see at times, he has tried to be subtle, but she can also see the way he looks at her, and she wonders if this is replicated in her expression when she looks at him.

She loved him once. This may be one huge mistake, she warns herself. She has made a life for herself, one that Mark does not know of. She is happy with her life as it is now. Why would she jeopardise that happiness now? There is a joy in her life. She is content. Yes, that's what it is, contentment. It is a state of being that she never attained when Mark knew the old Abriana. Mark is pushing the boundaries of this new life and it is making her feel uneasy. There is no room in this new existence for any element of her past that might threaten her happiness.

Who does Mark see when he looks at her, when he talks to her and when he eats with her? The Abriana she has banished, the one from her past? Or the one who has struggled with her demons? The one who has now made difficult choices and settled upon the decisions those choices have made? They have allowed her to turn her life around and give her, for the first time, the feeling that her life has substance, a state of existence that has become precious to her.

Abriana understands the aspects of her life that brought her success as a businesswoman, allowing her to rise through the ranks of the art world. Today, she is sure she would not like to meet that woman again. She has avenged that side of her life. Her life now defines who she has become.

She has anguished over that part of her life and she has concluded that although she hurt a lot of people, she too was a victim. She was focused on objectives and goals. That was her motivation. It propelled her to the summit, and she never gave a moment's thought to the carnage, the manipulation, the intimidating and the human cost. This was her business plan. She never considered that others were on the receiving end of her actions and decisions, not for once did she think of others as victims. They were just necessary collateral in the games she played. This was the price that others had to pay so that she could get to where she needed to be. She was on a crusade, Abriana was at war, and these were the battles that eventually won the war.

What she did not see, because she did not allow herself

to see, was that deep inside her, she was also at war with herself. Abriana was an actress, and she was good at it.

She now realises she isolated herself, she was tortured by her insecurities and her determination to get to the top of her game. To be a success in the art world was her way of escaping and avoiding who she really was. With the media revelation of her affair with Mark, the blackmail attempt, the sale of the painting to raise the funds for the blackmailer, the humiliation of her resignation and the realisation that her relationship with Mark was the ultimate casualty in it all, her world finally imploded.

Abriana just wanted to hide and curl up in an isolated ball. It paralysed her mind. The experience exhausted her. She cut herself off from colleagues and friends. She felt allergic to the art world, to aspiration, to ambition.

The thought of ever working again left her mind lethargic. She had left Rome, and all it represented for her and returned to Florence, her family home, her refuge.

Within a few months, she felt something she had never felt before, clarity and energy, and to her surprise, she found herself embrace, rather than resist, this newfound state. She hadn't noticed her body was aching with tension, her mind in discomfort until she began to mentally and physically relax. At first, the effects were subtle, but as time passed, this new feeling became more pervasive and she found her existence of constant exhaustion disappear. Abriana was inching her way forward to engaging with the social world around her. She was comfortable and became more confident in who she really was. She had found herself again. Sometimes we think we've changed. Sometimes what we were in the past is just that, the past... but underneath all the complexity, her past still walks with her in the present. How will she manage such an awkward and painful situation?

She is sitting on the bed and she checks her text messages. There are a few from the Uffizi Gallery that need her attention, asking for an update on her progress with Pavlos and one concerning Alan Sutton. A journalist from *The Telegraph* has contacted the Gallery, enquiring about the their interest in Alan Sutton's claim of ownership to a painting by John Sutton. The gallery had advised she press for an answer to her visit as the board of directors were averse to any unwanted publicity.

A sudden irritation forces her to straighten her posture. She presses her finger to her forehead. If she could, she would delete the last few seconds from her mind.

CHAPTER THIRTEEN

THE FORMING OF CONNECTIONS

Mark has decided that blue is his new favourite colour. He doesn't know if it is the same throughout Greece, but here on Zakynthos, he has not tired of the variety of shade. He is astonished at its depths. Its intrinsic beauty has the power to change his mood and shift his mindset. He can be thinking of the consequences he faces when he returns to Edinburgh, the scornful look on Joann's face, and the inquisition that will inevitably follow, and then, a walk in the garden will dissipate such thoughts, as if the heat of the day has melted them from him.

As he stands at the edge of the garden, looking out over to Zakynthos Town and its harbour, the shore is ringed by fringes of pure turquoise that dissolves into an aquamarine blue as it stretches further out to sea. The sea has a life of its own; he is sure of it. Nothing prepared him for this connection he feels to everything around him. He likens it to viewing a painting for the first time or walking into a new exhibition where the senses must filter copious amounts of visual information. It is a wonderful experience, and he has found nothing similar to compare it to, until now. It takes his breath away. It is such a profound and stimulating experience that Mark can only liken it to falling in love. It is the closest use of words he can think of to describe the sensation. He wonders if it affects everyone this way or only those that see what is around them. Each time Mark looks out over towards Zakynthos Town, the harbour, and further towards Mount Skopos, it is as if he is seeing it for the first time. Maybe it takes a certain type of person who feels such things.

So far, the thought of eventually returning home is a journey he wants to postpone. Even when Pavlos has finished his account of the painting's history, Mark would like to stay on for a while longer. At this rate, they will be staying a few more days, as Pavlos seems to tire quickly from relaying his account. Mark has been aware that Pavlos' cough, at first an irritation, has become worse the more he talks. However, the old man seems determined to impart his story, and he continues to be enthusiastic. Mark has also noted that Pavlos has a soft spot for Abriana. He smiles. The man obviously has taste.

The soft breeze feels like breath upon his skin. Mark was glad he came. The decision was not difficult to make. His interest was twofold.

Abriana is in his life again. He still finds the stretch of time incomprehensible. In himself, he knew, he wasn't going to let their opportunistic acquaintance slip from him. The short time he has spent with Abriana has reaffirmed one thing. All this time, he has been in denial; he has pushed from his mind what he truly feels. Now, it feels he has switched on a light and he can see with a clarity that previously eluded him; he is still in love with her.

Also, there is the unanswered question; who is the

rightful heir to the painting? Also, there is the desire, on his part, to find out about the woman who has had such a hold on him. He has struggled to make sense of it. He now knows her name, Alisha Hadley. Mark is sure of one thing. Through Pavlos, the painting is about to give up its secrets.

Every morning at breakfast and lunchtime, for the two days he has stayed, the same bird visits, always sitting on the same branch, in the same lemon tree, pruning its feathers and waiting. It has a distinctive dark marking on its neck, unlike the other birds of its kind that Mark has seen in the garden.

Mark has no idea what kind of bird it is, but to his untrained eye, the closest he can think of is a dove, but he can't be sure. Then, when it is ready, the bird flies from its branch onto the terrace and picks at morsels of crumbs, unperturbed, brazenly walking between their feet under the table, to Abriana's amusement. Its head continually bobs from left to right, assessing the situation, and then, with a flutter of wings, it's back on its branch, seemingly satisfied.

Mark has become attached to the predictability of these unremarkable events. It is a safe and comfortable feeling, and he knows that recently; such secure feelings have been missing from his life. Maybe this is why he looks forward to these visitations.

He lets his thoughts trail off and walks back to the terrace where Abriana is frowning at him.

'Have you been drinking my water?'

There are two identical bottles of water on the table, both opened and drunk from.

'No. That one's mine.' Mark points to an almost full bottle. He touches it. 'It's still cold. It's my second bottle today.'

'Good,' Abriana says as she picks up the other bottle and studies the label. 'There are 750 ml in each one. You've probably drunk a litre already.'

'That's good... is it?'

'You're supposed to drink a litre a day.'

'In this heat, it must be more. It's coming out of me as fast as I put it in.'

'The last thing you want is to feel dehydrated and no, coffee and alcohol don't count.'

He smiles. 'That's a shame.'

'We need to get a move on. I hadn't noticed the time. It would be unforgivable to be late for Pavlos' lunch.'

The Story of Alisha Hadley

London 1905

The concert is held in Alfred Beecham's ostentatiously grand townhouse. It has an imposing façade, three storeys tall, with maids and a butler. A large reception room adorned with two large tables with silver trays of sandwiches and canapes is set for a hundred people. The butler greets each guest and takes their hats and coats and offers them a glass of wine, champagne, or lemonade.

It is an exclusive and intimate affair. Alfred has only invited the influential business acquaintances and individuals of a certain standing and therefore of wealth with most male guests accompanied by their wives.

It is a concert, but mostly it is an opportunity for Alfred to entice potential investors to pledge their support and money to his venture.

Alfred is diminutive but large in bulk. His eyes are small and round, his cheeks red and veined, a wispy moustache and bushy sideburns dominate his face. He mingles among his guests, smiling brightly and caressing the females with his charm. Several maids move around the prodigious room, with silver trays of champagne, eyes sweeping from hand to glass, infused by Alfred's command that no glass is to remain empty.

John steps further into the room; above him, he notices two impressive chandeliers at either end. He can see several people that are familiar to him, one whose portrait he has painted is a conservative member of Parliament who he remembers, full of his own his self-importance. John had taken an immediate dislike to the man, and he hopes not to be re-acquainted with him. He feels uncomfortable with such gatherings; small talk, niceties and intellectual chest-puffing were the common currency. He feels an imposter among the laughter and raised voices that grow more intense in volume as the wine and champagne loosen guarded composures and tongues. He only accepted the invitation because it had come from Alfred, and Alisha would be performing.

'John, you haven't got a drink. Let me get you one.'

Alfred plucks two glasses from a tray and hands one to John.

'Here's to friendship.'

'Here's to the success of your new venture.'

'When are you going to paint me, John? I've been keeping space in my gallery for it.'

'Gallery?'

'I've got a room full of originals. I'll show you it later tonight once we finish here.'

'I'd love to, but I'm taking Alisha out for dinner.'

'Ah, that's a shame, maybe another time. I hear you are composing a portrait of the quartet.'

'I am, or I should say, I have. I put the finishing touches to it this afternoon, in fact.'

'I'd love to see it. Have the boys and girls seen it yet?'

'Not yet. I'd planned to unveil it before they leave. A private showing.'

'I see. Are you selling it? I'd like to buy it.'

'But you haven't seen it, Alfred.'

'There's no need. I've loved everything you've done, John.'

'You flatter me.'

'Nonsense. In fact, I'm going to commission you to do my portrait on my return from Europe. Would you need much preparation? I'm not familiar with the process.'

'I need to have an interest in the character of the person I portray.'

'Well then, I hope I pass on that one?' Alfred takes a swig of his drink.

'With flying colours. But it's not enough just to create an accurate likeness. I need to extract the character behind the face.'

'Sounds painful.'

'The light is important, of course, but I've failed if I don't capture a sense of someone. I convey this with attention to detail.'

'Warts and all?'

'I'm afraid so.'

'Well, we'll have to do my good side then.'

'Sometimes it's just as important to emphasise the detail of an eyelid or the folds of skin as it is to create a likeness. I try to communicate with the sitter's experience of life.'

'I've never thought about it like that, John. So much thought goes into it.'

'I haven't put you off, have I?'

'Not at all. Communicating the sitter's experience of life, I like that John, I like it very much.' Alfred pats John on the shoulder.

'How are the preparations going for your trip?' John asks.

'It's all slipping into place, finally. I'm hoping to be up and running by the end of the year.'

'Travel has become popular for those who can afford it. The competition has a head start on you.'

'Yes, others have already made inroads and are established, but it's a fruitful market. I'm offering something different, intellectual stimulation. I want to offer an experience that is educational, but also relaxing. There is room for us all, I believe.'

The distinctive sound of stringed instruments tuning forces John to turn. It is the first time he has seen Alisha since he arrived. She is wearing a white dress, her hair tied into a tight bun. As does Sara, who has a smooth round face, a heavier build than Alisha. She has thick lips; her hair is blonde and also tied in a bun. Both wear white glass beads. Rueben and Alex dress in dark suits, starched white shirts and black Dicky bow ties. On each side of the quartet, candles flicker in yellow light.

'I'll keep an eye on those two.' Alfred smiles.

'What?'

'Alisha and Rueben.'

'Whatever for? I don't understand.'

'Ah, I see. You don't know.'

'Know what? What are you insinuating, Alfred?'

'Oh, nothing,' Alfred says, anxiously.

'It can't have been, as you so guardedly eluded.'

'Your lack of knowledge on the matter has left me in rather an awkward situation.'

John's voice is suddenly sharp. 'I demand to know, Alfred.'

'Quite.' Alfred takes a long gulp of champagne. 'They were an item.'

'An item?' John repeats, struggling with this new revelation.

Alfred clears his throat. 'Yes. Some time ago now, obviously before you met Alisha and won her over.'

'She has not mentioned it.'

'Probably because it's unimportant now. After all, it was a few years ago.' Alfred coughs. He waves his hand dismissively. 'Oh, it was nothing, a little thing they had together when they were both studying at the Royal College of Music. It didn't last long; I'm led to believe. Anyway, they're just good friends now. Come, take a seat. It's time to enjoy some music.'

Before the quartet, there are several rows of seats. Alfred claps his hands and invites his guests to sit. He thanks them all for their attendance and enters into a prepared effusive speech he hopes will secure their support and sponsorship.

John has taken a seat in the back row. A fist grips his heart, and a momentary light-headedness comes over him. He can feel himself trembling. He longs to go outside into the fresh air, finding the mix of smoke and bodies stifling. An acquaintance recognises him and attempts to smile and then avoid the man's gaze. John's hands are fists on his lap, the knuckles white with tension. *Why did she keep this from me?*

They were lovers. He shakes his head. It feels like a furious thunderstorm is raging inside it.

Around him, the music is like voices floating amongst the audience, soft seductive tones, each eloquent note transcending into mood and emotion.

John navigates the images his imagination conjures of Alisha and Rueben together. A vehement rage crawls inside him; it is almost too much to bear. The room sucks the breath from him.

The music swirls gently, floating around the room like a delicate bird graceful in flight. The piece is warm, simple and textured, and the graceful arc of Alisha's and Sara's bow resonates with a hypnotic phrasing that captures the audience in an emotional attachment, a reverie of their own, where time does not exist.

John springs to his feet, the chair toppling behind him. He cries out, 'I will not be treated like a fool.'

Those around him are stunned by the ferocity of his voice. A woman seated next to John brings a hand to her mouth and screams, shuffling from him like a terrified creature. Alisha looks at him, bewildered. The music continues, but it is strained as John, choleric with anger, hastens from the room.

'Sir, shall I get your hat and coat?' The butler asks as John sweeps past him, wrenching the front door open. He almost stumbles down the stairs and onto the pavement, where he walks back and forth, drawing his hands through his hair.

Aimlessly, he walks onto the street. A horse-drawn carriage almost collides with him. He stares at it as the carriage continues along the street. He feels hypnotised by Alfred's sudden revelation. It is as if he is in a dream that has altered the course of this night. A couple walk past, arm in arm. They avert their eyes from him and quicken their pace, for he looks deranged, and they have no desire to engage him.

'John, are you ill?' Alisha stands at the top of the steps to the house.

'You have lied to me.'

'What are you talking about?' A flush of confusion streaks her face.

'Rueben!'

She shakes her head. 'It was a long time ago.'

'I have always been open and honest with you, always honourable in my intentions. I have no secrets from you, and this is how you repay me.'

'I didn't think it mattered. What is important to me is now, the present time and us. I have never enquired about your past; it has no bearing on who we are today.'

'That is where you are wrong. It is a matter of trust,' he says incredulously, his fists clench. 'Are you seeing him now?'

'Do I really have to answer that? What do you take me for, John? Do you not know me after all this time?'

'How can I believe anything you say?'

'This is madness, John.' Alisha shakes her head. 'The past is over with. I cannot change what has happened. Did you not think I may have had lovers before you? As you too have had before me. For God's sake, John, I am not a saint. We were young; it was a long time ago. Rueben is nothing but a good friend. You degrade what I feel for you with your accusation.'

John is stunned by the ferocity of her words. He recoils and then gathers himself. He looks at Alisha and she has straightened her posture. Her head tilts back as if to emphasis her words.

Just then, Reuben appears in the doorway. 'Is everything alright? The others are worried, and Alfred is keen for us to resume.'

'Ah, the good friend has impeccable timing,' John sneers.

'Leave us, Reuben, we are fine.'

'Are you sure, Alisha?'

'Yes, yes. Tell Alfred I will return soon.'

'As you wish.' Reuben is unconvinced, but all the same, he goes back into the house.

'I cannot go back in and join the others. I will get my hat and coat.'

'You are leaving?' Alisha asks.

John mounts the steps and brushes past Alisha, who follows him into the reception hall.

'John,' she pleads.

The butler is standing, waiting.

'Are you staying or leaving, sir?'

'I'll need my coat if you please.' John glances into the room where a cacophony of voices reaches his ears. For a moment, he is distracted, as he knows he is the subject of their chatter. He turns to face Alisha. 'I cannot forgive you, Alisha.'

Alisha steps back as if the implications of his words have physically pushed her. Her eyes widened in alarm. Her hand moves to her neck and rests on the beads. It is shaking. How it happened she does not know, but she must have pulled on the beads in frustration, and they are sent tumbling to the floor. Alisha turns from him; she will not let him see her tears; she will not give him the satisfaction.

. . .

'Oh! Alisha, you've been crying again. With time, it will get better, I promise,' Sara says.

'How do you know that?'

'Trust me, if it were not so, most of my friends would be permanently morbid.'

Alisha's eyes are red, blotchy and wet. She tries to blink away the tears, a failed attempt at preserving her dignity, but her tears have fallen onto her cheeks, leaving cold trails. She wipes them away.

Eventually, she finds her voice. She sounds calm, but a shiver tingles her spine. 'I can't believe John refused to see me, just ignoring my attempts to speak with him. Knowing I was leaving within weeks and still he kept his silence.'

'Men are strange creatures. I've never been able to work them out.'

Alisha becomes remarkably poised. 'I opened my heart and fell in love. I have lost him. He has gone from me and so has the person I thought I was.'

'Nonsense Alisha. You mustn't think like that. You are still beautiful, inside and out.'

'Well... I don't feel it. I feel I have fallen into an abyss.'

'John has always had an unquenchable moral conviction. It will be the ruin of him. I never liked that side of him and look where it has got him. He has thrown away a precious thing. The man is a fool, Alisha. Anyone who can hurt the person he supposedly loves because of something that happened before he met you is not worth the air we breathe. The way he has treated you is beyond reprimand.'

'You are mocking him, Sara.'

'He is mocking you, Alisha. He is not worthy of you. I'm sorry, but the man has infuriated me. And not only me, but Alfred is also furious with John. He almost ruined the night.'

Alisha could not perform after John stormed out of Alfred's house. Alfred's bewildered guests were treated to a performance, albeit, with an absent Alisha, who retired on the orders of an insistent Alfred, concerned for Alisha's welfare, but also racked by guilt that he was partly to blame for the night's conclusion.

Alisha feels sick, suddenly nauseous. She had always wondered if John suspected something between Rueben and her. Not that they gave him any reason to be suspicious. It was probably her mind playing tricks. An instinctive reaction perhaps, to the times that she wanted to tell him, but for whatever reason, the opportunity faded, or it just never seemed the right time, or for that matter, necessary to disclose their past. As time passed, the need disappeared. It was insignificant to the life she led with the quartet and the life she shared with John. That's how it seemed to her then, but not now.

John was an intelligent man, and she would have thought that jealousy was uncharacteristic of him. Intelligence doesn't always evoke compassion. She often found him to be guarded by his emotions, but never for once did she imagine he harboured a conspicuous concern about her work and those that it involved.

Possibly, his work was a distraction, she now considers. But, when she thinks of John and his work, the portrait was the catalyst for what was to proceed. There was definite friction between John and Reuben, so much so they could have started a fire between them. Alisha thought they clashed because they were both so self-opinionated and headstrong it would be unthinkable to back down. It was a weakness. Now, she considers, there was a definite glow of self-satisfaction about John when Reuben relented to John's vision of the portrait.

'Reuben has asked about the painting.'

'What about it?'

'Have you seen it?'

'No.'

'He thinks John will have destroyed it. Do you think he has?'

'It doesn't matter anymore. There is more than a painting that has been destroyed.'

'It would have been nice to have seen it, I suppose. Don't you think? It's not every day that one gets their portrait painted by one of England's finest painters, even if he is an ass.'

She is escaping. And the thought brings a combination of fear and exhilaration. Two opposite states that have a claustrophobic, yet perpetual motion about them. They come in waves.

The shock is considerable; the misery she has endured has left her feeling abandoned. She has struggled to make sense of it all, of that night that changed everything. It is almost impossible for her to think of how her life was.

Yet, she is escaping. She says it out loud to give the words confirmation. It brings extraordinary relief. She is leaving behind what her life has become. She will soon leave this place with all its constant reminders and what it has come to represent.

Sara has told Alisha her suffering is painful to watch. She needs to come to her senses; the quartet still needs to rehearse, and the others have been patient with her. The day of their departure will soon arrive and there is still much to do. Sara's words resonate with her. They remind her she has a purpose, still. Clarity has returned to her thoughts.

Nighttime is the hour her mind finally settles. The instant she lays her head on the pillow, her mind and body exhausted, succumbs to sleep. During the day, she sits for long periods, staring into space, remembering, alone except for dust motes, which catch her eye, floating gracefully in beams of sunlight. She wonders if John Sutton would recognize who she has now become. Is this normal?

When Alisha looks in the mirror, the face she knows, with all its imperfections magnified in her mind, is still hers. She has always seen herself as plain. She envies the women who look gracious and statuesque in their manner and posture. They always, to her eye anyway, look trimmer and taller.

She can make out dark circles around her eyes. She presses her lips together, attempting to stifle the ache in her throat.

Together, they had expectations of what a life shared could be like, endless possibilities stretched out before them, hopes and dreams intermingled. What will she do with the memories?

She brushes her hair methodically. She ties her hair up with combs. It is a ritual she performs each day without thinking. Lately, she has done a lot of thinking. John's anger showed the man he truly was. It stripped him bare of all his civility and propriety and exposed his hostility and jealousy. This was not the man Alisha knew, the man she loved, but that was the irony. He appeared to be something he was not; she understands that now, and the hold he had on her heart is now receding.

CHAPTER FOURTEEN

NO MORE PRETENCE

When she speaks, her hands move in animated gestures, she exaggeratedly nods her head, and her expressions are often extreme. She flicks her hair theatrically. He can watch her for hours. She entranced him. Periodically, she will glance at her mobile phone, checking emails and text messages.

She makes him feel guilty, a poisonous unease slips into him. He has not, nor does he feel the need to, check-in and catch up with Joann regarding the gallery. On the other hand, he has enjoyed the break from the ordinary and his mind is concerned with matters that he has methodically examined.

His interest in the painting and fascination with Alisha was immediate. The prospect of exploring whether they could start again after what happened made the decision to come to Zakynthos easier and because she instigated it. Abriana asked him to accompany her. He was confident it was the right thing to do, and still convinced of that.

'Pavlos just keeps getting better. It's as if he has written everything down and he's reading it to us. It flows so well. My worry was he'd only have a vague recollection. The more detail he tells us about the background to the story, the more I can record, which will help to build the evidence and hopefully a solid case.'

Their bottle of red arrives. Abriana insisted on choosing a wine from a vineyard on the Island, Ampelostrates Horses Vineyard.

Mark raises his glass. 'Here's to a positive conclusion that will wipe the smile off Alan Sutton's face.' They clink glasses.

'You don't like him, do you?'

'No. Not really.'

'Why not? You don't know him.'

'I don't know. It's just a feeling. Sometimes, you can take an instant dislike to someone. He looked too smug for me. I think he thought all he had to do was walk into your meeting and claim the prize. I must admit, you deflated his bubble rather well.'

'Let's just wait and see, shall we? You never know, Pavlos might confirm Alan Sutton's claim.'

'What then?'

'As I've said, the Uffizi will offer him a deal.'

'Ah yes, there is that offer.'

'It's a good one if it comes to that,' she says thoughtfully.

'So, all to play for?'

'Exactly.' Abriana thinks about the text message, the journalist, and wonders whether it was a mistake not to have told Mark.

'I'm glad we came out for dinner. It would have been a shame not to have sampled the local restaurants.'

'Have you eaten Greek food before?' Abriana asks.

'There are a few Greek restaurants in Edinburgh. I remember my first experience of going to one. I asked the waiter which part of Greece he came from. And he said, Turkey, would you believe?'

Abriana laughs.

Their meal arrives. Fasolada soup, chicken in a garlic sauce, pastitsio, and green dressed salad in vinegar and virgin oil. Abriana orders a vodka and coke.

'Are you finished with the wine? There's still half a bottle left.'

'No. I just want something a little stronger, that's all.'

'Are you alright?' Mark asks.

She sighs. 'I'm fine, Mark.' Abriana takes the lemon out of her glass and swallows a generous amount of vodka.

Mark looks sceptical, but thinks better to challenge her. 'This looks goods, I've never had pastitsio before, have you?'

'Once, in Thessaloniki, I remember because I was there just for a day and it was the only meal I had.'

'Oh, what were you doing there?'

'I was on holiday with some girlfriends. We were travelling around Greece, from one town and island to the next.'

'I'd like to do that someday.'

'What's stopping you?'

Mark shrugs. 'Life, I suppose, it keeps getting in the way.'

'That's just an excuse; people use it to justify not doing it in the first place.'

'I suppose.'

'You came here with me. Life didn't stop you. What's the difference? I'll tell you. You wanted to come, and life was just going to have to wait until you got back. That's the difference... motivation. You were motivated by something or someone.' She smiles self satisfyingly.

He takes a forkful of pastitsio. 'Mm... this is good. How's the chicken?'

'Stop trying to change the subject. It's delicious.'

'I'm not.' He shrugs defensively. 'I agree with you.'

'Good.' She takes another gulp of vodka.

'I think I'll order some water.' Mark catches the glance of a waiter.

'Have I told you I've got a dog?'

Mark looks at her as if she was mad. 'No. I can't picture you with a dog, or any animal for that matter.'

'Why not?' She feigns being hurt by his words.

'Do you take it out for walks, there a lot of hard work and dedication?'

'Of course I do. I was meant to look after him for a few days, for a neighbour and I ended up adopting him.'

'How did you manage that?'

'She went on holiday; met a man and the next thing I know, she's selling her house.'

'How did you end up with the dog?'

'The man she was in love with didn't like dogs. So, it was the dog or him.'

'What kind of dog is it?'

'A Labrador. Her name is Fee Fee. She's the most placid creature I've ever known. I love her to bits.'

'Who's looking after her?'

'My brother, the girls love her too.'

'You're full of surprises.'

'I got her on St Andrew's Day. She loves to sunbathe, she lies outside all day and sleeps and pants in the sun.'

'How did you know it was St Andrew's Day?' he asks sceptically.

She looks at him sternly and wonders if he is being serious. 'You've forgotten, haven't you?'

'What?'

'We met on St Andrew' Day, remember now? You said it was a good omen.' Abriana jabs a finger at him. She is smirking now.

'Ah, yes. Of course.' He smiles back, acknowledging the irony.

An image of St Andrew's beach and then Elie pops into his head. He remembers why he spent several weeks there, trying to escape the circus that erupted around him. No, that's not fair, he says to himself. Abriana suffered more than he did. Even though Abriana was in Rome... no, she was in Florence by then; he reminds himself; she had to face the accusations, the indignation, her life changed more than his. At least he still had his job. He returned to Edinburgh, to his home, to the gallery, and he resumed his life as it was before. Abriana lost her job, left her home in Rome, moved to Florence, a city she grew up in, but she returned to begin again. A new start. Mark's guilt is overwhelming. And yet, here they are, together again, he tells himself, not as lovers, not yet anyway, but she needs him, emotionally? probably... yes, she needs his support. He is fumbling about in his mind. For now, he tells himself; it is enough she wants his support, even his advice. If she were to make a physical advance, he would not turn her down. Mark is sure about that. So, no, this is not enough. He needs more than this; he wants more, much more.

'I wasn't expecting him to treat her the way he did. My God, John Sutton was a bastard.'

She's getting drunk. Mark can't recall seeing her drink this much. She's way past the tipsy stage, he is thinking.

Christ, that was quick. 'It was different in those days, I suppose, another mindset.'

'I'm not buying that. Poor Alisha and just when she was leaving for Corfu.'

'The timing could have been better. Imagine, she was in Greece. She was here. It's almost as if we have a connection with her, don't you think?'

'You can be a real sentimental softie, Mark. I've always liked that side of you.'

After their meal, Abriana suggests they go for a walk. When she stands, she feels dizzy and she must hold the back of a chair to steady herself.

'Are you alright?' Mark asks, concerned.

'I'll be fine.' She puts her hand to her head. 'Maybe I'll have some of that water, after all.'

'I think that's a good idea.' Mark hands her a glass, and she drinks it thirstily.

'Are you sure you're, ok? We could just get a taxi back to the villa if you want.'

'I'm fine. Honestly, I feel much better after that,' Abriana insists.

The night is sultry and even though it is almost midnight, Mark can feel his shirt stick to his back. He walks with his hands in his pockets and keeps a close eye on Abriana. They find themselves at the harbour where several yachts are moored. In some, people are finishing late meals, drinking and smoking. A woman waves at them, but as it transpires, she is acknowledging another couple who pass Mark and Abriana.

'How are you feeling now?'

'Much better, thanks. The air is doing me good. I'm sorry Mark; I don't know what came over me.'

But she knows why. Before they went out for their meal, Abriana received a text from the Uffizi Gallery informing her that, in the last day, it has come to their attention through contacts that the press is showing a growing interest in John Sutton's painting and the current dispute over its ownership. Abriana is sure Alan Sutton must have agreed to sell his story. Not only is Alan Sutton's claim to *The Lost Painting*, the header that will accompany the article, attempts were made to investigate Abriana's past and her current activities for the Uffizi Gallery. Mark has also been mentioned, although to her relief, only briefly. The gallery is considering pulling her off the case. Her involvement and the Gallery's interests are now compromised. She has lost control. It is now out of her hands and this is something Abriana finds incomprehensible. The shock has numbed her mind. This was not what she had planned. How long can she keep this from Mark? Her stomach is in knots.

'Have you enjoyed yourself?' Abriana asks, pushing her thoughts away from her.

'Yes. Of course, it's been a lovely evening.'

'I hope you're not just saying that... oh, I think I'm going to be...' and then, suddenly, with her hand resting on a palm tree, she heaves over the side of the harbour.

Mark tentatively places his hand on her back. She holds her hair from her face and attempts to apologise between waves of retching that empty her stomach.

After a while, the sickness subsides. Mark got napkins and a bottle of water from a nearby restaurant and Abriana dabs her lips and chin.

'Here, take a drink.' He offers her the bottle.

'Not the end of the night, I imagined.'

'If you are feeling better now, that's all that matters.'

'Thank you, Mark.'

'I didn't do anything. I'm just worried about you.'

'I know you are. What I meant was, thank you for coming here with me. It means a lot to me.'

'Are you feeling ok now?'

'Much better, thanks.'

They stand to face each other. Her eyes are watery, and he is not sure if they are wet with tears or with the sickness. She looks vulnerable.

Mark opens his arms. 'Come here.'

She moves towards him and slowly sinks into him. Mark wraps his arms around her. He catches the scent of her hair, her familiar perfume that has never left him, after all this time. He feels incapable of letting her go. Finally, he says, 'Let's get you back to the villa.'

The taxi ride back to the villa takes around ten minutes. During that time, Abriana is silent, her face tight with concentration. Around them, the landscape is glazed by a perilously bright moon and Mark can make out the contours of shaded hills and olive trees, as they leave the lights of Zakynthos Town behind.

He struggles to find words to describe what happened. He reflects, and he thinks of the things they spoke about; she certainly had an agenda, and it seems to Mark that Abriana had an overwhelming desire to drink as quick and as much as she could. He has never seen her like that. She is always disciplined and in control.

'You're quiet. Are you sure you're ok?' he finally asks.

'I'm just tired, that's all.' She can feel the beginnings of a headache.

When they return to the villa, Abriana goes straight to her room to shower. Mark pours himself a glass of wine and sits outside. Abriana's behaviour has disturbed him; it is so out of character he feels he doesn't know her anymore, not that part of her, anyway. Has she changed, or has he just never seen that side of her character? It is a question that is rhetorical because he has no personal experience with what her life is like now. Mark is unsettled. He empties his glass, which he drinks too fast, and goes to the kitchen for a refill. He is just about to pour the wine when he stops. Something inside tells him he has had enough, and he agrees.

Was it coincidence or fate that allowed them to meet again? Did Abriana engineer it? She sought him out. He feels a chill run down his spine. He is thinking too much. It is a response that finally settles him.

His bedroom is lit only by the light of the moon. He shuts his eyes, but sleep eludes him. He hears what sounds like an owl hoot. Can it be? Then he thinks, why not? Owls are not just restricted to Britain, but it is still a very British sound all the same. He wonders if Abriana is sleeping yet, then in answer, he hears the soft padding of feet, then a light knock on the door... it opens!

'Mark, are you still awake?' Abriana whispers as she moves into the room.

'Abriana!' He takes in a suck of air and sits up.

'I can't be alone tonight.'

As his eyes grow accustomed to the change in light, he can see she is wearing a silk nightdress before she closes the door behind her.

'What is it?' He can hardly believe she is standing before him.

'I just want you to hold me.' She moves closer to the bed and then before he can think of a response, astonishingly, she slides under the thin canopy of the sheet. She lays her head on his chest and he can feel the warmth of her body radiated against him. They lie in silence, their breathing the only sound in the room. He can feel her bare thigh against his skin, her warm minted breath on his chest, and when he looks, the moon's soft silver light catches the fine hairs on her forearm. Tentatively, he puts his arm around her shoulder. He can feel her body become heavier, her breathing deeper. He has often thought of this moment and this wasn't how he imagined the experience, the sensual and tactile.

'I'm sorry,' she mumbles.

'For what? Tonight?' And when there is no answer, he realises she is sleeping. He drifts his fingers through her long sleek hair and strangely, he doesn't feel disappointed that an opportunity has passed, irresistible as it is. Just to be lying near her is a satisfying recompense for all their months apart. In the morning, he will not ask her about tonight. It is enough that he is here with her.

He wakes with a jolt. The room is warm, and the sheet crumpled at his feet. Already, the sun has cast its light across the corner of the wall. He is confused, his mind struggling with a dream or reality. *Abriana!* There is still an indentation in the mattress and pillow. The feeling of her hair against his chest and her body next to him drifts to the surface. When he goes downstairs, Abriana is in the living room, talking into her mobile. She turns and sees him; he nods his head and gestures a drink with his hand. She smiles at him and he takes that as a 'yes.'

She sits down beside him on the terrace and reaches for her coffee.

'Thank you.' She holds the cup with both hands.

Mark struggles to find any words. He needs to be careful; he needs to say the right thing. In the end, there is no need, as Abriana speaks.

'About last night. I'm grateful, Mark. I was drunk. I feel ashamed of myself, actually. You acted impeccably and for that I'm... I have great admiration for that.'

'I restrained myself. God, I wanted to, I wanted you so much, just like it used to be,' he says with a relaxed smile.

'I have...' she pauses. 'I still have feelings for you, Mark. And I'm not blind. You're terrible at disguising it, but I can see the way you look at me sometimes.'

'It's that obvious?'

She smiles. 'I'm afraid so. Subtlety has never been your strength.

'Well...' he shrugs. 'No more pretence.'

She gives a small laugh, uneasy at his choice of words.

'What now?'

Abriana reaches out and takes his hand. 'Give me time, that's all I ask.'

The Story of Alisha Hadley

Corfu 1905

A Life, Full of Surprises

They take the train, the P & O Brindisi Express, on a Friday evening. From London, via Boulogne and Paris, they reach Brindisi in Southern Italy, fifty-four hours later.

They find the journey very civilised. Once the novelty of watching the passing countryside and towns wears off, they can indulge themselves with early morning coffee, lunch at noon, consisting of four courses, dinner at six, tea in the afternoon and the evening.

On their arrival in Brindisi, they stay overnight at the Grand Hotel International, conveniently situated at the harbour. The following morning, they board an Italian steamship. Alfred's secretary, a deliberate and austere man named James, with impenetrable eyes and hair that is oiled and combed back from his brow, hands their tickets to a steward, who then gives them the number to their berths. Their luggage is taken to the hold, and they are allowed to take a travelling bag and their instrument cases to their cabins. Alisha and Sara share a cabin, as do Reuben and Alex.

Once unpacked, Alisha and Sara take to the upper deck as the ship gradually distances itself from the coastline. Rueben and Alex are already there smoking the Italian cigarettes they bought that morning, pretending to enjoy the strong taste.

'Can you believe we're doing this? It feels real. Now we're on this ship.' Sara smiles disbelievingly.

Alisha's hair is loose about her face. It catches the breeze, and she holds it to her neck. 'It's like a dream, but we're really here.'

Alex inhales and then coughs. 'I must be getting a cold.' He glances at the cigarette in his hand and looks away.

Reuben smiles and shakes his head. 'In this climate, even the winds are warm. I don't think you're up to it, smoking these beauties.'

A waft of smoke blows into Sara's face. She flaps her hand vigorously. 'Oh, that's disgusting.'

'It's culture, my dear. It's European finesse,' Reuben smirks.

Sara covers her nose. 'Keep that thing away from me. It's like a chimney.'

Reuben tells unpalpable stories and rumours he has heard of the hotels in Greece, infested with fleas, bedbugs and lice. Sara squirms, unsure whether to believe him. Alisha tells her not to worry. This might be true of the inns found in the interior of the country, but she says with authority, in the main cities such rumours are unfounded. Alfred has stayed in Greece before and has stayed in hotels that are as agreeable as any first-class hotel in London. She tells Sara that when they get to Corfu, the first thing they will do is head to the drugstore and purchase Venetian *"Zampironi"* to stave off mosquitoes.

'I think Reuben's Italian cigarettes will do a good job of that,' Alex says, sullenly, gazing into the sea.

The coast of Albania is visible, a backdrop of mountains and small villages, smoke rising from roofs. Reuben asks after Alisha's well-being. Alisha seems paralysed with indecision before finally telling him she is over the ordeal, but, of course, he knows she is sparing him her true agonies.

'It's good to talk about it, Alisha. Everyone can see what he has done to you.' Reuben will not say his name. His mouth tightens. 'Although I must admit, you have been looking much like your old self these past few days.'

She doesn't look at him first. Alisha turns away and walks to a row of wooden seats. She sits down. Reuben follows her. She relaxes her gaze on the horizon. Luminous clouds scuttle across the sky. When he is beside her, she catches her breath. Eventually, when the words come, she can't stop. They spill from her.

'I've felt empty. I've cried so much my eyes are dry. Did I love him enough? Did I care enough? I waited, but he never came. When will I collapse? Sometimes I felt I couldn't go on. I felt drained of energy, of life itself. I walked around with a deep sense of disbelief; I swung from denial to anger. I questioned, why? I needed someone, something to blame.

'There have been times and they're becoming more frequent now that I've felt the glow of joy. I can laugh now. There are memories that make me smile. There is a glint of light inside me. I feel it radiate most days. Some days the light is weak, like a candle blowing in the wind, but mostly, it grows inside me, like today. Its embers flicker and sparkle, a warm sensation that spreads. It reaches into every sense, every thought and emotion. I'm being born again, cleansed of the pain and grief. I'm a flower spreading its petals in the light and temperateness around me.' Alisha looks at him. New confidence spreads across her face.

Instinctively Reuben touches her hand. 'I've often thought of you as a flower.' Reuben looks embarrassed; he braces himself, expecting a judgment of some kind from her. Alisha smiles warmly. He continues. 'We all care about you, Alisha, very much. Old Alfred is worried sick.'

'I know. I'll speak to him later today. What is that above your lip?' she asks Reuben.

There is a crop of stubble on his face. 'I'm growing a moustache; it's all the rage, apparently. Does it suit me?'

'Yes. I'd say it does. I like it.'

'Good. I'm glad you like it.'

'Why?'

'Because I respect your opinion.'

'What if I said I hated it. Would you shave it off?'

'Mm... maybe.' He laughs.

'Don't worry. I won't. But I might insist that you smoke

those awful cigarettes outdoors and not when we're rehearsing.'

'I promise.' He touches her hand again. It is enough for him just now. He tries to read her expression. There is a subtle shift in her, he is sure of it. She is examining his face.

'What is it?' He looks into her eyes and she holds his stare.

'I'm glad we are here, together.'

'You are full of surprises; do you know that, Alisha?'

She lowers her head. There is a moment of silence. Reuben wonders if she is searching for the right reply.

'My life, so far, has been full of surprises.'

'Corfu is the largest of the Ionian Islands. Did you know it has an area of two hundred and seventy-eight square miles? It's dominated by Mount Pantokrator. It gets quite a considerable amount of rain during parts of the year, which makes the countryside very fertile. The scenery is breathtaking.'

Alfred shares with everyone his knowledge of the island. They are all standing on the upper deck where they can see the dark silhouette of land ahead of them.

'It has a population of ninety-one thousand. Because of its colonial history, Italian is widely spoken. My Greek leaves much to be desired, so I'll get ample opportunity to practice my Italian. The capital is one of the most prosperous towns in the country. James, bring me the binoculars, there's a good man.'

Reuben leans towards Alisha. 'Alfred's in his element. I've not seen him this relaxed in a long time.'

Alisha smiles. 'It suits him.'

'As it does you. It's good to see you look so happy, Alisha.'

'It feels good, too. I've missed the feeling. I think I might take up drawing again. This scenery is so inspiring.'

'That's right, I forgot you used to draw.'

'Just sketches, really. I wasn't that good at it, but I enjoyed the feeling it gave me. When playing a piece on the violin, it's not permanent. There's a time when the music stops and, although it may give the listener joy, it ends. The sketch remains. It's visible. I like that.'

The passengers and their luggage are transported from the steamship by boats.

The harbour is larger than Alisha imagined, bustling with cargo boats preparing to leave alongside ships from Russia and England, with crates of grain and other goods being unloaded onto the quay. It is a world of chaotic activity, noise and smells.

Once through the custom-house, they take a carriage sent by their hotel, *Hotel D'Angleterre Et Belle Venise*, in the south of the town. Upon their arrival, they discover the hotel is opulent in design and architecture. Equipped with electric lights, a well-maintained garden and, most importantly, baths. The thought of sinking into a bathtub of warm water and the promise of undisturbed sleep in a comfortable bed is a welcome relief that both Alisha and Sara are looking forward to.

Rehearsals fill the first few days. Alfred has impressed upon them the importance that entertaining his guests is just as important as the business proposition they have come to hear. The first few nights are a success, and Alfred is delighted with the interest. Already, contracts among interested parties are in the process of being drawn up. After each day's rehearsal, the quartet is free to explore the town or relax in the hotel.

Alisha has never seen the sky look so vast. It is endless and so blue, stretching out to infinity, where no other colour stains her vision. In London, the sky was often low, a ceiling of cloud and sometimes fog amongst a wall of buildings, a warren of streets, dirt and noise. She remembers dead animals, horse manure, and running sewage that clogged the gutters and poisoned the air.

Alisha delights in inhaling deeply, filling her lungs with air that is clean, fragrant, and sweet. It purifies her senses, sharpening her nose. These past few days have transformed her. She has entered a world unknown to her. She felt like another being from afar off-planet. This foreign place is becoming familiar, and she is genuinely becoming attached to its curiosities. Corfu leaves her breathless with its perfection. Even if it has faults, which she is sure it must, yet evidence so far would say otherwise, it will not remove the glowing feeling in her chest. She has become intoxicated with this new country.

Alisha has now grown accustomed to her room. Over time, it has become familiar to her, and she considers it to be her space where she retires from the outside world.

The room consists of two large pieces of furniture, a wardrobe, and a dressing table, both made from dark wood that contrasts with the light that seeks out each corner. On the dressing table, there is a small mirror only capable of capturing the onlooker's face. Such are its limitations. There are paintings on the walls of sailing boats and a castle, all by the same artist, she thinks. The castle looks familiar and is possibly the one she has seen when she goes for her walk, in the late afternoon, around the town. Below one of these paintings sits her bed with its layers of sheets, which she peels from her body during the night. Hanging over her bed is a thin muslin curtain to protect her from mosquitos.

Her room is always still, in hushed silence, a quietness that reminds Alisha of her room in the boarding school, especially at night, when she lay in bed, thinking. Her young mind often wondered where life would take her. Alisha imagined playing in a famous orchestra or touring the world's stages as a solo artist. Sometimes, in her thoughts, she is married with children. She will have a handsome husband, who is a lawyer or works in a bank. She has maids to tend to the house and a nanny to watch over the children. In those days, at the boarding school, she often experienced a unique fulfilment, contentment that eventually resurfaced when she met John Sutton.

Today, the feeling has returned, and it is real. It is in this hotel room. It surrounds her when she steps outside into the piercing sunlight. It is reassuring and no longer unfamiliar.

Initially, she was hesitant to allow herself this joyous feeling, but gradually, her reluctance faded, as have the wounds John Sutton left on her.

After the incident at Alfred's house, she attempted to see John, but he ignored her requests. She sent him letters that went unanswered. Her despair and irritation grew with each new day of silence. Finally, she ran out of time and the day arrived when she had to leave London for Europe.

. . .

She has been for a walk in the hotel garden. Out of the heat, her room feels cool. It dampens the perspiration on her neck and Alisha dabs it with a wet cloth.

Alisha pulls on the sash window. It is heavy and stubborn. When it moves, in one fluent motion, a burst of air tickles the fine hairs on her forearms. She cranes her head and the sounds and smells of the street below flood her room as if they have become joined; they stir inside her, like music. It intoxicates her. It is a discovery she has not yet become used to. It stuns her each time and each day she yearns for this experience and she hopes it will never leave her.

The hotel is quite elegant compared to some which she has noticed in the town. She is thankful, for there is electric lighting, baths and a well-kept garden.

The reception is one of her favourite areas of the hotel. It is large and spacious, decorated with bouquets of flowers, leather chairs, and low tables, where often, men sit and read newspapers. There is a dining room, where breakfast, lunch and an evening meal are served. It is here, especially during the evening meal, that the dining room has become fertile ground to hear the latest gossip reverberating around the tables. Although they can have all their meals in the hotel, occasionally, they have ventured out into the town and taken a meal at a restaurant. It is Alfred's opinion that one cannot come to a country and omit to taste the local cuisine. To Alisha's surprise, in some of the restaurants they have eaten in, the food is half-French. The wine, on the other hand, is an entirely different proposition and is a matter of taste. She has tried an un-resin red wine called Kephisia. The Greek wine is mixed with resin, to keep it from going off longer and, if not accustomed to the taste, it is very unpalatable. Thankfully, to Alisha's relief, most of the good restaurants serve French wine.

She has learnt, when on her leisurely walks around the garden with Sara, that Reuben and Alex have been visiting the casino. This concerns her. Rueben influences Alex too easily. Sara has informed her, Alfred knows nothing of these clandestine excursions, which is fortunate, to say the least, as he would not take to kindly to the *'devils work'* being so enthusiastically indulged.

They have visited several cafes, and Alisha has noted that overall, most resemble the Italian style. Whenever they are out often, Sara and Alisha venture to the Esplanade, where coffee is served in small cups. It is left to cool and Alisha always drinks it with care as not to disturb the dark sediment at the bottom.

Often, she will have a Loukoumi, a Turkish delight mixed with pistachio nuts which she particularly enjoys, and it is quickly becoming her favoured choice.

She sits at the dressing table and releases the pins that held her hair. It tumbles around her shoulders and falls down her back in waves. She notices it is getting lighter from the sun, which prompts her; she must wear her hat more often even when she has her umbrella.

Alisha combs her hair, a ritual that relaxes her mind and she wanders through her thoughts. A knock at the door pulls her back. She opens it to find Reuben, standing there in a crème suit and white hat.

'Oh, it's you, Reuben. You look very... dashing.'

'Were you expecting anyone?' Reuben asks, his confidence fading.

'No.'

'I thought it would be nice to go for a walk and wondered if you'd like to accompany me.' He raises an eyebrow.

'I've just returned from one. I was out with Sara.'

'Ah. What about some tea, then, in the dining room?'

'That would be nice, but I'd need to freshen up first. I'm still uncomfortably hot from my walk.'

'Of course. I'll see you down in the dining room when you're ready.'

She smiles. 'You will.'

'How are you?' He takes a small silver cigarette case from his breast pocket and lights a cigarette.

'I'm fine. The same as I was during rehearsal this morning.'

'I didn't mean it like that. I meant are you still well within yourself? I just want to be reassured; you're not tormenting yourself?'

'I'm well. Thank you for your concern, Reuben.'

'I worry about you, Alisha, that's all. That's what friends do,' he says, seriously. He has crossed his legs and sits his hat on his lap.

'And I'm grateful for it, truly I am. It's a comfort to me, but I'm, well, really, I am, Rueben. Coming to Greece has been like taking an incredibly potent medication. My mind is relaxed. For the first time in weeks I feel a freedom, it's extraordinary. I feel born again.'

Reuben smiles and beams white teeth. 'Good. That's a relief. I can see that now. I love your smile, Alisha.'

Alisha takes a sip of tea and studies him over the rim. She has detected a keenness in his attention towards her, more than his normal demeanour. She thinks in pleasant anticipation of spending more time with Reuben. Maybe something else has changed in her, as well.

'I can't believe how lucky we are. Who would have thought that playing music would allow us to travel to the Mediterranean? We are privileged, Alisha, we truly are.' Reuben's voice is full of enthusiasm. He takes an avid suck on his cigarette and is careful to blow the smoke away from her.

A waiter asks if they are having lunch. 'Now that I think about it, I'm rather hungry.' He smiles and asks for the menu.

'Not for me, thank you.' Alisha waves her hand apologetically.

'Who would have thought, when we started playing together, we would end up here? We have Alfred to thank for that.'

'If it wasn't for Gloria, bless her, I shudder to think what would have become of me. Working in some dreadful factory, I suspect. She truly shaped my life.'

'You were responsible as well, Alisha. We all were. Without our initial promise of talent, we wouldn't have had the privilege of her vision and teaching.'

'I miss her. She was like a mother to me. I feel enormously sad for Alfred. As a couple, they had so much to give, so much to look forward to. Sometimes, I think he is lonely. That's why he fills his world with all of this.'

'Us, you mean.'

'Not just us. Don't you think this is all about filling the void she left?'

Reuben shrugs. 'I'm not sure. I know he's invested a lot of his own money in getting to this stage. It's a business opportunity for him. It's what he does.'

'My point is, he doesn't need to. He can let others do it for him.'

'I suppose. I'm glad he's here.'

'I am too.'

Just then, Alfred enters the dining room.

'Speak of the devil.' Reuben smiles, and he waves him over.

Alfred nods his head. 'Reuben, Alisha.' He pats Alisha affectionately on the shoulder. 'I hope I'm not disturbing you.'

'Not at all. Please join us, Alfred.'

'In that case, it would be my pleasure. You're both looking well. The weather must agree with you both, or it is each other's company?' Alfred looks at them shrewdly, checking their reaction. Alisha averts her eyes and takes another sip of tea. He pulls out a chair and sinks his large frame into it.

'Ah, that's better. I've been on my feet all morning and they've swollen to twice their size, I should think. It feels that way. I fear if I take my boots off, I won't be able to get them back on again.'

'Have you seen a doctor?' Alisha asks, concerned.

'No, no. It's not as drastic as that, not yet anyway. Don't worry my dear, if need be, I'll walk about in my bare feet.' He throws his head back and laughs. Alisha smiles, but it is for Alfred's benefit, as his humour doesn't abate her worry.

Alfred raises his arm and snaps his fingers, attracting a waiter's attention. 'What has a man to do to get something to eat around here? I'm starving half to death?'

During lunch, Alfred describes his impending trip over to the west of the island, where amongst the pine trees where the land slopes into a pretty cove, he has ambitions to build a small exclusive hotel.

'Would you like to join me? We leave tomorrow first thing after breakfast.' Alfred says between mouthfuls.

'Count me in,' Reuben enthuses.

'What about you, Alisha?' Alfred dabs the corners of his mouth with a napkin.

'I'd love to see the island.'

'That's settled then.'

Two great black horses whose coats shine in the morning sun pull the coach. Alfred is in a jovial mood and James, his secretary, sits next to him. Alisha can never tell what James is thinking, as he seldom speaks to anyone.

Reuben has spent the night at the casino, and they are not even out of the environs of the town when he has fallen asleep, his head bobbing from side to side as if it will come loose from his neck at any minute.

Alisha is enjoying being out in the countryside. They have spent most of their time in the town, apart from one day when Alfred hired a boat and they sailed along the coast for several miles.

'Look at that tree, there.' Alfred points out of the carriage window. 'It's called The Judas Tree.'

As the carriage rumbles along the rutted track, Alisha detects several more, peppering the road in purple bursts. The sea of yellow grass that carpets the dust and dried earth startles Alisha, where wildflowers sprinkle vibrant colours, like a radiant rainbow that has fallen from the sky. Along the way, to keep her amused, Alisha counts the cypress trees. These, at least, are familiar to her, as she recalls seeing them on the train, as they travelled through Italy, and she thought of them then, as she does now, as stabbing the cobalt sky.

Further along, luxuriant pines blanket hills, looming over secluded villages and the occasional farm.

'We're nearly there,' Alfred grins, and his eyes become like small black stones in his head. Reuben jolts awake. Startled, he looks around the carriage and sits back again, his eyelids still heavy and struggling with sleep. To Alisha's amazement, his hair, oiled and combed, has not moved out of place. It is stuck to his scalp, she amusingly assumes.

She is still contemplating this phenomenon when the horses pull to a halt, nostrils snorting and hoofs stamping at baked earth. As they disembark, the state of these magnificent creatures saddens her, their coats glistening with sweat. Then her distress abates when the driver appears with two sloshing buckets of water that he places at their feet.

'This way,' Alfred instructs.

Alisha fills her lungs with clear, ethereal air. She looks around, amazed at how green the landscape is. She mentions this to Alfred, who informs her that, on a day like today, it's hard to believe it can rain considerably out with the long hot summers.

The veritable cacophony of cicadas fills the air with their electric, crisp and synchronised rattle. Pine needles and wild thyme strewn the ground and as they follow Alfred, who walks with an enthusiastic shuffle. They come across a clearing, and suddenly, the view takes Alisha's breath away. Even from where she stands, she can hear the continuous lapping and rhythmic pulse of waves rolling onto a beach.

'This is where I intend to build my hotel. What do you think, Alisha?'

'It's spectacular. Imagine wakening up to this view every morning?'

'My thoughts exactly. When my life feels directionless,

all I have to do is look at the sea, and I always feel rejuvenated and the magic of it is, it's free. Of course, that's the only thing that'll be free in my hotel,' he says, grinning.

'Is it not a trifle far from civilisation?' Reuben asks, bemused. He lights a cigarette.

'That's the point. The hotel will be the best of its kind, much better than anything Corfu Town has to offer. It will offer luxury and seclusion, two for the price of one. Now, that's not bad. I must remember that.' He turns to James. 'Make a note of that, James. Look, down there, there's the beach. I don't think a human foot has touched its sands.'

'It's idyllic, Alfred.' Alisha touches his forearm. She notices a small blue rowing boat tucked in between rocks.

'Precisely, my dear. That's the point.' Alfred smiles broadly.

'Do you think Gloria would have liked this place?'

Alfred's eyes become momentarily sombre at the mention of his wife's name.

He clears his throat. 'I think she would have approved. In fact, I'm going to name the hotel Gloria.'

'I like that and I'm sure she would have too.'

Alfred turns from the sea and looks at Alisha. 'When the hotel is built, you'll have to come back, and stay, as my guest, of course.'

She smiles at him and nods her head. 'I'd like that very much.'

'As you know, Gloria and I were never blessed with children. The children who attended the music school were our family, in essence. I know I shouldn't be saying this, but you were my favourite. You'll always have a special place in my heart, Alisha.' He kisses her forehead. 'Are you hungry?'

Alfred has brought a lavish picnic, food never being far from him.

Amongst the pines, there is a small clearing shaded by the sun. James has laid out a chequered blanket and opened a wicker picnic basket. He sets out plates, cutlery and glasses. Before long, there is a small feast before them: cheese, bread, olives, chicken and sausages. James cuts the melon into pieces that remind Alisha of small boats and he places them neatly onto a china plate.

'Watch the juice doesn't drip onto the ground. The ants can be little buggers at times, here use a napkin,' Alfred says and then pours red wine into glasses which he hands out.

'One of my associates, back in London, is often fond of reminding me we learn more about ourselves as we get older. When I reach 80, I hope to know all there is to know about myself, but to do so, we all need a little help. In time, this will be a place where people can come to rediscover themselves, to rejuvenate their passion for living, indeed, for life itself...' he raises a glass. 'To Hotel Gloria,' Alfred beams, and they all clink their glasses in celebration.

Alisha thinks Alfred's vision is a noble undertaking and here in this place, she has already discovered her own *Hotel Gloria*, as Corfu has become, in such a short space of time, a mystical and soul-lifting island.

During lunch, there is a lot of small talk. Alisha delicately wipes her lips and then thanks Alfred for allowing them this opportunity to see such a stunning corner of Corfu.

After lunch, Alisha has a desire to see the views one more time before they leave. Her eyes take everything in as if she is seeing the world for the first time. The turquoise wash of the Ionian on a luxuriant expanse of golden sand takes her breath away. She is in awe. A light breeze displaces a strand of hair, and she fixes it in place. She is alert to someone coming up behind her.

'Alfred knows how to pick a spot. The view's stunning.'

'It is,' she agrees. She can see Reuben has rolled the sleeves of his shirt, his arms coloured from the sun. She thinks of her own arms, which are pale in comparison.

'It feels like we have got you back, Alisha. I can't tell you what that means to me. I thought we'd lost you... I'd lost you.'

'Despite what has happened to me, I'm happy. I'm all I've got, and I need to look after myself from now on. Life is too important. I'll never go back there again. I do have happy memories.'

'I don't doubt it.' He pauses. 'And can you love again?'

Alisha looks startled. It's an astounding question. She hasn't expected Reuben to be so direct; it throws her slightly. She pauses, collects her thoughts. Is it reasonable for him to enquire? She considers this. His interest is real.

'It's a subject I haven't given much thought to.' Her eyes skim his face, and she looks out towards the sea.

'If you felt the same way he felt about you, would you give him a chance to prove his worth?'

The sea is calm, reflecting the sun's light in contrast to the churning of her stomach.

'If he could see me for who I am and not for who I'm not.' Her words are a direct reference to John Sutton. The inference is not lost on Reuben. It stings him. It is a reminder he still comes between them, even here, even now.

'But what if he can already see you for who you are? He always has done.'

She touches his forearm. 'Oh, Reuben. This intrigue and

mystery doesn't suit you. Although, if I'm honest, it excites me, it's a change from your usual plain speech.'

'That's not a yes, then.'

'It's not a no either... I need time.'

It is a glimmer, and he clings to it.

CHAPTER FIFTEEN

REASONS

'Shall we take the car, or walk?' Mark asks standing poised with a spray of sun cream, wishing he had bought the cream variety instead, as he shivers at the thought of it, once applied, feeling greasy and oily on his skin.

'For all the time it will take, we could just walk.'

'Then I'll need to walk a few paces behind you,' he grins.

'Whatever for?'

'The view will be much better from back there.' He feels an uncontrollable urge to laugh.

'That's terrible,' she chastises him playfully.

'It's a compliment.' And then he laughs.

'Then I'll take it as such,' she says, smiling.

As always, the sea is not too far and the brilliance of colour, a translucent blue, lifts Mark's spirits. They are walking along a narrow road that connects the sparse array of new villas that populate this corner of the island.

'You could be here for two weeks and not see a soul,'

Abriana says as they walk past ancient olive groves that cast precise shadows on the dusty earth.

'I suppose that's the attraction of it.'

'I'm not sure I'd like that. It's good to socialise when on holiday. That's part of the experience, don't you think?'

'It depends on who you're with, I suppose. We're not on holiday, though.'

'No, we're not.'

They walk a little further. 'Did you make a list?'

'I did, but it's in my head: milk, bread, eggs, cheese, tomatoes, chocolate and wine, of course.'

'Any more than four things and my mind will stop working. I need my lists to be written down, well, on my phone, to be exact.'

Abriana shakes her head. 'Honestly, Mark, I don't know how you manage to run that gallery of yours.'

'I've got Joann for that. She keeps me right.'

'You're lucky to have her.'

'I know, in more ways than one. She's a good friend. I don't know what I would have done without her at times. Actually, I don't know how she puts up with me, to be honest. I've put her through hell at times. I'm sure of it.'

'Don't take her for granted. She might get fed up with it one day.'

'After what happened in Rome...well, when I came back to Edinburgh, she insisted I stay at her holiday cottage, just until things died down.' An image of the day he met Gill at Elie comes to mind. He pushes it away.

'That was thoughtful of her.'

'It's the kind of person she is.'

'Have you been in touch with her?' she asks, but what she really wants to say is, has Joann mentioned the article?'

'No, but she texts me the other day.'

'Oh. And how is she?' She looks at him discreetly.

'Fine, I suppose. A bit peed off. I didn't tell her I was off on my little trip. She used a few choice words that weren't very flattering. Put it that way.'

She waits. Finally, she speaks. 'I can imagine, but you can't blame her, especially with what happened.'

'I'm not going to hurt her feelings. She hasn't had any since 2005, as far as I can tell. That was a joke, by the way. Anyway, if there had been anything that needed my attention, she would have said. I'm sure of it,' Mark says with a reassuring smile.

'I suppose your right.' Abriana nods. 'I suspect once this all comes to its conclusion; they'll be some interest from the press.' She needs to test his reaction.

'Are you ready for that?' Mark asks.

Abriana shrugs. 'I'll try to keep out of it and let the gallery deal with it. They have people for that kind of thing.'

'You've already been bitten by them.'

'We both have. Doesn't that change things?' She's trying to persuade herself. He needs to know, but if she can, she will keep him out of it. After all, it is in the Uffizi Gallery's interest to deal with the press and, she considers, it's not unusual. In fact, it is to be expected that at some point the story of the painting will gain media interest. Her hope would have been not now.

'The thought has crossed my mind that the press may sense a story, or worse still, a bruised Alan Sutton might try to sell his story.'

She stalls. 'Yes. I suppose you're right,' she says, trying to sound unconcerned.

'Have you any thoughts on where Pavlos' story is going?' Mark asks.

'Reuben is an interesting character.'

'I think he loves her.'

She smiles. 'Of course he does.'

'A woman's intuition?'

'It has its benefits at times.'

'And Alisha, do you think she'll reciprocate this love?'

'Like all love stories, I think she will. If she doesn't, it'll come as a surprise to me and I'll have got her all wrong, but you can never tell. I'm looking forward to seeing Pavlos.'

'You're fond of him.'

'What is there not to like about him? He's a gentleman and a seriously good cook.'

'Yes. That lunch was something. He surprised me.'

'And the vegetables and herbs were from his garden. That made the difference, I think. I'd like to grow my own vegetables, be self-sufficient.'

'You, a gardener.' He looks at her, unconvinced.

'Why not? In fact, I think I'll ask Pavlos for some tips this afternoon.'

'It's not for me. That's what shops are for.'

'Wouldn't you get self-satisfaction? Preparing the ground, planting the seed, nourishing the plant as it grows and finally, picking the mature vegetable. It's like what we are doing now. Going to get the groceries, it's a domestic chore, but there's a satisfaction to it.'

'I'm not convinced.'

Abriana ties her normal cascade of hair into a bun on top of her head. She makes a slight adjustment.

'I've never seen you put your hair up like that.'

She smiles. 'It's hot.'

A small disc shape mark on the back of her neck draws his eye.

'Is that a tattoo?'

She laughs. 'Have I shocked you, Mark?'

'No. I'd just never thought you'd be the type.'

'And what type of person gets a tattoo?'

'Oh, I don't know. You know what I mean, usually young woman or a certain class.'

'Careful Mark, you're making assumptions, generalisations. You're in choppy waters,' she says, unable to suppress a note of amusement.

He asks her then, why did she get it done?

'When I moved back to Florence, I went to this little shop several times to buy scented candles. And I got friendly with the shop owner who one day told me about this sign which brings good luck. I thought about it for several months until I plucked up the courage to get it tattooed. It's a circle with two fish in it.'

'What does it mean?'

'That your thoughts are yours. You see, nobody can tell a fish where to swim. I like that.'

'You like being in control. For as long as I've known you, you've known your own mind. It's a virtue I like about you.'

'I like to make sure things get done the way I want. Sometimes that's a good thing and other times... let's just say it has its disadvantages.'

They walk a little further without speaking, then Abriana says, 'Is there anything you don't like about me? What annoys you about me, Mark?' she asks, obviously intrigued.

Mark thinks a bit. 'Sometimes you're guarded about what

you're feeling.' He pauses briefly. 'I'm not always sure what you're thinking.'

'Is that a problem?'

'Maybe that's the point, I suppose. If something is worrying you, you don't always share it. You keep it to yourself. Take, for instance, the other night. I knew you were upset about something, but I've learned to let you tell me in your own time.' He smiles at her reassuringly.

Abriana turns and looks at the sea that brims and melts into the sky. How can she feel such angst in a place that is so serene? She feels panic; the world she knows and cares about is shifting. She is not in control, as Mark thinks she is, and it is all her own doing, again!

She feels panic, and it is unsettling. It is not so much the thought that she hasn't told Mark about the press interest that has disturbed her-she has realised she can't let Mark get close to her again, not now, especially not now, even though she wants it to happen. She has her reasons. It would only get in the way; it would cloud her judgement and she knows she would question herself. She cannot have a semblance of doubt; her mind needs to stay clear. No, Mark would only get in the way and she can't let that happen.

'There are things I'm not sure about myself. I can't tell you just now. After this is all finished, you'll understand.'

'About what? You're speaking in riddles.'

'It's difficult, Mark.' A familiar weight descends upon her.

'Try me.' He tries to keep the irritation from his voice.

'Not now,' she says sharply, a little too much, which she instantly regrets.

'Like I said, in your own time, then.'

They are silent for a moment.

Regret prowls around her. She should never have asked him to come to Zakynthos.

The Story of Alisha Hadley

Corfu 1905

The nub of amber rosin, she uses to clean the bow, turns to a white powder that infiltrates the air. The beam of sunlight illuminates minute particles, like scores of fireflies, as she methodically rubs the length of the bow. They brought from London spare violin strings, but it worries her they may deplete their stock. She is hopeful they will last until Athens, where they can buy more if need be.

The performances are going well and each night; The Quartet is received with enthusiastic applause and appreciation. Their reputation is spreading beyond the *Hotel D'Angleterre Et Belle Venise* and if it wasn't for their strict schedule, Alisha is sure they would secure performances in the theatres.

She bends and places the violin in its case. She checks her hair in the mirror on the dressing table and secures a wide-brimmed hat in place. They meet in the reception and head out into the street where Alisha is in awe of the salmon-coloured sky. Reuben takes her arm and they walk along narrow alleys that twist and turn, separating Venetian houses, tall and elegant in red and yellowish-brown.

They pass shuttered mansions, many of them sleeping in the late afternoon heat. Soon, they come to the Esplanade. To Alisha's eye, the buildings look solid and grand. She likes the lack of architectural pretentiousness

and austere blocks, which, to her mind, would have under-
mined layers of Venetian influence and splendour, a
reminder of Corfu Town's past glories. They pass St.
George's Hotel and walk in the shade of the trees that line
the street. They stumble upon a market, where woven
baskets of fruit and vegetables are stacked under canvass
canopies. Reuben notices that it is mostly men and boys
who work here. They wear waistcoats and white shirts with
circular hats on their heads. They cross the street, paying
particular attention to the open-top carriages. Sailors in
uniform spill from a café bar, their voices loud and laughter
exaggerated, fueled by too much alcohol. One of them stumbles and narrowly avoids knocking over several baskets piled
on a table. The young men of the market mutter to each
other and, sensing the mood change, Reuben suggests they
leave.

The wide space of the promenade is a welcome relief as
they make their way along its expanse. Alisha enjoys the
light breeze from the sea where she can see several ships,
their sails ablaze with the setting sun that slips towards the
horizon.

A young woman, a nanny, Alisha suspects, walks a young
baby in a pram. Alisha looks upon them fondly and she is
aware of a pang in her stomach. In front of them, a few steps
ahead, another couple walk arm in arm. The woman shades
herself with a white umbrella, her dress swaying and skirting
the pavement as she walks. Her partner holds a cane that
moves with a sweeping motion as he walks, and Alisha can
tell by the look of admiration on Reuben's face, he will search
the shops of the town for a similar one.

A man on a bicycle approaches from the opposite direction; he waves his hat in greeting. Likewise, the man in front

waves his cane in return and Alisha's mood lifts by such civility.

They order some wine in a bar and sit outside, enjoying the last of the light, as the sky changes from orange and pink to a fire red. Soon electric light illuminates the street and a waiter lights a small candle in a glass upon their table. They discuss the arrangements Alisha hopes to introduce to their performances at the hotel, pieces by Vivaldi and Bach.

Reuben tells her that since they have spent time together, he has stopped frequenting the casino. It is news Alisha is glad to hear. In a few days, it will be Alisha's twenty-second birthday and Reuben tells her he has already bought her a present. Alisha stresses she doesn't want anything elaborate, but he just smiles at her and promises she will like it. His confidence surprises her. Above them in a star-studded sky, the moon gains definition. People sit around them, ordering dinner.

'Are you hungry?' Reuben asks.

She is feeling light-headed. 'Something to soak up the wine, maybe, but not a meal.'

'Some olives and bread, I think. Do you like olives, Alisha?'

'They're an acquired taste my palate hasn't acquired. It's fine though. I'll just have some bread.'

'Are you sure?' Reuben scans the menu.

'Yes, honestly.'

The waiter brings a basket of crusted bread and a bowl of green olives. Alisha has ordered a tea and Reuben another wine.

'One more week and we'll be in Athens,' Reuben says, picking an olive from the bowl.

'I'm looking forward to seeing the Acropolis. I've never seen anything as old as that. It fascinates me.'

'I'm just glad it's a city.'

'Don't you like it here?' Alisha is surprised at his tone.

'It's not London, is it?'

'Thank God for that. How can you not like Corfu, Reuben?'

'I didn't say I didn't like it.'

'It sounded that way.'

'It's just... the quicker we get to Athens, the better, that's all.'

'Are you in some sort of trouble?'

'It's nothing I can't handle,' he says, bringing his glass to his lips.

'What do you mean, Reuben? You're worrying me.'

'I owe the casino some money, that's all.'

'How much?'

'Not much.' Reuben frowns.

'Tell me, Reuben,' she insists.

Reuben looks uncomfortable.

'How much is it?'

'A substantial amount. Ten pounds.'

Her mouth drops. 'Reuben, how could you let that happen?'

'I thought I'd be able to pay it back with my winnings, but my luck ran out and the debt grew.'

'Have you told anyone?'

'Alex knows.'

'And Alfred?'

'Heavens no. I'm ashamed of it. You're the only other person I can tell.'

'Can you pay this debt?'

He looks sheepishly. 'I've got until the end of the week.'

'So, you don't have the money?'

'Not just yet. Alex says he has some put aside, but not enough to cover it.' He looks desperate, and he takes a drink. 'There's no getting away from it. I'm an idiot, I know. I'm sorry. As I said, I haven't been back to the casino. Luckily, I'm over all that now,' he says, his voice full of self-disgust.

'You must pay the money. You will be arrested.' She feels a rushing in her head. 'I have savings. I'll give you the money.'

'I can't accept it. It's too much, Alisha.'

'You don't have a choice, Reuben.'

'I feel ashamed.' He lowers his head.

'It's done. You can't change what has happened.' She reaches over the table and takes his hand. 'I'm not giving you the money out of pity, Reuben. I want to, that is the difference. It's what people do when they care about each other. In fact, I think, if I'm honest, we're becoming more than just friends.'

On the night of Alisha's birthday, Alfred takes the Quartet out to dinner in one of the finest restaurants in Corfu Town. Afterwards, when they return to the hotel, he treats them to the best champagne it offers. Once Alfred retires to bed, Reuben asks Alisha to meet him in the hotel garden, whilst he goes to his room to get her present.

She sits on a bench that looks out over the shrubs and flowers. Several lamps light the path that curve around the grounds and Alisha watches, as giant moths, attracted to the light, bounce off the lamps, and flutter again and again in a blind, frantic dance. She can feel her mind-numbing from the alcohol. She has drunk more than she is accustomed to and she straightens her posture, an attempt to still feel in control.

'Here you are.' He hands her a package. 'Open it.' Reuben smiles broadly.

She tears the paper to reveal a mahogany box with gold-coloured hinges. She lifts the lid and gasps with delight. Inside, sitting in their little holders, are twenty watercolour pencils.

'Do you like them?' He asks.

'Oh Reuben, there lovely. Thank you.' She leans forward and kisses his cheek.

'I've got another one.' He hands her another package.

She tears the paper to find a sketch pad.

'The pencils are no good on their own. You need paper to draw on.'

'I don't have any excuses now. Thank you, Reuben.' It is Alisha's turn to smile broadly.

'Did you enjoy tonight?'

'I did, although I wasn't expecting the attention. Alfred is too good to me.'

'It makes him happy to see you enjoy yourself, Alisha. I've been wanting to ask you... well, not exactly. I've wanted to tell you something that has been on my mind for a long time...'

Then, suddenly, she leans into him and kisses him, this time on his lips. It is short and soft. She stares into his eyes and her eyes are dancing as she looks at him. Reuben curls his fingers around the nape of her neck and guides her towards him again. This time, their kiss is longer, deeper, and he groans in gratitude. It is a release.

CHAPTER SIXTEEN

A SECRET REVEALED AT APOSTOLOS

'Oh my God, they became lovers.'

'I told you, Mark. The signs were there. Sometimes things don't have to be said.' Abriana smiles.

'This has come as a surprise to you?' Pavlos asks, forcing tobacco into his pipe.

'I could see they were fond of each other. Maybe Reuben was more than just fond now that I think about it.'

'I've lived with these memories most of my life. I could tell you what you really want to know in a second. The reason you came was to find out if this man in Edinburgh is the rightful heir to the painting. That would be wrong of me. I wouldn't be doing John or Alisha justice. I need to tell you their story, as it happened. It needs to be told and now that you are recording my words, there is evidence, there is proof.

'Speaking to you has helped me as well. All my life, it has felt I have lived with the ghosts of John Sutton and Alisha Hadley. I am now letting them go.' He gestures towards the

Dictaphone. 'You are responsible for them now. Look after them and do the right thing.'

'If the gallery wins the right to show the painting, your account of its history will accompany the exhibition of Sutton's work.'

'I would like that. And if it is not given to the gallery?'

'It will still be of interest to the art world. It will have a tremendous impact.'

Pavlos nods his head in satisfaction. He looks tired.

'These cakes are delicious, Pavlos,' Mark says.

'They are. I need to get the recipe from you. What are they called?' Abriana asks.

'Just a yoghurt cake. It has oranges and lemons, and it is garnished with a cognac scented syrup. It is called Yiaourto-pita. It is a traditional Greek cake recipe, made with yoghurt instead of milk, which makes it moist and tender. You have to use full-fat Greek yoghurt. You don't have to use the syrup, but I think it adds to the taste. You can take some with you. I'm never going to eat all of that.'

'I suppose we better get going. We'll drop by again tomorrow. I don't want to rush you, Pavlos, but the gallery is beginning to ask when I'll be finished here.'

'I understand. I like your company too much and it will be sad not to have these conversations. I miss having people around the house. The curse of growing old, everyone leaves you. I hate the silence.'

Abriana tries to muster a smile. 'Louis and Maria are only a walk away. You should visit them more often.'

'I know. I don't want anyone's pity. Louis is a good man; he visits when he can. I know he's checking on me, making sure I'm okay. He pretends he's interested in gardening and I play along. As I say, I like the company. We're fulfilling both our needs.'

'Right then, what shall we do with this cake?' Mark asks, getting to his feet.

'There is a container in the kitchen, the cupboard next to the sink if you don't mind getting it, Mark.'

As Mark disappears into the house, Abriana looks at Pavlos and decides to be frank. 'There are others who may be interested in your story. They will not just be interested in the painting. Let's just say they'll not only want to know about the ownership of the painting, but their questions may also be regarded as... intrusive. I suspect they'll be curious about Mark and me. You don't have to speak to them, Pavlos. Has anyone else been in touch with you?'

Pavlos shakes his head. 'No. I didn't realise there would be such an interest in my story. Do you know these people?'

'No, but nothing in the art world stays a secret for long. Don't worry, but if you are contacted, you'll let me know?'

'Of course I will.' His voice rises. 'I'll speak to no one but you.'

Abriana smiles. 'Good.'

'Here we are. That'll do. I'll return the container tomorrow,' Mark says, coming out of the house.

Abriana nods at Pavlos, as if to say, we're finished talking about it now.

'I thought we could find ourselves a little tavern for lunch.' Abriana says. Her pretending has become her normal, and she worries how easy it has become to slip into it.

'I know the very one. I've not been there for years, but if the owner is still Apostolos, tell him I recommended his tavern, you might get a discount.' Pavlos smiles, still holding his pipe between his teeth.

It fascinates Mark to see so many orange and lemon trees, their fruit glowing like lanterns. It's still a novelty to him, and he'll never look at an orange or lemon in the fruit aisle of Tesco the same again. On each side of the narrow road, ancient olive groves spill over the hillsides.

Mark smiles. 'Pavlos told me that if we were here in the winter months, the ground would be covered in green netting to catch the olives that are beaten from the branches during harvest time. He also said that Zakynthos is one of the largest producers of olive oil in Greece. You can see why the trees are everywhere.'

Abriana drops a gear as they approach several winding bends. She frowns. In front, a tractor, pulling a trailer, slows them down even more. Alisha edges out several times, but oncoming traffic forces her back in behind the tractor. Eventually, it pulls over in a layby. Allowing them to pass, Abriana sounds the horn in thanks and the driver waves. She glances in the rear mirror, just for a second. She lightly turns the steering wheel to accommodate a bend and then the unthinkable happens. A jeep is heading towards them on their side of the road. Abriana stamps on the brakes, the jeep swerves, there is screeching of tires, and their car veers off the road and into a ditch. The car jolts violently. There is a crushing wake of rocks and bushes. Just as the airbags inflate, the momentum throws them forward. Abriana feels as if her foot is crushing the brake pedal and her hands welded to the steering wheel. Then, eventually, the car is still. Around them, the silence is deafening.

Mark turns to her. 'Are you alright?'

She rubs her neck. 'Oh my God, we could've been killed. Oh, my neck's sore.'

'Did you see them? They looked about twelve.'

'No, I was too busy trying to miss them.'

Mark opens the door and steps outside. He inspects the car. 'It looks ok.'

Abriana carefully unfolds herself from her seat. Mark takes her by the arm and steadies her as she stands. She moves her head from side to side.

'I'm fine, it's not too bad.' Her face drained of colour is ashen. Mark touches her elbow.

'Are you sure?' he persists.

Just then, the tractor appears and rumbles to a stop.

'Can you help us?' Marks asks and then wonders if the man can speak English?

'Women drivers, eh?' The driver smiles in amusement, answering Mark's question.

Mark frowns. 'Did you see that jeep it almost killed us?'

The driver, a young man in his twenties, athletically springs from his seat. He raises his hands in a soothing gesture. 'Ah, I see. Yes, crazy people.'

'Would you be able to tow the car onto the road? I don't think we'll be able to reverse up the verge.'

'I have a rope in the trailer. It shouldn't be a problem.'

'That would be great. Thank you,' Abriana says.

Once the rope is secure, the tractor effortlessly manoeuvres the car back onto the road.

'I don't know what we would have done if you hadn't come along.' Abriana smiles gratefully.

'Are you going far?'

'I'm not sure. We're going to the next village for some lunch. To tell you the truth, I've lost my appetite.'

'Maybe I should drive?' Mark offers.

'I need to phone the car hire company. How do we get rid of the airbags?'

'Good question. I've no idea. We'll probably need another car.'

'The village is only a few miles away; I'm going that way. You can follow me, although my tractor is slow; she's an old lady now.'

'Don't worry, I won't be breaking any speed records. Behind you will be just fine.'

'Are you sure you want to drive?'

'I'm fine, Mark, honest I am.' Abriana turns to the young man. 'We're looking for a place called *Apostolos*. It was recommended to us.'

'Ah! a good choice. I know it well. Apostolos was a good friend of my granddad. He was at every family christening, wedding, and funeral. He is dead now, but his tavern isn't.' He laughs at his joke.

Mark studies the menu. 'What do you fancy? Let's see, there's grilled meats, seafood dishes, and various dishes called mezedes. One here has stuffed grape leaves, it's called dolmades. There are Greek cheeses such as feta, and dips and spreads. I like the sound of this one, taramosalata, and of course, tzatziki. I fancy a beer.'

'I think I'll just have some olives and bread. I've lost my appetite.'

Once they have ordered, Mark asks. 'How's your neck better?'

'It is thanks.'

'You're lucky. You could have got whiplash. That would have been nasty.'

Mark clears his throat. 'A second sooner and we could have been in the hospital instead of sitting here.'

'I know. It proves one thing.'

'What's that?'

'I've still got quick reactions.' She grins.

'I have to agree with you there. In fact, you've probably just saved my life.'

She seems to think for a moment and then sighs. 'It's not worth thinking about.'

Mark changes the subject. 'So, you're enjoying living away from Rome? I wouldn't have thought living outside Florence was cosmopolitan enough for you.'

'I am, actually. I love the countryside. I was brought up there. Tuscany's in my blood.'

They are sitting on the veranda of *Apostolos' Taverna*. It has a view of the sea which is pleasing to Abriana. The village has the look that it is sliding, in a collage of terracotta roofs and primrose houses, towards a ribbon of turquoise silk that is the Ionian Sea, today.

The tavern is only half-full, mainly couples having lunch, people on holiday, relaxed and contented, states of being that are as far from Abriana, at this time, as it is possible. She looks at them with a jealous eye and she realizes she can only accurately define a time in her life she has felt that way before when she was with Mark and recently,

returning to Tuscany.

Their lunch arrives, set out by a young waiter who proudly describes each dish as if he invented them himself.

'And you're enjoying working for the Uffizi Gallery?'

'It's a change. It's not as dynamic, but neither is my position now. I don't have the power or the influence I used to have. I'm anonymous, in some ways. It took some time getting used to, but there is less pressure on me. I'm grateful they took me on. They took a chance.'

'They knew what they were getting. They're fortunate, if you ask me.' He takes a sip of beer. 'This is refreshing.' Then the thought occurs to him. 'The gallery doesn't know I'm here with you.'

'No. I don't think they would have supported that.'

'What about the plane ticket?'

'It comes out of my expenses. I have a bank card.'

'Won't they question why you've booked another plane ticket?'

'They won't check my expenses until the job's finished. You'll be back in Edinburgh by then.'

'That'll put you in a difficult position once they find out who I really am.'

'Look. When I met you in Edinburgh, I could see how much the story and the painting had grabbed your interest. I couldn't see the harm in it. I saw an opportunity.'

'It could cost you your job. I don't want to be responsible for that... again. I've already been there, worn the t-shirt.'

'It won't come to that. Anyway, at this moment in time, how are they going to know? I'm not going to tell them. That's why you're not driving the car, because you're not here.' She smiles at him, trying to lift the conversation with some light humour. 'And anyway, you never asked.'

'Christ, why would you tell them my real identity? I suppose I was blinded by opportunity as well. I couldn't resist a few days away with you. I thought there might be a chance to... well, get to know each other again,' Mark says.

He remembers his willingness to help her in Rome, to put himself on the line and jeopardize everything he had achieved and worked for. He can recall the aftermath with such vividness it could have been yesterday. He wonders why he can't resist these lapses that are his weakness when it comes to Abriana. Why does she have such a hold on me? How does she undermine my commonsense in this way? It's not the first time he has asked himself these questions.

'This is not another *Rome,*' Abriana says. 'It's totally different. I'm here to get information, that's all.'

'So why ask me? I don't really understand that now. Why have you put yourself in such a vulnerable situation, from the gallery's perspective, by asking me here? Can you imagine the field day the art world would have, *the upwardly mobile art director, and the art dealer who stole a painting to pay a ransom have eloped to Greece.* It looks dodgy and suspicious.'

'But it's not.'

'I thought there was a chance for us again. Am I wrong?'

'It's complicated, Mark.'

'Not from where I'm standing, it's not. What's complicated about it? Do we have a future? It's that simple.' He's never asked her the question before, and many questions are going around in his head.

There is a tight silence.

'You don't know me, really. I don't want to hurt you again. I should have been honest with you from the start. Maybe, if things were different, we could have been good together. We were good together. This is not the right time, that's all.'

'In the last day or so you've been different. What's changed?'

'I have. It's not your fault. It's me.'

'Was I expecting too much? If I misread your intentions, I'm sorry.'

'That has always been your weakness, Mark.'

'What, seeing what I want to see?'

'No. Blaming yourself. I should have been honest with you. I will be honest. I do have feelings for you, Mark, and, if I had the luxury of hindsight and circumstances were different...' A turmoil of emotions slams into her. She takes a deep breath.

'Abriana, what is it? What do you mean, if circumstances were different? You can tell me.'

'That's my problem, I can't.'

'Why not? Don't you trust me?' He raises his eyebrows.

She purses her lips slightly. 'I do, of course, I do.'

'Then tell me.'

'It would change everything.'

Mark frowns. 'What are you hiding, Abriana?'

'It may change the way you feel about me. Are you ready for that?'

He looks at Abriana, scrutinizing her face.

She sits for a long time, as though sifting through her mind for the words to say. The words that will mean exactly what she has wanted to tell him all this time, but never felt she could. She looks away from him. It is harder than she thought.

Mark shifts in his seat. He is either impatient or nervous, she can't tell which. His eyes are narrow now and she bites the inside of her cheek. She lowers her head and her hair hangs around her face, like silken sheets. She combs her hair behind her ear. The feel of her hair on her fingers is reassuring, comforting. She touches her temple and tries to rub the tension away. Finally, she allows her eyes to meet his.

She takes a deep breath. 'I've stolen the painting and sold it.'

The Story of Alisha Hadley

Athens 1905

When she squints, Alisha can see purple mountains and at their foot what looks like a mass of shimmering, brilliant white. It reminds her of marble. Rising above this and perched on a hill is the Parthenon. As it has stood, she imagines, this view, one's first impression, unchanged since Aristotle himself, may have bathed his eyes on this very scene.

'Look, there it is. There is Athens,' someone shouts.

As the steamer continues to plough through the waves, a flotilla of boats, brown and white sails billowing in the wind, sail towards them. The steamer casts its anchor offshore and alongside, the boats have thrown ropes to be tied and their occupants have climbed on board and already they are bartering for business. Once a suitable boat has been chosen and their luggage safely secured, Alisha and her party tentatively take their seats and soon that great slab of marble, although still a distance away, is materialising into the familiar shapes and sights of a city that is revealing itself.

White-crested waves slosh against the boat and Alisha has the desire to trace her hand along the surface. She notices that on some boats, men are standing, facing the direction they are travelling and heaving heavy-looking oars through the dark sea, a rhythm, she considers, that looks graceful. Alisha can feel the spray from the sea move across her skin. She is glad of the wide-brimmed hats both she and Sara are wearing, and she remembers buying them on a drizzly wet afternoon with Sara in London. A time that already feels a lifetime ago. How different her heart feels today?

A railway runs from Piraeus into Athens, but Alfred insists on taking a carriage and haggles with a cabman.

'For you and your party, five Drachmas, there is a lot of luggage,' the cabman says in Greek.

'Nonsense, my man,' Alfred says in English and then in Greek. 'Three Drachmas and no more.'

'I'll give you a bargain. Four Drachmas. The horses will have to work twice as hard with the extra weight. You understand?'

The cabman bends to grab a suitcase as if to emphasise his point and as he does so Alisha got a whiff of garlic.

'I will not move from three Drachmas, or I will turn my attention to the next available carriage,' Alfred says, now becoming tired of the negotiating.

The cabman makes a tutting sound between his teeth. 'Three Drachmas it is then.'

'Good,' Alfred says with an accomplished tone. 'Ladies first.'

It is hot and stuffy. The air inside the carriage is oppressive and Alex loosens his collar. 'It's not even midday yet, and it's sweltering.'

The dust is everywhere. A light film covers the seats, floor and doors. Sara sneezes into her handkerchief, again and again, visibly exasperated by the experience.

'Are you alright, my dear?' Alfred asks, concerned. 'We'll soon be at the hotel.'

'I'm sensitive to the dust. I'll be fine once we get out of this confined box.'

To everyone's surprise, the carriage comes to a stop at a

roadside inn where water is drawn from a stone well and given to the horses. A man appears from the Inn, carrying a tray and approached the carriage door. He has glasses of wine, a yellow watery colour and cubed sized loukoumi. On the tray, there is also a small plate the size of a saucer, sitting next to a jug of water.

'I must have some water,' Sara commands.

The men try the wine and Alex baulks at his first mouthful. 'It tastes like tar.'

As they drink and eat, the man waits to receive their empty glasses. After they have given their glasses back and tasted their loukoumi the innkeeper stands with an expectant smile.

'I think we're supposed to pay him,' Reuben says.

Alfred drops a few Drachmas onto the small plate and the man leaves them, nodding in appreciation.

Rueben leans his head out of the window. 'It wouldn't surprise me, but I think we've just paid for the horse's water.'

As they near the city, the sun basks in a transparent blue sky. The houses are square and built of stone and stucco. Within the shade of the carriage, the brightness that radiates from them is glaring to the eye. Alisha notices some buildings are bleached a pale pink or tantalising blue. Every house is crowned in red tiles.

Alisha smiles. 'I didn't expect it to look so pretty.'

'It makes up for the dreadful dust. I hope it's not like this all the time,' Sara says.

'We'll need to get you some medicine, Sara. You won't be able to play a note if you're sneezing all the time. Although, I'd love to hear the sound you'd make.' Alex laughs.

'There's no one about. Where are the people?' Alisha asks, bemused.

The pavements and roads are deserted, save for the occasional foreign visitor struggling in the glaring sun and pressing heat, umbrellas and hats offering little respite from the blazing light. Glass fronted shops with their vibrant coloured shutters are devoid of activity. The carriages are idle, motionless in the shade, the cabmen resting or sleeping on top.

'What's happening?' Sara asks.

'It's mesimera time. Nobody comes outside at this time of day. They're all sleeping or resting,' Alfred answers.

'It was like that in Corfu, but because this is a city and bigger, it feels like the whole place has fallen into a deep sleep,' Rueben says.

The quartet's schedule allows them two free nights a week. Most days, they rehearse from midday to three in the afternoon, escaping the hottest part of the day. At night, they entertain Alfred's guests in one of the large reception rooms of the hotel.

Alfred's proposals that the rich English middle classes will fill the hotels and restaurants of Athens, hungry for the Mediterranean climate and antiquities, eagerly spending money has won him a considerable number of admirers and potential business partners. Alfred is in a buoyant mood most days.

One afternoon, Alisha walks in the hotel garden alone, needing time to think. Normally, she will pass a couple or two, taking a leisurely stroll, arm in arm under the protective shade of an umbrella. Not long ago, such a sight would have enforced her loss, forcing her to brace herself for the physical sensation that would pass through her overwhelmingly, tearing at her insides with such force that she would have to fight off her sobs. Thankfully, and to her relief, such pain has deserted her. She has once again embraced the prospect of celebrating what she has, that on a day such as this, in a garden bursting with colour and potent scents feels like an extraordinary life.

In the heat she feels flushed, so sits on the terrace, shaded by a covering of ivy. It is an advantageous position. She opens her pencil case and chooses a pencil. With her sketch pad on her lap, she studies the garden, for she can see most of it from where she sits. She enjoys the splash of red vines, apple blossoms, grape hyacinths and iris. She can see lavender and hear the buzz of bees growing into a frenzy. Little crops of succulents sprout from rocks. The garden has a lavish and ostentatious feel. There are straight lines and curves made from simple and smooth light-coloured stonework and warping paths. Before her, there is an array of terracotta pots and flowers, a little further, a marble fountain, sprinkles water, a touch of elegance she appreciates. Beyond the fountain, small cypress trees are trained to a white wall and if she squints, Alisha can make out rosemary growing tall and straight, their leaves thick and narrow. Thyme, sage, chives and parsley have colonised the garden, undoubtedly destined for the kitchen.

Some of her hair has fallen from its pin and as she fits it under her hat, an old man appears with a wheelbarrow, carrying garden tools. Each step appears a great effort, but as he draws closer, Alisha can also see several pots sitting in the wheelbarrow, all filled with earth.

His beard is silver, short and prickly looking. His skin is weatherbeaten, the lines on his face are like trenches but his eyes, different, an impenetrable blue like the sky.

'Kalispera.' He tips his hat.

'Hello. I'm sorry, I don't speak Greek.'

'Good afternoon,' he says, this time in English and then again in Greek. 'To hamoyelo sui ne iperoho.'

'You're speaking Greek again.'

'I am.' He smiles.

'Can I ask what it means?'

'I shouldn't have said it.'

'You'll have to tell me now.'

'You're doing it again.' The old man smiles.

'What?'

'Ok. Your smile is beautiful.'

'That's what you said?'

'I did, but it is true.'

Alisha lowers her eyes, embarrassed and unsure of how to answer. She is unused to such unguarded introductions.

'You are an artist as well as a musician.'

'Oh this, no. I just dabble. I'm not very good, I'm afraid. Is this all your own work?' Alisha asks in distraction. She gestures towards the garden.

He nods his head.

'Then let me return the compliment. Your garden is beautiful.'

'I try my best.'

'No, really, I've admired it since I arrived.'

'Thank you.'

She looks around the garden. 'I try to spend a little time here whenever I can. I look forward to it.'

'I'm happy it makes you feel that way.'

'It could uplift a heavy heart, I'm sure of it.'

'You've experienced this?'

Alisha averts her eyes.

'I've seen you several times in the garden. At first, I thought you looked sad, but as each day passed, it seemed to lift from you and I watched your smile grow. That's how I know you have a beautiful smile. I have heard your music and seen you with your fellow musicians.'

'Yes, the hotel management has kindly allowed us to rehearse during the day.'

The old man stretches, rubbing the base of his back.

'Are you all right?' Alisha asks.

'I'm ok. Just a little stiff.'

'Please, sit and take the weight off your feet.'

'Just for a minute then.'

'How rude of me! I haven't asked your name.'

'I am Andreas.'

'Please to meet you, Andreas. I'm Alisha.'

'Where are you from?'

'London. We're on a tour. We've already played in Corfu.'

'Ah, and what did you think of Corfu?'

'I loved it. I didn't expect it to be so green.'

'That's because it rains. Not so much in the summer months. How long are you staying in Athens?'

'A few more weeks.'

'What do you think of Athens it is different from Corfu? Have you been to see the Acropolis yet?'

'I find the city very charming. I'm going to the Acropolis on Saturday as it happens. I love it here. In fact, I think I'm in love with Greece.'

'It is difficult not to be, but I have a biased view on the matter.' He smiles, almost exultant.

Heat radiates from the garden. 'I love waking in the morning to the sun. It's not like that back home, not every day, anyway. Although, it can get hot here at times. It's not as bad as when we first arrived in Corfu. I couldn't believe how hot it was, especially at night, but now, I must be getting used to it, most days anyway.'

'I think you will like the Acropolis, Alisha. You can see all of Athens... and the sea.'

'You're English is excellent. Where did you learn to speak it so well?'

'It was a long time ago,' he says, quietly. Andreas tells Alisha the story of when he was a young man. He went to work for an English family who lived in what was then an up-and-coming area of new villas in Athens. The family was wealthy, and Andreas attended to the garden. They had a daughter, Elizabeth, the same age as he was and although he only knew a few words of English, they became friendly and time progressed, as did the language barrier between them, as Elizabeth taught Andreas English. In the beginning, she taught the lessons during Andreas' lunch break, but progress was frustratingly slow. So, on his days off, they met in secret. He was a fast learner and within a few months, he could talk to her about his family's past. Elizabeth told him of her life in England. This new connection to her brought hesitation and indecision. He desired to tell her of his feelings, the love he felt inside, but his restricted use of the language made his rehearsed attempts seem childlike and simple. Eventually, he could hold on to his impatience no longer and he revealed to Elizabeth what she meant to him. She smiled at him, laid her hand on his chest and to this day, he has never forgotten that first kiss. Andreas tells Alisha that he has never told another person his story, not even his wife, God rest her soul.

'So, what happened?' Alisha's voice was impatient.

'The family were never going to stay long in Athens.

Within a year, after that first kiss, they had moved back to England.'

'And you let her go? She went willingly?'

'Her father found out we were learning more than just how to communicate with words. I was sacked, and Elizabeth was forbidden to see me. When she left the villa, day or night, she was always accompanied by someone.'

'Did you ever see her again?'

'I did, but never alone. We never spoke to each other again.'

'That's awful.'

'It was a long time ago. I have four daughters and a son. I am a grandfather now. Life has a way of working things out. Nothing stops. Time keeps moving. It carries on, with or without us. It is the only permanent thing.'

'Yes. I suppose it is,' she says, smiling slightly. 'I've kept you long enough.'

'Yes. I should get back to work.'

'I've enjoyed speaking to you, Andreas.'

'It has been a pleasure to spend time with you, Alisha.' Andreas rises stiffly. 'Next time, you can tell me something about your life in London. I would like that. I have always wanted to go to London.'

Alisha bows her head and stares into her lap. 'Maybe. We shall see.'

'I get the impression this has made you sad. I'm sorry, Alisha. I did not want to make you unhappy.'

'It's fine, Andreas. Honestly. Don't worry. As you say, life moves on and we need to move with it.'

. . .

After breakfast, Alisha and Reuben take a tram into the centre of Athens. It is going to be a sweltering day. Alisha can already feel a slight sheen of perspiration on her forehead. She feels flushed, dressed in a lavender-blue suit and a wide-brimmed hat. Her jacket fits at the waist and her skirt hugs her hips and rubs the ankle of her boots. Reuben is wearing some cream suit jacket and trousers. Under his jacket, he has a white cotton shirt, and already he has loosened his tie. Concealed by his jacket, he has blue braces. She knows this because, at breakfast, Reuben took his jacket off, unlike the other men dining that morning, and hung it carefully on the back of his chair. She smiles at this and realises she likes his unconventional manners; she knows his idiosyncrasies, the way he always twitches his nose when he is thinking, his little rituals of which he is probably unaware, but she finds reassuring.

Alisha tilts her head, trying to shade her eyes with the brim of her hat. Reuben clears his throat. He is holding smoked coloured spectacles.

'I bought these the other day. I saw them in a shop and thought, I must try them out. It's amazing how much they are a relief to the eye. Try them on. See if they fit.'

Alisha is unconvinced. She takes the spectacles and inspects them. 'Are you sure they work?' she asks sceptically.

'Try them on and see.' Reuben is smiling. 'If you like them, we can get another pair, and then we can both wear them.'

She lifts them to her eyes and then hesitates. 'I'll look silly.'

'Nonsense. They are what all the Athenian ladies are wearing this summer. I have it on good authority that they are fashionable all over the Mediterranean.'

'Who told you that, the shopkeeper who sold you them?'

'It's true. Just yesterday, in the Place De La Concorde, nearly every young woman I passed wore them just like a hat upon their head.'

She smiles at him. 'Very well.'

'Well, what do you think?

'I can literally see their attraction. My eyes are my own again.'

'I knew you'd like them. Keep them on. They suit you.'

'Do you think so? You're not just saying that to prove a point.'

She looks at Reuben. 'You've changed colour. Your complexion is tinted.' Alisha laughs.

Reuben laughs as well. It has been his burning desire to hear her happy again and to see her feel the joy of living once more.

'I'm looking forward to seeing the Acropolis; I can't imagine something being that old,' Alisha says as they near their stop.

'According to my guidebook, it sits on a plateau of crystalline limestone and is five hundred feet above sea level. In Greek, it means *the sacred rock, the highest city*. It dates to the fifth century BC. I've brought my camera. I can't let an opportunity like this slip by without taking photographs.'

Alisha meets Reuben's eyes and there is a silence between them. At this moment, Reuben thinks she looks sensual and adoring. He reaches and touches her hand. 'I'll take a photograph of you when we reach the top and then this day will be preserved forever.'

Their walk is steep to the Beule Gate, which stands between two low towers, and then they ascend a marble staircase. Reuben takes Alisha by the arm and they continue, under the shade of her umbrella, carefully avoiding the many gaps. They reach a narrow platform and from there they progress up a steep gradient. Reuben asks Alisha if she needs to rest, but she replies she will rest soon enough when they reach the top. They pass the remains of a medieval castle and ancient wall, a large square pedestal that once held the statue of Marcus Vipsanius Agrippa, a Roman General and son-in-law of Augustus. Reuben consults his guidebook and informs Alisha the statue was erected when the general was still alive. They stop and observe several temples, Reuben adopting the persona of a tour guide explains the history of each and describes the dimensions in width and height of each pillar and features of the statues that are no longer in situ, but who can be seen in the Acropolis museum. Reuben takes delight in describing the friezes, the battles they depict, and the ancient gods, Zeus and Poseidon.

When, finally, they reach the top, Alisha fids the view enthralling.

'Look.' Reuben points. 'That is the Bay of Phaleron, the town and harbour of Piraeus and the island of Salamis. That dome-like rock is Acro Corinth, and you can see the olive plantations just over there, then if you look to the left, that is the coast of Attica, a splendid view spanning over thirty miles. And of course, before us, Athens, as you have never seen her. What do you think, Alisha?'

'I've never seen anything like it. It's beyond words.'

Where Alisha stands, she is on an elevated piece of stone and eye level with Reuben. He feels as if he has bubbles in his stomach. He can smell the mix of her perfume and, in the hot dry air, Reuben is almost certain he can smell her shampoo. He has waited so long for a moment like this. The urge to lean towards her and kiss her lips overwhelms him. He holds his breath and then she steps away and turns, facing the Parthenon.

'This is beyond my wildest expectation, just look at those pillars, and how symmetrical they are. I didn't really appreciate how tall and wide they would be. Reuben, you must take some photographs of it.'

'I will, but let me take one of you first.'

She turns and smiles at him. He fiddles with the camera and then raises it; it is a Kodak Folding Brownie, a number 3 Model A, the first of its kind, a portable camera.

'Just be yourself, be natural,' Reuben instructs.

Alisha straightens her spine and places a hand on her hip. She smiles at the camera. It is a posture that takes him back years to a room in his lodgings at the music college. He feels her body beside him, soft and warm. She whispers to him and he can hardly breathe.

'Have you finished?' Alisha asks, impatient to explore further.

'Nearly. You've still got the spectacles on, take them off.'

Alisha laughs. 'I forgot all about them. See, I'm used to them already.'

Reuben also encourages her to take off her hat, and she does so, pressing her hair into shape with her fingers.

Reuben takes several more photographs before Alisha insists he takes some of the Parthenon. Reuben is satisfied he has captured her essence, an impression of her beauty will surely adorn the photographs. He is sure of it.

Once they have seen all there is to see, they swing down the white dusty track and visit the Acrolois Museum. They wander through *The Room of the Bull*, where fragments of porous stones depict animals fighting, flying eagles, Hercules and chariots, Zeus and Athena enthroned and all still with fragments of the original colouring.

They move through the rooms at a leisurely pace. Alisha enjoying being out of the heat and not having to shelter under her umbrella. In another room, unnervingly named, *The Room of the Tripled Bodied Monster*, where they discover Hercules fighting with Triton, Zeus overpowering Typhon with its three human heads, wings and body of serpent's coils, Alisha holds on to Reuben's arm, much to his delight.

In *The Room of the Marbles,* they view fragments of Athena fighting, marble fragments, architectural fragments in terracotta, porous stone and marble, again all with traces of the original paint. Alisha is aghast at the scenes of violence and says to Reuben that if the remaining rooms are filled with similar themes, she would much rather seek the civility of a café and quench her uncomfortable thirst. Reuben promises there are no more surprises. In one room, Alisha finds attractive a statue of a youth carrying a calf, graceful female statues, archaic horse's heads and mounted horsemen.

In another room, larger than most they have viewed, busts, torsos and full statues are the major themes. In front of them, there is a group of people and they can hear the guide describe how these statues were discovered to the west of the Erechtheion, near to the north wall of the Acropolis, in what was essentially a rubbish tip that dates back to the Persian Wars.

Finally, in *The Parthenon Room*, they marvel at the preserved fragments of the Parthenon Frieze. After this, Reuben suggests they have some lunch. When outside, they encounter a blazing glare of light and Alisha gratefully puts on the spectacles.

'I think I'm going to have to buy another pair, after all,' Reuben teases.

After a lunch of garlic chicken and swordfish, Alisha having the latter, they head towards the market. When they get there, a group of young boys loiter outside the market, waiting with baskets strapped to their backs.

'What are those boys doing?' Alisha asks, intrigued.

'If you're going to shop in the market, you choose one of them. He'll then follow you around the market as you deposit your shopping into the basket. Once you have finished your shopping, he'll take your food to your house or in our case the hotel, for a price, of course.'

'How do you know all this, Reuben? You sound like a native.'

'It's in my guidebook. I wouldn't go anywhere without it now. It's the best investment I've made since I arrived. I wish I'd had one when we were in Corfu.'

The market is under a glass roof, which feels like a greenhouse. Alisha finds it a cacophony of noise and vibrant colour. On tables, laid out the entire length of the market, there are seasonal fruits and vegetables, clams and a multitude of fish that populate the Mediterranean. Every variety of meat is on display: boar, deer, lamb and goats. On one stall, they view every form of poultry known to Greece hanging from hooks: pigeon, woodcock, partridge, chicken, turkey and duck. They use the market as a slaughterhouse where they slice the throats of animals without ceremony, that slump to the hard floor, blood spilling onto sawdust, drained of life itself. Reuben shepherds Alisha away from it.

It is not long before Alisha learns the market is a conundrum of contradiction. It is an assault on her senses, from the sweet aroma of ripened fruits to the earthly hue of seasoned vegetables. The smell of salt, seaweed and iodine of the sea accompanies the fish stall. The coppery tinge of meat is mixed with the smell of fear and death wielded by the butcher's knife.

Once out into the air, Reuben takes Alisha's hand and feels liberated in the anonymity that the city brings.

'I love being able to take your hand while we walk without having to think about someone might see us.'

She smiles at him. 'I like that too.'

'Do you think the others know?'

'Sara has her suspicions, I'm sure of it.'

'And Alex?'

'What do you think?'

'I think we'd have to spell it out for him.' Reuben grins and then adds. 'Do you feel ready? I don't want to rush you.'

'I worry about what others might think.'

'It's got nothing to do with them.'

'I know, but they might think it too soon.'

'Let them think what they like. What do they know?'

'I'm sure Alfred would be pleased. He has virtually said as much.'

'Has he?'

'Yes. In his own way.'

'I'm glad about that. It will mean a lot to me if he approves... I just want to shout it out to the world; I love Alisha Hadley.'

'Is it not enough for now that I know you love me and that you know that I love you in return?'

'Oh Alisha, it means more to me than life itself.' He looks at her seriously. 'I would gladly die for you, Alisha.'

'I know you would, Reuben, but I'll never ask you to.'

She takes his arm in hers. 'Not just yet, anyway.' She laughs, and it lights up her face. He wants to kiss her then.

Phaleron is a holiday resort where most Athenians take in the sea air and spend the summer months swimming in the sea. The beach is easily reached by tram or carriage. Dotted with screens made from shawls or clothes, women, men and children alike, change into swimming costumes and swim and play in the warm sea.

On their day off from entertaining Alfred's guests, the quartet escape the city and take an open tram to Phaleron. They are full of excitement as they travel towards the little resort. The last time they had enjoyed the sea was in Corfu, where they took for granted their excursions to the beach or just seeing the sea on a daily basis. It is different in Athens. The city is big, and although the sea is near, it is not always visible, unless one is close to the harbour or on higher ground. So, daily, the sea is rarely prominent in one's thoughts or vision.

'When we get there, I'm going to buy everyone ice cream,' Alex says generously.

'Do they sell ice cream? I hope so.' Sara smiles at the thought.

'You're feeling flush, Alex,' Rueben says.

'I had some luck in the casino last night. You should try it sometime, Rueben. In fact, I thought I saw you there the other night, but after a bit, I gave up looking for you.'

'I've never been that way inclined. I prefer to spend my money in return for something I want, not give it away and be able to buy the occasional ice cream. How much money did you lose?'

'Reuben!' Alisha says, chastising him. 'You won't be wanting that cold refreshing ice cream then.'

'I wouldn't go that far. I can indulge myself and celebrate Alex's luck, just like the rest of you.' He pats Alex on the shoulder. 'Next time, you might be able to stretch to a meal.'

Once on the beach, the girls are eager to get into the water. Both Reuben and Alex hold towels, shoulder height, around the girls, shielding them and their modesty, as they dress in their swimming costumes.

'No peeping now,' Sara reminds them, just in case.

'As if I would,' Alex says, feeling slightly affronted.

'You'd better not or your life won't be worth living,' she replies.

Alisha is facing Reuben. For an awkward second, they avoid each other's eyes. He is looking away and inside; she is daring him to turn and face her. He has averted his eyes; it is the right thing to do; he tells himself, allowing her some privacy.

Around them, children run to the sea, and shout and scream excitedly, under the watchful eye of parents and grandparents. Similar scenes pan out along the beach.

'Don't feel uncomfortable; try not to, anyway.' She reaches and brushes his fingers; whose knuckles are white and tense against the cloth of the towel. Her touch is light and feathery.

Considering her eyes, he can see only Alisha; lost in her look. His thoughts are a mix of temptation and resignation, a desire to drop his eyes and a desire to remain locked in hers. If he looks, how will she feel?

To her surprise, she relishes the look on his face. There is a slight tremor to her fingers as they fumble with the buttons of her dress. She doesn't feel the flush of embarrassment she would otherwise attune to; instead, she can feel a warm glow in her stomach. Is it because they are not strangers to the intimacies of the past they have both shared?

Reuben's eyes are clear and sharp. Alisha can't read the expression on his face, but she can see his pupils dilate and there is something quite different about him.

To everyone's relief, the girls soon change into their swimming costumes and then it is their turn to wait on Reuben and Alex. When they are ready, they all run towards the sea as if it will disappear at any minute. Alex is the first to reach the water and as he gets further into the depths, his legs seem to work in slow motion, growing too heavy for him to move. He fears he'll stumble into the sea at any moment. With an effort, his arms push the air and then he dives into the waves, submerged, before reappearing and turning onto his back, smiling towards the others.

'Hurry up, the sea's lovely.'

Rueben is next to dive in. When he reaches Alex, he cups the surface of the sea with his hands and throws it towards Alex, forcing him to dive backwards. Reuben increases his momentum, sending wave after wave. Rueben is laughing and even though the saltwater is stinging Alex's eyes, he too is laughing, and trying dismally to retaliate.

'They're just like boys, really. Look at them,' Alisha says, shaking her head.

'As long as they don't come near me. I've no intention of getting that wet. This will do me.' Sara looks at her feet as the water laps around her ankles.

'Oh, come on, Sara, you can surely go a little further. What was the point of all that trouble getting into a swimming costume?'

'Maybe just a little further than.'

Alisha takes her by the hand. 'It's lovely and warm. Look how the sun sparkles on the surface.'

They move tentatively into the water. 'Look, it's up to our knees already.' Alisha encourages.

'It's actually quite nice. Oh, what are those little things? They might try to eat my toes.' Sara stops abruptly and looks terrified.

'They're just tiny little fish. They're probably more scared of you than you are of them. Look, when we walk towards them, they swim away from us.'

'I still don't like them.'

'Just a little further, that's all.'

Reuben has noticed the girls. 'Come on, girls.' He shouts enthusiastically.

'This is far enough, Alisha. I don't want to go any further.' Sara's hand tightens on Alisha.

'Are you alright, Sara?'

'If I stay here, I will be.'

'But it's not deep. Look at Ruben and Alex, the water is only to their waists.'

'I know, but that's not the point. To me, it's deep.'

By now, the boys have made their way back to the girls. Their hair soaked and flat against their scalps.

'Come on, you two,' Reuben coaxes and he moves towards Sara, stretching to grab her arm. Sara panics and steps back to avoid Rueben's hand, and in doing so, she stumbles and screams. Her arms flap aimlessly, and she falls, like a felled tree, into the water. She can taste the salty water in her mouth and, to her shock, she swallows some. When Sara manages to stand upright, she heaves, close to being sick. Sara gulps for air. She is close to crying now.

'I can't believe you did that, you idiot.'

'Did what?' Reuben turns his palms to the sky.

'I can't swim. Yes, I know it's ridiculous, but I've always had a fear of deep water.' She spits the sea salt from her mouth and wipes her chin. 'And look at me, I almost drowned and worst of all my hairs soaking. It's a mess.'

Everyone can see the funny side of it, except Sara.

'You should have said you couldn't swim, Sara. I was almost dragging you into the water.' Alisha grins and then laughs.

'Come on, we'll get you dried off.'

Reuben laughs. 'Am I supposed to be a mind reader? How was I to know you couldn't swim?'

Once Sara has dried herself and tied her hair up, they sit on the picnic rug they have brought with them.

'Do you miss London?' Sara asks.

Alisha shrugs. 'I haven't thought about it much. So, I suppose not. Do you?'

'I thought I might have done, but no. I'm enjoying myself too much... mostly, that is when I'm not rolling about in the sea.' She laughs, and Alisha laughs with her. Sara stretches her legs out in front of her and crosses one over the other. 'When we arrived in Corfu, I was worried, well, anxious really.'

'Whatever for?'

'I'm ashamed to admit it now, but I was worried about the sanitation and possible disease from mosquitoes. I thought we'd be lucky to get a bath and when I felt the heat, I thought that would be unbearable. My first instinct was to wonder if there would be shops with modern clothes and perfumes. That just goes to show how insular I've become. I really thought nothing of worth exists outside London, well, England. I suppose I thought like that because it was all I knew. Now, my God, the thought scares me about leaving here and going back to England. I'll miss this wonderful climate.'

'I don't want to think about that right now.' Alisha looks away.

'I suppose it has helped you, being here, you know, getting away from what happened.'

'You mean, John. You can say his name in front of me, you know.'

'I know, it was just, well, I wasn't sure, that's all. You seem so different now. You're back to your normal self, I suppose. I was just being cautious, silly of me, I know.'

Alisha smiles. 'You're right. Recently I've been able to gain a clear perspective. Being so far away from him has made me finally realise that without him in my life I'm still the same person I always was. That hasn't changed. In fact, I'm stronger now. I'm more determined to make something of my life. I'm not entirely sure I would have come to that conclusion if I'd stayed amongst everything and everyone that reminded me of him. Coming to Greece has shown me that life continues. Here, there is no John Sutton and the sun still rises in the morning and sets at night. Life goes on and people continue to live and experience their own journeys. I feel I'm on my own journey. I don't know where it's taking me, but for the first time since that night at Alfred's, I feel good within myself. I like who I have become. I like who I am.'

'You seem so self-assured now and confident. I'm so happy for you, Alisha. You are finally living.'

Alisha takes Sara's hand. 'No. It's more than that. I'm over him now. I have survived, and I have Reuben.'

'Yes, I have noticed the two of you are spending more

time than usual together. Is there something you want to tell me, Alisha?' She smiles a wide smile, not showing her teeth.

'We care about each other.'

'Is that all? I care about Reuben too.'

'We are close. We are getting to know each other again.'

'As friends, or something more? Come on, Alisha. What are you scared of? Why won't you say what your eyes give away? I'm not blind.'

'He loves me, and I love him.'

Sara squeals and claps her hands. 'I knew it. I just knew something was going on between the two of you. I do worry about you, Alisha, but my mind is at ease now. Oh, this is wonderful.'

'We haven't told anyone yet. You're the first.'

Reuben and Alex are walking towards them, both smiling broadly and dripping with seawater.

'I've got that out of my system. Now all I want to do is just lie in the sun and let Mother Nature dry me off.' Reuben says, throwing himself down beside Alisha.

Sara is still smiling, and she directs it towards Reuben.

'What?' Reuben asks.

'I know your secret.'

'Well, it's not one now, obviously, is it?'

'What's this, a secret?' Alex looks bewildered. He mouths the word 'casino' towards Reuben with raised eyebrows.

'That's all been fixed, old boy.' Reuben takes Alisha's hand. 'We're together, Alisha and I.'

'You mean as a couple?'

'I'm sure that's what they call it these days. Yes, as a couple.'

'About time, as well.'

'What about those ice creams you promised us, Alex?' Sara asks.

Alex rolls his eyes upwards. 'Let me get dried first.'

They spend the afternoon on the beach, reading, napping, and talking. Alisha is relieved that she has spoken frankly to Sara. She feels relaxed. A weight has lifted from her.

'Let's play a game.' Alex smiles broadly.

'What kind of game?' Sara asks.

'I've just made it up.'

'This sounds like fun,' Reuben says sarcastically.

'Come on then Alex, how do we play this game?' Alisha asks, intrigued.

'Ok then. We have all to think of a word. It has to be a proper noun or an abstract noun.'

'What's an abstract noun?' Sara asks, looking lost.

'They refer to concepts and ideas, things that can't be concretely perceived.'

'That doesn't help.'

'What I mean is words like love, peace, nationalism...'

'That sounds a bit pretentious; it doesn't sound like it'll be fun.'

'I'm not finished yet. Once you have decided on your word, so a proper noun can be a place, like a city or a person and as I said...' he looks at Sara to emphasize his point. 'An abstract noun is something you can't see, feel or hear, so it would be things like freedom, a political system etcetera, then you get one minute to talk about it without saying the actual word, you have to use the word, *blank,* instead, and the others have to guess what it is. If no one can guess your word, then you are the winner.'

'What if none of us can guess any of the words?' Reuben asks.

'Then there isn't a winner.'

'But surely that's the point. Someone has to win.'

'Not necessarily.'

'Then there's no point. You haven't really thought about this, Alex. Have you?' A self-satisfied grin blazons across Reuben's face.

Alex shrugs. 'Then we keep playing until someone does.'

'What if we guess everyone's words?'

'Oh, stop it you two. Come on, let's give it a try. It could be fun,' Alisha mediates.

'As long as the words are not too hard,' Sara sighs.

There is silence amongst them as each is lost in their thoughts.

'I've got one,' Sara beams, pleased with herself and at the same time surprised that she is the first.

'Are we ready?' Alex asks.

'Who goes first?' Reuben enquires.

'Oh, I never thought about that,' Alex says.

'Right, you close your eyes, Sara,' Alisha instructs. She points to each of them in turn, giving them a number from one to four. 'Now, Sara, open your eyes and pick a number.'

'Four.'

Alisha smiles at Sara. 'That's you.'

'Me!' Sara squeals, flapping her hands excitedly. 'Right, here goes. Oh, this is so exciting. So, *blank*, was a child prodigy...'

'Mozart.' Reuben smirks.

Sara stares at him in disbelief. 'How did you get it so quickly? That's so unfair,' she says, bewildered.

Reuben laughs. 'I didn't make the rules up, Alex did, it's his game, blame him.'

Alisha tries not to smile. She looks away, stifling her laugh.

'Right, pick another number, Sara,' Alex says.

Sara frowns. 'Three.'

'Reuben, it's your turn.' Alisha sounds upbeat. 'Come on, Sara, you can get your own back now.'

Reuben's attempt lasts the whole minute, much to Sara's irritation, who sighed wearily throughout it.

Reuben smiles. 'Ah, I like this game.'

It surprises Sara that she doesn't feel annoyed, and then she laughs at seeing the funny side of it.

Then it is Alisha's turn. 'There are various kinds of...' She nods her head to illustrate the word in question.

'Actually, I'm going to use the word '*blank*,' when I'm referring to the word that is missing. That will make it easier.'

She straightens her posture. 'There are various kinds of *blank*. There is the one you have for your family, for your husband or wife, your children, your lover, your country, religion, music, art... but no matter what kind it is, it affects us the same. It tugs at our heart, our emotions, and feelings. It can pierce our souls... our very being. To live is too *blank* and to *blank* is to live. Without it, we are shallow and empty, walking in shadows, never basking in its light and heat. Our *blank* for certain things, or people, can fade or die, but its essence is always present, manifesting in new discoveries... even old ones. It can allure us to false hopes and drastically change our lives, ruin us, take us to places that are dark; it can hurt like a knife and tear out your heart. In time, it can resurrect us; roll away the rock that encloses us in our tomb. Grabbing us with its instincts; its sensibilities, it feeds us hope with all its beauty and passion. It can be like a piece of music whose melody is heard for the first time, yet it is also familiar.' Alisha's eyes glistened as she speaks.

'Your minutes up,' Reuben says. He is genuinely stunned. 'I wasn't expecting your description to be so... poetic.'

'I've had a lot of time to think about it recently and that was my conclusion,' Alisha says lightly. 'You know what my word is.'

'I do.'

'And you didn't say.'

He hesitates. 'No. I wanted to hear your description to the very end. I'm glad I did. *To live is to love and to love is to live.* I agree it's a beautiful phrase. It allows for second chances?' He swallows and draws in his breath.

'As I said, the melody is familiar.'

Reuben lets out a small laugh.

'You cheated, Reuben,' Alex complains.

'Oh, Alex, sometimes you really have no idea at all.' Sara squeezes Alex's arm and restrains an impulse not to laugh.

In the early evening, couples and families walk along the promenade, alongside tables set for dining and drinks.

A small group of musicians play on a bandstand on a platform that sits over the sea. As it gets dark, lights illuminate the promenade and restaurants, where diners sit outside, to the faint whisper of waves and classical music accompanying their meal.

Reuben has suggested they stay for dinner. Alisha and Sara find the thought of not being able to wash and change into evening dresses unsettling, but their worries soon dissipate, as it feels like half of Athens has come out to walk and eat.

Their meal is more French than Greek, and Reuben tells them he has read in one of Alfred's books that the waiters are addressed as '*garcon.*'

They have soup with egg and lemon, roast beef, potatoes and vegetables. They order two bottles of wine and finish with coffee and cheese.

After dinner, the four of them walk along the promenade. Sara insists on walking arm in arm with Alex, much to Alex's embarrassment, who tries to wriggle from her clasp, but Sara insists, a woman needs a chaperone and anyway, she doesn't want to walk under such a beautiful night sky, without enjoying it with her second-best friend.

Reuben is aware his hand is almost touching Alisha's hand. If he were to stretch his fingers, he could almost touch them.

'I hope I didn't embarrass you earlier on the beach. I got ahead of myself. I have spoken too plainly.'

'I wasn't prepared for your honesty, especially in front of Alex and Sara.'

'I'm sure it didn't come as a surprise to them.'

'No. Sara has been trying her best not to ask after my feelings for you, but Sara, being Sara, she often can't help herself. I could almost hear her screaming inside of herself. I could tell it was a relief for her to hear it out in the open. As it was for me, as well.' She looks at him and curls her fingers around his.

'I wanted to take your hand, but lacked the courage in case...'

'I've been waiting for you to take it. You don't need my permission.'

Reuben's heart swells and he lightly squeezes her hand.

Reuben can feel himself relax in her company. The

pretence he has performed, for what seems like a lifetime, is now gradually slipping from him. He has always been tentative in his approaches, hesitant with his intentions, cautiously gauging her reactions, observing each gesture, each word for her acceptance. The knowledge that she has finally let him come close and share her journey of recovery, acknowledged his feelings and to have them reciprocated gradually over time, is a response that brings indescribable joy.

Alisha closes the door to her room. She stands in the dark for a few seconds, her eyes adjusting to the change in light. Every morning she wakes, Alisha tells herself the walls are the blue of the Greek sky. She walks over to the dresser and sits. She prefers to sit in the dark and relies on the luminous moon to look at her face in the mirror.

Since she broke up with John, she has sensed a willingness about Reuben to be delicate and polite, always persistent in his concern for her. This change in him is pleasing to her.There is an attraction to this softening. It is the Reuben she knew before John, the Reuben who was so much a part of her past and who now occupies her present.

She wonders if these things would have developed if she had still been with John. Would his motives be the same? Looking back, Reuben was full of resentment and grudges towards John. She realises now, these were gestures of defiance. Reuben is now enshrouded with sympathy, sincerity and, she thinks, remorse. She is surrounded by complexities.

Her affair with Reuben at the music college, if described as such, lasted a few months. It was innocent, as they were. They were teenagers, tentative, inexperienced, frightened of being physical and intimate with one other. They never professed their love, but she is certain that is what it was.

There have been times, recently, when she wishes they had expressed that love, for it would, in some way, that she is not fully able to understand, give John justification for his actions. She does not blame Reuben for what has happened to her. She blames John Sutton.

Alisha feels perfectly at ease when she is in Reuben's company. Though unspoken, she can tell, by the way, he looks at her; he wants more. Is she ready? She hesitates. Why the indecision? She hadn't anticipated this reaction. She stands still and listens to the world around her. From outside, a dog's bark, a horse and carriage pass in the street below and then there is a stillness, silence returns. And then, almost immediately, she is thinking; *I have been in the darkness. Without hope, he offers stability; he accepts me for who I am. He knows my vulnerabilities, my weaknesses; he is a light in my world. I will not extinguish it. I could be happy again.* It feels like a logical progression. Instantly, she feels a weight lift from her.

In the early evenings, before performing with the quartet, Alisha will often find a place where she can look upon the slopes of Hymettus, just as the sun slips from the sky, washing it in a vibrant violet hue. It is at this time of the evening that the vivid white of the city's buildings and houses become brushed in a soft pastel flush. In the *kafenions*, men play dominoes, discuss politics, drink black coffee, smoke cigarettes. Sets of tables sit outside rows of cafes and bars, many filling up as people come out to eat late into the night.

Several nights, she wanders up and down streets and lanes, observing the locals go about their business. She passes shops, bakers, butchers, some closing for the day; others remain open like the Pantopoleion –the Grocery Store. She often wanders inside and spends her time leisurely and inquisitively browsing amongst the many shelves lined with jars of hard-boiled sweets, herbs from sage, to thyme, rosemary and mint and olives packed into tubs. There are rows of pungent-smelling cheeses, ham, pasta and usually an impoverished collection of wine. It is a sensual and tactile experience.

Sometimes, on the street, she comes across ramshackle stalls, displaying baskets of fruit and vegetables. On occasions, she has bought oranges and delighted in the novelty of the juice trickling down her chin as she heads back to her hotel.

She often inhales the smells of the city and the musky scents of the early evening and realises she is becoming sentimental about the sights and sounds of Athens. She is sure that if Alfred was to find out about these expeditions, he would forcefully vent his disapproval and forbid her from such pleasurable visits. If the truth is told, she agrees. He has a point. She is aware she has been fortunate, so far, not to have encountered or attracted the attention of thieves or unruly strangers. She knows it is not advisable for a foreign woman to be roaming the city at such a time of day and resigns to the fact her solitary excursions are inhaling their last breath.

In the hotel's garden, the flowers bloom in vibrant colours. The effect is stunning. Alisha finds them irresistible, bending to inhale their fragrance. As she walks along the stone path, a murmured breeze carries on its gentle breath a trace of thyme and rosemary. The sun's heat is gradually subsiding as she sits in what has become her usual spot on the bench under the sprawling branches of ivy. On most days now, she meets with Andreas as he goes about tending to the garden. She looks forward to these meetings. Over the short time she has known him, Alisha has become fond of Andreas and it was her intuition that Andreas also enjoys their time together.

'They'll soon be flying the nest. They're getting bigger every day.'

Alisha turns, eyebrows raised, questioningly.

Andreas is pointing to a nest, wedged under a balcony. Four little dark heads appear from inside the nest, their beaks opening and closing, searching the air for their mother's return.

'I've never noticed it.'

'The cats have.'

Three scrawny cats sit in the shade, their unflinching attention trained on the nest and its occupants.

Andreas sits on the bench and smiles at Alisha.

'I hope they don't fall out of the nest,' Alisha says.

'If that doesn't kill them, the cats surely will.'

Alisha frowns, wrinkling her nose. 'Then you'll have to move them, Andreas.'

He rolls his eyes upwards. 'I can't interfere with nature. It's survival of the fittest. The cats have to eat as well.'

She looks at him pleadingly. 'Please, Andreas.'

'Alright, alright. As if I haven't got enough to do. I'll keep an eye on them, but I can't move the nest. That's going too far.'

'Thank you.'

'Are you performing tonight?'

'Yes. Alfred has some new prospective investors attending. It's important that the evening goes well and then they'll probably all get drunk.'

'Is it going well... for this, Alfred?'

'It is, yes. He has secured several investors, and that was the purpose of us coming here. We're almost coming to the end of our stay.'

'Ah, is this good or bad?'

Alisha looks away.

'It is bad then.'

It paralyses her with indecision. 'Sometimes, I find myself thinking about home and I look forward to resuming my normal life. Then other times I wonder, what is a normal life? Do I like 'normal' my 'normal?' Sitting in this garden, walking around Athens, that has become my 'normal' now. I feel disengaged from London... I'm frightened that those feelings that are now just memories will return again. I can't go back to that. I just existed. I don't want to be that little sparrow again.'

'Then be the eagle,' Andreas says, simply.

'I'm scared. That's the truth of it,' she says, with an awkward laugh.

'Listen, Alisha. I'm an old man. That doesn't mean the advice I give is right. But I'll give you the benefit of what I've learnt, anyway. You can spend years trying to unpick and make sense of what has happened to you. You can live your life with regret, or you can try to make the best of what you have and look forward. This is your life Alisha and you only get one chance at it. You are not responsible for what this man did to you, but you are responsible for what you decide to do now.'

Alisha's throat constricts. She looks down, and she has a feeling of being transformed. 'Your right, Andreas. I think I just needed to hear it from someone else.'

'You have a soft heart, Alisha; you are vulnerable because you are human. The world is full of people like John Sutton, but he doesn't need to be in your world anymore.'

'I never really knew my father. I don't even know if the memories I have of him are real, or if my mind just made them up to compensate for not having any. I was too young at the time to understand what was going on. Alfred was the closest I had to a father figure. What I'm trying to say is if I did have a father, I would want him to be like you, Andreas.' Alisha's voice quivers.

He waves his hand dismissively.

'It's true, Andreas. You are kind and wise, and your advice is always spoken with a soft air of authority. It's laced with sentiments that wrap around me up like a blanket.' There are tears in her eyes.

'You flatter me, Alisha.'

'No, I think it's the other way around. I'm the lucky one in all of this.' She pauses. 'I've met someone. Well, I've known him a long time, actually. We have been good friends, but it's becoming more than that now.'

'Ah. And do I know this lucky man?'

'You do.'

'Who is he then? Is he Greek? The probability would suggest he is,' Andreas says, alarmed.

'No. Don't worry, he's not Greek.'

'Thank God for that. You almost gave me a heart attack. I have experience in that area, remember? It didn't turn out well.' Although he is warning her, Andreas' voice hints at nostalgia.

'I know. I remember how it ended for you. He is English, and his name is Reuben.'

'The same Reuben who plays in the quartet?'

She nods.

'But how is that possible, after all this time? You have known him for years; you have told me so.' Andreas scratches his head.

'It's true, we have known each other for a very long time since we were children, really.'

'He has a handsome face. And I get the impression you are happy.'

'I am. I'm really happy. I almost forgot how it feels,' she assures him.

'So, tell me how this came about. I'm not very clued up on the modern way of doing these things.'

Alisha tells Andreas how she and Reuben met their fledgeling affair at the Royal College of Music and their subsequent friendship. She takes her time and is careful in the words she chooses to impart her story. Andreas, on his part, listens thoughtfully.

'We have been playing together for several years. I now know Reuben struggled with my relationship with John. He has told me so, but he could see how happy I was, so he kept his true feelings to himself. He put my happiness above his.'

'A sacrifice indeed.'

'I know he loves me.'

'Do I sense doubt on your part?'

'I know how I feel. That's not the issue.'

'Then what is?'

'I'm scared to get too close again. Abandoning my inhibitions is a state of mind that I'm not sure I'm quite ready for.'

'Do you love this Reuben?'

'I believe I do. When I watch him, and he doesn't know I'm looking, I feel an instinctive, overwhelming, near-unbearable surge of love for him. After John, I didn't think I could love again, but I've surprised myself. I think I've realised I've always wanted this to happen. Does that make sense?'

'It is all you need to know. You have answered your doubt. If he loves you, like you say he does, he will accept the way you feel and allow you to take things at your own pace. He should be respectful of that.'

'I'm sure he would be,' she says the words as a whisper.

'If things are to progress, you need to face this fear, Alisha. That is all it is. It is a fear and fear can be conquered.' He smiles.

'Oh Andreas, I've been so confused. You make it sound as if it's the most natural way to feel. You are always able to simplify things. I really do need these chats of ours.'

She looks at him with her eyes twinkling. 'You are special to me; you do know that?'

'If you compliment people, they believe anything you tell them. Of course, I believe I'm special,' he teases her.

She takes his hand. It is rough and callus, a working hand. 'Earlier, you asked how I felt about going home.'

Andreas nods. Now there is a serious look on his face.

'It pains me dreadfully to think this is coming to an end. Our time together in this garden. The thoughts and secrets we've shared sitting here with you have been a source of comfort.' Her eyes well up with tears and her restraint deserts her. 'Oh Andreas, what am I going to do without you?'

He squeezes her hand. 'You will have Reuben with you. You will be busy planning your new life together. A life full of possibility.' He wipes an eye and smiles at her. 'I must have got dust in my eye.' She looks at him sceptically and they both burst out laughing.

'*Hermes*' is the main area for shopping and named after the God of commerce and barter. In this area of Athens, the shops sell fashionable clothes imported from London and Paris, which are popular amongst the ladies of Athens.

It suffuses her in a sensation of utter contentment. With Reuben on her arm, she flits from shop to shop,

He shakes his head in amazement. 'Do you never tire of it?'

'Shopping? Never. I think we ladies are addicted to it.'

'I like a fine suit, like any other man, but this feels like an expedition.' His mouth tightens, and he tries not to smile.

They discover a small Byzantine church. Reuben consults his guidebook and proclaims it to be one of the smallest in the city.

'I'm amazed.'

'Yes, it's rather pretty,' Alisha agrees.

'I never expected to see so much gold and the colour of the paintings are so intense and vibrant. It's like walking into a gallery.'

'It definitely puts our churches in England to shame.'

'I wouldn't know. I've never been in one. This is my first time.'

Alisha looks at him in surprise. 'You've never been in a church... you mean, never?'

'No. I've never felt the need.' He grins. Alisha suspects he is playing with her.

'Do you believe in God, Reuben?'

'I do, of course.'

'Then why have you not been in a church?'

'Because I'm Jewish.'

Alisha feels foolish and embarrassed. 'I never knew. I've known you for years, Reuben. It doesn't matter to me, of course, but...' she struggles to find the words.

'It was never important. Didn't my surname give the game away, Bentov?'

'I thought it sounded Russian.'

'My parents lived in St. Petersburg. My father was a tailor. They had no choice but to leave. My brother was four at the time. They feared for their safety, their lives. Russia, especially, St Petersburg was a hotbed for political extremists and the Jewish population was always seen as scapegoats for everything wrong in Russia. Thousands were killed and displaced from their villages and towns. My parents fled with what they could carry and eventually ended up in London. My father was lucky enough to open a little tailor's shop. My parents got by. Life was better in London. My father never spoke about their life before London. When he died, eventually my mother told my brother and me about our family history.'

Alisha touches Reuben's arm. 'Oh Reuben, how dreadful. Your mother must have been proud of you when you were accepted to study music.'

'She told me that apart from giving birth to her children, it was the proudest day of her life.'

She looks at him and she can see that speaking of such things has registered emotion so intense that it has watered his eyes. 'And she would have been proud of the man you have become.'

'Do you think so? I'm not that special.'

'Are you saying I'm a bad judge of character, Reuben Bentov,' Alisha says with emphasis and strokes his cheek.

'Never, Alisha. I'd never doubt you or mock you, for that matter. You mean too much to me.'

At that moment, an old woman and a young girl emerge from the church door. The old woman stares at them whilst the young girl runs innocently towards the candles that burn like small torches at the foot of an icon of Christ. Alisha can feel the old woman's scorn and suspects her intimate gesture towards Reuben is perceived as a display of disrespect or, worse, blasphemy.

'I think we've upset her,' Reuben whispers.

The old woman crosses herself and mutters something in Greek.

'I don't know what she said, but I don't think it was very complimentary towards us. We should go.'

Reuben doesn't argue, and when they reach the street outside, they both look at each other and burst into fits of laughter.

They come across a street where every shop front and shop window are adorned with candles of every size. Reuben consults his guidebook. 'Huh, guess what this street is called? The street of Candles.'

As they walk further, they notice silver and gold icons also for sale, not only of Christ and the Virgin Mary but every conceivable saint: Spiridon, Nikolas, George, Elena...

'There's a lot of money to be made in the name of religion,' Alisha says. 'Look, Reuben. There are little arms and legs in the windows. They're like broken dolls.

'Ah, these are models of the human body, internal organs also. Look, that's a heart, there's a leg and there's an arm.'

'But why?' Alisha asks.

'Well, according to my little book here, if a person has a diseased organ or something wrong with a limb, they buy a model of an arm or a leg, whatever it is and then hang them up in church and pray to a saint or the Virgin Mary for their intercession.'

'Look, there's one of a baby. Do you think it works?'

'I don't know, but superstition can be a powerful motivator and good for business, it would seem.'

'I think it's rather special that people have so much faith.'

'I'm not convinced,' Reuben says sceptically. 'I'm starving. Do you fancy some lunch?'

'I'd love a cup of tea.'

'Let's see what's down here.'

They walk a little further and come to a square; several cafes have tables and chairs outside shaded from the broiling sun by canopies. They consult a few menus before settling on one and take their seats. Reuben takes off his jacket and rolls his shirt sleeves. A waiter takes their order and Reuben lights a cigarette.

'That's better. You wouldn't believe that it ever gets cold here. It's so hot today,' Reuben complains.

Alisha takes off her hat and places it on the table. She unbuttons the top button of her blouse. Her face is flushed, and she dabs her forehead with a napkin. She places a stray strand of hair on top of her head and fixes it in place with a pin. She pats her hair with her palm and, satisfied, places her hat back on her head.

'Are you missing London, Reuben? I mean, are you homesick?'

'I wouldn't complain if it rained. I never thought I'd say it, but I'm missing the rain. I don't think it's rained since we set foot in Greece,' he says with faint dismay. 'What about you?'

'Finding Greece has been the best thing that has happened to me. Present company exempted, of course.' She smiles at him.

'I'm glad to hear it on both counts. You look like and sound like the Alisha of old. You have returned to me, Alisha. When I wake in the morning, the first thing I want to do is see your face, hear your voice, and surround myself with your beauty. I'm enticed by your intelligence, the strength of character you have shown these past months. You have exuded a confidence that is infectious. I just want to be with you, Alisha.'

From across the table, he takes her hand. A tide of emotion floods through him. 'You are the most precious thing in my world. It has been unbearable, torture even, knowing that you were with that man. I won't degrade you with his name. At times...' he pauses, his voice cracks with the weight of emotion. His throat constricts. He lifts her hand to his lips. 'At times, I had to detach myself from what was going on around me. Every day I saw you and you were a constant reminder of my loss. I felt as if I was living two separate lives. The one you saw each day, the Reuben in the String Quartet, he was not me. I became proficient at pretending; I was an expert liar. All I wanted was to feel you next to me. Touch your hair, your beautiful hair. Every night, all I desired was to feel every inch of your body lying next to mine. I gazed at every expression, every smile, and every little gesture that to others would appear insignificant, unimportant even, but to me, it was life itself. And when you spoke, I felt so much joy; your voice was music to my ears. Mozart didn't come close. I remember it all. I'll never forget.' He kisses her fingers, one by one. 'There, I have done what I longed to do all this time. Now you know.'

Reuben is still holding her hand, and Alisha rests her head there. She is wailing, a deep mournful sound.

'My dear Alisha, what have I done to you? Forgive me, please.'

She waves his apology away. 'It's not you, Reuben. I didn't see what was in front of me all along. I failed you with my pride. I was blinded by a life promised to me by circumstance, a life that others had and eventually, I grew to want. It was a love of possession, of standing, of which others would envy. It was not real. It was an illusion.' The memories come rushing at. She recalls the night at Alfred's. The memory of it is so clear that when she describes it to Reuben, she could be detailing a photograph. Sutton's words return to her, like an earworm, mocking her.

'I'm ashamed of myself,' she says, truthfully.

'There is nothing to feel shame about. My love for you will wash it away, I promise. There is one consolation; you will never have to feel pain like that again.'

She turns her head, not wanting him to see her reaction. There is a slight pursing of her lips.

'When you mourned the loss of that man, for at the time that is what I believed it was, I wondered about your rage and grief, and I came to the conclusion that it scared me.'

'Why would you feel that way?'

'I feared you might never be the same again. I thought your mind might be numb to life itself. Mostly, I thought I'd lost you.'

'I never knew these things, Reuben. You don't have to worry anymore.'

'I can see that.'

She touches his face. 'Despite what has happened, I am so happy.'

He stares at her impenetrable eyes and all he wants to do at this very moment is make love to her.

Since the day on the beach, she has spent a considerable amount of time with Reuben. Alisha knows Sara is happy for her, but she detects a hint of jealousy now that she has been sparingly lending her attention towards Sara.

Alisha is experiencing the joy of being in love. Has she always been? Could it be that John Sutton was merely a distraction to the inevitability of an attraction that has spanned years, and therefore, not extinguished itself?

She remembers when she first saw Reuben; it was his skill as a musician that she appreciated. His ability fascinated her. Now, as she contemplates this, she realises she felt inferior, exposed and unsure.

Most of the pupils' upbringing had involved their needs being indulged by nannies and servants, spoilt was not too strong a word for it. Reuben was different. There was an easy familiarity about him, and he believed in her. He accepted her worth amongst the others and acknowledged her natural abilities as a musician that later, distinguish her from her peers.

His eyes are watery blue, and she tells him how lucky he is to have such long eyelashes, but being a man, he says, the thought has never crossed his mind.

There are times she is shocked at her feelings for him.

She catches herself wanting to touch him; it comes over her as natural as the tide rolling in. She tries to make sense of these thoughts and understand her reasoning. She decides these are not intellectual responses; they are a primaeval corollary of desire and her need for sensual exploration. His features and scent are now as familiar to her as her own. They have lost their innocence and modesty.

Alisha studies the plains of his face. She reaches out and traces the outline of his lips.

'My love,' she whispers, and he kisses the tip of her fingers. She finds the sensation extraordinary.

Reuben moves onto an elbow, lifting himself, and the bed creaks. Even though the window is open, the temperate afternoon air is sultry and still and the sheet sticks to Alisha's thigh.

Sometimes, he believes their love is fated. He visits her room every day now and every day they make love. He cannot think of life before this time. Only now matters. Only now has substance. Only now has meaning.

'You are the anchor in a world full of storms.'

'That's dramatic.'

He considers how to tell her. 'It's not, it's true. I fear I would not be the man I am today if I did not have you in my life.'

'What do you mean?'

'I can only describe it as my mind was not my own. You have brought me back to my senses. Before we came out here, I was going mad. I was consumed by a rage that would not subside; my anger was overwhelming. When the portrait became everyone's focus and all they could talk about was seeing the completed version I was at my worst, I think.'

'But, whatever for?'

'I didn't care about a stupid painting. It meant nothing to me, but I could see that it was important to the others and you had made great concessions. I know he wanted to paint you; we were nothing to him. He did it out of respect for you.'

'This is true, he did.'

'So, I held my tongue. I tried so hard to bury my loathing for the man. I lived each day knowing that he was closer to your affections than I could ever be. When I think back to that time, I'm ashamed that I could feel such abhorrence for another human being. I loathed the man and everything about him.'

Alisha is shocked to hear Reuben speak this way.

'He took you from my world, Alisha. He took the most perfect person I had ever known and locked you away from me. You were untouchable. I had lost you to him.' Reuben smiles sadly. 'I'm sorry. I'm making you sound like a possession. You're not, of course.' He rubs his head.

'I was going mad. I was ill. The thing is, as I've said before, I became good at hiding it, acting normal in front of everyone. My thoughts were incoherent. They just went around and around in my head, and that's when I started to gamble.

'At first, it helped me to escape my thoughts. It was the only time my mind wasn't consumed by you. It freed me from my torment, from the worm of jealousy that was boring itself into my soul. So, I began to visit casinos, just a few times at first, but then it became every other day.

When I won, it was the most incredible feeling and I chased that reaction because it blocked out reality. It was numbness. It was a reprieve for a while. It never lasted.'

Reuben feels his stomach spasm at the memory. 'I'm over it now. You do, believe me, Alisha?'

'Oh Reuben, my love.' Her tone soothes him. She lays her hand on his chest.

'I wanted you to know. I don't want to hide anything from you. I'm ashamed of what I did, what I felt, what I became. I need to be honest with you. I need to be honest with myself.'

Reuben feels her hand in his hair, and he looks into her eyes, and there are tears there. He moves his head towards her, and she kisses him willingly, lacing her fingers through his hair. Reuben is thirsty for her. He holds her face close to him, in case he is dreaming, and she fades from him. He kisses her again, this time more softly. He feels an exultant sense of love for her. She presses herself against him and he can feel the soft swell of her breasts against his chest. At that moment, he experiences the most profound sense of elation, and every nerve in his body tingles in sublime pleasure.

There is a wrap on her door, then another. 'Alisha, are you awake?'

It is Sara's voice and for a second Alisha thinks she has overslept, but Sara's voice is shaking. It alarms her. 'Alisha, quickly, it is Alfred. Something has happened.'

Alisha throws the cover from her and fastens her dressing gown. She unlocks the door.

'What is it, Sara?'

'There's a commotion in Alfred's room. They won't let me in.'

'Who?'

'I think there's a doctor with him.'

They run along the corridor and meet Reuben, whose face is grey and gaunt.

'I've been told by James that we have to assemble in the hall in ten minutes. He has some news for us, it concerns Alfred.'

'Is he alright? What has happened?' Sara is almost hysterical.

'I don't know. I'm sure we'll find out. Don't worry; he's probably just off colour, probably had too much to drink last night.'

'But why call a doctor?'

Reuben meets Alisha's gaze. He answers lightly. 'As a precaution, maybe.' His expression is unconvincing.

Alisha changes as quickly as she can and when she enters the hall, the others are already waiting. She can see their music stands and their sheets of music placed on them. The rows of chairs where the small exclusive audience sit each night appear as they always have done unmoved. Everything is as it should be. Everything looks normal, but it doesn't feel that way. There is a palpable tension lurking amongst them.

Reuben offers Alex a cigarette and nervously lights his own. He inhales deeply and paces, occasionally looking out of one of the large windows. Sara is sitting with her hands in her lap. Alisha sits next to her.

'There's something wrong. I don't like this.' Sara's bottom lip quivers.

Alisha touches her on the arm. 'Let's just wait and see, shall we?'

For an unbearable minute, they are silent. Reuben musters an encouraging smile in Alisha's direction.

Sara rubs her forehead. 'I've got a terrible headache.'

Suddenly, James appears. With him is the hotel manager. They both look sombre in their suits. James' mouth is set firm and Alisha notices beads of sweat on his forehead. Alisha and Sara stand.

James' voice is uncharacteristically soft, almost a whisper. 'I'm afraid I've got some terrible news to tell you.'

Sara groans.

'Alfred passed away last night in his sleep. The doctor thinks it was a heart attack. Thankfully, it was peaceful.'

Sara screams and falls to her knees, covering her face and muffled sobs.

James stares at her. The hotel manager looks like he wishes he was somewhere else. James blinks nervously. Such a display of raw and naked emotion throws him. He is unprepared, so he continues to speak, a defence mechanism, a distraction.

Alisha cannot recall what James said then. Her world turns in on itself, collapsing, as does her resolve. Later, all she remembers is the familiar scent of Rueben, as she buries her head in his chest.

The garden is her sanctuary where she can be enclosed by the inner world of thought and reasoning, of choices and judgements. She comes here to escape from the real world, just for a short time. It is like a friend she can turn to; it brings her clarity; it brings answers to her questions and there is often Andreas, a rock amongst the stones of the world.

'Do you fear death, Andreas? Are you afraid of dying?'

He thinks for a moment. 'I fear nonexistence. Before you are born, you have no knowledge of that, no memory, no emotion. You did not exist. I fear going back to that because I have experienced existence, this thing we call life. I know how it feels. I know only this life.'

'Would you like to live forever?'

'Knowing that I am going to die, whenever that will be, probably sooner rather than later, helps me to focus on the things that matter, to get things done, to concentrate on what is important to me. If I was to live forever, there would always be a tomorrow, not a today. Today, there is a here and now. That is why it is important to live in the moment, to express what we feel, not tomorrow or the day after, but now.'

'You speak as if you don't think heaven exists? I'd like to think Alfred is finally with Gloria.'

'You need to believe in God first.'

'You don't believe in God. Greece is a Christian country.'

'That doesn't mean anything. No. I don't believe in God, but I believe in humanity, and I believe in goodness and compassion and that the earth should not belong to the few but be a home for us all.'

'I like the sound of that, but I don't think the politicians of my country and yours, for that matter, will have any enthusiasm for such an idealistic perspective.'

'That doesn't make it wrong. Believe me, Alisha, there is a change that is sweeping Europe and it may come to England as well. The workers of the world are rising; there is a new dawn, a new way of thinking. I've waited for it all of my life.' His tone changes and sadness replaces his enthusiasm. 'The world belongs to the young, not us old, people. I sometimes fear about the world we are leaving you. And you Alisha, you will now be leaving sooner than you expected.'

'Yes, I will. I can't believe I won't see Alfred again.'

'If he is in your heart, he will always be with you. He will never leave.'

'I hope so, I really do. And you, Andreas, you are in my heart.'

'Then I will always be with you.'

She draws in a long breath. 'I hope so. I really do.'

'Do you know when you are going back to London?'

She has no idea. It depends upon the legal necessities and protocol of returning a body to its homeland.

Alisha shakes her head. 'I honestly don't know when it will be. James is seeing to everything.' She feels hot tears in her eyes just thinking about leaving Athens and never seeing Andreas again.

CHAPTER SEVENTEEN

THE ANGEL HE SAW AND OTHER DRAMAS

There is something about the air. Abriana settles on the notion that it is spiritual, like breathing incense in a church. She inhales a sweet, warm fragrance; it hints of mint and there is a definite lacing of lavender. It settles on her in a warm embrace, like a lover. Around her, a serene tract of pristine landscape, of pine trees, cedar, cypress, olive trees and palms unroll before her in glorious and gratifying honeyed light. Her spine tingles as she watches the sun, a blazing pearl, spread a cone of golden light on the shimmering water and melt like liquid into the Ionian. She folds her arms across her stomach, luxuriating in the soft tinge of heat in the early evening.

Keeping her intentions from Mark had affected her. Was it right to have told him in the way she did? Was it right to be so arbitrary? Abriana has felt weighed down; she was tired of keeping up the pretence and because of this; she envies him. She was fearful of his reaction, but he pushed her too far this time and she is now glad of it. There is an inward sense of relief. She despised her confinement of the truth, but now such feelings have dissipated like fog. She remembers the disbelief on his face at *Apostolos' taverna.*

'You've stolen it, for fuck's sake, Abriana. Why?' Mark had asked incredulously. And then, as if he had just remembered. 'Who did you sell it to?'

'The Roma Gallery. Not me personally, Geoffrey Buchanan did.'

'The current owner?'

'Yes.'

'But why? Why would you do such a thing?' He looked at her as if he had been slapped.

'If Alan Sutton or The Uffizi Gallery are given ownership of the painting, The Roma Gallery will have to return it to either one.'

'And they will have lost what they paid for it, a fortune, and their reputation. I see now. This is all about what they did to you, isn't it?'

'You don't get it, Mark. How can you even begin to understand? I lost everything, my identity, the person I was. They took that from me. They tore my heart out and trampled on it. I was humiliated and used. Protecting their brand and their position in the art community was all that mattered to them. It was more important to them than I was. I was nothing to them. I had given them everything. I was just a fly to be squashed. I wasn't worthy of their protection. You have no idea how that feels.' There was a tautness behind her eyes.

'Have you lost your mind? It's insane. What makes you think you can get away with it... Why?' He shook his head vehemently. Suddenly, Mark stood up. He walked off, pent-up frustration coming to the boil.

After a while, she went over to him. He was sitting on a stonewall. His expression was as featureless as a slate. Behind him, houses were framed with hints of family life, washing hanging limply in the heat, children's bicycles lying at abandoned angles, terracotta pots sprouting every flower imaginable, creeping bougainvillaea, long stem roses, a flurry of purple and orange bloom and coiling vines. His stone face and the ache that had settled around her heart didn't belong there. She examined his face. She waited. He looked up at her.

'You want to humiliate them? I get that. You want retribution. Do you want it so much that you're prepared to risk everything? The life you have now?'

'After this is over, I'm finished with the art world. I'll walk away from it happy, with a sense of completion.'

'And do what?'

'Who knows, I might write a book about it.' There was a little truth to her distraction. 'I've always wanted to write.' At that very moment, she felt a desire to embrace him, in a way, she thought, to show him she wasn't going mad. 'I don't want the money, Mark. Geoffrey Buchanan is now a rich man.'

'Why hasn't he sold the painting before now?'

'The thought never occurred to him. It's been in his family for years. He didn't know its value. I just planted a seed. I told him the painting was worth a lot of money and I had the perfect buyer. He had debts. He needed the money. I just opened a door that held an opportunity for him. Greed is a powerful motivator.'

'So, all of this time you've known the painting was going to be sold.'

Abriana looked away from him.

'You told Pavlos his story would be told.' She was taken aback by the look of distrust in his eyes.

'And I meant it. Once the rightful owner is established, The Roma Gallery will be duty-bound to return it. They'll have no option, unless they prefer an expensive court battle, but that won't happen. They won't have the appetite for that. They'll have been humiliated enough. Eventually, the painting will be returned to the heir. Pavlos' story will be told, one way or another. I'll make sure of it.'

He rose to his feet. 'Your sense of justice begins.'

She touched his arm and felt him flinch. It hurt her. It felt like a bomb detonating inside her. Mark sighed.

'There's one more thing.'

Mark turned and looked at her. 'Should I be worried?'

'Remember, in Edinburgh, I told you about Buchanan, and how he let the BBC researchers look at the painting? Well, part of their research involved getting an expert in the scientific analysis of paintings to examine the painting. That's how we know the necklace was added to the painting at a later date, but they found something else. A game-changer, really.'

'What?'

'Human hair stuck in the paint.'

Now he was curious. No. More than that, she had snagged the art dealer in him.

'As you know, the paint should have preserved the hair from light and moisture. If they could get reliable DNA, they could compare with...'

'A relative,' Mark interjected.

'Yes, a male relative. In fact, any male relative will

provide conclusive proof, due to the unchanging nature of the Y chromosome.'

'So, let me get this straight. What you're saying is, if there is reliable DNA from the hair, which we suspect came from John Sutton, it can demonstrate a parentage link down the male generations.'

'That's the science.'

'But you have a problem. You have to prove the hair belongs to John Sutton. You need a swab from a male relative.'

She was smiling at him.

'And you've found one?'

'Sutton's father had a brother and there's a male descendant of that line living in New York. Remarkably, the lab was able to extract reliable DNA from the hair and he agreed to provide a sample.'

'Has it been done?'

'It has.'

'And?'

Her lips curved into a slow smile. 'It was a positive match.

'Jesus.'

Abriana sensed his mind working.

Mark's eyes narrowed. 'So, we didn't need to come to Zakynthos?' He didn't know whether to be angry or intrigued.

'It all really happened the day we arrived. That's why I've been the way I have. When the gallery told me they had located a distant relative of Sutton, I panicked. I knew it would only take a day or two to get the results and if the hair was from John Sutton, they would request a swab from Alan Sutton in Edinburgh. It would only take another twenty-four hours to get the results. The Roma Gallery was being obstructive; they started to stall. I thought they might have learned of the DNA tests. You see, the Uffizi haven't made their interest in any of this public. But, just the other day, while all of this was going on, a newspaper article hinted at it. It added to my recent un-rational behaviour. I lost it, evidently. I'm sorry for putting you through that. I was running out of time. I wasn't in control.' Abriana's lips tighten.

Mark began to pace; he scratched his head. She stared at him, bright-eyed. He turned and looked at her, scrutinizing her face, his brain a confusing state of supposition. 'I don't know what to think, Abriana.'

'I shouldn't have brought you here.' she said apologetically.

'It's too late for that.' He realised then, in a burst of self-awareness, that Abriana was defining her life around the painting just as he had defined his life around her.

'So, how does it feel now, knowing it has been sold?'

'It's just begun. I need to see them humiliated... and they will be.'

'Where does old Pavlos fit into all of this now?'

'His story is just as important as it always was. As far as the Uffizi is concerned, it can only be a bonus. If Alan Sutton fails the DNA test, they will also have a firsthand account of the history of the painting. That, in itself, is a precious commodity. That's why we're still here.' Her head was upright, there was a determination about her posture. 'I wouldn't blame you if you left, but being in Zakynthos isn't about us, is it? It's about letting Pavlos tell his story, knowing that his words will live on, well beyond any of us.'

Mark's expression softened. 'I need a drink.'

. . .

On the table, outside on the veranda, Pavlos has set the table with olives, hummus and bread. A large bowl filled with chunks of chicken breast sits in the centre with sliced avocado, tomatoes, cucumbers, bell peppers, red onions capers, feta cheese, over greens. Around this, he has placed stuffed grape leaves, spinach cheese pie spanakopita, oven-roasted potato and rice pilaf. There is a jug of water with ice and a bottle of red wine.

'What's all this?' Mark asks as he and Abriana walk from the car.

'We are celebrating.' Pavlos replies, easing himself into his usual chair.

'This sounds exciting, celebrating what?' Abriana smiles, as she leans towards him and kisses him in greeting on the cheek.

'The story is coming to an end.'

Pavlos' revelation tightens Abriana's chest. She is eager to discover the outcome, but sadly, their time with Pavlos is almost over.

Mark smiles. 'That's quite a spread.'

'I hope you're hungry?'

'Always. And wine. That's a shame. Abriana can't have any. She's driving.'

'She can have a small glass.'

'No. I better not. Some lemonade would be nice.'

'There's some in the fridge.' Pavlos says, directing his words towards Mark.

When Mark leaves, Pavlos looks at Abriana. 'How are you?'

She sits in a seat and flicks her hair. 'Good. I'm enjoying your lovely island.'

'I'm glad... but you are not yourself. Something is wrong, I can tell.'

Pavlos' sudden interest in her takes her aback, and she wonders if she should tell him. 'What do you mean?'

'I might be old, but I'm not blind, not yet. Since you have both been coming here, I have never seen him walk in front of you, and just now, you would think he was walking towards me on his own. The body language between the two of you is strained. You haven't looked at each other since you arrived.'

'We've had an argument, that's all. Nothing to worry about.' She smiles, relieved, hoping to convince him.

'Here we are.' Mark places the glass on the table.

'Thank you.'

Mark swings his gaze towards Pavlos. 'Shall we open the wine?'

'You do the honours, and come on, eat the both of you.'

'John once told me. '*I saw the angel in the canvass and painted until I set her free.*' I didn't know until years later; he had borrowed that saying from Michelangelo.'

Mark smiles. 'I saw the angel in the marble and sculpted until I set it free.'

'You know it.' Pavlos grins. 'That is how he painted. He wanted to reach into her face and draw out her characterization... the angel he saw.'

The Story of Alisha Hadley

Athens 1905

She walks with no purpose, her umbrella protecting her from the glare of the afternoon sun. She is uncomfortable in her dress; the lace sticking to her skin. After a while, she becomes aware she has been in a trance that is as close to being asleep as one can get while awake. Her mind clouded, as if in a fog. It shocks her, her vulnerability all-encompassing.

How could she fail to register her surroundings? The shops, the café bars, the scruffy boys selling fruit and veg from rudimentary stalls and baskets. She had crossed a street and her dress almost trailed in a mound of horse manure. She was deaf to the noise of carriages and trailers; her sense of smell dulled to the city around her. Alisha's dreamlike state engulfed her.

Sweat trickles down her spine. Suddenly, she feels an urge to unfasten her buttons, remove her hat, and unpin her hair. Alisha is registering herself in space. Her throat is dry, and her eyes slide from face to face. She is aware of an ache in her forearm. Where it bends, it is stiff; the tendons pulling tightly, and she changes the umbrella to her left hand, stretching her free arm. Animated voices float around her, becoming louder and brisk, a language whose sound is now familiar, but still foreign. She can smell the baked aroma of bread and pies, and she is slowly rising to the surface.

Alisha passes a kiosk at the entrance to a park where boys and girls with cupped hands drink water from a well. Women stroll by, smiling and chatting, their floppy hats bouncing with each step. Suited men slouch on park benches reading newspapers. She can hear the distinctive vibrating sound from the strings of a fiddle.

Alisha stops at the corner of Rue du Strade and the Rue du Korias. Her eyes scan the Hotel D'Athenes. She recognises the impressive façade of the Finance Ministry. The sun glistens upon the details of grand buildings, a visual representation of friezes, pediments, cornices, and architraves. She strolls on. A numbness settles over her. At the Place de la Constitution rows of tables and chairs are set out, and at the Café Zachartes, exhausted, she slumps into a chair. She sits for a while twisting her hands, a pain tightens in her chest and then, like a tsunami, the loss of Alfred overwhelms her.

Around Alisha, Athens buzzes, like any other city, but in her head, there is a silence. Her world has stopped. It doesn't move; it is blurred at the edges. She can't imagine what it will be like, or feel like, not ever seeing Alfred again, or hearing his joyous voice bring colour and stability to her world.

Her nose twitches and she scratches it. It is a mannerism that Alfred would always tease her about. Now she would give anything to be the butt of his joviality. She flicks stray strands of hair from her face.

A waiter approaches and tentatively offers her some napkins. He smiles nervously, hoping the young woman's sobs have subsided. The waiter is unsure what to say or how to offer comfort. He would rather be taking orders or clearing tables. These are tasks that only call for small talk if needed, and he has built up a repertoire of phrases he uses. But the head waiter insists he attends to her and moves her on quickly, as she will deter any prospective customer with her melancholy looks.

So, he stands there, shifting his weight from time to time, searching his mind for an appropriate phrase that will offer her some comfort. What would his sister or mother say in a similar situation? Their words would come to them and flow naturally, without a second thought, but not him. And then she speaks after wiping her eyes and nose.

'Thank you. I'm embarrassed. I didn't mean to make such a fuss.'

She is English, he thinks, and pretty. He only knows a few words of English. He likes the sound of her voice.

'You better, now,' he says, a little awkwardly.

'I'm feeling much better, thank you.'

'My English is not good. I speak French.'

'Oh, so do I. I said, I feel much better now. I'm sorry for picking your restaurant to cause such a scene,' Alisha says in perfect French.

'Your French is excellent. Have you ever been to France?' The waiter asks, his shyness deserting him now that he can adequately reciprocate.

He can feel the stern looks of the head waiter upon him, who is expecting the woman to leave, but Alisha's apparent recovery has encouraged him to ignore his senior's stare.

'No. I learned it at the school I went to in London.'

'I had no idea French is taught in England.' The young waiter is astonished at this newly discovered revelation.

'It wasn't then, but my school was different. It wasn't like most other schools in England at that time. It was a private school for children who were promising musicians and the lady who owned the school loved French culture, and she wanted us to have a practical knowledge of the language.' Alisha can feel tears at the lid of her eyes at the memory. 'You also speak good French.'

'My mother is French, and my father is Greek.'

'Ah, I see. And what is your name?'

'Sebastian, and yours?'

'Alisha. Pleased to meet you, Sebastian.'

He nods his head. 'It's a lovely name,' he says, now lowering his eyes and wishing he hadn't been so bold.

'Thank you, Sebastian.' Alisha smiles.

Sebastian thinks his name falls from her lips like petals.

'Would you like a drink? Tea or coffee? Something stronger, maybe?' It is all his inexperienced mind can think of saying.

'No. I'm fine. I really need to get back to my hotel. Yes, I need to be going now.' Alisha looks at her hands and her feet and wonders if she can stand.

'Are you sure you will be alright? I get off in five minutes. I could walk you to your hotel.'

'No. I will be fine, honest. I feel much better now. I wouldn't want to put you out of your way.'

'I don't mind, honest. If you change your mind, it will be my pleasure.'

Alisha smiles at him. 'Merci, Sebastian.'

'I would feel much better if you were to let me walk with you, just until I know you have reached your hotel.'

'I feel silly. No. I don't want to be a nuisance to you.'

'You won't be. My mother would never forgive me if she found out I didn't make sure you got home safely. Honestly, it would be easier walking with you. Better for my health, believe me.' Sebastian grins.

Alisha smiles, playing along with him. 'Well. I suppose I can't have your mother think badly of you, especially since you offered.'

'Good. Let me get out of this apron. I'll just be a few minutes.'

When Sebastian returns, he asks, 'What is the name of your hotel?'

She tells him, and his face brightens. 'Ah, it is this way, not too far.'

As they set off, Alisha notices that Sebastian has an attractive face. His features are smooth and youthful, his slim build pleasing to her eye. She asks him his age.

'I'm eighteen, but I've been shaving for years.' He cringes at his choice of words. Oh God, why did I say that? She'll think I'm a child trying to impress her.

Alisha can see his embarrassment. 'I didn't mean anything by asking. I was just curious, that's all. How long have you worked as a waiter?' she asks, attempting to change the subject.

'Nearly a year now. I used to work in the market, but it doesn't pay well. My father is friendly with the owner, who offered me a job on a trial basis, and I've been there ever since.'

'Do you enjoy it?'

'Each day is different. I get to meet a variety of people. Although, we have our regular customers and I've got to know them and their day-to-day worries and often the good things that happen to them.'

'It certainly sounds interesting. I bet there's never a dull moment?'

Sebastian smiles at her, unsure of what to say next. They walk a little further in silence. It has been prodding at his curiosity why Alisha was crying. He debates with himself if he should ask her and veer into the personal, then thinks it would be rude of him. But, at that moment, it is the only thing he can think of saying and fearing the silence between them more than a personal enquiry he counts down from five and quickly says before he changes his mind, 'Why were you upset?' Now that he has spoken the words, his stomach seems to fall from him.

She thinks it a reasonable question and to his relief, Alisha explains recent events. She tells him about the quartet, Alfred's passion for opening Italian and Greek experiences to those who can afford such travel, his vision of offering exclusive tours and building a grand hotel in Corfu. It all seems like another world from the life Sebastian knows, and he is transfixed by her descriptions. She tells him of Alfred's sudden death and how it has devastated her. Finally, when she has finished, Alisha realizes she hasn't been paying attention to the buildings and streets around her and it is only now that she recognizes the frontage of her hotel, less than a hundred yards in front of her.

'Oh, we're nearly there.'

'We are,' Sebastian says. He is unable to disguise his sense of disappointment.

'This will do fine. I don't think I'll get lost now. Your mother will be pleased.' Alisha smiles. 'I'm truly grateful, Sebastian.'

'Will you be leaving for London soon?'

'In a few more days, I'd think.'

'Then I hope you have a safe journey home, Alisha.'

'Thank you, Sebastian. Before I do, I may visit your restaurant for some tea. Sara would love to meet you.' Alisha holds his gaze.

'I'd like that,' Sebastian says, lowering his eyes.

'Well, I'll say goodbye then and thank you once again.' She touches him on the forearm, kindness in her touch. 'You're a true gentleman, Sebastian.'

He blushes then. He tries hard to summon a smile and

watches intently, his eyes bulging, as Alisha walks towards the hotel. Sebastian's chest is burning. Each cell in his body is alive. Alisha's face imprinted on his mind.

He is not ready to let her go from his sight, so he follows discreetly from a distance, between the trees that line the street. He feels ashamed that he is watching her without her knowledge.

Alisha crosses the street and heads towards the hotel entrance. Then, quite unexpectedly, a man appears. Alisha stops, and Sebastian can see they are talking. There is something about the man's posture that alarms him. He is leaning towards Alisha and moving his hands in rapid succession. It is the gesticulation of someone agitated, bordering on angry, even. Sebastian stands behind a tree. He is reluctant to move, as he has the advantage of not being seen. He can see Alisha take a step backwards.

'So, who is he?' Reuben asks.

'His name is Sebastian.'

'Why were you with him?'

The accusation in his tone pricks her. 'He offered to accompany me to the hotel, as I was not myself.'

'What do you mean?'

'He is a waiter. I was lost. I know it was silly of me, but I went out for a walk and I became upset. I realised I would never see Alfred again; he was not coming back. I found myself standing outside a restaurant. Sebastian was concerned for my welfare and he offered to walk me back to the hotel.'

'He was probably waiting for an opportunity to take advantage of you. He knows where you stay.'

'You know quite well I would never let that happen. It wasn't like that. Sebastian is not like that.'

'How do you know what he is like? He can speak English, then?'

'We spoke in French, actually.'

This revelation seems to add to Rueben's boiling frustration. 'You should have told me you were going for a walk. I would have accompanied you. You are obviously in no fit state to be out on your own.'

'I don't need a chaperone, and I'm perfectly capable of making my own decisions. Do not degrade my intelligence in assuming I'm not capable of coming to a decision on the substance of someone's character.' Alisha is furious with him.

'I was merely worried, that's all. And by the looks of it, I had every right to be. You don't know what could have been on his mind. I know what men think about. A young woman on her own, distressed and lost. It doesn't take much to surmise what this Sebastian's motives were. For God's sake, Alisha, don't you think we have all been through enough trauma with poor Alfred's passing? I will find this fellow myself and make it clear he is to keep away from you or I shall not be responsible for my actions.'

'Oh, Reuben. There is no need for that. You are taking this too far.'

He looks at her, aghast. His mouth drops, and she can tell his mind is contemplating possibilities.

'Why would you not want me to warn him off? Is there something I should know? Are you hiding your true intentions from me?'

Alisha shakes her head. 'Listen to yourself. What has gotten into you, Reuben? We have all been upset, but you seem to be taking your grief out on me.'

'I've suspected you have been keeping things from me. You have been distant with me; you have not been yourself and I'm not referring to your sadness over Alfred. I have felt a reluctance from you towards me. A physical reluctance. The other day, I was outside your door and I was about to knock when I heard you being sick, so naturally, I thought the reason for your withdrawal from me was because you were ill, but now, I have had confirmed with my own eyes the real reason for your lack of interest in me.' He pauses, letting the gravity of his words sink in.

'You should be ashamed of yourself. How dare you accuse me of such a thing?' The force of Alisha's words and her piercing eyes stab him, like a hot poker. It is not the reaction he expects.

'I am going to my room now and I do not expect you to follow me. In fact, it would upset me greatly if I were to see you at all.'

'So, you don't deny it.' Even as he speaks, he can see the hurt on her face. It is a look of devastation. And, at that moment, it brings him back to his senses, but he cannot retract his words' implied meaning.

'How could you, Reuben? How could you, of all people, think such a thing of me? You have the eyes and words of John Sutton about you.'

She walks towards the entrance to the hotel when she turns. 'Do you think I would jeopardize what we have... what I thought we had?'

'Alisha, I...'

'I have a life growing inside me. I'm pregnant with your child.'

I am alone, utterly alone.

Her loneliness is all-encompassing. The slightest thing

can trigger her grief. She knows the others are hurting just as much as she is, yet inside, she has only dwelt on her loss. Grief can be a selfish, intrinsic state.

Alfred has occupied a vast space in her life, and her mind is having difficulty computing. He no longer fills that space. She cannot let him go.

Alisha has begun a process of self-evaluation. What was her last conversation with Alfred? She can't remember, and now it means so much. Everyone she has cared about or loved has left her: her father, Gloria, John, Alfred, and now Rueben. They are all murmurs of another life. It makes her fear ever giving over her thoughts, feelings and self to another again because eventually, they will all leave her.

Her mind is full of conflicting emotions. The partition between allowing herself to get close to another and fearing their excruciating loss, eventually, is thin. She wonders about her physical and mental attachment to Reuben. The closeness she thought they shared would have been a shield to protect her. Only uncertainty occupies her thoughts now.

The only thing of substance she has left is her water-coloured drawings. Alisha draws because she enjoys the experience of being creative. The pleasure of drawing is aesthetic, spiritual, escapist. It offers her a challenge. It awakens her to self-awareness, to her thoughts, her feelings. It is the expression of human nature. It is life itself. It illuminates the virtues of curiosity, patience, and contemplation. It is a mirror that reflects the value of living. It is life itself. She can confront the world around her and evaluate it with honesty. Alisha feels it is her responsibility to record what she sees in this way. She desires to step outside of her orbit. And this is all transmitted when she opens the wooden box that holds her rainbow of colours, to the soundtrack of harsh whispers and the hushed glide of her pencil.

They have all been summoned by James to meet in the dining room, just before dinner at 6 o'clock.

Alex, Sara and Alisha arrive first. Rueben enters and, seeing that Alisha has crossed the room to fill a glass with water, he walks towards her, glancing nervously.

'Have you told the others?'

'Is that all you have got to say? No. I have told no one.'

'I am ashamed of myself. My reaction was unforgivable. And then your news, well, that was... unexpected, to say the least. It came as a shock, but a good one. Please forgive me, Alisha. I wasn't myself.'

She is still angry with him. 'No. You weren't. How could you accuse me of such a thing? You Rueben, of all people.'

'I know, I know. I'm an idiot. I wasn't myself. We need to talk. I feel terrible about the way I treated you. I don't know what got into me or where those words came from. I was jealous, that's the only thing I can think of. When I saw you with him... Sebastian, it was as if a mist descended upon me.'

Alisha stares at him.

'I need to talk to you. We need to talk. There is so much to discuss now,' Reuben pleads. He thinks Alisha looks tired. 'I can't believe you are going to have a baby, my baby.'

'Thank you for coming,' James says. He looks pristine in his suit, starched collar and tie. 'I know this has been a difficult time for everyone. For my part, I have made it my duty to ensure all the necessary arrangements have been put in place. Unfortunately, such a process takes time, it can't be rushed. Now, I'm glad to inform you all that everything is arranged and our passage back to England is secured.'

'When will we be leaving?' Sara asks.

'The day after tomorrow. So, I would advise you to make sure you have packed your luggage the night before, as I have arranged for the hotel staff to transport it to the ship.'

'What will happen to Alfred?' Alex asks.

'His body has already left. There are specific procedures that need to be adhered to.' He takes a sip of water. 'As I have said, I appreciate this is a sad time for us all. When we arrive in London, I have been charged with being the executor of Alfred's will and seeing that his estate is dealt with according to his wishes. I think it would be wrong of me if I did not allude to the fact that your circumstances have changed, and you can no longer expect to enjoy the privilege of Alfred's patronage. You will, of course, continue to be paid until the end of what would have been this trip, thereafter it is my sad duty to inform you that thereafter, you will have to ascertain other means of employment. It remains to be seen if Alfred has provided for you all in his will.'

There is a mechanical drone to James' voice, devoid of emotion as if he is merely reading from a prepared script. There is no apology or empathetic sentiment, and James leaves the room in an air of accomplishment.

Sara looks stunned. Alex has his hands buried deep in his pockets and stares at his feet.

'It hasn't come as a shock, has it?' Reuben offers. 'It had crossed my mind, with Alfred gone.'

'This is awful. What will we do now?' Sara is close to tears when her attention is drawn to Alisha. 'Alisha, where are you going?'

'I need some air,' Alisha says, as she brushes past Reuben and leaves the room.

In the garden, Alisha closes her eyes and takes a deep breath, tears roll down her cheeks. By the time Reuben has reached her, she is sitting on her usual bench, staring into space.

'Here you are. You had me worried.' He sits beside her and takes her hand. She tries to yank it from him, but he enfolds it with his free hand as well.

'Alisha, please don't do this. If you want to punish me, don't do it with your silence. I couldn't bear it. I will not abandon you. No matter what is in Alfred's will, it does not matter to me. I love you, Alisha, you must believe me.' He reaches towards her face and turns her head so that he can look into her eyes.' I will never hurt you again. I promise. I want to protect you and keep you safe. I would do anything for you. I would never abandon you or our baby. Knowing I am going to be a father has made me confront what life would be like without you. The possibilities are alien to me. I will not lose you, Alisha, not again. I will not let you. I cannot contemplate my life without your presence in it, without the light you bring to it. I want to... I need to be a part of your life, and our child's life.'

He lowers his head; he feels mentally exhausted. When he looks at her, he is sure he can see a softening in her eyes.

'I was brought up to believe, and it has always been my firm belief, that motherhood is a woman's most important role. But I can see now how such a belief is totally misguided. It's not just a mother, but a father as well. It has to be shared in the loving security of a family. This is what I'm trying to say. I want us to be a family, Alisha. I dedicate every living breath to you and our child.'

Alisha's eyes are puffy and red. 'Everything is changing so quickly. I don't know what to think anymore. One minute, I'm contemplating what life might be like on my own, with a baby spurned by society. And you, Reuben, you have promised me before you would never let any harm come to me. Here you are, trying to repair the damage you have inflicted on my heart. And Alfred, dear Alfred.' Her voice cracks now and her throat aches. Alisha closes her eyes and fresh tears fall. She places her hand on her chest. 'I'm struggling with all of this. My life has changed beyond recognition.'

Reuben leans into her and kisses her lips. Alisha does not push him away, her consent encourages him. He can taste her tears and he presses her to him. A sound escapes her, and he knows he has won her over again. It is the most erotic moment of his life.

Her nose runs, and she gently pulls away from him. 'I must look awful. How can you kiss me?'

'Because you are beautiful, and I'll never tire of reminding you.'

Reuben runs his fingers through Alisha's hair. They are lying on Alisha's bed. Reuben has propped himself up on his elbow. Every time he touches her skin, it feels like electric passing through his fingertips. The sensation is enthralling. He traces his fingers along her shoulder, down to her forearm, and with circular motions he drifts across her hand, and eventually, each knuckle and then finger, resting on her thigh. Her fingers are long and elegant, musician's fingers. He smiles. He knows she is deliberately attempting to cover the tiny white stretch marks that lightly run across her milky skin, but he does not care, for he is in love with each inch of her body. He lifts her hand and her look of protest elicits a smile from him that implies, 'It's alright.' His lips delicately brush against the white scars. And then he presses his lips against her, covering her thigh in soft kisses. Alisha runs her finger along Reuben's taut skin that covers the vertebrae of his curved spine.

'We have created a life together, you and me. How wonderful is that Alisha?' Reuben says, mellifluously.

Already, there is a faint swelling to her stomach and Reuben kisses her there too. Alisha still can't believe there is a life growing inside of her. She thinks it will not be until her body changes its shape that she will fully appreciate the significance of it.

'Will you still find me attractive when my stomach is large, and I walk like an old woman?'

Reuben lifts his face towards Alisha's. 'I'll love you even more, if that's at all possible.' And then he kisses her deeply.

'Are you happy?' Reuben asks.

'When I'm with you, yes.'

'And that's the way it is going to stay.'

'It will soon be morning. What time is it?' Alisha yawns.

Reuben leans over her and stretches his arm. He picks up his pocket watch that is on the bedside cabinet. 'Six-thirty. It's still early.' He replaces the watch and, as he moves his weight to lie back on the pillow, his hand brushes her hair. He looks at the mass of waves that flow from her face and around her shoulders. Rueben finds it amazing to see her hair fall naturally around her shoulders as he is so used to seeing it held up with pins. He takes her hair in his fingers and feels its weight. It reminds him of silk as the strands slip from him like water. When up close, he can see hints of various shades that her hat often hides.

'I thought I knew all there was to know about you, Alisha. But I was wrong. I've been wrong about so many things lately. It's funny how the eye becomes accustomed to the things it sees daily, yet I wasn't really seeing you. What I mean is, it's easy to take the person you love for granted. I was blind to what was in front of me. I stopped seeing all the little things, like how you always think of others and put them first before yourself. It comes naturally to you, unlike me. I realised it's these little things that mean the most. These are the qualities I admire in you.'

Reuben lets the strands of hair slip through his fingers and they fall over her breasts, concealing them from his view.

Reuben thinks for a moment, then a smile crosses his lips. 'Have you ever watched the sunrise?'

It is a question that lingers until the sudden realisation dawns on her. 'Actually, now that I think about it, I haven't. I'm ashamed to admit, really.'

'You're not the only one. I suspect most people don't think it is important. It's probably the last thing they'd think about when they awoke to start their day. It's a marvel of nature that happens every morning. People have become immune to it because of their busy lives. It's the most wonderful display of nature. Have I said that?' He grins. I would go as far as to say it has a spiritual quality to it. And each morning gives birth to a different sunrise that colours the sky. It's like a canvas that is redefining itself every minute, every second, even.'

Reuben gets out of bed and pads over to the window. He opens the shutters and just as he hoped, he can see over the rooftops and there is not another building tall enough to spoil the view. He climbs over the bed and takes Alisha in his arms. 'That was a bit of luck. We're facing east. Now just watch, it shouldn't take long.'

Alisha can see the rooftops stretch out before her in a gray hue. Several dark silhouettes fly across the roofs. She can hear the morning call of birds against the pulsing beat of Reuben's heart. His chest is warm against her cheek, and she can feel an excited anticipation rise inside her.

Just as Reuben had said, the light changes into a pastel hue. She can detect a thin streak of yellow beneath the clouds. Then, afraid to blink, she watches, her eyes wide and bright. The sun's light defuses the cloud cover in fiery orange and crimson, a silver halo banding their edges. Then, gradually, a transcendental salmon dilutes the sky as golden rays spread out, combing the sky.

'What do you think of it?' Reuben can't stop himself from smiling.

'I can't believe I've missed this every morning.'

'We're privileged to witness it. Doesn't it make you appreciate each new day? It also makes me feel how small and insignificant we are.'

'It does, it really does.'

'I'm glad you think of it that way, too.' He kisses the top of her head.

The light in the room is sharper, the sun reaching onto the bed, its growing heat falling onto their bodies. Reuben watches as the fine hairs on Alisha's legs glow in the soft silver light.

'What do you think will happen when we get back home? What about us, Reuben? How will we support ourselves and the baby?'

Reuben takes a deep breath. He tries to dismiss the

thought that life will be different, uncertain and full of difficulties. 'We'll work something out. There's still the possibility we can continue to make money with the Quartet. I mean, all we need to do is secure regular engagements. It's not as if we don't have a reputation in London. I'm sure we'll be able to work and receive a regular income.' He tries to sound upbeat... hopeful.

'Do you think so?'

'Of course. We're one of the best in London, if not the entire country.'

'It was only through Alfred's continued support that we were fortunate to earn a good living and afford luxuries. Now I don't even know if I can afford the roof over my head.'

She looks up at him, her eyes wide. 'It's a constant worry, Reuben, and now there will be the baby to consider.'

'Try to not trouble yourself, Alisha. We'll work something out. If all else fails, I'm sure Alfred will not have abandoned us.'

'You mean we may prosper from the will?'

'I'm sure of it... Look, look at how the sky has changed now. The sky is a democracy. It allows every colour to have its limelight, every tone to shine.'

Alisha feels an enormous need for him. It is spontaneously engulfing. She loves looking into his eyes; it reminds her they are part of his charming smile.

CHAPTER EIGHTEEN

ANOTHER LIFE AND OTHER STRUGGLES

Abriana places her phone on the table and takes a drink of water.

'Was that important?' Mark asks.

'It was a text from the Uffizi. There have been some developments.' She glances at Mark, trying to sound businesslike.

'Positive ones, I hope.'

'He has agreed to the test.' She looks at Mark and raises her eyebrows and gives a secretive smile.

'When?' Mark asks.

'Within the next twenty hours.'

Pavlos looks at them, confused and vague.

Mark sighs. 'I think he has a right to know,' he states plainly.

Abriana knows by the look on Mark's face that if she doesn't tell Pavlos, he will.

'Know what?' Pavlos looks at her. 'Abriana, what's going on?'

She hesitates before answering. 'I haven't been entirely honest with you.'

Her admittance, she realises, may push Pavlos away from them, from her. He may even distrust her now, and she can't bear the thought of that. What if he refuses to cooperate? Even if proven that Alan Sutton is a relative of John Sutton, the Uffizi Gallery will still want Pavlos' account. They need it. But, importantly, apart from these concerns, she needs to know how Alisha's story ends.

She has no choice. By telling Pavlos the truth, she is allowing him to see her vulnerability; her need for revenge. By being complicit in the sale of the painting, she has deceived Pavlos and Mark. She is tired of hurting those she cares about. She knows how much the painting and its story is a part of Pavlos' life, his history, and what it means to him. Abriana realises now how important Alisha's story has become to her, and she cherishes her fondness for Pavlos. To lose them both is something Abriana finds incomprehensible. It feels like a void is opening in her heart.

She looks at Mark for support and his expression tells her, 'You are doing the right thing.' When their eyes meet, Abriana's eyes are wide and frightened. He feels an irresistible pull towards her, and he feels guilty now for pushing her in this direction. If he could, he would take this burden from her.

Abriana starts at the beginning: Rome, Mark, their affair, the blackmail attempt, the sale of Mark's gallery painting, the refusal to give in to the blackmailer, the fallout that occurred, her resignation and the beginning of her revenge.

She spoke with affection about moving to Florence, her new job at the Uffizi Gallery, and the discovery of John

Sutton's lost painting. She told Pavlos it was, then she started planning her revenge.

There were tears in her eyes when she described meeting Mark again, and her feelings that resurfaced. She looks at Mark. 'I tried hard to suppress them,' she tells him. It was a complication she welcomed but dreaded at the same time. To an extent, she gave in to it. She could see how much Mark was interested in Sutton's painting, especially Alisha and her story, so, in a way, against her better judgement, they both came to Zakynthos. She needed to be focused on the task at hand, but events moved faster than she had anticipated, and this affected her rationale. There could be no compromise. The changing developments around establishing a family link through John Sutton's DNA could have jeopardised everything, the sale needed to be made to the Roma Gallery if she was to inflict humiliation and her revenge on that establishment. She found it incomprehensible, unbelievable even, that justice would not be hers.

'Alan Sutton's claim to the painting rests on the evidence that the painting was stolen from John Sutton, therefore it remains the property of his family. Now, all he has to do is take the DNA test to prove once and for all his claim is genuine.'

She can't deny it, there is no point, and she knows deep within herself, the consequences of her actions held her no fear. One thing alone could cause her alarm, the prospect of failure. That is, until now.

When she has finished, she sits quietly, her eyes glistening. Pavlos holds her in his stare. To her horror, he begins to cry, silently, tears staining his cheeks. Remorse engulfs her.

'It is a terrible thing you have done. How could you let that man sell the painting?' Pavlos says accusingly. He wipes his tears with the back of his hand. 'I brought you into my home. I welcomed you. I shared with you the most precious thing I have, my memories. I would give anything to gaze one last time upon John's painting of Alisha and the others. You have used them, all of them, Alisha, John, Reuben... for what? Revenge. Revenge is for the weak. It is underestimated, Abriana.'

'I'm sorry, I'm so sorry, Pavlos. Believe me, I wish I could change what I've done.'

'And so do I, but you can't.'

There is no point in trying to deny it. He is right. 'No, I can't.'

She reaches over to him, her eyes pleading, 'Please forgive me, please try to find it in your heart to forgive me. I was wrong, so wrong. I can see that now. You're right, Pavlos, I don't feel how I thought I would. I just feel shame and worst of all, I have caused you so much pain and you have been nothing but kind to us since the day we came.'

She stares at his bent head. 'I have lied, betrayed and broken trust. What have I become?' Her voice drops to a whisper. 'Please say something, Pavlos.'

He looks up. 'What do you want me to say? *I forgive you.* It hurts Alisha, doesn't it? It's not my forgiveness you need. Can you forgive yourself? That's what matters. If it helps, I understand why you did it. Such things are as ancient as the world itself. History is littered with it, as are our own personal histories. None of us is innocent, Abriana.' He takes her hand then and says, 'It seems to me you're running away from something. What are you running away from?'

She looks at Mark. How can he ever trust her again? And then at Pavlos, who is holding her gaze, and in his old face, she can see a look of compassion.

There is now a lightness in her heart, and wiping her tears with a napkin, she says softly, 'From me.'

Mark is slightly disturbed that he has not been aware of what has been a personal and emotional struggle. 'Abriana, you should have said something to me.'

'I've struggled for so long. It's been a nightmare. Some days I just cry. From nowhere, it just comes over me. I didn't realise how bad it got, until once, just before I got involved in this case, it went through my mind...' she gulps some air. 'This is so hard.' She bites her knuckles.

'Take your time.' Pavlos' voice soothes her.

'I took a bottle of Paracetamol and vodka.'

'You took an overdose?' Mark gasps.

She combs a hand through her hair. Her hand is shaking. 'Almost. I had them out on the kitchen table. By that time I had drunk a lot of vodka. All I had to do was take the pills.'

'And then what happened?' Mark asks, still struggling to believe what he is hearing.

'The phone rang.'

'And you answered it?'

'No. I let it go onto the answering machine.'

'And who was it?'

'It was the Uffizi. They wanted me to go to Edinburgh, and interview Alan Sutton about his claim to a newly discovered painting. I had been involved with the case for about two weeks by then.'

'And that stopped you.'

She closes her eyes and takes a deep breath. 'No. you did, Mark.'

'Me. I don't understand.'

'Yes. Edinburgh had a personal significance. You were

there. I felt this immense urge to see you again. I felt relieved.'

Mark doesn't know what to say. The magnitude of her words strikes him forcibly.

'In a way, you saved me.' Abriana can feel her handshake. She is finding this an effort, but she needs to tell them.

'By then, I'd lost all my confidence. Oh, I was good at not showing it in public, but when I was alone, that's when this incredible feeling of self-doubt came over me. I laughed at the jokes in the office, I smiled, and pretended to be interested in people, their holidays, their dogs, their complaints about work. I was an excellent actor. That's all it was. Inside, I screamed. I wanted to be alone. This thing inside my head clouded my mind. I'd lost all my motivation, my drive was non-existent, I just went through the motions. The parts of my job that I identified with, that made me get up in the morning and go to work, didn't have the same pull anymore. I could have quite easily let others take on my roles within my job. I struggled to find the person I was, I struggled with the person I had become.'

'Abriana, if this is too hard for you, just leave it. You don't need to upset yourself. It can wait,' Mark says.

She dismisses his concern with a wave of her hand. 'I want you to know you, of all the people, you deserve to know the truth. I now know I had depression... have depression. At the time, I knew there was something wrong with me. I didn't know what depression felt like. That happened to other people, weak people, not someone like me. I just knew I wasn't in control of my feelings. They controlled me, and I couldn't change how I felt. I was digging a black hole, and each day, it got deeper and deeper, and it was swallowing me.' She wipes her tears. 'I had a few weeks before I was due to travel to Edinburgh. So, after that phone call, the thought of taking those pills really scared me. I got help. I went to my G.P. and was put on anti-depressants. The doctor wanted to sign me off work, but I made up a story that I was going on a four-week cruise, so there was no need to. I needed to be at work because by then, that's when it all came to me. I hadn't done this to myself. The Roma Gallery and its precious sanctum of respectability and their untouchable brand were responsible. Those people changed my life, they ruined it. I thought some of them were more than just colleagues, some were my friends also, or so I thought. In my head, I had devised the perfect plan. I would ruin their reputation. I would humiliate them. I would make them pay.' She pauses. This was who she had become and saying those words only deepened her sense of remorse and regret.

Mark is looking at her mouth, watching as the words tumble from her. How could he have not known it was that bad? He can't even comprehend what must have been going through her mind. Even now, after all this and what is yet still to come, he knows he still loves her, and he can't help but think she has the most beautiful mouth he has ever seen.

Abriana catches her breath. 'By that time, I had been in contact with Buchanan. We met several times as part of my research. I learnt the measure of the man, and it wasn't too long before he was telling me about his money worries. He fell into my hands. In the end, I didn't need to persuade him to sell the painting, he couldn't wait to.' The thought of it now pains her.

'And how are you now?' Pavlos asks, lightly.

'I'm feeling better. I take each day as it comes. Some are better than others. I realise now... well, as you said, Pavlos, I can't change what has been done.'

'But you have begun to change.'

The relief is so total and unexpected. Mark notes that Abriana hesitates before she nods her head. 'Yes, I suppose I have.' The softness and gentleness of Pavlos' voice make her want to cry again. 'I'm afraid,' Abriana says truthfully.

The tension that was in the air no longer exists. Abriana's large almond eyes glisten with a wave of fresh tears, and Mark rises from his chair to comfort her. As he embraces her and the fragrance of her hair fills him, a tremor of regret, bottomless and crushing, moves through Mark's body. A few hours ago, he thought, coming here was the single worst decision of his life. It might have been, he thinks now, the reason that saves them both.

Pavlos coughs into his handkerchief, a deep rattle evident.

'Are you sure you're alright?' Mark is concerned. He has noticed Pavlos' cough has worsened by the day.

'It's just a cold, a silly cold.' He turns to Abriana. 'What happens when this man takes the test?'

'If the test is positive, Alan Sutton has a claim to the painting. But, if it's not, he is no longer our concern. His claim is void. So, you see, Pavlos, Mark and I, being here, is still as important as it always were. In a way, it's more important now. Whatever happens, you are a first-hand witness, the only person alive today who knew John Sutton. Your account of that time is invaluable to art historians and the art world. They'll write books about it.' She smiles.

'It doesn't matter what happens, or what this Alan Sutton says. I know the truth. Only I know the truth. After all, I was there, with John and...' he trails off.

'You said John, and there was someone else, wasn't there?' Mark asks.

'There are certain things you don't know, not yet, things that happened. It is difficult for me to talk about.' Pavlos sounds regretful and sad. 'It was such a long time ago.' He pauses. 'Another life.'

'Pavlos.' Abriana hesitates. 'You don't have to tell us about it. We don't need to know.'

'But that's just it. You need to know. I have to tell you. You will know the results of this test by tomorrow?'

'More than likely.' Mark nods.

'Then we don't have long.'

'Are you sure you want to continue? We can come back tomorrow,' Abriana says.

'No.' he nods his head. 'It's more important now than ever.'

The Story of Alisha Hadley

Athens 1905

She finds the church by chance. Turning a corner, it stands in front of her. It is smaller than most she has seen in Athens, but similar in construction: whitewashed walls and terracotta tiled roof. The polished wooden doors are open, an invitation to enter. She thinks a few minutes of escaping the heat will be time well spent.

The interior is a surprise to her. It is large and not what she expected. She sits in a pew and her first impression is one of amazement at the richness of colour that lights the walls, depictions of saints, Our Lady and Christ, emblazoned in the yellow and golden light. The walls are shielded in a dark wood, intricately carved and styled.

She has a moment of panic. She is alone and feels like an intruder. The church has a life of its own and soon as she sits; it has a calming effect. A cloak of solitude rests upon her and she embraces the silence she has willingly entered. She has escaped the imprisonment and restrictions of the outside world, and it is enlightening. For the first time in what has seemed a lifetime, her mind is still and quiet. The incense is overpowering, but at the same time, it is emancipating, freeing her worries and anxieties, thoughts that have plagued her and she finds herself inhaling its scent with deep satisfaction and fulfilling breaths.

The eyes of the saints, Mary and Christ, look down upon her in an emblazonment of rich colour, so profound in its effect, she feels the eyes of God himself upon her.

The altar shimmers in yellow and gold. A glimmer of heaven, perhaps. She still has her faith. It is absorbed in her human condition, and it brings down the walls she builds, brick by brick, revealing its infinite condition.

Recently, she acknowledges, her eyes have been closed, blocking out the hurt in her life. But, in the here and now, in this church of Orthodoxy, of burning candles, icons and ancient scriptures, it is impossible not to see clearly, through a vision of clarity. And then a strange thing happens. The resolve she has been trying so hard to maintain for so long now suddenly gives way.

When she steps out into the blistering sunshine, something inside her has changed. Suddenly, she feels light and weightless, and events are carrying her like a kite in the wind.

That night, in her room, Alisha reluctantly packs her trunk. She is careful with her dresses, folding them with care, trying to avoid creases. In the wardrobe, she has left her favourite dress. She will wear it tomorrow at the start of her journey home. She remembers Alfred had passed comment on how he thought the colour suited her complexion. It is a garment of deep sapphire. She can feel tears well in her eyes. At times she feels furious with Alfred, for leaving them, for never returning. She shuts her eyes and they sting.

She glances around the room; it is a wrench to leave. She is not ready to go. Alisha sits on the edge of the bed and smooths the sheets with her hand. She tilts her head to the ceiling and wonders how her days spent here have turned so quickly into weeks. She can feel a tension building behind her eyes.

It surprised her, and at the same time, pleased her, that she has adjusted to living in Athens. Her mind has acclimatized to the sounds, the smells, the food and the heat. There is something about the light, it was the same in Corfu, where it often polished the soft stone and stucco of the tall and slim Venetian houses, peeling pastel paint, blemished and faint, amongst narrow streets and lanes where washing hung from balconies, like multi-coloured flags. She often thinks of her time in Corfu, especially the sea with its myriad hues of blue and green.

Her mind has also accommodated the slight suggestion of a rounded stomach, and she has spoken at length with Reuben regarding the difficulties they will surely face on their return to London. She cannot think about what lies ahead of her without feeling a rush of lightheadedness and the loud beating of her heart. It contrasts with the hush of the room around her.

She could not leave without saying goodbye to Andreas. That would have been unforgivable.

. . .

In the garden, Alisha luxuriates in the soft tinge of heat in the late afternoon. The trees cast precise shadows as she sits in her usual place, hands placed on her lap, whilst she waits. Andreas usually passes through the garden on his way home and she has met him here many times now. As she waits, Alisha trains an eye along the branches of one particular tree. She is relieved to see the young chicks are still there and growing stronger by the day. Alisha's face loosens. It brings a small smile to her face. Life carries on. It doesn't stop. Its energy is consistent.

'Kalispera Alisha.' Andreas sits down slowly; his back is stiff and his muscles ache.

'You look tired, Andreas. This is a job for a younger man. You do too much, more than is expected of you.'

'I can't change my nature. What would I do all day and anyway, if I didn't come each day to work, I wouldn't see you? You are like a summer's day in a storm. You bring a heat to my heart that radiates throughout my day.'

'You sound like you've swallowed a book full of poems, and poor ones at that.' Alisha grins and it brings a reprieve to her heavy heart.

'I'm sorry, it was dreadful, you're right, but it's true.'

She looks at Andreas. 'Are you alright?'

'My grandson is going to America. He has bought his ticket for the ship. I can't blame him, really, but his mother is beside herself. There is nothing here for the young. I have a brother who lives in Boston. At least he will have somewhere to stay.'

Alisha averts her eyes, and Andreas observes she is troubled.

'You're leaving too?'

She nods her head; her voice has deserted her.

'When?'

'Tomorrow morning.'

'Ah, so this is our last time together in our little garden. There was always going to be an end, you knew that.'

'But it doesn't make it any easier. Why is it that every person I love eventually ends up leaving me? It's only a matter of time before Reuben does.' Her voice cracks.

'Nonsense. Any fool can see he adores you; you'd have to be dumb and blind not to know, and anyway, I'm not leaving you.'

'No. I'm the one that's leaving.'

'I will always be with you, Alisha, and you will always be with me.' Andreas places his hand on his heart. 'In here, always.'

She takes a handkerchief from her sleeve and wipes her eyes. She closes them briefly.

'The pain is terrible, Andreas. What has happened is unimaginable.' She cannot imagine surviving another day and then she thinks of the life already growing inside her. And that is all she can do is think, because it has not announced its presence yet, with a little flurry, like a butterfly in her stomach. Alisha has the presence of mind that she hasn't told Andreas yet.

She stops herself. She had thought she would tell him, but now, as she sits with him, she hesitates, unsure of what his reaction might be. She doesn't want to put him in that position, even more, Alisha could not forgive herself if her revaluation upset or angered Andreas, especially now, as there will be no time to repair it. She is not ready to tell others, not even those close to her.

'I'll write to you.' And then she thinks. 'Can you read English?'

Andreas smiles. 'Yes, I can. I learnt a long time ago.'

Alisha remembers the girl he loved in his youth. 'Was it Elizabeth who taught you?'

'It was. An English girl taught me to speak and read her language and because of that, another will be able to write me letters from England. Life has its way of making things happen. It has its reasons.'

'I'll never see you again.'

'You might find your way back here one day,' he says, his face creasing into a smile.

'At this moment in time, it doesn't feel like that.'

'What will happen to the Quartet when you're back home? Will you continue to play?'

'I hope so. I've no other way to earn a living. It's all I know. Reuben thinks we'll still be able to perform. To be honest, we haven't really spoken about it, together that is. I think we're all still too shocked by what's happened.'

Andreas nods his head. 'Well, with what I've heard, and I'm no expert, but I'm sure people will still want to hear you play.' He looks at her seriously. 'Will you promise me one thing, Alisha?'

She looks at him and tries to lock the image of his face in her mind. 'Of course.'

'Be happy, find contentment, whatever that may be. Don't waste a single day worrying about the things you can't change or what other people say, or do, or what they may think of you. Be true to yourself. You're a beautiful person Alisha and I'm honoured to have spent time with you. This garden won't feel as lonely if I know you're happy.'

She takes his hand in both of hers and squeezes it. 'I

promise, Andreas. Oh, how I am going to miss you.' She tries hard to smile, but she can no longer hold back her tears.

'And I promise to look after your little birds until they have grown.' He nods towards the tree and smiles. 'There's going to be a few disappointed cats around here.'

Alisha awakes and sits on the edge of the bed; the floorboards are freezing under her feet. She slips her feet into slippers and walks over to the window. She wonders what time it is, as the room is shrouded in that intermediate and muted luminosity of not quite dark, but still not light. She moves the heavy curtains just a little, and the grim appearance of silver threads of rain soaks the London streets.

'I think it has been raining all night.'

'Come back to bed. It's too early to get up,' Reuben mumbles.

'I can't sleep. The baby keeps moving.' She strokes her rounded stomach; it has become a habit she performs instinctively. Her ritual.

'I'll make some tea. Do you want some?'

Reuben pulls the covers over his head and she shivers in the chill. Alisha puts on her dressing gown. She remembers it is Sunday, and she hopes the rain will clear, so that they can walk in the park after lunch, but other thoughts chill her heart.

In the kitchen, she starts a fire, fills the kettle and places it over the fire to boil. She can feel her worries kindle in her stomach.

It has been seven months since their return from Athens. For Alisha, this feels like a lifetime away. She shivers and wraps a shawl around her shoulders. When she coughs, it feels as if her lungs are being stabbed. The pain is sharp and intense.

They returned to London and attended Alfred's funeral, which was an ostentatious spectacle of wealth and privilege. It troubled Alisha, as this was not the Alfred she knew and loved like a father. No one questioned James. In fact, he acted like a man absorbed in his duty as executor of Alfred's will, to which he implied he was following by the letter. He emanated an aloof aura and Alisha had loathed it; she told Rueben so.

A week after the funeral, Alisha learnt Alfred had specified that in the event of his death, she was to receive a yearly sum of money. The sum disclosed in due course. Weeks passed without a word from him. When she spoke with Reuben and told him she was becoming increasingly troubled. At first, he was not duly concerned, but as Alisha expressed her worry, he too felt something was not quite right. They informed Alex and Sara about their concern. Both had not seen nor heard from James either. Alisha felt her stomach being pulled from the inside. Her instincts were now insistent something was terribly wrong.

Eventually, the four of them met with Alfred's lawyer, a man of careful and methodical habits called Joseph Fleming, and when they gathered in his office, it was evident he was troubled. They listened to him, fearing the worst. He echoed a man defeated and professionally ruined. He was vociferously insistent that in all his thirty years of practising law, such shame had never fallen upon him; it had ruined him. The matter was now a police concern. The circumstances and details of how James executed his theft were, as at that moment, being investigated by the police. An adrenaline-fuelled panic seized Alisha. Did she ask how much had been stolen? She could not bring herself to voice his name. Only Alfred's properties remained, and the money in overseas bank accounts. *But how is it possible? How can this be? How could you let this happen? Alfred put his trust in you.* Alisha was incredulous. Joseph averted his eyes, his embarrassment was unmistaken, and it was apparent it shamed him.

They walk arm in arm in the park. The sun is low in the sky; it has made an appearance from behind the clouds and warms their backs against the chill of the air. The baby is due any day now and the occasional pram being pushed by a smiling woman, accompanied by a doting husband, is a reminder, they too will be a family.

'I know I don't say it as often as I should, but you know I love you, Alisha.'

'You don't have to; you tell me every day by the way you look at me. I see it in your eyes.'

'You do. I didn't know.'

'That's what makes it special.' She smiles, and she snuggles into his arm.

'I forgot to say, Alex sends his love. He is being posted to India. I'm not sure he'll be suited to army life, but he seems enthusiastic enough. He said the training was a bit rough, but there's a chance he'll get to play in the military band. He always said he preferred the trumpet to the violin.' Rueben is smiling, and he lights a cigarette. 'Have you heard from Sara?'

'No. Not for a while now.'

'What was that chaps name again?'

'Bertie Bullins.'

'That's it, I remember now. His father's a lord or something.'

'He is. They have an estate near Southampton. Sara was sure he was going to ask her to get engaged, seemingly he hinted on several occasions, but I've not heard from her in a while.'

Rueben gestures with his cigarette. 'I knew she would land on her feet.'

'What does that mean?'

'Well, you know.'

'No, I don't.'

'No one was ever going to be any good for her unless they had a lot of money.'

'That's unfair. She wasn't like that.'

'Then we're talking about a different person. Lady Bullins. It doesn't really have a ring to it, does it? I'm sure that'll disappoint her.'

'Reuben, you're being unkind.'

'It's the truth.'

'I know.' They both laugh, and it feels like a reprieve.

They walk in silence for a while. 'What are you thinking about?' Reuben asks.

'You'll have to accept The London Orchestra's offer. We have no choice. Soon we'll have no money.'

'I'll be away for six weeks. How will you manage on your own with a newborn baby?'

'I've no option. I'll just have to.'

Reuben sighs. There is no reply he can make. Without the money from this job, they could not afford the rent for Alisha's house. The thought of them being homeless is too much to bear. He remains silent. His belief that the quartet could secure regular bookings on their own merit when they returned from Greece was, in retrospect, optimistic at best. Now, in the cold light of day, he realises how foolish he has been.

He can sense Alisha is tiring.

'We could go back now if you want. It's not a good idea to walk too far.'

'I'm fine. I'm enjoying the air.'

'What if we sit here for a while, then?'

They sit on a park bench. Alisha's face, drawn and pale, worries Reuben.

'I'm supposed to protect you, keep you safe. How can I do that? I feel helpless.'

'Just having you with me every day is enough. Knowing that you are there for me is all I can ask for.' Alisha flinches.

'What is it?'

'Just a pain in my back.'

'I knew this was a bad idea. We should have stayed indoors.'

'I'm tired of staring at four walls all day, Reuben.' She coughs and covers her mouth with a gloved hand. She bends forward and her chest and lungs heave. The pain in her back is sharp and a muscle spasm feels like the worst cramp she has ever experienced. Reuben puts a hand on her shoulder. He has been worried for days about her worsening condition.

'This is madness, Alisha.' He stands and guides her to her feet. 'We're going home now, and I'll get a doctor to see you. This has gone on far too long.' His mind is driven, his thoughts compressed, he is panicking.

'We don't have the money for a doctor.'

'The hospital won't turn you away. Yes, we need to go there.'

'It's too far.'

'I'll get a carriage.'

'No.' She is insistent. 'I want to go home.'

'You have to think of the baby.'

'It's healthy and strong. I feel it kick all the time. Please Reuben, just take me home.'

Against his better judgement, he relents.

'Your sweating, Alisha.'

She can do nothing now but nod her head. 'Just take me home.'

He undresses her, as she has not the strength to lift her arms. He helps her to bed and wipes her forehead with a wet cloth. He slides the back of his hand over her cheek. Unexpectedly, her skin is hot and sticky. He straightens her hair along the pillow and over her shoulders. It is an act that tries to bring a sense of normality to the room but fails. He pulls the sheets over her. Her eyes, normally large and full of expression, are now dull and hollow. She closes her eyes, and it feels that too is an effort, a struggle for her. If she looked at him then, Alisha would see an astonished and alarmed expression on Reuben's face. His eyes are strained, and Reuben rubs them, hoping to erase this face before him which at this moment scares him, but in which he also finds beautiful. All he can think about is how suddenly her physical health has declined in front of him. It feels like he is in a dream and he will wake from this nightmare any moment now. His head feels hot and tight.

'I'm thirsty. I need some water.' Alisha's voice is faint and whispery. He notices then that her lips are dry.

'I'll be as quick as I can.'

In the kitchen, he is in a blind panic, frantically opening

cupboards, searching for cups, a glass, anything. His normal rational thought processes and functioning skills are disabled. They have quite extraordinary, abandoned him. Eventually, he fills a cup with water. From the window, he can see his neighbour hanging white sheets on a washing line.

He rushes outside, and it is then that he notices it is raining. Mrs Gillis is taking her washing in, not hanging it out. From the kitchen, this fact didn't register with him. His voice chokes. 'Mrs Gillis! Mrs Gillis!'

Her head appears from behind a sheet. 'Hello, Reuben. Are you alright?'

'I need a doctor. You need to get a doctor. I can't leave her.'

Reuben's expression alarms Mrs Gillis. 'Is the baby on its way? Do you need the midwife?'

'Just get a doctor, please. As quick as you can.'

Mrs Gillis has seen this look before, many times, as a nurse on the wards of London's hospitals. It is an expression that infuses an urgency about her. She abandons her sheets. 'Don't worry, my dear. Arthur will get the doctor; I'll be right round. You get back indoors. I'll just be a minute.'

Days have passed as a continuous sequence. Reuben has lost track of time, existing only in the moment. He has eaten little and has only drunk the tea that Mrs Gillis makes for him when she stays to watch over Alisha. He sleeps in their bedroom, sometimes in the chair, or when Alisha is settled, he lies beside her. Only occasionally will his mind allow his body to succumb to sleep. Even then, his sleep is shallow, and he wakes often to calm himself and check on Alisha.

Alisha is lost to him. When she is not sleeping, she is incoherent. She surfaces into his world, only to stare at the ceiling. When she coughs, she now brings up blood. Her breathing is rapid, and he watches her chest rise and fall, willing it to continue. He speaks to her constantly. He doesn't know if she can hear him and he isn't conscious of what he says. Most of the time, he just talks to her. He wants her to hear his voice, so she knows he is there with her, and she is not alone. He holds her hand and gazes at her eyes in concentrated attention, watching to see any movement, any flicker of recognition, or movement in her hand, however slight, that would convey she can hear him. His heart is left heavy.

The doctor visits each morning at eight, and by chance, and a fortuitous coincidence, Reuben learns, he regarded Alfred as a close friend. It transpires the doctor often attended many of Alfred's dinner parties and always looked forward to The Quartet's performances, which he told Reuben he enjoyed immensely.

He has waved his fee. Not from an obligation of charity, which he was at pains to express, but as an expression of his gratitude for the many hours of pleasure their music gave him. It was the least he could do; he told Reuben.

Reuben has no means to pay him by. It is a blessing Reuben gratefully receives. It is the only thing that eases his mind.

Reuben glances out of the window. The sun is bright and low in the sky. He notices rain marks on the glass, running its length, and beyond, in the street, people go about their business. Reuben wants to scream at them and jolt them out of their ordinariness, their contentment. He wants to stop them from putting one foot in front of the other and bring an end to their mundane day, their monotonous existence, their indecisions and thoughts. He wants to scream at them. His world is ebbing away from me, lying lifeless in a bed.

There is a moment, he thinks, he should join them, he envies them. A wave of grief replaces the anger that pushes and bubbles. Reuben leans his hands against the sink and bends forward. He muffles with his hand a noise that comes from deep within him, an unintelligible sound. He has the presence of mind not to let the others hear.

A panicked voice carries from the other room. It is calling his name. His eyes are uncertain and wide.

Mrs Gillis stands in the doorway. Almost reluctantly, she crosses the room and moves closer to him, placing a hand on his shoulder. 'It's started. The midwife said it would be best if you stayed here. I just need to get a few things.'

He is momentarily confused. The baby. How can she give birth? It is unthinkable? Reuben collapses into a chair and holds his head in his hands. He is exhausted, but the ache inside is worse.

He knows the second he sees Mrs Gillis' face that something is terribly wrong. 'Oh Reuben, I'm so sorry.' At that moment, his legs go from under him. He holds on to the table for support. There is a noise in his head. It seems to block out the world around him. He sinks to the floor.

Mrs Gillis is speaking, and he tries to take her words in. He thought he had prepared himself for this. It was always on his mind, but the reality is different. Reuben is not ready; he would never be ready. He tries to comprehend that Alisha no longer breathes; she is not with him; she does not exist. He sways backwards and forwards and wraps his hands around his head. He moans, 'No.' and slaps the side of his head with the heel of his hands.

Mrs Gillis bends her knees stiffly and kneels next to him. She takes his face in her hands and turns his head, so that he is looking at her. 'Listen to me, Reuben, listen. You need to think about the baby now. The baby is what matters.'

'The baby?' He gulps air and looks at her, trying to organise his thoughts.

'Yes. The baby, Reuben. It's a boy.'

This new information dazes him. It is almost as if Alisha has come back from the dead.

CHAPTER NINETEEN

A LETTER

Abriana and Mark sit in silence. Pavlos' sonorous voice is still.

'She died,' Abriana says in disbelief. 'Poor Alisha. Oh God, how sad. I thought she would get well. I'd hoped, anyway.'

'Was it pneumonia?' Mark asks.

Pavlos nods his head. 'In those days, it wasn't unusual for a healthy woman to die in labour. Alisha was too ill by then. I don't think it would have come as a shock. Even Reuben would have known this. Saving the baby was probably the priority.'

It feels like they have just heard the news of a friend's death. That is how much the story has affected them. Abriana is clearly upset.

'Are you alright?' Mark asks.

'I feel silly. She's been dead a long time.'

'It's like watching a film or reading a book. You become attached to the characters. If it makes you feel any better, I had a sneaky tear in my eye that I wiped.'

'Did you?'

He nods his head. 'I feel close to her. I know that sounds weird. But I do. The second I saw her in the painting, it was like I knew her, that I had met her before. She was familiar to me. I can't explain it, really.'

'I know what you mean.'

Pavlos is smiling.

'What? What is it?' Abriana asks.

'It's nice to see you make up. It suits you both. I prefer it when you are talking to each other.'

She can sense his relief. 'I'm sorry, Pavlos. Were we that bad?'

Pavlos packs tobacco into his pipe. 'I'm afraid so.' He smiles, apologetically. Pavlos looks at them carefully. 'I haven't said before, but you look good together. When I first saw you for the first time, I thought you were a couple.'

'Really?' Abriana says, amused and touched.

'Yes, you're both relaxed with each other. There's an intimate air about the way you talk to each other. You have a certain familiarity with each other.' Satisfied with his analogy, Pavlos lights his pipe.

Just for a moment, Alisha's eyes are bright with tears and she tries to regain her composure. She is an emotional wreck, with her revelation about her troubles and then the sadness of Alisha's story.

Mark reaches out and touches her hand. 'I'm sorry.'

'For what?'

'Judging you, blaming you, instead of listening to you.' He is filled with a sense of unfulfilled longing.

'You, of all people, know me better than anyone, but I wasn't myself. When I look back at that time, even I don't recognise myself. Don't blame yourself. I don't blame you for how you reacted.'

Mark hates his stubbornness, his judgemental snobbery. 'What gave me the right to act the way I did?' His reaction was so predictable, he now thinks. Her smile encourages him. 'I'll make it up to you, I promise.'

Abriana laughs. It is the first time Mark has seen her so relaxed in days. 'What's so funny?'

'It sounds like a proposition.'

'Well, maybe it is.'

'Good. I'll look forward to it then.'

'Have you two finished flirting? I've still got a story to finish, remember?' Pavlos says with a wry smile. 'And come on, eat up, this food needs to be eaten, or it will just get thrown out.'

'I'm on it.' Mark grins, popping an olive into his mouth.

Abriana looks embarrassed, but today has transformed her, and her determination to make things right between Mark and herself has doubled. I still want you; she tells herself.

'Alisha never got to see her baby. How awful. Life can be cruel, can't it?'

'It happened a lot in those days, mothers dying in child-birth. I remember, in my village, we lived in the hills, and I don't think there was a single family who was untouched by the death of a newborn or its mother,' Pavlos says.

'I hope she was happy. Do you think she was? She was with Reuben, so I suppose she would have been,' Abriana says brightly, convincing herself.

Mark thought for a while. 'I think it would have been tough for them. It sounds as if Reuben didn't get much work.'

'Poor Reuben, having to bring up a baby on his own. How did he manage? Do you know, Pavlos?' Abriana asks.

'He didn't, I'm afraid.'

'You can't blame him, I suppose,' Mark says, trying to be generous.

'Why, what happened?'

Pavlos puffs on his pipe. He coughs, this time slightly too long for Mark's liking.

'You need to get that cough seen to it's getting worse.'

'It's nothing.'

'Smoking that thing won't help. How long have you had it? You've coughed every day.'

Pavlos thinks. 'A week, maybe no more.'

'Promise you'll see a doctor, Pavlos,' Abriana says.

'I will, I will. I promise. I want to show you something.'

'What?'

Pavlos leans to the side and picks up a cardboard box the size of a shoebox. He places it on the table.

'When the Germans arrived at John's villa, he had the presence of mind to hide belongings that were special to him. Just small items. The paintings were too big. We hid things all over the villa. Anyway, when the Germans left, I remembered about this box. I've kept it ever since. Sentimental value, I suppose. It's my connection to the villa, to John and Lysander.'

'Who?'

'Lysander Sutton.' Pavlos' voice almost fails. It flounders. He smiles at them both. 'He is the reason you are here. He is the answer to your question.'

. . .

Pavlos explains Reuben had two choices. He either stayed to look after the baby, or he took the job with the orchestra. Apprehensively, he asked Mrs Gillis if she would take the baby for him. She agreed, as it was on the condition of it only being for six weeks. On Reuben's return, after the six weeks, he told Mrs Gillis that he had been offered a permanent position, playing in the orchestra. It meant that he would be touring the country for weeks at a time. He asked if she would continue to care for the baby. Mrs Gillis was adamant that she could not commit to such an arrangement. She and Mr Gillis were too old and besides, a child needed its actual parent to form an attachment. It needed to know who its father was. Reuben could feel his happiness drain from him. Although the money was not much, it was a secure income, something he had not enjoyed since he returned to London. He also relished the social comradery amongst his fellow musicians. It was his opportunity finally to make something of his life. He was determined. This may be his only chance.

To say that he didn't struggle with his conscience would have been unfair. But as each day passed, he became more frustrated and angrier. He knew, deep inside, he had already made his decision. If anything was to undermine his intentions, it was the thought that he was not just about to abandon his child; It was Alisha's child too, her flesh and blood.

He sat down with pen and paper. At first, he could hardly glance at the sheet in front of him, as he tried to formulate the words that would be persuasive in describing why a father abandons their child of only two months. With each word, his eyes became moist and as he expanded on and grasped the essentials as to his reasons. His eyes became fiery with tears because it exposed the man he really was, the man he could no longer hide from, this weak, shameful man.

Pavlos opens the lid of the box and takes out a brown envelope creased with age. Abriana notices a name and address written on it. Pavlos places the envelope in the middle of the table.

'Is that the actual letter?'

Pavlos nods.

Mark leans forward. 'It has John Sutton's name on it and a London address.'

'Take the letter out, read it.'

Abriana takes the envelope in her hands. She opens the flap and slowly takes the letter out. As she opens the sheets of paper, she hesitates; it seems inconceivable that she can feel, between her fingers, the actual letter. She is aware it is a document of great importance. She looks at the handwriting, the way each letter curls at the edges. A flick of the pen exaggerates certain letters. Towards the last few lines, the writing feels hurried, the letters smaller, as if the author is impatient to finish, or he has lost his composure. The words dance before her eyes.

'What does it say?' Mark asks anxiously.

She clears her throat and reads the letter out loud. 'Dear John, I'm aware that this correspondence will take you by surprise and, quite possibly by astonishment. This is a difficult matter for me to write about and it puts us both in an intricate position. It is with a heavy heart that I must inform you of Alisha's passing...'

The letter describes Reuben and Alisha's life in London, her pregnancy and illness. He is at pains to defend his decision to place the baby in a workhouse, where he hopes it will be nourished and given the care, he cannot afford it. Reuben hopes John will find it in his heart to forgive him; it is a choice that, if Alisha was alive, he would not have to make, and it will live with him and shame him every day. Reuben writes the address of the workhouse in hopeful anticipation that one-day John might find it within himself to spare the child a life of poverty that is undoubtedly ahead and take it in as his own.

Abriana's mind freezes. She finds it inconceivable that a father could do such a thing.

Abriana continues to read. 'I have written an account of Alisha and I's time in Corfu and Athens and our return to London. You will find it with this letter. For whatever reason, I don't know why, but I felt it was the right thing to do, and if I am honest, which I have tried to be through this letter, it has helped me greatly. It is my desire that it gives you a sense of how happy Alisha was and how she had an affiliation and a deep love of the country that is Greece. It may help to ease your loss, for I know, on my part, it has made me realise it was a moment in time I was privileged to share with her and it will live with me until my dying breath. It brings me so much contentment that I could watch Alisha flourish and blossom. I will forever hold the memory in my mind. It is my comforter.

'It is with a great amount of soul searching that I have come to my decision. You may struggle to see the logic in it, and even hate me. I would not blame you, let me assure you, it was not taken lightly. The arrangements have been made and the baby will be leaving tomorrow, whereupon I will depart London. It would ease my conscience greatly if you could find it within yourself, and are moved enough, to spare the child and myself this ordeal, by taking it into your care. I will understand if you find such a prospect impossible and abhorrent. I would not blame you. I merely ask as I feel it is my duty to do so. If such a thing were possible you have my blessing. It might interest you to learn that before Alisha became too ill, she had chosen the name, Lysander if the baby was a boy...'

Abriana stops reading. Her face is stony. She places the letter on the table and sighs. Mark knows exactly what she is thinking.

'So, you see, Abriana. This is how I know Alan Sutton is not who he thinks he is. He's related to Lysander, his great-grandfather, there's no disputing that, but he's not related to John Sutton. John never had children.'

'But that's not the name on the birth certificate. We have a copy. The name of the child was Fredrick, there was no surname recorded either.' Abriana is bewildered.

Pavlos smiles. 'I know, and I will explain it all in good time.'

'So, John went to the workhouse and took this child... Lysander into his home.' Abriana thinks out loud.

'Well, not exactly. It took him a while.'

'What do you mean?'

Pavlos explains it came as a great shock to John, learning about Alisha's death and the baby. He was still in love with her, he always was. The memories of their time together came flooding back. He had tried so hard to erase her from his mind, but his attempts were futile.

He felt unimaginable guilt; he blamed himself for her death. If only he hadn't let his pride get in the way, if only he had gone back to her and apologised, begged her forgiveness. He had made the worst error of his life. He should have persuaded her to stay, he knew, deep inside, he would have then asked her to marry him. She would have stayed and not gone to Greece. She would have still been alive. It could have been his son she gave birth to, and they would have been a family.

He felt Reuben had humiliated Alisha; he had deeply dishonoured her; it appalled him. It unsettled his concentration; he trembled with emotion and at the same time, it eventually transformed him.

The Story of Alisha Hadley

London 1906

It takes John over a week to come to terms with the fact he can't live another day knowing Alisha's baby is in a workhouse.

Once he arrives, he meets a stern-looking woman with sharp features and scowling eyes who escorts him along a long corridor. They pass small wards, overcrowded, little rooms, no more than cells, with a floor of wooden blocks. John tries but fails not to look, his stomach hollow with pity and disgust. As they progress up a staircase, John senses a redolence of hopelessness that seems to seep from the tiled walls.

The governor's office is a small room with books on philosophy, history and religion lining the walls. He is a large, framed man, balding, with a neatly trimmed beard. He observes John over silver-rimmed reading glasses. John notices he has been reading a file, which is still in his hand.

'Mr Sutton, what a privilege it is to finally meet you. I

must tell you, I'm an admirer of your work.' The Governor who stands up walks around his desk and welcomes John with a firm handshake. He introduces himself as Robert Darwin.

He gestures with his hand for John to sit, before settling into his chair opposite and tapping the file. 'A tragic case, but sadly, all too common. I believe you knew the gentleman.'

'I knew the mother. We were... good friends.'

'I see. Then I'm sorry for your loss. Welcome to Greyfriars, Mr Sutton. We're very proud of the place. Did you know, we are the newest built institution in London, the country, for that matter. Greyfriars comprise seven parallel three-storey pavilions separated by 80-foot-wide yards; each pavilion has space for 31 beds, a day room, a nurse's kitchen and toilets. As you will have seen, it's built to an impressive standard. We have two steam boilers with automatic stokers supplying heating and hot water throughout the building, a generator to provide electricity for the institution's 1,133 electric lamps, and electric lifts in the infirmary pavilion.'

John notes he says nothing of the unfortunate people who live in the workhouse. 'Your enthusiasm for the building is plain to see, Mr Darwin, but I'd like this matter to be concluded tonight.'

'Of course, as you wish. There is a note in the paperwork that stipulates the father, a Reuben Bernstein, sees it proper and fit that in the event of a certain John Sutton requesting custody of the child, he gives his full consent and support. He goes on to say, that in the event of this custody being granted, he, Reuben Bernstein, would find this an acceptable conclusion.' Robert looks at John closely. John has detected a tone of diplomacy in the Governor's voice.

'I would require written assurance that he would never contest this.'

'He was already one step ahead of you.' Robert pulls a sheet of paper from the file and hands it to John. He opens his hand with an invitation for John to read the contents.

'I presume this meets with your approval and sets your worries at ease.'

'Quite.' John hands the sheet back to Robert. 'I'd like to take the baby with me tonight, if that is possible?'

Robert smiles. 'Of course. There is just one more thing, the question of your generosity.'

'You will find it is the agreed amount. You are welcome to check.' John pulls an envelope from his inside pocket and hands it to Robert, who opens it.

Robert can't keep the grin off his face. 'Your charitable donation will go a long way to continue the good work we strive to emulate each day. Every man, woman and child, under our roof, would thank you personally, if they could.'

John is beginning to feel a distinct dislike for the man with each sentence Robert speaks.

John sucks air over his teeth. 'I have your word then that this guarantees my anonymity? because I will hold you responsible if this transaction, for that is what it is Mr Darwin finds its way into the public domain. I don't have to remind you of the consequences that would fall upon you personally.'

Robert's eyes widen, and an ingratiating smile makes John distrust the man even more. 'I give you my personal assurance, Mr Sutton. I am a man of my word.'

John does not want to stay a second longer than he must.

'Is he in good health?'

'He is. Positively thriving.'

'And he is ready to leave?'

'He is. You do know the child has been named. It is on the birth certificate.'

'Yes. I'm aware of that fact.'

'Will that be a problem?'

'It is the name his mother chose, so it will be the name he is known by.'

Robert shifts in his chair. The colour runs from his face.

'Is there a problem, sir?' John asks.

'That depends. You see, Mr Sutton, when the father came to us with the child, he was in such a state that he left without telling us the child's name. There was no birth certificate. These things must be official. We need a birth certificate, we have procedures. I was the informant, so I named the child Fredrick. I didn't know the father or mother, so I was unable to put a surname.'

'I see. This is most unfortunate. I hold you responsible. It is incompetence on your part. Has the child been baptised yet?'

'No. Not yet.'

'That is the only agreeable thing that has come out of your mouth. Then the child will be known by the name his mother gave him. He will be called, Lysander.'

'Excellent. Well then, I presume your carriage is waiting.'

'It is.'

'Then I won't keep you any longer than need be.'

'My housekeeper will see the child to my carriage, she is waiting in your reception area.'

Robert extends his hand. 'Then all that remains is for me to wish you well. Mr Sutton.'

John ignores the gesture and nods his head. 'Likewise. I shall see myself out.'

John stands above the cot in the room he has had decorated into a bedroom and nursery. He has never held a baby. John strokes its head, surprised at how delicate it is to the touch. He looks down into its tiny face and it is unmistakable how the baby's features remind him of Alisha. The curve of its small mouth, the shape of its nose, its closed eyes fringed by long eyelashes. It feels as if she is in the room, her presence a tangible thing. His heart bleeds. John holds the baby's tiny hand, he crooks a finger, and the baby squeezes it with a firm grip. John smiles and then an involuntary surge of buried and repressed grief bends him forward. 'Oh Alisha, forgive me, my love.' His voice cracks, his chest heaves, and finally, his tears fall. He muffles his sounds in fear of waking the baby, whose serene face his eyes can't leave. 'I promise you with all my heart, I will love Lysander as my own flesh and blood, and he will...' his grief overcomes his words. In his mind, he wonders if Alisha eventually forgave him and now, he could see the irony of it all. For as Rueben betrayed her, by his monumental abandonment, he has also brought John an overwhelming comfort, because, through Lysander, a part of Alisha will always be with him.

CHAPTER TWENTY

REVELATIONS

Pavlos pours more wine.

Mark raises his hand. 'That's enough for me. I need to keep a clear head.'

'So, now you know. John raised Lysander as his own and as far as Lysander was concerned, John was his father.'

'Did he tell Lysander who his actual parents were?' Abriana asks.

'Eventually, when he was old enough to understand. He told him everything.'

'Did Lysander ever want to find Reuben?'

'No. Even if Lysander wanted to, John never heard from Reuben again and he never tried to contact John. It seemed he just disappeared. He must have had his reasons, hard as they are to understand.' Pavlos pauses. He looks at Abriana. 'Lysander's birth certificate is in the box. It's a copy. Also, there's a photograph of Alisha, the only one that John had when he was in Florence. It arrived by post several weeks after his visit to the workhouse. There was no accompanying letter. We can only assume it came from Rueben.'

Abriana's heart jumps. She breathes in deeply and tries to calm herself. 'A photograph of Alisha.'

Pavlos lifts the lid from the box and hands the photograph to Abriana. She stares at it for a long time. Alisha is standing holding a hat and then Abriana notices she has what looks like glasses in her other hand. Her posture is straight but relaxed, and although her hair is tied up, Alisha can see that if released, it would be thick and wavy.

'She's beautiful, just as I thought she would be. It's taken at the Acropolis in Athens. This must have been when she and Reuben visited it. Remember, he took her photograph.'

'You can see the likeness to the portrait. John captured her perfectly, don't you think?' Pavlos smiles.

'Yes, he certainly did.' She traces her finger across Alisha's face as if by doing so, she can feel her skin.

'Look, Mark.' Abriana hands the photograph to him. 'She looks so happy, so content. I feel like I know her now.' A thought crosses her mind. 'Do you know where she is buried?'

'No. I'm sorry. John told me before he left for Florence, he visited her grave with Lysander, but I don't know where. Why? Is it important?'

'No. Not for this. But I'd like to visit her one day, that's all.'

Mark looks up from the photograph and smiles. 'If you do, let me know. I'd like that too. Just to pay our respects. We owe her that, at least.'

'What made John leave London for Florence?' Abriana asks.

'He was tired of London. He had very few real friends. He knew his wealth and fame were what people were attracted to. He was a private man. He didn't want Lysander exposed to that world. Also, his asthma got worse. His doctor advised an environment with clean air. He knew Italy well; it was an easy choice to make.'

'He sold up, everything?' Mark says, leaning forward.

'It was a one-way move. He had no intention of returning to London.'

Pavlos explains, John bought the villa without seeing it, recommended to him by a politician who had rented it one summer from a wealthy Italian. Lysander was six when they arrived. John brought with him his housekeeper and her husband, who was a handyman come butler, but less formal. In London, the townhouse had no garden, but acres of lush vegetation and orchards surrounded the villa. Over the years, he employed locals to tend to the garden.

When Pavlos' father died from his accident, Pavlos was desperate, and returning to Greece was not an option. There was little work, if any, in his village. He would have to go to Athens or Thessalonica, any large city where there might be the prospect of work. So, he stayed in Florence.

Pavlos explains he learned that an Englishman, an artist, who lived in a villa not far from Florence, was looking for a gardener and handyman. The only gardening experience Pavlos had was when he helped his father grow the occasional vegetable at home, but he was good with his hands, and he had an eye for building and fixing things. The job came with lodgings, food and a little money. To Pavlos' astonishment, John offered him the job. By that time, John's reputation as a landscape artist was well established.

Mark makes a mental calculation. 'That would make Lysander... let me see, thirty-seven, thirty-eight, maybe.'

'Yes. Something like that.'

'And he was still living with John.'

'Oh no. By then, he was married to an Italian woman, much younger than he was. They met in Milan. Four months later, they married. Lysander owned a bookshop in Florence. He visited John often.'

The climate was agreeable to John's health. He adored the villa, and he grew fond of Pavlos. He often told people that visited him. He now regretted he lived in London so long and wished he'd moved sooner. John found the landscape to be an inspiration. It became an extension of his paintbrush and infused in him a newfound lease of expression. It was a creative period that saw him paint every day. Pavlos often accompanied John when he ventured into the countryside to paint. On these occasions, John spoke to Pavlos with great seriousness of his time without Alisha. He lost his confidence and fell into what he now knows was a depression. When he spoke of happier times, his face was expressive, he laughed, he smiled, his eyes were alive, his face transformed.

Pavlos cherished their companionship. He loved John's humour; he found it infectious. He hung on John's advice, his counsel, and his guidance. John replaced the great gulf Pavlos' father left, and it was a time that Pavlos experienced great happiness. There was another reason, too.

Pavlos takes a sip of his drink. 'I loved him.'

'Friendship is often stronger than family. My relationship with my best friend has outlived the one I had with my brother. We don't see each other much, not now. He lives in Australia,' Mark muses.

'I mean, I really loved, Lysander. We were lovers.' Pavlos smiles.

Mark looks at him, momentarily stunned. 'Jesus, Pavlos, I wasn't expecting that.'

'I can tell by your face.'

'I'm sorry, I didn't mean to react like that, but...'

'You don't have to apologise, Mark.'

'I do.' Mark could see Pavlos was genuine and relief rinsed over him.

'No. It's fine. I took you by surprise. We had to keep it a secret. You know, after all, he was married and, well, those were different times, not like it is today. I had been working and staying at the villa for two years by then when Lysander and I met.'

'How old were you then?' Abriana asks.

'I was eighteen.'

Pavlos tells them how they first met. He was working in the garden and Lysander was strolling through the orchard. Pavlos was shy and Lysander polite. He asked Pavlos about his home in Greece, he offered his condolences regarding Pavlos' father. After that first meeting, every visit Lysander made to the villa, he made a point of meeting Pavlos. He remembers their first kiss. Lysander was tender, delicate and his touch was gentle. Pavlos had never kissed a man before and he tells them his heart never quite recovered. As the months progressed, Pavlos was deliriously happy and came to think of the villa as his home.

'He was much older than you.'

'He was, but that didn't matter to me, nor him.'

'I think it's wonderful, Pavlos.' Abriana touches his arm affectionately.

'We could never have told, John. That would have destroyed him. So, in a way, we both deceived him, but at the same time, we sheltered him from the truth.'

'So, what happened?' Mark asks, leaning forward.

'We were together for two years and then Lysander's wife had a child. He ended it then.'

'How did you feel?' Abriana asks.

'I knew he would never leave her. After that length of time together, I accepted it. We were both happy. I suppose we were fortunate to have kept it from everyone for so long. We spent our last night crying in each other's arms. After that, he took his family to London. John had invested money into a bookshop Lysander was opening, and I never saw him again.' Pavlos says with a certain sadness. He looks at Abriana. 'It was a very long time ago. I suppose knowing about this Alan Sutton has brought it all back to me, after all, he is Lysander's great-grandson. Lysander still affects me. He influences my life, even now.' He wipes a tear.

'Oh, Pavlos.' Abriana stands and folds her arms around him.

Finally, Pavlos says, 'It's not as if I've not led a rich life. I have. It has been full of surprises, achievements, hopes and many dreams. It has had a purpose. I've loved others, but not like I loved him, Lysander. I knew nothing of his life in London, and that hurt me. I don't even know the day he died.'

When Abriana sits back in her chair, Pavlos says gently, 'So, you see, this is my story, just as much as it is, John Sutton's story.'

Abriana exhales, only now she realises how hard this must have been for Pavlos. She looks at the photograph on the table. Alisha gazes out at them and she wonders what she would have made of all of this. More than a hundred years have passed since she died and yet, it feels as if she still walks amongst them; she has touched so many people in different ways, even in death.

Abriana thinks for a moment. 'Did you ever get a photograph taken together?' She notices the darkness under his eyes.

'No. It didn't seem important at the time.'

'I wonder if Alan Sutton has a photograph of Lysander when he was older?'

Pavlos touches his head. 'I still have him in here. I often see him in my dreams, even now. He's still young, he never grows old.'

'Maybe you should keep him that way.'

'I think I will.'

A cockroach scurries along the tiled floor, and Abriana doesn't notice it. Mark knows, if she had done, she would have screamed and almost jumped onto his lap. He smiles with raised eyebrows towards Pavlos, who, catching his meaning, keeps his eye on it and watches as it disappears into the garden.

'The day the German's came to the villa changed all our lives,'

'It must have been frightening, and you were so young at the time,' Abriana says.

'By then, Mussolini had fallen. German troops entered Rome, General Badoglio and the royal family fled to Brindisi, in southeastern Italy, to set up a new antifascist government. I was used to seeing the German soldiers, but they had never come to the villa. John was an Englishman, but a famous one, who had embraced Tuscany, the language, even the religion. He had converted to Catholicism and invited to weddings and baptisms. His connections with the Uffizi Gallery brought him many influential admirers. He was sympathetic to the ordinary Italian. He could see how they had suffered, and his political leanings supported them. John was not a fascist, as some have suggested. He cared about the people he knew; he wanted a better life for them. John thought Mussolini was mad. He didn't like the man. He called him the bald little Caesar. He knew how dangerous it was. How could he go back to England? John regarded Italy as his home Also, he knew he was living on borrowed time. By then, his health was failing, he was often short of breath, and by the time the Germans came to the villa, he was getting pains in his chest.

'I was the first to see them. I knew there were a few vehicles by the dust they created. I saw a jeep in front and several lorries. I knew they carried soldiers, and I feared this was different. John gave me this box.' He touched the box on the table. 'He told me it held objects that were valuable to him. I was to hide it in the villa. I remember asking him about Alisha's portrait. I knew then, by his look, he knew this was what they were coming for. He had learned that the Germans were collecting art, stealing it really, paintings in particular. John knew what they were coming for. He also sensed that his time had come. They were coming to arrest him.'

Abriana looks shocked. 'What happened?'

'John insisted that I left and get as far away as possible. He gave me money and said I was to return to Greece; it wasn't safe for me anymore in Italy.'

'What did you do?' Mark asks.

'I did as he said, up to a point. I didn't want to leave him, but I could see the panic on his face. I knew he was right. A voice inside told me, don't be stupid, run, escape. So, I ran as fast as I could, and I could hear the rumble of the engines, the German voices, the crunch of boots on the ground and

John's voice, calm and assuring amongst all the confusion and noise.

'I kept off the main road and tried to hide amongst the trees and shrubs. The further from the villa I got, the more trucks full of soldiers I saw. I knew this was different. Something had changed. I decided it wasn't safe anymore, so I hid in a field amongst the long grass. I don't know for how long, but it felt like an eternity. And then, this feeling came over me, at that moment, I decided there and then, I could not leave John. I had stopped thinking about the danger, the soldiers, and the war.

'It was almost dark when I thought it was safe to enter the villa. There were no lights on, but I could see the soldiers had ransacked every room. There was nothing left untouched. I ran to John's studio. The floor was littered with brushes, paint, overturned easels and jars. I stood amongst the devastation and knew the portrait was gone. My heart sank. I knew they had ripped from John his only reason to live. It was then I remembered the box. To my great relief, it was still where I'd placed it, behind a loose brick in the garden wall. This very box.'

'Did you see John again?' Mark asks.

Pavlos shakes his head. 'No. They had taken him to be questioned. John died a few days later. A heart attack was the official cause of death. Of course, there were many rumours, but I remembered what he was like the days before the soldiers came and I believe it was a heart attack.'

'What did you do?'

'I had friends in Florence. I stayed with them for a few days. They organised my escape. I was helped by the Italian Resistance. But that's another story. It took months, eventually, I made it home.'

'I had no idea it was like that. I can't imagine how that must have been.'

'I had a few lucky escapes. There were others like me. I wasn't the only one, just lucky, that's all. After the war, I received a package. It came from my friends who had taken care of me in Florence. Written on it was my name, my village, and Zakynthos, Greece. Whether it was by chance or the skill of the Greek postal service, I'll never know, but it arrived all the way from Florence.'

'The box?' Mark asks.

'This very one.'

'Incredible.'

'I'd like you to have it, Abriana. Give it to the gallery. I'm sure they would like that.'

'But it's part of your history, Pavlos. It belongs to you.'

'I've kept it long enough. I want it to have a use, not shut away in the dark. It's part of the history of the portrait. It feels right that they will finally be reunited. John would have approved.'

'Yes. I'm sure he would.'

Mark checks his watch. 'I didn't realise that was the time. Where did it go? We should think about getting back.'

The sky has softened into a violet hue, and the sun had slipped, half-submerged into the horizon when Abriana's mobile rings.

'It's the Uffizi.' She sits back. 'Ciao.' She listens intently and then replies in Italian. Mark notices Pavlos is listening and nodding his head and it occurs to him then that Pavlos would have learned Italian as a young man.

Abriana smiles at Mark. 'There was no match.'

A satisfied smile lights up Pavlos' face. 'Did you ever doubt me?'

'No, of course not.'

'Has Alan Sutton been told yet?' Mark asks.

'As we speak. It's over.'

'How do you feel?' Mark looks at Pavlos.

'Sad. I'll miss you both, your company and cooking for more than one. I looked forward to your visits. You'll be leaving Zakynthos soon?' He directs the question to Abriana, and he can see she is close to tears.

'I'm afraid so. The villa is booked until the end of the week, but I'll need to get the recording of your story to the gallery as soon as I can. We could probably stay until tomorrow. I'll need to book flights, but I'm sure we could stay an extra day or two.'

'I'd like that.' Pavlos smiles.

'We all would, I think.'

'I'd love to stay and really explore the island. We haven't really had the chance to see it properly.' Mark announces his intention to return to Zakynthos at a later date, possibly visit the other Ionian islands, Corfu and Cephalonia. As he speaks, a soothing feeling comes over him. Lately, it has felt like he has been juggling bubbles. Mark feels guilty that he has been complacent about his attitude towards Joann and the more he thinks about his impulsive decision to come to Zakynthos, he revises his nonchalant attitude. He decides he will phone her, and apologise, and accept with grace any scorn she cares to throw at him. He meets the thought that she will forgive him, with no great optimism.

'I think we should help you with the tidying and washing up. You look tired Pavlos.'

'I'm fine, Abriana. Don't worry about this lot, get yourself off and enjoy what time you have left on Zakynthos.'

'If you're sure?'

'It'll take me five minutes. I insist.'

'Okay. We'll drop by tomorrow. I'll know by then about our flights.' She stands, leans forward, and kisses Pavlos on the forehead. 'You're not going to get rid of me that easily. I'm coming back to visit you.'

Now it is Pavlos' turn, as his eyes well up with tears. He swallows. 'I'm looking forward to it already.'

They walk to the car, and Mark takes her hand. Pavlos smiles in adoration and a certain feeling of satisfaction, as he waves their car goodbye. They deserve to find happiness with each other; he tells himself. It is a reminder of what could have been.

When he thinks of the patchwork of his life, Lysander was the thread that connected each event, each transition, each experience. He looked for him in each new relationship; he was the barometer, the gauge each one had to attain and invariably failed.

Pavlos eases himself into his chair and slides an old, faded photograph from his breast pocket. He looks at it appraisingly. He raises it to his lips and gently kisses it, as he has done so, every night.

Pavlos breathes the scent of the rosemary and sage and mint he has planted in his garden and sitting on the veranda; he is aware of the great weight he has carried for years, has lifted from him. He has let Lysander go. After all these years, it has come as a surprising relief. This sudden shock meets him like an unsuspecting punch. It is so unexpected. He closes his eyes and feels the tears run down his face.

Pavlos draws in his breath. He finds solace in the stillness around him. Only the occasional intermittent birdsong breaks it. He takes in the skies dying performance, transforming light and cloud with red and purple, until the monochrome sights of the night establish themselves with the closing curtain of darkness.

They sit in silence for a while. The white light of the headlamps illuminates a small patch of tarmac in front of them. Beyond this, there is just darkness.

'I don't know how I feel. Now that it's over with, it's weird.' She glances at Mark and then back at the road in front.

'It's changed us, don't you think? It's changed me, anyway,' Mark says.

'In what way?'

'This sounds corny, I know, but I feel like I've been on a journey. I really do. I think we both have.'

She flicks a stray hair from her face. Her expression is serious, and Mark can tell she is still struggling with remorse.

At that moment, he feels courage and confidence. He rests his hand on her arm and says, gently. 'I'm here for you. Don't shut me out.'

She turns her face to him and then back to the road in front. There is something in her look. It worries him.

'Sometimes, I don't know who I am. I'm scared of myself. Only when I'm with you do I feel safe from myself. That's quite a responsibility to put on someone, I know. I'm sorry.' She smiles. 'You did say, you didn't want me to shut you out.'

Despite his concern, Mark smiles too. 'It's nice to be wanted. Seriously Abriana, I had no idea. I can't even begin to understand what you went through. God, I'm sorry, but I'm here for you now.'

'You won't always be, Mark. I know I can't get through this on my own. Don't worry, I'm not going to try to kill myself again. I'm going to get help when I get back home. There are nurses and psychiatrist and goodness knows who else who would love to get inside my head, I'm sure of it.'

'That's good. I mean about getting help, not the looking inside your head bit.'

She laughs, and he does too.

'I'm learning to talk about it and that's good. It helps. I've made a big step in the right direction. Coming here, meeting Pavlos, spending time with you, yes, just seeing you every day has been like therapy, in a good way.'

'I'm glad to hear it.'

'Really! I've not put you off me by now? I know I would be.'

'Why would I do that, Abriana? Don't worry, you won't get rid of me that easily. I'm like a life sentence. I'll always be here if you need me... if you want me to be.'

'I do, Mark. I do. I just worry, that's all. Especially with what I've done. I hate myself for that. It's unforgivable. My mind was blind. I lived for revenge. I can see now how sad I must have looked. I'm trying to cope with the shame. The look on Pavlos' face when I told him the painting had been sold. I felt burned by that look. At that moment, I realised innocent people had suffered because of my vendetta. Up until then, it had been all about me, all about how I felt. What a selfish bitch I was. I never thought for one minute, people I didn't even know, might be affected by my actions. I'll never get that look of betrayal out of my mind, never.'

'These things take time. What's important is you now know it was wrong, and remember, Pavlos doesn't blame you. He understands why you did it. Remember that.'

She bends her head slightly and says in a flat voice, 'I'm trying.'

As they approach the lights of Zakynthos Town, Mark asks, 'Do you want to get something to eat?'

'I don't mind,'

'Or would you prefer just having something at the villa? There's plenty in the fridge. We bought enough food for two weeks.'

'Actually, a nice shower and a glass of wine sound perfect.'

'I'd like that too. There's salad and moussaka. Five minutes in the microwave is all it'll take.'

'Good. I didn't realise how hungry I was until now.'

'I'm not surprised. You've hardly eaten a thing today.'

'I hope there's enough, Moussaka, for two?'

'Why?'

'Because if there's not, you're having the salad.'

'There's plenty of cheesecake. I won't starve.'

'Cheesecake as well. How could I forget about that?'

'I remember. It's your favourite.'

She turns to him. 'What?' she asks, seeing his incongruous smile.

'I've just remembered the game we played. It involved a cheesecake in Rome. Remember, we didn't use plates when you ate it. In fact, I was the plate.'

'Ah.' It is the unmistakable acknowledgement of recognition. 'That one. I'd forgotten about that.'

'Abriana, how could you? You were the one eating, after all.' He fakes offence.

'As I remember, it was pleasurable for both of us.'

Mark finds this sparring of words and innuendo daring in its sexual flirtation. 'It was. I've never thought of cheesecake quite the same.'

They have moved into another phase. How easy that was, Mark considers.

They passed along the harbour, St Dionysus Church and the neon glow of restaurants and tavernas. The sight of the silver disk moon hanging in the night sky, rubbing the faint outline of Mount Skopos enthrals Mark.

'The moon's glow on the water looks like molten platinum. It's amazing. Look Abriana.'

'I would if I wasn't driving. Everyone's determined to cross the road in front of me! How have these people lived so long?'

'I think you're needing that glass of wine.'

'A big one. We can celebrate tonight.'

'What are we celebrating? That Alan Sutton has no claim to the painting or that the painting will soon hang in the Uffizi along with their collection of Sutton's landscapes?' Mark thinks once the likely court case has happened.

'No. None of them.'

'What then?'

'Us. You and me.'

CHAPTER TWENTY-ONE

HER HAPPINESS IS INFECTIOUS

In the moonlight, her features are translucent. He sees she is smiling, and he can feel himself relax into the chair. The remnants of their meal set before them, Mark picks at a bowl of olives with a toothpick. The lights from the pool splay a soft light over the surface, changing colour every few seconds from red to turquoise and indigo.

Abriana lifts her glass to her lips and Mark watches her Adam's apple move slightly as she swallows. He observes as her tongue moves over her glossed lips; he finds it sensuous, and he needs no conscious prompting on his part for his imagination to cast vivid possibilities.

'What's that smell? I've smelled it every night.'

'It's night Jasmine.'

He breathes it in. 'I think it'll define my stay here. The smell will always remind me of Zakynthos. Do you think I'll be able to grow it in Scotland?'

'I doubt it. It would probably struggle with your summers.'

'What summers?'

'Exactly.'

'I'll just have to come back, then.'

'Do you think you will?'

'As I said, I'd like to travel around Greece. It appeals to me. What about you?'

'Maybe, but not just now. I'm missing home.'

'I'd like to see what home looks like.'

'I've got a photograph on my phone. I'll show you.'

It takes her a few seconds to find it. 'Here it is.'

He studies the photograph. 'It's a beautiful house. I wasn't expecting it to be so big.'

'I'm just renting it for now. The owners thinking about selling it. It's two hundred years old. It was originally a farmhouse.'

'Would you buy it? It looks a bit isolated. Although I love the shutters, it has that typical Italian look. You can definitely tell it's in Tuscany.'

'I've been thinking about it. I love its situation. I like that it's on its own. My nearest neighbour is about half a mile away.'

'Is it far from John Sutton's villa? I meant to ask you that, as he lived near Florence,' Mark asks.

'The villa's not there anymore.'

'What do you mean?'

'I didn't have the heart to tell Pavlos, and I'm relieved he hasn't asked me, as it was completely destroyed by a fire, just after the war.'

'That's a shame.'

'It is.'

Mark notices she looks sad.

'I'd love to have seen it, especially now. It feels like John's life has been rubbed out.'

'There might be a photograph somewhere,' Mark says.

Abriana sips her drink. 'This wine is lovely.'

'I got it at the little store.'

She tilts the bottle and reads the label. 'It's Greek.'

'You seem surprised.'

'No, not surprised, it just confirms what I love about this place.'

'What's that?'

'It seems to catch me with its diversity and contradictions. It can look to the outsider to be such a simple country, but that's just being short-sighted, in my opinion. In fact, I was probably one of them.'

'It looks like that's changing.' He raises an eyebrow.

'Oh, you're empty.' She pours a generous amount into his glass.

'Did you meet the little old lady who owns the shop? she has a son who works there too, I think it's her son, anyway.'

'I did. She's nice and very friendly, in fact, she recommended the wine, told me all about it. I was beginning to think she had shares in it.'

'She knows, Pavlos. I spoke to her this morning when I went to get bread for breakfast. She thought I was on holiday, but when I said I was visiting someone, she asked who? She likes to know everyone's business. Anyway, she said I was the second person she'd spoken to where Pavlos' name had come up.'

'She did?'

'Yes. She spoke to a lovely young man, very nice looking and Scottish. She'd like to marry him off to her daughter. He was that good-looking.'

'She never did?'

'She was very animated.' Abriana laughs at the memory.

'God, how embarrassing. I'm middle-aged, look I'm starting to get thick around my waist. I'm not that good looking.'

'She was funny with it, but I do agree with her,' Abriana says, amused that he doubts his looks. Mark feels slightly taken aback.

She takes another sip of her drink. 'I haven't even dipped my toe in the pool. Do you fancy a swim?'

'What now?'

'Yeah. Why not? It's our pool. We can swim in it whenever we want.'

'I suppose we can.'

'Well then, is that a, yes? I'm going in, anyway,' she says, decisively.

Abriana stands and strolls over to the pool. She bends and runs her hand over the surface. 'It's lovely and warm.'

She unzips her dress, lets it fall and steps over it. She sits on the edge of the pool and slides like a fish into the water.

She surfaces. 'Are you coming in?' She starts to swim and then flips onto her back; her hair looks like an oil slick floating around her.

'The water feels like silk against my skin. Come in. I'm getting lonely.'

'Alright, I'm coming.'

It is a surreal image, Abriana floating in the pool, at night, in only her bra and pants, rivulets of water on her skin, glistening like diamonds. Her happiness is infectious.

CHAPTER TWENTY-TWO

CLOSER

Sunlight suffuses the room. They must have slept late. She glances at the digital clock on the bedside cabinet. 8.23. She has slept soundly. Her first full night's sleep in as long as she can care to remember. She watches Mark sleep and listens to his breathing. She wishes this little pocket of time could last forever, but she knows it will end soon.

For no apparent reason, the portrait enters her thoughts. Echoes of a different time. It has touched and influenced her life in so many ways.

The shame returns to her. Abriana cannot conveniently change what has happened. She feels her hollow stomach return as she remembers Pavlos' quizzical frown, that quickly turned to disappointment and disapproving scorn. She felt stunned, disoriented. In her worst moments, she knows his face will haunt her.

Abriana instinctively understands the past is still a vivid reminder of a version of herself she wants to banish. She is a work in progress. She reaches out and strokes Mark's hair; she smiles then, a reassuring smile.

She remembers last night and his expression as he walked towards the pool, desire veiled by a modest restraint. In one swift motion, he slipped into the water and then he was beside her.

He wrapped his arms around her waist, and she made no effort to release them. She could feel his breath warm on her lips and she remembered his words then. *'Life always has the potential to surprise us. It can scare the shit out of you, or it can be the best thing that ever happens to you. What has happened in the last few days has shown me there are certain things I can't live without.'*

'And what would they be?'

'Happiness, love and you, I want all three. I want all of you.' He kissed her then, his mouth thirsty for her.

She remembers her fingers laced in his, as he took her up the marble stairs to the bedroom. Droplets of water fell from her hair and onto the floor, recording their progress.

She remembers the touch of his lips when his hand brushed her wet hair and he kissed her below the nape of her neck and carried on down her spine. And his voice, a mere whisper, his breath shaky, 'You are so beautiful to me.'

She has made breakfast and set the table on the terrace when Mark joins her. He ruffles his hair and yawns. 'God. I must have needed that. I didn't even hear you get up. I've never slept that late for years.'

'I was quiet. I didn't want to wake you. Would you like a coffee? There's some on the table?'

'I'd love a coffee. Did you sleep well?'

'I did, thanks.'

She sits opposite him and lets Mark pour her coffee.

Mark grins.

'What is it?' She smiles.

'I was thinking about last night.'

'Me too.'

'Are you Ok with what happened?'

'I'm still here.'

'Yes. You are.'

'And you?'

He smiles. 'I'm still floating.'

She raises her cup to her lips and blows over the rim.

'What happens now?'

'I'm not sure.'

'It's complicated.'

'Only if we let it be,' Mark says, after a pause.

'Are you sure this is what you want?'

He nods. 'I've never been surer.'

'Do you think we can make it work, Mark?'

'We can try.'

'There might be a court case.' She looks away.

'I know. I've thought about that.' Mark turns his gaze to the sky. It is cloudless, wide and blue. 'And there might not be.'

There is a tight silence between them.

'I wonder if I would've liked him.'

'Who?' Mark asks.

'John. What he did was a courageous and selfless act. He found it unimaginable to abandon her child. It was because he loved Alisha, even after everything he had been through with her. He was a decent man, after all.'

'The important thing is, he was happy. I think in

Florence he found his real home, and he was able to share that with Lysander.'

'And Pavlos.'

'Yes. And Pavlos.'

CHAPTER TWENTY-THREE

GUARDIANS

When they turn off the road, Louis, Pavlos' neighbour, is clearing the dishes from yesterday's meal on the veranda. 'Something's wrong,' Abriana says startled. Her chest tightens, and she brings the car to a sudden stop.

Louis looks up and raises a hand in greeting, but his expression is flat, his face gaunt.

'Louis, what are you doing here?' Abriana probes him as she rushes towards the house. She watches for his reaction.

'Abriana, Mark.'

'Why are the dishes still here? What's going on, Louis?' She touches her forehead. Adriana can see Pavlos' pipe on the table. She braces herself.

'It's Pavlos... I'm sorry, he... he passed away last night.'

'What!' A tidal wave of shock hits her

'I often check on him, most nights, just to make sure he's alright, but he wasn't. I knew the minute I saw him in the chair. It was dark, and he's never outside at night.' Louis shakes his head. 'He had a pulse. It was light, but there. I don't know how long he had been that way, but I phoned an ambulance and did CPR. By the time they got here, it had been too long. I went with him to the hospital, but he never gained consciousness.'

'Oh, God. Poor Pavlos. 'I...' words desert her. Her world spins.

Mark takes her by the arm. 'I can't believe it; I knew he had a cold or something. I didn't think it was this bad.'

'It was a heart attack, and not his first,' Louis says.

'Let's get you a seat, Abriana.' Mark directs her to a chair.

'He was ill?' Mark asks Louis.

'Pavlos was on medication. He had a heart attack three years ago. It almost killed him then. It should have done, but he was lucky or blessed. Either way, it didn't stop him from working in his garden and walking miles every day. It was part of his recovery. He embraced it, as he did with everything in life... I'll miss him.'

Mark remembers then that Louis has lost a dear friend. He has known Pavlos for years, as has his family.

'He was like a grandfather to my kids. Our house used to be owned by a woman called Anna, a character larger than life, so she was. Pavlos and Anna were old friends, they went back years. That's how I got to know Pavlos...' He shakes his head. 'I'm sorry. You don't want to know about all of this. I just can't believe he's gone.'

'No. It's fine, honest. It must have been a shock. I mean, finding him,' Mark says, still trying to take it in himself.

'I don't think it's hit me yet. I really should get all of this cleared up and get back to Maria. She's quite upset as well.'

'We'll see to it. Off you go.'

'Did you get what you came for?' Louis asks.

'We did, and much more.'

'Good. At least I know Pavlos' last few days were happy ones. He told me it meant a lot to him, telling both of you his story. He said he was passing it over to you. You were now the guardians of the truth. That was his words and he couldn't have wished for it to be revealed to such a perfect couple.'

'He said that?'

'With a smile on his face. You made a big impression on him. We'll clear this away together; I need to lock the house up.'

Abriana reaches out and touches Pavlos' pipe. 'I can't take this in. He's gone. He was sitting in that chair only yesterday talking and eating.'

Suddenly, nothing matters anymore. She closes her eyes briefly, her thoughts consumed with images of him. When she opens them, she can see Pavlos' box on the table. It is still where he left it the day before.

She takes a breath to control her emotion. Since they arrived in Zakynthos, they have shared so much, stories of loss, betrayal, love and of being loved. Pavlos' story has shone a light on the past, bringing it to life in her mind. She feels she has heard other's intimate thoughts, witnessed brutal turns and twists. She has heard secrets told, listened to the spectrum of human relationships where unforgivable things have been done in disastrous circumstances.

Moments of refined beauty and sensibilities have enthralled her, as has love expressed with honour and courage, forgiveness and the generosity of the human spirit.

Above all, Pavlos' with his words has illuminated and touched the hearts of the living.

'Oh, I found this photograph. It was lying next to Pavlos.

You might know who it is. It's quite an old one.' Louis hands the photograph to Abriana.

She looks at it and smiles.

'If it's ok with you, I'd like to go home and check on Maria. I'll come back later and lock up.'

'Sure Louis, you get off. We'll see to this lot,' Mark offers. As Louis leaves, Mark looks at Abriana. Her face lights up.

'Who is it?' he asks.

'I think it's Lysander.'

'How can you be sure?'

'Call it intuition. Look, how handsome he is. Of course, it's him. Who else can it be?'

Mark leans in and looks at it. 'I think you're right.'

Just then, a car turns into the driveway. They all turn to look at the newcomer.

A woman steps out of the driver's side and runs her hand through her hair. She wears a sleeveless dress and sunglasses and walks towards them with an air of confidence in her stride.

'I thought that was you. Hello, Mark. It's nice to see you again,' she says, cheerily.

Mark can see Abriana struggling to comprehend what had just happened. She turns to him. 'You know this woman? Who is she?'

'Gill. What are you doing here?' Even as he is saying the words, his stomach churns.

She reaches them, takes her sunglasses off and kisses Mark just off the mouth. 'I was about to ask you the same question. And this must be Abriana. Aren't you going to introduce me?'

. . .

Mark tries to keep his voice level, and matter of fact, as he tells Abriana that Gill is a friend he met in Elie when he was staying at Joann's cottage. Mark thinks about and then decides against telling Abriana how friendly they were, and wonders if this is a mistake? As he looks at Gill, he thinks, this is incredible, but he has an intuitive understanding of why she is here. His mouth feels dry and he can feel his shoulders tense. He is not lying to Abriana; he is just keeping the truth from her. For now, he hopes. All the time, he is thinking this is his worst nightmare.

'Why are you here? I thought you were in New York.'

Gill lifts her chin. 'I was. I'm working on a different story now.'

Abriana stares at her.

'In fact, I'm here to speak with the old man, Pavlos. Is he in?'

'No.'

'Oh. That's a shame. I'll come back later, then.'

'They'll be no need. He died last night.'

'Shit, that was quite inconsiderate of him.'

Abriana touches Mark's arm. 'I want her to leave.'

'That Alan Sutton is a weird little man. He's got quite a chip on his shoulder now. Doesn't care much for you, Abriana. Oh, and Geoffrey Buchanan, now he's an interesting man, quite the opposite from weirdo Alan. He wasn't pleased with the attention he's getting since he sold the Sutton painting to the Roma Gallery. He had a lot to say. No matter who I speak with, your name just keeps coming up, Abriana.'

'You don't have to pretend. I know why you're here.' Abriana feels sick.

'It's a shame about Pavlos. I was hoping to get the icing

on the cake. But maybe I still will. You can balance this all out and give me your side of the story, Abriana.'

For a moment, there are tears in Abriana's eyes. 'You'll write what you want, anyway.'

'I'm sorry you feel that way. You've hurt me, actually,' Gill says, although it isn't strictly true. 'It's your choice. It would have been an unexpected coup on my part. Either way, you're fucked. It's the beginning of the end.'

Gill turns as if to leave, then looks at Abriana. 'If you do change your mind, I'm staying at the Diana Hotel in Zakynthos Town. I'm leaving the day after tomorrow. And since he probably won't tell you, Mark and I were more than just friends, weren't we, Mark?' She pauses and then smirks. 'I know where his birthmark is. In fact, I've seen it several times.'

'You were very restrained, polite even.' Mark says sheepishly.

'It's a pity she wasn't. So, you made love to her.' Abriana tilts her head.

'No. We had sex, that's all it was.'

'You were on the rebound, as they say.'

'I've no excuse. It wasn't my finest moment. I'm not proud of myself.'

'No, and so you shouldn't be. You could have picked a nicer person. Is she always like that?'

'She surprised me. She was never that way.'

'Obnoxious you mean.'

If Abriana was angry, she wasn't showing it.

'I feel responsible.'

'Why?'

'It's because of me that she's here.'

'I guessed that part.'

'Joann warned me this would happen.'

'It's because you see the good in people, although I don't know what you saw in her. Well, I do actually.'

'What?'

'Her breasts, she's rather well gifted.' Abriana smiles.

'You're taking this well.'

'What part. That you fucked her, or that I'm fucked. None of it matters anymore.'

He didn't like her speaking this way. He longed to hold her. 'So, what happens now?'

'We leave tomorrow. You return to Edinburgh and I'll go home. My position is untenable, you must see that. I'll resign before this all blows up. I'd be the first casualty, anyway. I'd rather be in control of that than give someone else the satisfaction.'

'So, people like the Roma Gallery and Gill have won?'

'It was just a battle, never a war. Anyway, I'm a pacifist now. Pavlos taught me that.' She rubs her eye with the heel of her hand.

'I don't want this to be the end for us. I've walked away from you once before. I promised myself I'd never do that again.'

'Sometimes we make promises because it feels, at the time, it's the right thing to do, but some promises we just can't keep, no matter how hard we try.'

'Don't do this, Abriana.'

'It's already been decided for us, Mark.'

CHAPTER TWENTY-FOUR

RESILIENCE

'You've come on your own. I didn't think she'd come."

'Why, Gill?' Mark looks at her scathingly.

'It's not personal, Mark. It's my job.

'What, ruining people's lives?'

'I don't always enjoy what I do.'

'It looked like you were enjoying yourself.'

'As I said, it's just a job. She's not innocent. She knew what she was doing. She's got a track record, remember?'

'That doesn't make it right, Gill. God. I trusted you. I'm to blame for all this.'

'Look, Mark. Once it's found out that she's implicated in the sale of the painting, she becomes an accessory to a potential crime. She knew that. She's not stupid. She's calculated. She knew what she was doing, she knew the consequences.'

They are sitting at a table on the rooftop bar of the Diana Hotel. Around him, Mark stares at the terracotta roofs of Zakynthos Town, the treetops basking in white and yellow sunlight, across the harbour towards Mount Skopos, rising majestically above Argassi. And just beyond Argassi, along a road rising through the olive groves, is Pavlos' house. Although it is warm, he feels a coldness grasp him. The house that he loved to visit will now be forever associated, not with the wonderful stories Pavlos told, but with the day a visitor from his past brought his life crashing down around him.

'When I saw you in Edinburgh before you went to New York, you were already involved in this, weren't you?'

Gill stiffens in her chair. 'I wanted to tell you; I really did.'

'You can stop this, right here and now.'

'It's not as simple as that, even if I wanted to.'

'You mean you won't.'

'I can't. I'm not cold-hearted,' she protests.

Mark decides it is pointless and he should never have come.

'I'm jealous of her.'

'Abriana?' Mark says, incredulously.

'Yes. I always have been.'

'But, why?'

'She has something I want but will never have.'

'What?'

'You, Mark. I loved you... I still do.'

Mark looks at her intently. He glances away and then looks back. His hands are trembling. He stands up. 'I never want to see you again,' he says sharply. 'I detest you. Do you hear me? You are nothing to me.'

She looks at him silently, her eyes full of tears.

Her reaction catches him, and he is forced to sit down.

'Tell me you felt something for me, that I meant something to you.' Her voice chokes on her words.

He turns away and sighs.

'I just need to hear you say it.'

'You want me to lie to you?'

She pulls a cigarette from its packet, lights it and takes a deep drag.

'You took me by surprise, Mark. I never thought for one minute I'd fall in love in Elie. You saved me from myself.'

'I seem to have a habit of that. How do you imagine I feel?'

'I'm sorry. I don't know what else to say.'

There is silence between them.

'Ok. I'll be honest with you; you deserve that at least. It wasn't love; it was just sex. I was infatuated with you.'

'Are they not the same thing?'

'No. I believe one to be unconditional and the other a thirst that follows desire.'

'So, you were attracted to me? I can live with that. I can tell you love her. It's in your body language. I could see it when I saw you with her. You might find it hard to believe. I do admire her. She's a strong woman, unafraid.'

Mark agrees. She has a toughness about her, a resilience that almost defines her. Suddenly, Mark feels a need to be near Abriana. The thought occurs to him that she might have already left the villa. Nausea crawls in his stomach.

'What is it, Mark?'

'I need to leave, Gill. I think Abriana has already gone.'

CHAPTER TWENTY-FIVE

GONE

There is a plane ticket on the kitchen worktop. He has checked the entire house. There is no visual evidence that she was ever in the villa. It makes the last few days swirl into a dream-like state.

He was happy here. Her voice filled the space and warmed the vast rooms. The silence in the kitchen is deafening.

He thinks of their conversations on the terrace, lazy mornings and long breakfasts, the warmth of her body next to him, seeping into his skin. He thinks of her dark eyes, the curve of her glossed lips, into a beautifully formed smile.

She was happy. This place soothed her and caressed her. It animated her. Yes, she found contentment here, not always, but when she was happy, it quenched Mark, and she brought a glorious light to his world.

He can see her still and hear her feet on the tiled floors. But mostly he fears what will become of her.

He knows he will find leaving monumentally hard. With

an effort, he picks up the ticket and looks at it; he has three hours until his plane leaves.

The track descends through olive and orange trees dripping with heavy fruit. Around him, the warm smells of plants and herbs perforate the air where butterflies flutter in dazzling colour. He doesn't have to walk too far before he comes across what he is looking for. Just off the track, Mark finds the spot that Abriana loves.

In front of him, a canopy of green, tall cypress, giant oak and pine trees intertwine and descend towards the sea, dipping and merging into pools of turquoise.

Mark attempts to frame the scene on his smartphone. He holds it perfectly still. He fears that if he blinks, it will vanish. Click, click, click. Three should be enough, he hopes. He studies his work and the results please him.

Before he walks away, his eyes take it in one last time, the scene Abriana loves. He feels the sun's heat radiate around him. He marvels at the essence of the light; it is a magical mystery to him; it has a quality he struggles to describe. For once, words are inadequate.

He lifts his gaze towards the sea and imagines holding her hand, and the scent of her hair filling him with desire. His chest suffuses in a sensation he recognises as a feeling of release. He knows himself to be in love. The ache is astonishingly refreshing, but ridiculously painful. Without her, he is lost. What will become of her? The feeling is devastating and absolute.

EPILOGUE

Mark's commute to the gallery is not his normal one. He usually takes the tram or taxi, his two preferred modes of transport. Instead, Mark decides to walk. It is a glorious autumnal Edinburgh that meets him, as he steps from his front door in Eglinton Crescent. He can see the three spires of St Mary's Cathedral, looming large, above the chimney pots, like arrowheads piercing the sky. There is a confidence in his stride and although the sunlight slants off the roofs, there is a definite chill in the air that forces his hands deep inside his pockets.

He crosses the street and saunters along Rothesay Place. A row of skeletal trees behind a trimmed hedge splits the street and above him, there are black wrought iron ornamental balconies, each one sitting below a row of three windows. To Mark's mind, such features are exclusive to this street, there is nothing like it in the rest of the city that he is aware of.

The morning traffic grumbles at a steady pace as he enters Randolf Crescent. He has loved this part of Edinburgh since he was a child. It resonates with him and its history has always intrigued him. Built in the eighteenth century, Edinburgh's new town is a spectacle of neo-classical style, wide cobbled roads, spacious squares, sandstone block facades and black wrought-iron railings.

He stops abruptly and stares at the grandiose Grecian pillars. It inspires his thoughts with a flashback of a garden, a pool and a glass-fronted villa. He runs his hand through his hair. The vivid image pulls at his heart.

He recalls the small garden wall, twisting and curved shaped olive trees, silver trunked fig trees and the scents of blooming flowers and wild herbs raiding his senses daily. A panoramic view of rolling emerald sloped towards salmon coated houses where an imposing church steeple, red doomed, pushed its way towards the sky.

He remembers the harbour wall, stretching like a finger into the incredible peacock blue sea, calm and welcoming. Mount Skopos, sitting over the bay and undulating against the sky, Greek blue, he murmurs to himself, words that spilt from him in awe, every time he stepped into the garden.

It is blazed in his mind. It fills him with a warmth he has rarely felt since his return to Edinburgh. He realises he is not only pining for a physical place, every day it has been the same. He thinks of her face, the voice he longs to hear, the skin he has touched and luxuriated in that brings its own unique cravings. When he thinks about it, he knows it was happiness, contentment, which he has lost.

He exhales and continues to walk along Ainslie Place and Moray Place, glancing inside the sashed windows with tall ceilings and decorative friezes and trimmings inside. On Heriot Row he quickens his stride, glancing to his right, now and again, at Queen Street Gardens. Shortly, he stops and waits for a break in the traffic before breaking into a soft jog over to Abercromby Place and virtually on the corner of a Georgian building, between two white opened doors, he enters his gallery.

'I just made a coffee; would you like one?' Joann asks.

'That would be nice. It's lovely out there,' Mark says, taking his jacket off and hanging it on a coat stand.

'You can't beat this time of year. The colour of the trees is gorgeous,' Joann says, as she makes the coffee.

'I know. Queen Street Gardens was a spectacle all on its own.'

She turns to him. 'How do you know?'

'I walked into work.'

'You. Walked.'

'I did. I've been getting lazy; I need the exercise. So, I decided to do something about it.'

'You'll be telling me you've joined a gym next.'

'I don't know if I'll go that far. It's amazing the things you see. I wasn't aware of how much I take for granted. We live in a beautiful city, Joann.'

'You've just noticed, then.'

'No. But I've seen it in a different light.'

'Why would that be, then?' She hands him a mug.

'Thanks. I took the time to look around me for a change. A lesson I learnt in Zakynthos.'

'You liked it there, didn't you?'

'I did.' He looks down at his mug.

'Would you go back? Are you thinking of going back?' She slumps into her chair at her desk, opposite Mark.

He leans back in his chair and brings the mug to his mouth. Habitually, he blows over the coffee. 'I was told it's really nice in the spring, March and April. I'm thinking of going then. In fact, I might take in a few islands.'

'I'd like that. I've never been to Greece,'

'Who would look after the gallery?'

'It won't be much fun going on your own.'

'That depends. I'll have to wait and see.'

'On what, exactly?' She prompts.

'I've decided to go to Florence, after all.'

'The Sutton exhibition. What changed your mind?'

'I don't know. I suppose I'm hoping it feels like closure. The Quartet portrait is the jewel in the exhibition's crown. I invested a lot of myself in that painting. I feel I owe it to myself. And I really want to see it up close, be in the same room with it. It's weird, but I feel it's a part of me now. I feel like I have a personal relationship with it. I know it's history. I'd like to be part of its present.'

There is a moments silence, then Joann smiles. 'That's deep shit.'

It is Mark's turn to smile. 'I know, but that's how it is. What happened in Zakynthos affected me on so many levels. It was not just all about the painting. We became closer again, Joann.'

'And she buggered off back to Florence and left you without saying goodbye.'

'I know. She had her reasons, you know that. It was a difficult time for both of us.'

She can see a glimmer in his eyes.

'Have you heard from her?'

He shakes his head. 'What makes you say that?'

'I've known you for a long time, Mark. You're hiding something.'

'I've not heard from her since the trial.'

'Are you sure? I'm warning you, Mark. Don't go back there. You'll only get hurt again. I can see it coming.' She shakes her head.

'I'll try not to... I'm only kidding.' Mark begins to think about such a prospect and his excitement begins to build. 'It's different now, anyway.'

'In what way?' Joann sighs, unconvinced. 'Do you know what? You really piss me off. When it comes to your love life, you've made it a habit of yours to ignore every morsel of advice I give you, so do you know what? I don't care. Let it be on your head.'

'You've already convinced yourself I'm going to see her.'

'How long has she been out of that jail? Five minutes and you're off to Florence.'

'Coincidence. That's all.' He looks at her. Joann frowns.

'Promise me one thing.'

'What?'

She leans forward. 'Look, you know there's no love lost between me and her. So, if you see her... When you see her, tell her from me, I still think she's a bitch for what she did to you, again, I may add. And the three months she got for her little escapade was a fucking joke.'

'You're overprotective.'

'And you're an idiot, I keep telling you this, but do you know what, I can't help myself, I'll always be here for you.'

'I know. You're the only stable person in my life.'

'It's a life sentence, believe me.'

Mark stands at the entrance to The Uffizi Gallery. On the expansive pavement, banners flutter gently, imprinted with an image of the Quartet and the title, The Lost Painting. For a moment, he pauses. It was a question he asked himself. How would he feel once here? This is where she worked. This is where it all started. From this building, Abriana and John Sutton's portrait came into his life. The sensation in his stomach feels like liquid running through him, elation and trepidation soaked into one. He lifts his face to the sunshine and looks at the building. It's very impressive, just how he'd imagined.

A woman passes him, and as she does, she glances in his direction before entering the gallery. It jolts him into a sudden walk, and he is past the threshold and in a modern reception area. It's busy with people and Mark looks around for a sign that will tell him where to go to see the exhibition.

A well-groomed man in a dark suit speaks to him in Italian.

'Sorry, I don't speak Italian.'

The man speaks again, in Italian, this time frowning obstinately.

'He's asking if you have your invitation?' Her tone is casual, her accent thick. It's the woman who passed him outside.

'Oh, I do. Let me get it.' He reaches into his inside jacket pocket and presents his ticket. The man casts his eye over it, tears a slip off and hands the other half to Mark.

'Ciao,' Mark says.

'Prego,' He replies stony-faced.

'Thanks.' Mark smiles at the woman. She is young, attractive and he can tell her suit dress is expensive.

She looks at him and smiles. 'Is everything alright. I saw you outside just now. You looked a little lost.'

'I'm fine, thanks again.' Just then he spots the entrance to the exhibition and already, a large heading of people is moving that way.

'You're here for the exhibition?'

'Yes, I am.'

'Are you familiar with John Sutton's work?'

'A little.'

'Most people are here to see, The Quartet. Do you know it?'

'I'm familiar with it. And you?'

'I work here. I was involved in setting up the exhibition.'

'Oh, I see.'

'In fact, this is my first one.'

'So, you haven't worked here long.'

'A few months. I'd worked in smaller galleries, but nothing on this scale. I was lucky the job became available when it did. My big break really. My predecessor was implicated in the sale of The Quartet to a rival gallery. It was quite a scandal. She went to prison. Did you hear about it? It was covered a lot by the press at the time.'

'I vaguely remember it.' He attempts to appear disinterested.

She hesitates then, 'Anyway, I'll let you get on. It's just over there.' She combs her fingers through her hair. 'It was nice speaking to you. I hope you enjoy the paintings.'

'Thanks once again, I'm sure I will.' When she walks off, he gives a sigh of relief.

He follows the crowd through the glass-fronted doors and into a large room with four decorative arches on each side that lead off into other viewing rooms. The features of the room that appeal to him are the waiters with trays of wine and soft drinks. He opts for the red. Italian has always been his favourite.

The paintings vary in size, some are vast, while others would fit on a wall in a house quite snuggly. Mark stands with a wine in hand. His eyes feast upon sweeping fields and rolling hills, vineyards next to villas and farmhouses. There are sunflowers and poppy fields, clipped hedges, cypresses, poplar and parasol pines standing on the crest of hills. The geometry is tidy and orderly, the style elegant and disciplined. It strikes Mark that there is a lack of people in the compositions, as if Sutton had abandoned his faith in humanity for the brilliance and textured colours of the Tuscany landscape. Every composition is a landscape except the centrepiece of the exhibition, The Quartet.

Mark stands for a while in front of the painting. It is larger than he expected. Mark contemplates the figures of Alisha, Reuben, Sara, and Alex. He feels he knows them well, in a way, personally. He is familiar with their story, their journey. Mark has learned of their worries, their fears, their weaknesses, their loss and the joy of their friendships. He can identify with those they loved, and those they lost. He knows their times of happiness and their betrayals. Mark knows the lived experience, and it phrases his understanding of this painting differently, unlike the others, who file through these rooms, and analyse and construct an impression of its subjects. For he has been privy to the words of a gentle soul who illuminated their story with humility and a generosity of spirit few attain, or others have the honour of knowing.

It is almost impossible not to see himself in these faces of paint and canvas. There is a connection, and that is what strikes him the most. And, as he stands in the gallery conceptualising the paintings' influence on his life, he personalises it through space and time. The moment in its history that extends back to John Sutton dipping the brush in paint and applying the first stroke. Its abandonment, as John learned of the secret Alisha had kept from him. As time passed and events softened him, it became his connection to Alisha, a constant reminder of his love for her and his dreadful loss. It was his constant companion in his years in Tuscany. Where a young Greek man heard the Portrait's story, which John told him while painting the compositions that now hang on the walls around Mark. It has been subject to the tyranny of German soldiers who took it because they could. It became a trade-off for a few crates of wine and then a wedding present, passed down from father to son, its past forgotten, lost in time. He met Abriana for the first time since Rome. He learned of the painting's chronology and the dispute over its ownership. But mostly, Alisha intrigued him and he wanted to know her story. It brought Mark and Abriana to Zakynthos, where Pavlos opened a door of time, revealing normal lives, plighted by loss and suffering, but also sustained by love and friendship, but most importantly, it brought him closer to the woman he loves. The portrait's vast reach has taken him aback. It has touched the lives of so many. Finally, it has brought him to this gallery, where they meet for the first time. He has a lot to thank it for, this painting that has seen trials and tribulations but given so much in return. It has shaped and changed the lives of those it has touched, its influence has been momentous. It has defined the struggles and joys of the human spirit. It has captured what it means to love and be loved. This will be its legacy.

Mark smiles. He realises now how he feels. As he turns to leave, he wears his happiness like a new pair of shoes.

. . .

The café is just as she described it. As he approaches, he can see a waiter placing two cups on a table where a woman is sitting reading a paper in the shade of a parasol. She looks up and a smile lights her face, like sunshine, he thinks. When he draws nearer, she stands and kisses him on the cheek. Habitually, his arms embrace her and as he pulls her into him, his world feels balanced once more. It feels right.

'Oh, how I've missed you,' he says once he lets her go. This time, he kisses her on the lips.

'Let's sit,' Abriana suggests. 'The coffee has just arrived.'

He looks at her, taking all of her in. She has lost a little weight. 'I can't believe I'm here. I've imagined this every day since Zakynthos. How are you, Abriana?'

'I'm good, now.'

'I heard you didn't hold back at the trial.'

'No. I think now that was a mistake. It might have given the judge an excuse to give me a few extra weeks.'

'I was going to come, but I didn't see any good coming out of that. I'm not sure I would have coped.'

'I'm glad you didn't. As the days passed and I saw you weren't in the courtroom. I relaxed, as much as I could.'

He looks at her again, as if to make sure she is opposite him. He can see the light has come back to her eyes. 'I missed you.'

'I thought of you every day.'

'Why didn't you want me to visit you? I would have come over. You know that, don't you?'

She nods her head. 'That would have been too much for me. I didn't want you to see me in that place. I had to concentrate on getting through those months. You would have been... a savoury distraction.' She laughs at her description and Mark does, too.

'Does anyone know you're here?'

'Only Joann. She thinks I'm here just for the exhibition. She would have sent her love if she knew.'

'I doubt that. You're a terrible liar, Mark. She must have quizzed you.'

He smiles. 'She did.'

'She knows?'

'No, she doesn't. I was convincing, honest.'

Abriana laughs. 'I'm sure you were, but she'll know, believe me.'

He tries to imagine what it must have been like for Abriana, a thought that has plagued his days and nights.

'I'm so glad you look well. I was really worried about you. The thought of you in a prison cell played with my head.'

'You shouldn't worry, Mark. I've not lost everything. I still have my house and my savings, but most importantly, I have you.'

'You always will have. That's why I'd like to see where you live. I've tried to imagine how it looks. I've got an image of an old Italian house surrounded by groves and cypress trees.'

'Not a bad description and close. You'll see it soon.'

'I can't wait.' He says, with a wide grin. Mark takes a sip of coffee. 'Mm, this is nice.'

'Of course it is. It's Italian and you're drinking it in Florence. What is there not to like?'

'I don't need convincing.'

There is a silence between them, the first since he arrived.

'You saw the portrait?'

'I did.'

'And?'

'It was special. I'd be lying if I said it didn't touch me. I certainly felt like I knew them, The Quartet. And Alisha, the likeness is incredible when you see the painting up close. There was a crude attempt at a description of the painting's history. It was lacking... let's say, it felt detached.'

'I'm glad.'

'I knew you'd like that.' He scratches his chin. 'Why the photograph? Why did you ask me to send it to you?'

'I had to know you agreed with me and would do what I asked. I knew that when my plane landed, the possibility of being arrested was very real. If that happened, the authorities would have confiscated my phone. Even if you had sent a text and I deleted it, I'm sure it can still be retrievable. Somehow, maybe not, but I couldn't take that chance. So, that's why I asked you to take the photograph of that view and send it to me. I thought it was the only safe way to find out if you had agreed to help me. You knew what that view meant to me. To anyone else, it was just a photograph of a beautiful view. To me, it was everything. Also, I really wanted to see that view again. When you sent it, I was so relieved, you can't imagine. Did you doubt yourself?'

'When I came into the villa that day and saw you were gone, I didn't know what to think. But then, I noticed your note inside the plane ticket. When I read it, it brought a smile to my face. I knew then you hadn't given up. This was your one last act of defiance. Without Pavlos' account of the true story behind the portrait, the art world had lost, the Uffizi Gallery's exclusivity was weakened, and you had won. It was a nice touch, burying the Dictaphone at the tree we always stood at. You always reminded me; it was the best place to stand to appreciate the view. I knew it was the right thing to do. Pavlos would have wanted you to tell the real story, not a gallery full of businessmen inflated by their own self-importance. It would have just been a marketing exercise for them, a coup. You have lived through the experience, you have owned your emotions, you're emotionally connected to the story of the portrait, especially Alisha's story. That's what really matters. That's why I knew you were doing the right thing. I knew I had to help.'

'Thank you.'

'Why did you bury it? I always wondered about that.'

'I wasn't sure you'd take the Dictaphone back to Edinburgh with you. I buried it in a place I knew I could easily find and that wasn't going to change unless the tree got chopped down.' She laughs then.

'How did you explain you didn't have the recordings or any transcripts? There must have been a lot of very pissed off directors at The Uffizi.'

'I said I lost it. I turned the villa upside down. I couldn't find it anywhere. It seemed to have vanished into thin air.' She gestures with her hand.

'And they accepted that?' he looks genuinely surprised.

'No. I don't think they did. But what can they do? They're waiting for me to make a move. I know that.'

He places the Dictaphone on the table. 'Then it's your move.'

Abriana's heart jumps as she takes the Dictaphone and presses it to her chest. 'This means everything to me, Mark. Now I can finally begin to write.'

'Have you thought of a title for the book?'

'I have, actually.' Abriana takes Mark's hand and looks into his eyes. 'The Girl in the Portrait.'

'I like it.'

Her eyes shine. 'I knew you would.'

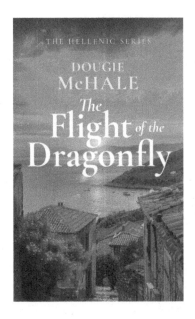

vinci-books.com/dragonflight

What if the person you love is the last person you should trust?

Turn the page for a free preview...

THE FLIGHT OF THE DRAGONFLY
PREVIEW

The Past

The Beginning

She slipped through my fingers. I lost my child and there was nothing I could do about it. But that's not how it began.

I loved the way he looked at me. His smile could melt the coldest heart. There was a definite feeling that we belonged together; our friends named us *the soul mates*. Sometimes, it uneased me that I could feel such a bond with another. He mesmerised me. That's not the word. It implies we weren't equal. We connected, physically and emotionally. That's what it was. I was the hand that fitted his glove.

We met at a party. I hadn't been invited to it, but my friend Jasmine had, and she didn't want to go on her own, so she asked me to go with her. I wasn't exactly dragged along. I quite liked the idea of going out and the chances were I'd probably know someone there, anyway. It was at a house in

Corstorphine, a nice house, in a nice suburban area. I remember walking along a wide street with mature trees on each side. It must have been autumn, because golden and copper leaves littered the pavement. It had been raining, and they stuck to the soles of our shoes. The front door was painted black with a large silver knocker. It's funny how we remember certain details and others are obscured by time. I can't recall the host's name, but I've never forgotten him, after all, it was he who introduced me to Jamie that night.

My first impression of Jamie was he was shy, not painfully shy where he struggled to make conversation, but reserved. I suppose that's a better word. Yes, that's a better description. He asked me my name, and when I said, Grace, his eyes lit up; it had been his mother's name. Then, he refilled my glass and enquired about what I did for a living. He seemed interested in my work, either that, or he was good at pretending to listen. I know now it was a bit of both.

I was a researcher at Edinburgh University, and we had just started a major project on the effects of plastics polluting the sea and its catastrophic effect on sea life. Looking back now, I probably did speak a lot about it. I was brimming with enthusiasm about the prospect of getting my academic teeth into it. Jamie asked all the right questions and smiled a lot. I remember he smiled.

I did eventually enquire about his job. He said it wasn't as interesting or globally effective as researching the environment, but he enjoyed it. He was a policy adviser for the Scottish National Party at Holyrood, the Scottish Parliament. He must have seen something in the look on my face, as he almost apologised by saying it wasn't as grandiose as it sounded.

'So, you're one of them?' I asked.

'One of who?' he grinned.

'You know, a tartan warrior in a kilt who hates anything to do with the English, anything British.'

He looked at me with his piercing eyes and as he took a drink, he said, 'Not really.'

'I'm sorry.' It was my turn to apologise.

'What for?'

'Judging you. I didn't mean to generalise.'

'Don't worry. I don't have the legs for a kilt.'

I laughed then. We both did. In a way, it broke the ice between us. I asked where he lived. He told me he had just bought a house in St John's Terrace. He asked me if I knew it and when I said I didn't, he told me it was a nice unassuming cul-de-sac not far from where we were.

I lived in a flat in Lonsdale Terrace. Opposite The Meadow. It was handy for walking to work and nowhere near Corstorphine, where Jamie lived.

'So, I can assume you're not a fan of Nicola?'

'Nicola?' Should I know this Nicola, I thought, and then it came to me. 'Oh. You mean Nicola Sturgeon. Your boss.'

'Who else?'

'Let's just say I respect her because she's a woman in a man's world and doing well. In fact, she's doing much more than that. She's widening the parameters, but that doesn't mean I have to like her. I much prefer Ruth Davidson. She's a more likeable character, but I don't agree with her politics.'

'That's a relief. I never had you down as a Tory, anyway.'

'Why? Do they have a certain look?'

'No.' He smiled. 'Although they are irritating.'

'I'm glad you don't think I am, then.'

'Are you interested in politics?'

'I wouldn't call it an interest, but I've always had a soft spot for the Lib Dems.'

He pulled a face and rolled his eyes.

'I know. I know. But in their defence, their public image is improving.'

'It can't get any worse.'

I combed my hand through my hair.

'Are you hungry?' he asked.

That smile again.

'I saw when we came in, they've got a little buffet set up in the dining room.'

'There is, but I'd like to take you out, for dinner.'

'When?' I could feel my heart beating in the back of my throat.

He leaned forward. 'Now.'

The Present

Lesvos, Greece

Grace is looking at a mannequin in a shop window. It is wearing a dress she has admired for over a week now. Each morning, she stops and admires the cut of the dress, and the way in which the fabric hugs the curves of the mannequin. It's a statement. Yes, that's what it is. Wearing such a dress, Grace thinks, is a measure of one's own confidence in who one is. It defines who you are.

She is not ready to be clothed in such refinery. It is too soon. There was a time she would have bought the dress the minute she laid eyes on it, but not now. Back then, she was indomitable: fiercely independent, driven and resourceful. She had a prepense determination to be optimistic, positive... she turns away from the shop window and sighs under her breath.

'Grace, I thought it was you.'

Grace spins around. 'Oh. Hello, Monica.'

Monica touches Grace's arm. 'Have you got time for a coffee?'

Grace checks her watch. 'I suppose so.'

'Good. I'm glad I bumped into you.'

Monica is in her late fifties and well presented. Her face is taut, and her skin has a polished sheen to it, a waxed complexion that reminds Grace Monica is not averse to the surgeon's knife. They sit outside under the shade of a parasol. The café is popular with the locals, which means the beverages and food are of a good quality.

'Have you settled in now?' Monica asks as she takes her smartphone from her bag and lays it on the table. She looks at it and frowns. 'I'm expecting a call... you don't mind, I hope?'

Grace shakes her head. 'No. Not at all.'

'So, the apartment is up to scratch?'

'Yes, I'm so lucky. There's a few bits and bobs that need my attention, but apart from that, it's perfect.'

'I'm glad. There's nothing worse than moving to a place you haven't seen. I know it's just bricks and mortar, but it's more than that, don't you think? It's important to feel a sense of belonging, I feel.'

'Yes, you're absolutely right. I feel an attachment to it already, even though it's just been a few weeks.'

'Time flies, don't you think?'

'This past year has, that's for sure.'

'At least you're rid of him.' Monica smiles and then looks embarrassed. She glances at her phone.

Grace wonders if she is willing it to ring. 'Oh! thanks for the kettle.'

'You're welcome. I was glad to get rid of it. It was just taking up room. I had two sitting in the cupboard. God knows how I managed to acquire all those kettles. You don't want another one, do you?' Monica laughs.

A waiter approaches them, and they order two coffees.

'Would you like a cake or a pastry?' Monica asks as she scans the menu.

'I wouldn't know what to get. Why don't you order for both of us?'

Monica sets her mouth. 'Mm... I think we'll have a slice of *Melopita and let me see... a baklava.*'

The waiter nods his head in approval before leaving them.

'You're not on a diet, I hope?'

Grace smiles. 'Not this week, anyway. What did you just order?'

'The *Melopita* is part custard, part cheesecake, it's a Honey Pie, you'll love it. Now, the Baklava is a classic. It's basically Greek pastry made with flaky dough and layered with a cinnamon-spiced nut filling and sweet syrup. It's very decadent, but it tastes like heaven. You'll love that too. We'll have half of each.'

Once the coffee and cakes arrive, Monica cuts the cakes into four pieces.

'Oh my God, that's delicious.' Grace dabs the side of her mouth with a napkin.

'Better than an orgasm?'

'What is that?'

'Has it been that long?'

Grace suddenly feels guarded, but she can tell she has caught Monica's curiosity. She hesitates before nodding.

Monica sighs. 'And is it important?'

'I'm enjoying my own company. I'm comfortable with how things are.'

Monica looks at her, as if weighing up the implications of Grace's words. Then, after a pause, Monica smiles and lifts her cup to her mouth. 'Then that's all that matters.' There is an awkward silence. 'So... you've settled in then, that's good.'

'I have. I've surprised myself.'

'It took me a while. I thought I'd never be happy here. The biggest mistake of my life, I kept telling myself. Eventually, I stopped missing London. I'd never go back now. This is home. It's been eight years now.'

'I didn't realise it was as long as that.'

'Yes. Arthur's been dead three years now, but as you know, I'm not on my own. Georgios and I are... very fond of each other.'

Grace thinks it is quite an old-fashioned word for someone like Monica to use, especially when referring to Georgios.

'I'll need to ask you over for dinner, Georgios as well, of course.'

'I'd like that.'

'Me too.' Monica's presence has been a comfort to Grace. In fact, she doesn't know how she would have coped if it hadn't been for Monica's continued support. 'I can't tell you how grateful I am.'

'We stick together. Especially in times of crisis. We muck in. I wouldn't have it any other way.'

'You've been a great support, Monica. I wouldn't have lasted five minutes here if it wasn't for you.'

'Nonsense, you don't give yourself credit enough. I've watched you change. You're not the woman you were when you first came here.'

'I suppose not,' Grace muses. She takes a sip of her coffee. 'But there're days when I just don't want to get out of bed. The thought of facing another day... it's like... well, it's hard, you know.'

Monica takes Grace's hand and locks her eyes on her.

'You're doing just fine, believe me. I could never have done what you have. I don't think I've got the courage.'

'I just don't feel the person you're describing.'

'And that's why you need to start having a higher opinion of yourself, Grace. Stop bringing yourself down all the time. You were like that as a child.'

'I can't help it. It's in my DNA, I think.' It's a statement that is instinctive. It's her default, but all the same, the familiarity sits uncomfortably on her tongue.

Monica rolls her eyes. 'Well, that needs to change.'

The Present

Something of Worth

The sun trickles through the shutters as Grace rises towards the surface of sleep, and just for a moment, she is in her bedroom in Edinburgh. Her heart pounds in her chest and she turns to see if he is really there, lying beside her. She can feel the cold dampness of sweat run in the dip between her breasts.

She remembers his eyes, piercing her resolve and staring down at her. He holds a knife in his hand. She tries to scream, but he has silenced her voice. He grabs a handful of her hair and hacks at it, viciously.

She closes her eyes. It was a dream, just a dream. The terror does not leave her. It fills the room. She does not want the memory of it to stain this new day, this new beginning, this new place.

After a shower, Grace makes a breakfast of toast and black coffee and sits outside on the balcony, just big enough for a chair and table. She watches as small groups of children, with sports bags strapped to their backs, make their way to the local primary school. It is a building she came across the other day. She wondered how many classes it had, as, like most of the buildings, it was small and only two storeys. At the rear was a basketball court which surprised her, and she remembers thinking if basketball was popular in Greece.

The children smile and laugh; they are always talking with each other. It is uplifting to see children this happy. Such innocence stirs fond images of her own childhood and a convivial warmth spreads through her.

A father, she assumes, passes below her, with a girl sitting on his shoulders. She has long dark hair that bobs with each step. Unlike the others, the girl's face is set, almost determined, Grace thinks. Her face has the look of natural beauty, like the young girls often portrayed in television adverts and magazines. The father looks up, more by chance than any interest in Grace and, to her surprise, smiles a reserved *hello*. Grace returns the gesture. She resists an urge to raise her hand. Her modesty restricts this, and she straightens up and pulls the soft collar of her dressing gown around her neck.

She presses her back against the chair and watches as they continue down the street. Grace releases her hold on the dressing gown and absently fiddles with the cord tied around her waist, as the man and child turn down a small lane that Grace knows will take them to the school gates.

It is already warm, and she can feel her shins tingle from the sun's glare. This morning, they look a bright red, burnt from yesterday's overexposure. She won't forget to cover them in sun cream today.

It has always been one of surprise and wonderment when, every morning, Grace gazes over the terracotta roofs towards a sensuous sea, cerulean blue, constantly amending and sprinkling diamonds like shattered glass. Her heart flutters by the dazzling brightness and decorated surfaces of colour that adorn each archway, house and structure in luminous blue, alluring mauve, and brilliant white.

The baker's shop is only a few feet away, and she smells the sweet aroma of freshly baked bread, pastries and cakes that transforms the air into a riotous bouquet that the ovens have fired. Each morning, smells, tastes, sights and sounds are becoming familiar, but always experienced new and unique to this space and time.

Grace decides that this morning, she will buy a loaf of freshly baked bread and then some jam from *Sofia's Delicatessen*.

She steps from the shade of the doorway and immediately feels the heat of the morning sun upon her shoulders. Grace crosses the street where it is sheltered, checks her bag for her purse and then ambles at a slow pace. She turns a corner that takes her down a steep hill where, in front of her, she can see tall masts and a myriad of boats, all shapes and sizes, hugging the harbour wall. She has forgotten the surreality of her dream and its residual impact, and now, amongst the sea air, she feels revitalised. Amongst the palm trees, traffic and pedestrians, the sun gleams off the pavements. She puts on her sunglasses and pulls her bag further up her shoulder. In places, weeds appear between the paving slabs, and skeletal cats lounge in the shade of doorways and under tables, where people sip coffee, and tea, and eat English breakfasts with chips, a peculiarity she can't get her head around.

Grace smooths her hair and readjusts the clasp that keeps it in place. She enters the delicatessen and slips her sunglasses onto her head. She takes a moment to adjust her eyes. Sofia is a slim woman, with dark wavy hair. She wears her make up discreetly, and it compliments her features. Grace would place her in her forties. She knows she has a daughter; Grace has seen them together.

Sofia is reaching into her display and rearranging pastries and cakes when she looks up and smiles. 'Good morning.'

'Kalimera,' Grace replies.

Sofia's smile widens. 'You're learning Greek?'

'I'm trying. I can only say a few words.'

'It takes time and practice. I admire that, learning to speak the language.'

'Your English is excellent. Where did you learn?'

'I went to university in London in my twenties. I was able to improve my English every day, just like you will.'

'I don't think I'll ever be able to speak Greek like you speak English.'

'I thought that, too. You'll be surprised how quickly you'll learn. You'll pick up new words every day.'

'I hope so.'

'What can I get you?'

'I was hoping you had jam.'

'I do. My friend makes it. She has her own business.'

Sofia points to a shelf full of jars, each with the same logo emblazoned on the front. 'It's just over there. You'll find quite a variety.'

'Oh, I'm not that adventurous. I'm looking for raspberry.'

Grace picks up a jar. 'The jars are quaint all by themselves. It would be a shame to throw them out. I think I'll take two.'

'You haven't tried it yet.'

'I don't need to. It's worth it just for the jars.'

Sofia takes the jars from Grace with a confident half smile. 'I'm sure you'll like the jam. I love it myself.'

'Well, that's all I need to know,' Grace says, unzipping her bag and taking out her purse.

'That's six euros. Do you want a bag?'

'Yes, please. I'm going to the bakers. I'll use it for that as well.'

'Very environmentally friendly.'

'It was my job.'

'Really? What did you do?'

'I was a sustainability researcher at Edinburgh University.'

'Wow! How interesting!'

'Really? I don't normally get that kind of reaction.'

'It's a passion of mine. In fact, if you're interested, there's a group of us who clean the beach of plastics and rubbish every week. You're welcome to come along... if you want?'

Grace's eyes light up. 'I'd love to. When is it?'

'Tomorrow, in fact. We meet at the beach in the morning, around nine.'

'Perfect. I'll be there.'

Sofia hands Grace the plastic bag. 'This will be one of the last plastic bags I give out.'

'Oh! Why is that?'

'I'm changing to paper and encouraging customers to bring their own bag.'

Grace nods in approval. 'That's a great idea. The supermarkets back home have been doing it for some time now. If you want a bag, you must pay for one. It encourages people to use the same bag each time.'

'That's what I'm hoping to achieve.'

'Well, good luck. And I'll see you tomorrow.'

'Until tomorrow. Enjoy the jam.'

'Oh, I'm sure I will.'

When Grace leaves the shop, she feels uplifted. She thinks she will like living in Molyvos. She attributes this to having a purpose again. She is not just going to be engaged in the small things in life, she has found something of worth, something she believes in.

The Present

An Englishman in a Hat

The next morning, Grace strolls through the town on her way to the beach. She passes the bank, the church with its bell tower and the school. She smiles at an old woman in a headscarf, dressed in black.

The sun is a golden disk in the sky and already, the rising heat makes Grace feel flush, but she is happy.

As her shoes sink into the sand, Grace can see a group of people up ahead. Someone is handing out what looks like large bags.

Sofia touches her lightly on the shoulder. 'Thanks for coming, Grace. I hope you're not allergic to latex?'

'No, not that I know of.'

'Good, take these then.' Sofia hands her a pair of blue latex gloves and smiles. 'Health and safety. You'll be surprised at what we find.'

Grace glances over the beach. Ahead, there are rows of umbrellas and sunbeds descending to the sea. Even at this early hour, sun worshippers pepper the beach, lacquering their skin with sun cream.

Grace estimates there are about twenty men and women of various ages readying themselves to begin. A keen enthusiasm spreads through the group and an older man in a straw panama hat raises his voice above the chatter.

'Right folks, we all know the drill. Our newcomer,' he nods towards Grace, 'can stay close to Sofia. She'll keep you right. What's your name, my dear?'

'Grace.'

'Well, Grace, welcome to our motley crew. Okay, let's get started.'

'We walk in a row along the width of the beach and pick up the rubbish lying around. Sometimes we come across condoms, pardon the pun. So, keep the gloves on. If you find money, give it to Peter at the end of the clean-up. We use it to buy the gloves and bags. Anything sharp goes in the yellow tubs.' Several people are carrying yellow containers. 'We dispose of the glass we find and sometimes needles, I'm afraid, separately.'

Grace raises her eyebrows. 'I see.'

'Is there anyone here you know?'

'I don't think so.'

And then Grace sees a man bending forward, reaching with his hand into the sand. He is familiar, she is sure of it, yet she can't pinpoint how she knows him.

By the time they have finished, Grace's muscles are aching. She places her hands on her lower back and stretches.

'Well done, Grace. You did a grand job.'

'Thank you, Peter. I enjoyed it. I think I've used muscles I didn't know I had.'

'There's nothing like the sense of achievement. It gets easier. Will you be joining us again?'

'Try to stop me.'

'Good, we need all the help we can get. Please excuse me, I need to help with loading the bags onto the truck.' Peter tilts his hat and moves off.

'I forgot to ask,' Sofia says. 'Did you like the jam?'

'It was delicious.' Grace peels off her gloves. 'Do you open later in the morning, after this?'

'The shop's open now. I've got an older lady, Angeliki. She works a few hours in the morning.'

'Ah, I see.'

'What are you doing today?'

'I'm trying to keep out of the sun for a while.' She lifts a leg, slightly, to show Sofia her sunburnt shin.

'Oh, that looks sore. Best to stay out of it. The sun ages your skin, you know. Always wear a hat and keep out of the midday sun. In fact, when you come next time, remember, wear a hat.'

'I will. When is the next time?'

'Tomorrow morning. Not everyone comes each day. Most people have their regular days, except Peter, that is, he's here every morning.'

'He's English.'

'He is. You can't disguise that posh accent, but he's lived in Greece longer than he ever did in England. He used to be a tour guide on Zakynthos, you know. He's retired now.'

'I could imagine him being a tour guide and a good one at that. There's an authoritative yet friendly presence about him.'

'Well, I've been told he was one of the best. Zakynthos must be a poorer place without him.'

'How did he end up here?'

'You'll have to ask him that,' Sofia replies, smiling.

'I love his hat.'

'Oh, the Panama. I've never seen him without it.'

The Past

Wishing Well

Edinburgh had always been home. I had never lived anywhere else. We bought a house on Colington Road. It badly needed renovating. The previous owners, an old couple, had lived in the house since the fifties and the décor hadn't changed much since then. It had a large garden, populated by mature trees and a fish pond. When we viewed the house, I was adamant the pond would be the first feature to go.

We acquired the house at a good price, a bargain, considering the inflated property market in Edinburgh, but we had to spend a small fortune on the renovation of every room.

I loved my house; we had made it our own, stamped our identity on it. It was always going to be a home for our children, our family.

The house was a short walk away from the Union Canal built to link the centre of Edinburgh with the Forth and Clyde canal at Falkirk. I loved to walk there. It also exercised my mind, amongst the dog walkers, joggers, cyclists and parents with toddlers on tricycles and youngsters on skateboards. Sometimes, canoes would spear through the dark murky waters, scattering ducks, as the solitary swan, I had never seen another, continued to glide gracefully amongst the reeds.

The canal flowed almost straight and narrow through the city and it had become a common walk of several miles I took most weeks into Tollcross, adjacent to Fountainbridge. I often bought wine gums at the Tesco Express for the walk back home, but before then, I'd visit Loudons, an all-day café and an artisan bakery for a fruit scone with clotted cream and jam.

Occasionally, at the weekends, and if the weather was fair, both Jamie and I would walk the canal into town. We often went for lunch at a favourite bar or café, in the grassmarket, or along Lothian Road, before doing some shopping, and then, depending if it had started to rain, we'd wander back, at a leisurely pace, talking about our plans: holidays, weekends away and starting a family.

We had a small group of friends that we shared. Really,

they were my friends before I met Jamie. After several get-togethers, Jamie started to warm to the husbands and partners and we soon became part of the group, a couple, invited to parties, nights out and meals on the weekends.

It was a happy time for us both. When I think back, I could never say *no* to him, and that was my problem. It became our problem.

We went on long weekends to Skye and The Kyle of Lochalsh. We climbed Munros and ate lunch in little pubs, in villages, without a Post Office, whose names I couldn't pronounce. To be fair, I enjoyed most of it, not the weather, it always seemed to rain, and if it didn't, the sky seemed to be lost in a continual mist that seeped into my skin. All I really wanted to do was take long weekends in Rome, visit Venice or London.

We went to Majorca one year: Puerto Pollensa. A week in a four-star hotel, bed-and-breakfast. We didn't go full board, because Jamie wanted to eat out at the local restaurants and eat authentic Majorcan cuisine.

We hired a car and toured the island. I hadn't realised it was so big. I loved the weather. It was hot and sunny for the whole week, even though it was early October. Olivia was conceived on that holiday. We had been trying to start a family since January of that year, and I was despondent at our lack of success. Jamie, on the other hand, was more relaxed about it, saying it can take some couples a year or two. I think he was enjoying the sex too much. By that stage, it was not lovemaking. It felt mechanical and purposeful. There was to be a product at the end of it, after all. I know you can't compare a baby to that kind of thing, but, well, that's how it felt at the time.

One day, we took a car trip to the historic village of

Valldemossa. It was a charming little place with steep pedestrian streets and buildings with old stone facades. I remember it was mountainous and very green. On the way there, we passed gorgeous beaches and coves. Below the hilltop town, I remember a quaint little harbour at a little fishing village. We ate lunch there and the seafood, freshly caught, or so we were told, was delicious. I wasn't sure if it was a marketing ploy, or the truth, it didn't matter. I'd never tasted fish like it, or since.

After lunch, we visited the magnificent 14th-century Carthusian monastery. It housed a large well, and it was the tradition for visitors to make a wish and throw money into its water. So, I did. Whether it was coincidence or not, my wish came true. It wasn't until, weeks later, when I knew I was pregnant, that I made the calculations, and then it dawned on me, our child was conceived that night after I made my wish.

Get your copy:

vinci-books.com/dragonflight

ABOUT THE AUTHOR

Dougie lives in Dunfermline, Fife, with his wife, daughter, son and golden retriever.

Thank you so much for taking the time to read my novel. It really does mean everything to me. My novels are inspired by my favourite city, Edinburgh and my passion for Greece, her islands, people, landscapes, sea, light and ambience, all of which are important themes and symbols in my writing.

My books encapsulate themes such as love, loss, hope, coming of age, and the uncovering of secrets. They are character-driven stories with twists and turns set against the backdrop of Edinburgh and Greece.

I never intended to, but seemingly, I write women's contemporary fiction and since 95% of my readers are women; I suppose that is a good fit.

Since all my books are set in Edinburgh and Greece, you will not be surprised to know that I identify with a physical place and the feeling of belonging, which are prominent in my writing.

Edinburgh is one of the most beautiful cities in the world, it is rich in history, has amazing classical buildings, (the new town of Edinburgh is a world heritage site) and it also has vibrant restaurants and café bars.

Greece occupies my heart. Her history, culture, religion, people, landscape, light, colours and sea inspire me every day. There is almost a spiritual quality to it. I want my novels to have a sense of time and place, drawing the reader into the social and cultural complexities of the characters. I want my characters to speak from the page, where you can identify with them, their hopes, fears, conflicts, loves and emotion. I hope the characters become like real people to you, and it is at that point, you will want to know what is going to happen to the characters, where is their life taking them in the story.

The common denominator is, I want my novels to be about what it means to be human through our relationship with our world, our environment and with each other. Most of all, I want them to be good stories that you, as a reader, can identify with and enjoy.

ACKNOWLEDGMENTS

Heartfelt thanks to Sheona, my wife, for her continued support and constant encouragement. Thanks to Tracy Watson, Maggie Crawshaw, Anne Clague and Lisa Richards, who have been with me from the beginning. As my advanced readers, they have given me invaluable feedback on this novel. Finally, I am indebted to Margaret McGlade for her editorial skills, advice and time.